FIRE IN THE DESERT

DOUG PETERSON

'Shea Books

To Nancy: Over 50 years of marriage, you have made our home an outpost of the Kingdom of God.

Fire in the Desert

Cover illustration by DogEared Design

Map by Santiago Romero

Published by O'Shea Books

Champaign, IL 61821

www.bydougpeterson.com

ISBN: 978-1-7358151-4-5

NOVELS BY DOUG PETERSON

KINGDOM COME SERIES

Book 1: *Thrones in the Desert*

THE FIRST 12 CHAPTERS of the Book of Luke, as seen through the eyes of five fictional characters—a slave, a guard in Herod's palace, a Pharisee, the daughter of a Zealot, and a tax collector. They all encounter Jesus, who overthrows the thrones in their lives.

Book 2: *Swords in the Desert*

Book 2 follows Jesus's footsteps as He heads steadily toward Jerusalem. *Swords in the Desert* also continues to follow five fictional characters.

Book 3: *Fire in the Desert*

Book 3 follows the same characters as they experience the world-changing events of the Book of Acts. *Fire in the Desert* covers the first 12 chapters of Acts, from the descent of the Holy Spirit to the Road to Damascus.

NORTH-SOUTH SERIES

Book 1: *The Vanishing Woman*

Ellen and William Craft escape when Ellen poses as a white man while her husband pretends to be her slave—a true story.

Book 2: *The Disappearing Man*

Henry "Box" Brown mails himself to freedom. He ships himself in a box from Richmond to Philadelphia—a true story.

Book 3: *The Tubman Train*

Harriet Tubman's name is legendary, but most people do not know her complete story. *The Tubman Train* is one of the first novels to tackle her remarkable life.

Book 4: *The Lincoln League*

John Scobell, the first African-American spy for the U.S. intelligence service, operates deep within Confederate lines during the Civil War. Based on a true story.

Book 5: *The Dixie Devil*

André Cailloux is the forgotten first black hero of the American Civil War. This is the story of André and his wife, Felicie, as they try to survive in the turbulent world of New Orleans.

ANNIE O'SHEA MYSTERIES

The Puzzle People

A suspense novel that spans the rise and fall of the Berlin Wall. Inspired by real events.

HOLY LAND IN THE TIME OF ACTS
GALATIA
Pisidian Antioch
Iconium
Lystra
Derbe
CAPPADOCIA
CILICIA
Perga
PAMPHYLIA
Tarsus
Antioch on the Orontes
Seleucia Pieria
SYRIA
CYPRUS
Salamis
Paphos
THE GREAT SEA
Damascus
Capernaum
Paul's Road to Damascus
Caesarea Maritima
Joppa
Jerusalem

CAST OF CHARACTERS

Main Characters

Eliana—The daughter of a Zealot freedom fighter

Asaph—A former tax collector

Sveshtari—A former bodyguard for Herod Antipas

Keturah—A woman who escaped slavery in the House of Herod

Nekoda—A priest and member of the Sadducee party

Supporting Cast

Zuriel—Childhood rival of Asaph

Abel—A friend of Sveshtari's and former thief

Judah—A Zealot freedom fighter and father of Eliana

Lavi—Eliana's dog

Babette—Keturah and Sveshtari's oldest daughter

FIGURES FROM HISTORY

Jesus—The Messiah, the Son of God

Saul (Paul)—The champion of the Gospel

Peter—A fisherman and disciple of Jesus

Joanna—Wife of the manager of Herod's household

Herod Agrippa—The last king of Judea, grandson of Herod the Great

Stephen—One of the Church's first deacons

Ananias—A devout Christian in Damascus

I.

THE BOOK OF ACTS, CHAPTER 1

ELIANA: JERUSALEM, JUDEA, MONTH OF IYYAR (LATE APRIL), 30 A.D.

THE ROOFTOP WAS THE ideal place to sleep on hot nights in Jerusalem. The air was stifling, almost suffocating, without a trace of wind. Eliana rested her head on a stack of soft, folded fabrics, looking up at the stars and breathing in the smells of the night—spices and flowers.

Turning onto her side, Eliana stared at a vase holding bright red flowers on a nearby table where they had taken dinner earlier in the evening. "The Blood of the Maccabees," the flowers were called. According to legend, they bloomed wherever the blood of Maccabean rebels had been spilled in their fight against the Greeks hundreds of years earlier.

The blooms stirred thoughts of another person's blood recently spilled just outside the walls of the city. Eliana had been there, at the foot of the killing tree, and she had forced herself to look up at Jesus to absorb every moment of his agony. She was a witness.

These flowers also reminded her of the morning, two weeks ago, when her friends discovered the empty tomb. The disciples said they saw Jesus in the flesh, and she had no reason to disbelieve them. To rise from the dead seemed beyond human reason, but she, too, had run to the tomb that morning and found it empty. The body couldn't have been stolen because it was heavily guarded by soldiers who faced the ultimate punishment if the body was snatched on their watch. Those soldiers had since been executed.

A throbbing began on her right side, so she shifted onto her back and stared once again at the swarming stars, trying to calm her mind for sleep. But a thumping noise followed by a groan in the alleyway behind the house distracted her.

Her forty-year-old knees creaked as she rose and crawled toward the edge of the flat roof, peering down on the alley below. She saw no one. Had she been hearing things? It wasn't unusual for people to be out and about in the night, although it could be dangerous to venture too far in the dark. Jerusalem had more than its share of thieves and murderers. Many of them were in positions of power.

After the dramatic events of Passover, Eliana, her father, and Asaph had been welcomed into a family compound under the covering, or protection, of a man named Shechem. Asaph was still recovering from a deep stab wound he had suffered on the day Jesus was crucified. He and her father occupied one of the four rooms of the compound, while Shechem's family and Eliana spilled into the other three rooms.

Just as she was about to pull back from the edge of the rooftop, Eliana noticed that the door leading from the alleyway into the courtyard was slightly ajar. Surely, the door hadn't been left that way when the family had gone to sleep. This deserved investigation, so Eliana rose to her bare feet and padded to the ladder leading down to the second floor. She moved quietly, a talent she had learned over many years on the run from the Romans. On the second floor, she passed by a small storage room where another ladder led to the first floor.

She went halfway down the second ladder before pausing. She thought she heard the faint sound of shuffling feet. Thieves? If so, how many? She thought about calling out a warning, but she would feel foolish if she woke the entire household for nothing.

Eliana felt exposed going down the ladder with her back to the courtyard. She would make an easy target. When she reached the ground, she turned, still moving as silently as a cat. She scanned the courtyard—and saw the movement of a single shadow. There was a little light from the moon, enough to see that the shadow carried something in his right hand. It was the shape of a sword.

"Who are you! What are you doing here?"

The shadow whirled in her direction, and the flash of steel confirmed that he carried a weapon. The man hesitated and stared at her, but only for a moment. Then he charged, sword raised, but Eliana was quick on her feet. She catapulted over the low stone wall that enclosed the pen where sheep and goats were kept.

"Help! Thief! Help!"

Eliana's voice ripped through the air, surely waking every soul in the house—including her dog, Lavi. The shadow jumped onto the top of the stone wall, and he raised his sword high, preparing to deliver a fatal blow. Eliana picked up a thick piece of wood from the nearby stack just in time. As she held it in the air with both hands, the blade sunk into the woody flesh.

By this time, the household had been roused.

The attacker tried to pull out the blade, but it was stuck, and for one bizarre moment, she was face-to-face with the man. The man's face was covered in cloth from the nose down, but his eyes seemed oddly familiar. The man's eyes spoke hatred, and before Eliana knew what was happening, his fist came out of the dark like a striking snake, battering her in the nose. Jolted by shock and pain, Eliana staggered backward, blood gushing.

Eliana's attacker tossed aside his sword, still stuck in the wood, and drew out a knife. As he closed in on Eliana, she hurled another piece of wood at him, but he swatted it aside easily.

Eliana backed up until she could go no farther. The attacker jabbed with his knife, but she danced to the right. However, the blade nicked her shoulder, leaving a stinging slice. He closed in on her.

Before he could thrust his knife again, a fast-moving shadow darted from behind and launched itself onto the attacker's back. It was Eliana's dog, Lavi. Letting out a roar, the attacker knocked the medium-sized dog to the ground and sprinted for the courtyard door, giving one of the men of the house a stiff-arm to the chest as he passed. Eliana watched Lavi dart underfoot and sink his teeth into the attacker's leg. The man sprawled forward onto the ground, and Eliana wondered if Lavi would tear him to pieces. Her dog had killed before.

But the attacker slammed his free foot into Lavi's face, and her dog let go. Before Lavi had a chance to recover and pounce on the man's neck, the attacker was on his feet and through the gate. He slammed it shut. The attacker was gone in an instant, sprinting down the alleyway and into the Jerusalem maze.

"Eliana!" It was the panicked voice of Asaph, who had an oil lamp in his hand. "Eliana, where are you hurt?"

"I'm fine. I'm all right, Asaph."

"Are you sure? You don't look it," came her father's voice from the darkness.

As Eliana slowly took stock of her condition, she realized why Asaph and her abba must have thought she was mortally wounded. Blood streamed down her chin from her nose, and her robe was stained by the blood from the slice to her shoulder.

Asaph and her father crouched beside her, examining her for any sign that she had been stabbed. “Did you see who did this?”

A chill ran up Eliana’s back, and she began to shake and shiver.

“Never mind, don’t speak,” said Asaph. “You need a warm blanket.”

Eliana laughed, and the men must have thought her mad. But she found it strangely funny that she would be shivering on such a blistering hot night.

“He carried a sword and knife,” she said as Asaph raised her to her feet and led her toward a back room, where several women and girls awaited. “He came to murder.”

Lavi shadowed her every move as one of the women, Rhoda, drew her into the room. After they sat her on a chair, Lavi got up on his forelegs and began to lick the blood from her face.

Asaph nodded toward her. “I’ll leave you to Rhoda and Bilhah, who will tend to your wounds and clean you up.”

“But I have no wounds, other than a bleeding nose and a superficial cut.”

“With so much blood, we must be sure the knife didn’t do more.”

“I would know if I had been cut deeply.”

“You are in shock. Let the women tend to you.”

“Lavi is already doing a pretty good job.”

“I think he’ll need some help.”

With that, Asaph leaned over and gave her a soft kiss on the side of her head. Then he left, and Rhoda began to dab at Eliana’s face with a washcloth. She dipped the cloth in a bowl of water and wrung out the blood.

Asaph

Asaph was amazed that Eliana had no serious wounds, other than a small cut and what might be a broken nose. When he saw her covered in blood, he was certain she had been mortally wounded.

He knew about mortal wounds, for he had nearly died on Passover when his childhood enemy, Zuriel, drove a sword into his side. The doctor, Luke, had brought him from the brink of oblivion. He wasn't resurrected in the miraculous sense, but nearly so. Now, he could move about with some normalcy, but the wound was still sensitive. He had to be careful.

"We're quite the pair with our wounds," he said to Eliana after the women had cleaned her up. It was still the dead of night, but no one was prepared to go back to sleep any time soon. Neighbors, awakened by the ruckus, had come to find out what had happened, but Asaph and Eliana slipped away from the crowd.

They sat next to each other in the courtyard, perched on the stone wall encircling the sheep enclosure. Asaph took both of Eliana's hands and looked down at the sword that had been used to attack Eliana. The blade, which lay next to them on the rock wall, had been removed from the piece of wood.

Asaph spoke softly. "Did you see his face?"

Eliana hesitated.

"If you don't want to speak of what happened tonight, I will understand," he quickly added.

"No, no, I was just trying to picture the man's eyes. I could see only his eyes, but they seemed familiar."

"What was the man doing when you first spotted him?"

"Heading toward the rooms. *Your* room," said Eliana.

"He didn't seem intent on robbery?"

"He had his sword drawn. I think he was intent on violence."

"Do you think it could have been Zuriel coming to finish what he started?" Asaph asked. "Were those the eyes you recognized?"

Not only did Zuriel try to murder Asaph on the day Jesus was crucified, but he had killed Chaim, a friend and fellow follower of Jesus. Zuriel had no hesitation in committing violence.

"Perhaps it was him. It was hard to tell. Everything happened so fast. It could also be a Temple guard hoping to slay any followers of Jesus the Christ."

The Christ. The Messiah. One month ago, Asaph wouldn't have believed the stories of Jesus rising from the tomb. But after the strange happenings on Passover, anything was possible.

"We may be putting Shechem and his family at risk by staying here," Asaph said. "Maybe we should return to our home village."

Both Asaph and Eliana were born and raised in a small village in the Judean hills not far from Jerusalem—John the Baptist's hometown. Asaph's parents were long gone, but he still had extended family there. But would they welcome back a relative who had once exchanged the Jewish life for Roman ways as a tax collector? Would they embrace the follower of a resurrected man who claimed to be ushering in a new kingdom?

Eliana shook her head. "I will not desert our fellow believers here in Jerusalem. But you may be right about putting Shechem's family in danger. My father and I should find lodging with other followers of the Way. I'm sure you could do the same."

Large numbers of Jesus people were being added to the fold every day in Jerusalem as word of the resurrection spread. Followers of the Way were generous with their money, food, and lodging, so Asaph and Eliana would have no problem being welcomed into other homes.

"Do you believe in the resurrection of Jesus?" Eliana suddenly asked.

Asaph hesitated, but only for a moment. "I do."

"But you have doubts? I can see them in your eyes."

"Don't you have doubts?"

"Sometimes. But our teacher told us he would be raised on the third day."

Asaph didn't deny the possibility of resurrection, as the Sadducees did. But he had always feared that existence after death would be nothing more than a misery in Sheol, a dreary, gray place that people trudged through for eternity.

Eliana sighed. "I feel suddenly weary. It is time to find rest, and you too need your sleep, Asaph. You are still healing."

"I plan to keep watch over the house the rest of the night."

Asaph could sense that Eliana was going to insist he sleep. But she just smiled and held her tongue.

Asaph gave her a kiss on her head. As she departed for her room, he picked up the sword that the attacker had wielded. Staring at the blade, he wondered if it could be the same weapon his enemy Zuriel had used only two weeks earlier to try to kill him. He examined the sword in the feeble light of the oil lamp. Was this the sword that had been driven into his side? It's possible.

He put his hand to his scar and winced. It was still tender to the touch.

Sveshtari: Capernaum, Galilee

Sveshtari strode along the Sea of Galilee on a beautiful spring day with a dagger hidden in the folds of his clothing. He didn't think the other followers of Jesus would approve, but he wasn't about to give up all weapons—not when he knew that he and Keturah were being hunted by Roman authorities.

A cool breeze blew in from the lake, which mirrored the blue sky, and all around were plants at their peak. Off to his right was a cluster of deep-pink sword lilies with their multiple blooms climbing up the stalk of the plant. To his left was the *kalanit*, or the "little bride," with velvety, blood-red petals.

Passing by these lilies of the field, he entered Capernaum, nestled on the northwest corner of the Sea Galilee, and he strode past the home of Peter, the big fisherman. Much of Peter's extended family still lived there, although the disciple spent much of his time in Jerusalem. Recently, however, Peter and the other ten remaining disciples (Judas Iscariot was dead) had traveled north to Galilee, where spring brought out lush colors, a welcome change from the desert-brown landscape to the south in Judea.

When Sveshtari saw several men up ahead in a heated discussion, his right hand went instinctively to the handle of his dagger. It was a force of habit from years of serving as a bodyguard in Herod's palace. In his old world, heated arguments often led to bloodshed, but that wasn't true among these Jewish men. They argued all the time, and yet they never lashed out in violence. Very peculiar, he thought.

The arguing men clustered in front of the local synagogue, a stone's throw from the home of Peter. Sveshtari's friend, Abel, was among the men arguing, and his voice was the loudest. No surprise there. Abel was a small man with a big presence.

"The Scriptures say that the casting of lots puts an end to strife," Abel said, rising on his toes. He stood a head shorter than most of the other men. "When decisions are made by casting lots, what is there to fight about?"

"But when Jesus chose his twelve closest followers, he didn't cast lots to make his decision," said another man, Simon, gesturing wildly with his hands.

"What is going on?" Sveshtari asked. He never participated in these raucous debates because, as a God-fearer and former pagan, he knew little about the Jewish faith. But he wanted to learn.

"Peter and the disciples are planning to find a replacement for Judas Iscariot," said Abel. "They are not complete without twelve to mirror the Twelve Tribes of Israel. So, they are planning to cast lots to choose the replacement. Don't you think that's reasonable?"

Sveshtari didn't dare venture his own opinion. He hesitated just long enough for the man named Boaz to answer for him. "There is too much chance involved in casting lots!"

"Not if you bless the process with prayer," said Abel. "God works in every little thing that happens in our lives—including the casting of lots. Do you really think casting lots is only chance? Is *anything* in life really chance?"

"But lots have also been used for evil," Boaz said. "Haman cast lots to decide what day they would kill our Jewish ancestors!"

"Just because something can be used for evil doesn't make it inherently wrong," piped in yet another man. Benjamin was his name.

"That's true," Sveshtari said. "Is a sword inherently evil?" Because Sveshtari made it a habit to stay out of Jewish arguments, he didn't know what made him say this. The words just tumbled out.

Sveshtari's question brought the argument to a screeching halt. All five men turned toward him and stared. Sveshtari felt suddenly foolish. He grinned awkwardly.

"He's exactly right!" Benjamin suddenly shouted, breaking the spell. "Swords can be used for good or evil, and so can lots!"

Sveshtari crossed his arms and said nothing, taking it all in. My, these men loved to argue. Sveshtari was used to physical combat, but he was intimidated by verbal battles. Every so often, his friend Abel would glance over, as if inviting him to join the fray. But he remained mute.

Then a new and urgent voice intruded on their entertainment.

"Come quickly! Come and see!" A man suddenly came sprinting toward them, shouting like a herald of news. "It's *Jesus*! He's here!"

Sveshtari sensed the hairs on his neck stand up. The man's words captured everyone's attention.

"What are you saying, Eli?" asked Abel.

"Just what I said. Jesus is here!"

"Jesus of Nazareth?"

"Who else?"

"Where?"

"Down by the water! Hurry! Before he vanishes!"

Then the man was off again, sprinting down the streets of Capernaum, shouting the good news. The five arguing men looked at each other for a moment before Abel took off running. All followed, including Sveshtari. There had been stories about Jesus appearing to his disciples and others in Jerusalem and even here in Galilee, but he didn't know what to make of those reports. Now, here was the chance to see with his own eyes.

Sveshtari pulled ahead of the other men, and he felt weightless, as if running on air. People streamed out of the town to see for themselves. Women, men, and children. A father carried his sick daughter in his arms as he ran. If Jesus were truly present in the flesh, he would bring healing in his wings.

Ahead, hundreds of people had already gathered by the shore. Sveshtari realized he should have gone to find Keturah and bring her with him, but the entire town was emptying out, so she was probably in the crowd somewhere. As he closed in on the shore, he estimated there were several hundred people jostling for position. But still no sign of Jesus.

Then a man emerged from the masses and began to stride up a slight rise—a grassy hill. The man had a beard, and he looked about the same height as Jesus. But Sveshtari would need to get closer to confirm. He tried to squeeze through the crowd, but everybody else was trying to do the same. The eleven disciples attempted to keep back the crowd. What good would it do for Jesus to rise from the dead, only to be trampled by a mob?

The man on the hill held up his right hand, motioning everyone to settle down. The crowd obeyed, and people began to take seats on the rocky ground along the water. Sveshtari remained standing, trying to get a clear view, but a couple of people behind him told him to sit down. He obeyed.

Then the man began to speak, and the acoustics of the seaside worked wonders. He could hear the man's voice as clearly as if he were standing next to him, speaking into his ear.

It was the voice of Jesus.

Keturah

There was no longer any doubt in Keturah's mind. Jesus was alive. He stood only twenty cubits away. Keturah was among the first to hear the news of his appearance, and she rushed to the Sea of Galilee shore alongside Joanna and several other women. She carried her three-month-old child, Babette, in her arms.

People pressed in on all sides, with the disciples serving as a human barrier to keep Jesus from being crushed. Then the Master moved up the grassy hill so all could see, and he began to speak. He talked about the kingdom of God and how he would be with them for a short time. He also said he was sending a helper, a counselor, when he leaves.

"What will this helper look like?" asked one man. "How will we recognize him?"

Keturah didn't really understand Jesus's answer. To be honest, she was too distracted by his presence to remember a lot of what he said. The last time she had seen Jesus, he was hanging on a cross, his body crisscrossed by whip marks, and a crown of thorns pressed into his scalp. She couldn't believe he was standing here before them, healed and complete.

How was this possible?

Keturah scanned the crowd for any sign of her betrothed, Sveshtari. She should've gone to him first with the news, but she was too excited to think straight.

Suddenly, Jesus moved within an arm's length of her, and she tensed. He was standing so close that she could reach out and touch him. Should she dare? Was he a material body?

Then he reached out to the child in Keturah's lap—the child she had rescued from a trash heap. *Babette.* "Promise of God." Jesus crouched to Babette's level and smiled. Babette stared back intently. Then Jesus put his hand on the child's head and gently rubbed her wisps of hair. Instantly, a smile appeared, so naturally and tenderly, on Babette's face; her eyes narrowed, and her cheeks rose. A look of merriment. Then Jesus said the words he had spoken to Babette a month earlier:

"Let the little children come to me, and do not hinder them, for the kingdom of God belongs to such as these. Truly I tell you, anyone who will not receive the kingdom of God like a little child will never enter it."

As Jesus continued to smooth the soft hair on Babette's head, Keturah noticed the scars where the nails had penetrated bone and flesh.

"Master, welcome me into your kingdom," Keturah said, tears welling. Then he turned to look at her, and Keturah diverted her eyes downward. She felt his hand gently on her head, the same as he had done with Babette.

As she raised her head, she felt the same urge to break into a smile. Men should not touch the hair of an unmarried woman, but Keturah knew there was nothing inappropriate in the touch.

He then placed two fingers on her forehead and said, "If you hold to my teaching, you are really my disciples. Then you will know the truth, and the truth will set you free. Be free, sister."

When Jesus withdrew his hands, Keturah's fingers flew to her forehead. She traced her fingers across her skin. Did Jesus know that when she had been recaptured after escaping from slavery, Rufus had tattooed her forehead with the words "Arrest me, for I have run away"? Sveshtari had helped her to remove this tattoo, but she continued to feel the ghost of those words, like an unhealed burn on her skin.

But no longer. She no longer sensed the shame and the fear that had been tattooed on her forehead. Keturah broke down in tears and bowed until her forehead touched the ground. Jesus had bestowed on her a crown of beauty instead of ashes, the oil of joy instead of mourning, and a garment of praise instead of a spirit of despair.

She entered his kingdom with rejoicing.

Keturah and Sveshtari sat side by side on the shore of the Sea of Galilee later that afternoon, feeling the touch of a soft breeze. They were perched on a large boulder with Babette asleep in Keturah's arms.

They had spent the last hour talking about the miracle they witnessed. When Jesus had finished talking to the people, he mixed in with the crowd, as if he wanted to allow each person to see, up close, that he was alive. He wanted *hundreds* of witnesses. Then he departed with his disciples.

"I must return to Jerusalem," Sveshtari said out of the blue.

"What about me?" Keturah asked.

"It's too dangerous for you in Jerusalem. You'll be safer here."

"But we're betrothed."

"We will do it the Hebrew way. When a man and woman become betrothed, the man goes away to prepare a home. Then he comes back to his bride, maybe as long as a year later. I will come back for you."

"I don't understand. Why this sudden decision to go back to Jerusalem? Does it have to do with Jesus's appearance?"

"Yes. He told his disciples to return to the city. So, I must go, no matter what the risk. His kingdom has arrived."

"Are the disciples going to raise up an army for this kingdom? Will there be war in Jerusalem?"

"I don't know," said Sveshtari. "But if there is going to be a war, I want to be there to fight for his kingdom. You should stay here where it is safe."

"Where you go, I go."

"We are God-fearers, so we can marry the Hebrew way. Being apart during the betrothal is normal."

"Then maybe we should marry the Roman way. The betrothal doesn't have to be as long, and we can still be together."

"Why would we want to do *anything* the Roman way?"

"To be together, of course. I'm not asking you to worship Caesar."

"But the Romans do not legally recognize marriages of non-citizens."

"God will recognize our marriage."

Sveshtari scowled. Since their betrothal, he had come to expect that she wouldn't question his opinions. The Jewish way was for the wife to come under the husband's covering, his protection, but she didn't think that meant she had to agree with everything he said. She had seen plenty of Hebrew wives speak their mind.

"The Romans are looking for me, too. I need your protection," she said.

She knew those words would hit this former bodyguard where he was most vulnerable. Sveshtari had the heart of a protector.

"I don't think the Romans will come this far to seek you or me," Sveshtari said.

"What do you mean? There is a military garrison just east of Capernaum."

"But those aren't the Romans who are seeking us."

"Babette needs your protective arm as well."

Those words penetrated his armor. Although Sveshtari initially opposed Keturah's decision to rescue this baby from a Roman ash heap, he had come to dote on her. He treated her like his own flesh and blood.

Sveshtari stared at Babette and groaned as if in pain. "Then we will travel to Jerusalem together. I have spoken. It's decided."

"Yes. It's decided. Will we go through the marriage ceremony in Jerusalem?"

"We will," Sveshtari said, as if trying to wrest control of the decision-making process. "And we will be married in the Hebrew tradition. Beneath the canopy."

"Agreed." Keturah hid her smile. She gladly gave him that decision, especially since it was what she too desired. She sought it more than the world.

Nekoda: Jerusalem

The smell of burnt offerings wafted across the Temple Mount like incense. The first lamb had been sacrificed—its neck slit and the blood captured in a cup, which was passed from hand to hand before being splashed on the altar.

Nekoda, a Sadducee priest, had participated in the morning sacrifice, and it brought back painful memories of the tragic events of Passover. He had sacrificed a lamb on the afternoon that Jesus of Nazareth hung on the cross. It was a bloody day, but not only because of the death of Jesus and the death of thousands of Passover lambs. His brother, Chaim, was murdered that day, and Nekoda was determined to find out who had done it.

Nekoda stood in the shade of Solomon's Porch—a massive colonnade with a double row of pillars stretching along the eastern side of the Temple Mount. Its stone was as white as the wool of the lambs being sacrificed nearby. He stared at the men debating the finer points of the Torah and spotted Zuriel making his way through the crowd.

Zuriel's beard was long and thick, and the hair on his head was tightly curled. A beard is considered a divine quality, and the wearer is expected to show heightened compassion for the people around him. But Zuriel was short on compassion, undeserving of such a glorious beard. As the man neared, his smile blossomed. Nekoda could smell the aroma of clove and cinnamon, probably the anointing oil used in Zuriel's glistening beard.

He wanted to smack the smile off Zuriel's face. Nekoda was meeting with him for one reason only. Zuriel said he had witnessed the murder of his brother, Chaim. He had information.

"Shalom," said Nekoda.

"Shalom, brother. Blessed be the Lord's glorious kingdom, forever and ever."

Nekoda refused to respond with a blessing of his own. He turned to stroll the colonnade, and Zuriel fell into step alongside him.

"Do you know why I asked to meet?" Nekoda said. No small talk. Right to business.

"You want to know what happened to your brother, and I understand completely. I am sorry for your loss, Nekoda. Chaim was a good man."

Nekoda agreed. His brother was a good man, but Nekoda had consistently failed to see it. When Chaim started walking in the footsteps of the rabbi Jesus of Nazareth, Nekoda had nothing but scorn. Now he had nothing but sorrow for a brother who was no more.

"Thus far, I have not been able to locate any witnesses to my brother's murder," Nekoda said. "All I know is that he was killed during the pursuit of Sveshtari—and that you were part of that pursuit. What did you see?"

Zuriel bowed his head as if in sorrow. It came across as play-acting. But everything Zuriel said and did seemed artificial.

"I saw your brother, bless his immortal soul, arguing with Asaph."

"Asaph? The former tax collector? Why would they be arguing?"

"Because Asaph was trying to prevent Chaim from helping in the pursuit of Sveshtari."

"Why would my brother, Chaim, help anyone pursue and arrest Sveshtari? He was friends with Sveshtari."

"I wouldn't call them friends. Your brother decided that Sveshtari was a dangerous man and had to be arrested."

It was true that Sveshtari, a former bodyguard in Herod's palace, was a dangerous man. He was implicated in the freeing of several Zealot prisoners, during which several guards were murdered. He had also helped a slave girl escape from Herod's palace and had killed a fellow guard. He had blood on his hands.

"Asaph is a friend and ally of Sveshtari. He wanted to stop your brother, as well as Rufus and myself; he wanted to keep us from pursuing Sveshtari. I tried to intervene in their argument, but Asaph drew a knife. There was a scuffle, and before I could do anything to stop him, Asaph stabbed your brother."

"And what did you do?"

"I wanted to run after Asaph, but I felt it was more important to tend to your brother's wounds. I was by his side when he breathed his last."

This fit what little facts Nekoda had gleaned. He had been told that a man was with his brother as he died.

"We must find Asaph and bring him to justice," Zuriel said.

"But why would Asaph kill my brother? They too were friends."

"Friends?" Zuriel laughed. "They were *rivals*!"

"Rivals?"

"They both loved the same woman—Eliana. With Chaim out of the picture, Asaph has Eliana to himself."

Nekoda felt a tremor in his breast. He wanted justice for his brother. Someone had to pay. Someone needed to be killed; their throat needed to be slit and their blood captured in a cup and tossed on the altar.

"Why didn't you come forth with this information sooner?" Nekoda asked. "Why did you wait for me to summon you?"

"I told the authorities what happened to your brother, but I'm sorry . . . No one seemed to care about Chaim because he was a follower of Jesus. The Nazarene's followers have been accused of stealing Jesus's body, so the authorities have other concerns."

That part was true. When Nekoda began his investigation into his brother's death, the other priests in the Temple seemed obsessed with Jesus's missing body. There were stories about Jesus being seen alive and moving about in Jerusalem; stopping those rumors ranked higher than the murder of one of the Nazarene's followers.

"So, where is Asaph now? Has he fled the city?"

"I don't think so. People tell me they have seen him here in Jerusalem."

"If he killed my brother, why didn't he flee?"

"Because he's a radical follower of Jesus. He probably wants to remain in the city to catch a glimpse of the man whom they falsely claim rose from the dead. He probably thinks it's worth the risk."

"Can you find him?" Nekoda asked.

Zuriel sighed and said nothing. Nekoda knew what he wanted.

"I will pay."

"Then I will find him. Would you like his head on a platter?"

"If he killed my brother, then beheading would be too merciful. Bring him to me in one piece. I'll tear him apart."

Nekoda vowed to wield his sword in judgment. He will take vengeance on his adversary and repay those who have done him wrong. He will make his sword drunk with blood.

Eliana: Jerusalem, Month of Sivan (Late May), 30 A.D.

The Upper Room was packed. Eliana stood, like most people in the room, reciting psalms along with Asaph.

Over 100 people filled the place, the same space where the disciples and Jesus shared their last meal before the crucifixion turned Jerusalem on its head. The story of Jesus's resurrection had swept through the city, like fire through parched fields, and people flocked to the disciples.

It was still day, and while light poured in through three windows, the room was cloaked in shadows. With all the bodies concentrated in one open room, it was hot and saturated by the smell of scented oils. Believers knelt, arms raised, while others leaned against the large pillars, as if their prayers held up the roof. The walls were decorated with simple artwork—the picture of a shepherd and sheep on one wall, a dove with an olive branch in its beak on another wall.

The room was not divided by the sexes, and a surprising number of women, such as herself, mixed into the crowd. Up front were the eleven remaining disciples: Peter, John, James, Andrew, Philip, Thomas, Bartholomew, Matthew, Simon the Zealot, James son of Alphaeus, and Judas son of James. The other Judas was gone, of course. With the money he earned for betraying Jesus, Judas Iscariot had purchased a field, where he hung himself. When they cut down his body, it burst open. Everyone was calling that field *Akeldama*, the Field of Blood.

Peter stepped to the front and began to talk about Judas.

"For it is written in the Book of Psalms: May his place be deserted; let there be no one to dwell in it; and, may another take his place of leadership."

"I don't understand," Eliana whispered to Asaph. "Why do they feel the need to choose a twelfth apostle?"

"Because they must preserve the twelve—a holy number, reflecting the Twelve Tribes of Israel," he said. "They *must* replace Judas."

"That I understand. But I don't know why the *disciples* are the ones choosing the twelfth person."

Asaph cocked his head. "Who else should choose?"

"Why doesn't Jesus select the new disciple? After all, he chose the original twelve."

"But how can Jesus . . . ?"

Asaph's question trailed off. Eliana sensed that Asaph was about to say, "How can Jesus select the twelfth if he's no longer with us?" It probably dawned on him that Jesus *was* still with them.

"Who are we to question Peter and the others?" Asaph asked.

The disciples had nominated two people to fill the twelfth place: Matthias and Joseph called Barsabbas, who was also known by his Gentile name, Justus. Eliana knew them both.

"Barsabbas" was the "son of the Sabbath," because some say he was born on the Sabbath. Matthias, meanwhile, had been following Jesus for a long time; he was one of the seventy that Jesus sent out from Galilee, a time that seemed a thousand harvests in the past.

Eliana had a difficult time peering above the heads of the crowd, so Asaph had to tell her what was happening.

"They're casting lots," he said, standing on tiptoes.

She heard Peter's voice rise above the murmur of the crowd. "Lord, you know everyone's heart. Show us which of these two you have chosen to take over this apostolic ministry, which Judas left to go where he belongs."

Where Judas belongs? Eliana knew what that meant. Where he belonged wasn't good.

"Have they selected the stone?" Eliana asked, tugging on Asaph's sleeve like a child pestering a parent.

"They have," Asaph said. "Peter is holding it high."

"The Lord has chosen Matthias!" Peter announced, igniting a roar of approval.

"Did I miss something?" came a voice to Eliana's right, and when she spun around, she couldn't believe her eyes. There stood an old friend.

"Sveshtari!"

She had not seen Sveshtari since he and her closest friend, Keturah, left for Galilee many weeks ago. She didn't expect to see them again for years, if ever.

Asaph gave Sveshtari a holy kiss, and then Eliana flooded him with questions.

"What are you doing here? Where's Keturah? Did she come to Jerusalem with you? How is Babette? How have you both been?"

"Keturah is outside," he said. "She didn't want to bring the child into this crowded space."

Sveshtari hadn't even finished his sentence before Eliana was off. She bolted for the stairway leading downstairs. When she burst through the door, into the brilliant sunshine, she spotted her friend sitting on a stone bench and bouncing baby Babette on her knees. The child had grown in just these few weeks apart.

"Keturah, my sister!"

Keturah looked up and broke into a smile. Then she rose to her feet, Babette in arm, as Eliana threw herself into a full embrace. The tears broke loose, a fountain of joy.

Keturah

Keturah continually marveled at her friendship with Eliana. They had met several years earlier on a dusty road leading north to Galilee from Herod's palace in Machaerus. At that time, Eliana was infested with demons and threatened to murder Keturah in her sleep. Now, they were sisters.

"What brings you back to Jerusalem?" Eliana asked her after giving Babette a soft kiss on the forehead.

"Sveshtari decided to return with the disciples." Keturah passed Babette into Eliana's arms. "Things happened in Galilee. Strange things."

Eliana cocked her head—like her dog, Lavi, might do.

"We saw Jesus," Keturah added.

Eliana stood up straighter and blinked. Her mouth opened, but no words came out. She took one step backward, studying Keturah, looking at her in a new light.

"Say something," Keturah said. "Do you believe me?"

"Believe you? Of course I do!" Eliana hooked her arm with Keturah's and led her down the street. "Tell me every detail."

As they headed east toward the Lower City and the Pool of Siloam, Keturah explained how Jesus had appeared along the Sea of Galilee to 500 people, and how he had even blessed Babette and said we needed to be like children to enter the Kingdom of God.

When Eliana finished pelting her with questions, Keturah had a question of her own. This question had been burning in her mind since the day she saw Jesus, alive again.

"Do you think he really died on the cross that day?"

"We were both there, at the foot of the cross," Eliana said without hesitation. "He was dead. To be sure, the soldiers drove a spear into his side. We saw them do it, and we were there when he was taken down from the cross. I've seen plenty of dead bodies in my life and so have you. He was dead."

"I know . . . It's just . . . It just seems so dreamlike seeing him. If I hadn't been standing beside hundreds of other people when I saw Jesus, I might not have believed my eyes."

"That's probably why Jesus appeared before so many."

"That's exactly what Sveshtari said. But I don't understand . . . Does this mean Jesus is the Messiah you've talk so much about?"

Eliana sat down on a stone wall and rubbed her cheek against Babette's cheek. Keturah's little girl was unusually well-behaved.

"Some say he's more than the Messiah," Eliana said. "Some say he is divine."

Keturah had heard similar stories, but she always brushed them away. "You mean like Zeus or Apollo?"

"Not at all like Zeus or Apollo. First of all, he exists. Those are imaginary and petty gods with all the flaws of humans, only heightened. Zeus and the other gods see humans as their playthings. But you saw what Jesus did. He came to serve . . . to die . . . to give. Does that sound like Apollo to you?"

Keturah laughed. Eliana had a point: The idea that Jesus was like one of the gods, especially Apollo, was ludicrous.

"Apollo had many lovers, including the nine Muses. He also chased after Daphne, who turned into a laurel tree just to escape him. So, I suppose you're right. Jesus is not Apollo. He's so much more."

"He is our King," Eliana declared.

Keturah nodded, unsure how to respond. As a former slave in Herod's palace, she had lived among Hebrews for much of her life—but she was still baffled by these peculiar people.

"I so wish I could have seen Jesus as you did," Eliana said. "I'm a bit jealous to be honest."

"Maybe you will still see him here in Jerusalem."

"I don't think so. Didn't you hear?"

"Hear what?"

"Jesus took his disciples east of the city and then left. He was taken up into a cloud."

A couple of weeks ago, Keturah would have laughed at such a statement. But after seeing Jesus in the flesh on the shores of the Sea of Galilee, she couldn't deny the possibility. Her skin prickled at the thought.

"He's gone?"

"The disciples think so. He ascended on the fortieth day after his resurrection. *Forty.* The number of completion. His work here was done, but he told the disciples to remain in Jerusalem to receive the baptism of the Holy Spirit."

"Now I'm even more confused. I have no idea what you're talking about."

"The Holy Spirit is the Spirit of God, but I'm not sure what he meant by a *baptism* in the Spirit. He told the disciples they will be clothed in power."

"What kind of power?"

"We will see. But tell me more about what happened with you and Sveshtari since we last saw you."

Before Keturah could answer, Babette began to wail.

"She is still being fed by the wetnurse, so I better return to the house where we are staying."

"And where are you staying?" Eliana asked, handing Babette to her mother. "Asaph and I can visit, bring food and gifts."

"That would be—"

At that moment, Sveshtari's friend, Abel, came rushing up to them. He was out of breath. Agitated. Sweating.

"Shalom, Abel!" Eliana said. Abel responded with a quick "Shalom" before asking, "Where is Asaph?"

"Still in the Upper Room, I presume," said Eliana.

"Then lead me to him."

"What's wrong, Abel?" said Eliana.

"I will tell you if you come with me. Please. There is no time to lose."

"Now you're scaring me," said Keturah. "What happened?"

"The Temple guards are coming. And they intend to arrest Asaph and charge him with murder."

"Murder?" Keturah said. "Murder of who? Gershom?"

"No. Chaim."

"We must warn him!" Eliana said before bolting for the Upper Room.

"That's what I've been trying to say," added Abel, jogging alongside.

Keturah followed, but with Babette in her arms, she had a hard time keeping up with Abel and Eliana. Babette's wailing grew louder.

2.

THE BOOK OF ACTS, CHAPTER 2

ASAPH: JERUSALEM, PENTECOST, 50 DAYS AFTER PASSOVER, MONTH OF SIVAN (LATE MAY), 30 A.D.

SEVERAL OXEN LUMBERED ALONG at the head of the procession, their horns gilded and their heads covered in olive wreaths. The music of a flute announced the coming of the firstfruits, the *bikkurum*, being carried in baskets by men and women, whose heads were also covered in garlands.

For two days, Asaph had been in hiding, ever since Abel brought word that the Temple guards were hunting him. But on Shavuot, the Feast of Weeks, he came out of seclusion, figuring he could lose himself among the multitudes streaming into Jerusalem to celebrate the firstfruits—the harvest of the grains. This was the second of the three great feasts that drew pilgrims to Jerusalem every year.

Women, dressed in white with belts of red, lifted up the baskets filled with the firstfruits of seven agricultural products—grapes, pomegranates, dates, figs, olives, barley, and wheat. An overflowing abundance.

It had been fifty days since Passover and fifty days since Jesus had died. With every day that passed, Asaph was more and more convinced that Jesus of Nazareth was ushering in a new kingdom. He wished he could have seen Jesus's post-resurrection body, but he held on to the memory of witnessing the day that Jesus was baptized by John—an event that meant nothing to him at the time but all the world today.

As Jerusalem exploded in celebration, Asaph trusted that God would protect him from the false accusations of murder. So, he mixed in with the crowd, which included people from all over the land. He basked in a Babel of languages, spoken by Parthians, Medes, Cretans, Arabs, and Elamites, as well as people from Cappadocia, Pontus, Phrygia, Pamphylia, Egypt, Libya, Rome, Mesopotamia, and even from parts of Judea where other languages thrived.

"What does Shavuot have to do with your Law, given at Mt. Sinai?" asked Sveshtari, who stayed by Asaph's side as they pressed through the jubilant crowd. Ever the bodyguard, Sveshtari promised Eliana he would stay by Asaph's side to protect him from the Temple guards. As a God-fearer and former pagan, Sveshtari had no shortage of questions for Asaph about every aspect of Hebrew life.

"Yahweh gave us the Torah on Mt. Sinai on the Shavuot," Asaph explained. "It was on Mt. Sinai that he also gave the marriage contract to his bride, Israel."

"You lost me," Sveshtari said. "Israel is Yahweh's bride?"

"Yahweh's covenant with Israel is like a groom with a bride, and the giving of the Law was the signing of the *ketubah*."

Sveshtari laughed. "Everything to you is like a wedding, isn't it, Asaph? You've got marriage on the mind. Have you sat down with Eliana's father to hammer out the *ketubah*?"

Asaph nodded. "I plan to discuss the marriage contract with him soon. But it's true what I say about Israel being Yahweh's bride. Yahweh hammered out a marriage contract with Israel on Mt. Sinai—the Ten Commandments. That's what all Hebrews believe."

"All right, all right, I'll take your word for it."

"Do you plan to follow Hebrew marriage customs when you marry Keturah?" Asaph asked Sveshtari.

"We have talked about it, but we still have much to learn about Hebrew customs."

"Then stick close to me, and I will tell you more," Asaph said.

"That I plan to do. I told Eliana I would stay by your side to keep you alive for your wedding day."

Asaph's eyes flicked to Sveshtari's waist, where a sword was strapped. Asaph still possessed the sword used to attack Eliana—the very sword that might also have been used to kill Chaim. Asaph had witnessed Zuriel's cold-blooded murder of Chaim, and he was outraged that authorities were trying to arrest him for the killing of his good friend. He was the one who comforted Chaim as he died in his arms. The injustice ate at him, but the glorious day of the firstfruits of harvest was one of thanksgiving, not anger, so he tried to rein in his passions.

Asaph and Sveshtari moved with the flow of the procession. Some pilgrims carried gold, silver, and willow baskets containing live doves. These doves would become burnt offerings. As they approached the Temple, however, Sveshtari put a hand on Asaph's shoulder to hold him back. Sveshtari nodded to the right. There, several Temple guards stood at attention, scanning the crowd.

"They're keeping the peace, not looking for me," Asaph said. "Besides, they wouldn't even know what I look like."

"No. But *he* does." Sveshtari pointed at the man lurking in the shadow behind the guards. It was Zuriel. "Turn around. *Now.*"

Asaph wasn't going to argue. But as he spun on his heels, he noticed another familiar face coming down the street. It was Chaim's brother, Nekoda, a tall man who stood above the crowd. Sveshtari pulled Asaph down a side alley. When Asaph accidentally plowed into a stranger, knocking his basket of figs to the ground, he wanted to stop and help. But Sveshtari grabbed him under the arm and yanked with tremendous force. Asaph thought his arm was going to come out of its socket.

"Out of the way! Make way!" came voices from behind. Asaph knew he shouldn't slow down by taking even a momentary look, but he couldn't help himself. He glanced over his shoulder and saw four Temple guards shoving their way through the crowd. They were close.

By this time, Sveshtari had his sword drawn, and people cleared a path for him. But they were also clearing a path for the Temple guards, who clutched swords as they pushed through the crowd. Asaph rebuked himself for not bringing along his own weapon.

As they made a left turn and began running south through the city, they were stopped by the blast of a deafening sound. It was like a mighty wind, a howling tempest. They didn't feel any wind, but the sound was exactly like that of a storm. It all was very strange and unworldly.

Eliana

Eliana was just outside the building where the disciples were praying in the Upper Room when she heard a sudden roar. The sound seemed to come from the sky, but the low-hanging clouds did not look threatening. One moment, the street was filled with the normal bustle and babble of human activity, and the next second all she could hear was this tempest blast. It was like a mighty wind, or a tremendous blast on a shofar.

Immediately, everyone in the streets stopped what they were doing and looked around for the source of the sound. Thinking there was actual wind coming, she held on to the garland wreath on her head. But no wind accompanied the booming sound. The sound seemed alive and moving, and it concentrated its power on the building where the disciples regularly met in the Upper Room.

"Is Babette safe?" Eliana shouted to Keturah above the roar. Keturah clutched her child wrapped within the folds of her clothing.

Several people dropped their baskets, containing bundles of wheat and barley, and raced to the northern part of the city. Others crouched and held their hands over their ears. Eliana sensed that something important, something strange and singular was happening, so she forced herself to raise her head and open her eyes. A man pointed at the house where the disciples were praying.

"Fire!" he shouted.

Eliana stared upward and saw what looked like flickers of red and yellow visible through two open windows. If a fire had broken out inside the house, and if this sound was just the forerunner of an approaching wind, those flames were going to sweep across the city in a matter of moments.

Was this the judgment of God? But why would Yahweh burn Jerusalem on this day of all days—on Pentecost, on the Feast of Weeks when his people showered him with thanksgiving? She could hear the disciples inside the house shouting, but she couldn't make out their words. Were they being burned alive?

As the sound of a mighty wind reverberated inside and outside the house, several tiles fell from the roof, nearly hitting a man below, and an unearthly glow remained visible through the windows on the upper floor—like dozens of Sabbath candles. But she could not smell anything burning, and the flames didn't appear to be spreading and growing. If anything, the light coming from inside was beginning to dim. As it did, the roar of mighty wind, the shofar blast, began to die down as well. People ventured back outside from their homes and stared at the Upper Room and the sky.

All went oddly quiet. People looked around at each other, wondering the same thing. What had just happened?

Suddenly, the disciples burst from the building, wild with excitement. Their eyes glowed, and they were laughing and babbling. Were they drunk?

"What happened?" Eliana said to Bartholomew, the disciple closest to her. But when Bartholomew answered, he didn't speak in Aramaic or even Hebrew. It sounded like the language of Egypt, but she couldn't be sure.

The disciples, all twelve of them, made their way through the streets, heading north toward the Temple. Curious about what was happening, people followed close behind. Eliana was one of them.

As the streets thickened with people flowing from the opposite direction, the disciples finally came to a halt and began talking excitedly with onlookers. But they were using words of different languages!

Most people spoke Greek, Aramaic, Hebrew, or Latin. But the disciples were speaking languages other than those four. She watched as John came face-to-face with five pilgrims and began speaking in the words of the Elamites. The five pilgrims seemed to understand him completely. Had they traveled all the way from Elam, the land far to the East, across the Syro-Arabian Desert?

Meanwhile, the disciple Matthew chatted to another pair of men, speaking a language Eliana was not familiar with. What in the world was happening?

"It's like Babel," said a woman standing next to Eliana.

"Like Babel?" Eliana sensed a prickling of her skin on her arms and neck. "No! It's like Babel has been reversed! The languages aren't being confused! They're being sorted out!"

"I don't understand." Keturah came up beside Eliana with Babette nestled in her arms. The child smiled and gurgled, as if she too were attempting to speak. The way this day was unfolding, Eliana wouldn't be surprised if Babette suddenly started speaking Egyptian.

Eliana motioned toward the madness. "I think God has enabled the disciples to speak in many tongues."

Eliana had been disappointed that she never got to see Jesus resurrected in the flesh, as Keturah and Sveshtari had. But this! This more than made up for that. Jesus told the disciples he would send God's Spirit in power. It had come to pass.

Falling to her knees, Eliana began to ululate, raising her arms high and singing with her own form of unrestrained and reckless praise. All around her, languages swirled and twirled—a bounty of words, overflowing and spilling from the disciples' lips like the abundance of fruit and grains that had been brought into the city in overflowing baskets. The firstfruits were the choice of the harvest, the first and best of the crops that had been gathered and given to the Lord. The Lord had responded in kind by giving the disciples his firstfruits, his abundance, his language. He had given the disciples his Word. This language tied the people together, like cords around a sheaf of wheat.

Languages usually separated people from one another, but not today. Words had taken on a life of their own, and they poured from the disciples' lips. Although Eliana didn't know the various tongues they were speaking, she knew what they were talking about. They were speaking of Jesus, the Messiah, the Risen One, the Nazarene, the Prince of Peace. And the people seemed to be responding.

Eliana bowed to the ground, again and again, overwhelmed by the glory flaming all around her. She knew what it must have felt like for the ancient Israelites to follow a cloud by day and a fire at night as Yahweh led them out of Egypt and through the wilderness.

The fire she had seen in the windows was a holy fire, a refining fire. *Ruach*, the breath of God, was like the sound of the wind that roared through the streets of Jerusalem, breathing life into the pilgrims in the city, and into Eliana. She hadn't felt this power, this kind of cleansing, since the day she was delivered of demons on the shore of the Sea of Galilee.

She only wished that Asaph could be here at her side to share the experience.

Sveshtari

The people pressed in on all sides. Something was happening just ahead, and everyone strained to see. The commotion was taking place just outside the house where the disciples held their regular prayer meetings.

"Stay with me, Asaph!" Sveshtari shouted, trying to keep his head above the surging mob. In the confusion and madness, they had lost the Temple guards, but Sveshtari kept his eyes peeled in case the soldiers sprouted up from nowhere.

There seemed to be no end to the strange occurrences since Passover and Jesus's crucifixion. Sveshtari was nearly knocked off his feet by a powerful sound, like a lion letting out a roar.

When Sveshtari finally fought his way close to the disciples' prayer house, the sound had abated, but he was met by yet another astonishment. The disciples were talking eagerly with people, but other languages came out of their mouths, including the Thracian language.

Sveshtari came from Thracia, a province just north of Macedonia, but he didn't often hear his language spoken in Judea. He whirled to his left and came face to face with one of the disciples—Andrew, Peter's brother.

Andrew put his hands on both of Sveshtari's shoulders and spoke to him with urgent words. Thracian words. "Our Lord our God is very great, he is clothed with splendor and majesty. The Lord wraps himself in light as with a garment; he stretches out the heavens like a tent and lays the beams of his upper chambers on their waters!"

"Why didn't you tell me you spoke Thracian?" Sveshtari said, using his native tongue for the first time in a long while.

"I didn't know I spoke it until now!" Andrew exclaimed. And then he continued to gush praises in Sveshtari's native language. "The Lord makes the clouds his chariot and rides on the wings of the wind! He makes winds his messengers, flames of fire his servants!"

"Did the Lord send that powerful sound?" Sveshtari asked.

"Yes! And he sent fire too!"

"Fire? Where?"

"Tongues of fire in the Upper Room! As we were praying, my heart grew hot within me, and the fire burned. Then I spoke in languages I never heard before."

"Can you teach me to do that?"

"I don't think it can be taught. It's something you open yourself up to. You need to immerse yourself in the Lord's Holy Spirit, like a *mikveh*, like a baptism. Have you ever experienced a *mikveh*?"

"Once," Sveshtari said. He didn't want to admit that the only reason he and Keturah had immersed themselves in the water of a *mikveh* was to hide from pursuing soldiers—not to be cleansed.

"Then you know! You know what it's like to be surrounded by the water, to be completely immersed. That's the only way I can describe this. It's like being immersed in God's Spirit. God above me, God below me, God to the right, God to the left!"

As Andrew spoke, nearly shouting, he shook Sveshtari by the shoulders. Then he embraced Sveshtari and moved on, speaking to another person in another language. Sveshtari was left standing there, speechless. Six months ago, he was a follower of Mars, and now he was a God-fearer—a believer in One God. Six months ago, he never would've believed he would find himself embracing the Hebrew God. But now . . . He was so confused. He needed to ask Asaph about this strange experience.

Asaph.

In all the commotion, he had completely forgotten about Asaph. Anxious, he looked around, bobbing up and down amidst the crowd and calling out Asaph's name. He retraced his steps, but there was no sign of his friend. However, there was no reason for concern, he told himself. Asaph had probably been carried away by the miracles swirling all around them on this street. He too had probably been swept off his feet by the Spirit of the Lord.

Up ahead, he spotted Eliana kneeling in the middle of the road with Keturah standing next to her and holding Babette. Maybe they had seen Asaph. At least he hoped so. He prayed so.

Asaph

Asaph spotted Sveshtari in an intense conversation with Andrew, one of Jesus's disciples. As he made his way forward, it was like swimming against the current of the Jordan River. But before he could reach Sveshtari, a hand gripped him under his right arm. Then another hand latched onto his left arm and yanked him backward.

"Sveshtari!" he shouted, but in this hubbub, there was no way his friend could hear him.

Then Asaph felt the prick of a knife, needling him through his clothing. "Be quiet or this blade goes in further," came a voice in his right ear. He turned to see a stocky man with a broad face, thick, black eyebrows, and an ink-black beard. His grip was iron.

"Who are you? Where are you taking me?"

"No questions," came a voice on his other side. The second man, who kept a python grip on his arm, was much taller than his partner and as strong as an ox.

Asaph glanced over his shoulder for any sign of Sveshtari as the two men hurried him past market stalls, his feet barely touching the ground. He thought about shouting for help again, but the blade was pricking the skin of his side. He could feel blood oozing out. Couldn't anyone see what was happening?

They passed by the aqueduct and moved into the lower city—the southeastern corner of Jerusalem, into the Tyropoeon Valley. Here, the crowd thinned, and the two men picked up the pace. Then they made a sharp left turn, and the men shoved him through the open door of a square, stone house. Asaph stumbled and fell to his knees, onto the stone floor. Off to his left were a few sheep and a goat, nibbling on hay and eying him.

The tall man took a handful of Asaph's hair and yanked him back to his feet. His scalp burned. The man pulled him across the room and shoved him onto a stone bench. Asaph's head struck the stone wall behind him.

"Please. Tell me why you have taken me here."

"As if you don't know," said the stocky man.

"I don't know."

"You're wanted for murder," said the taller man.

"Murder? I haven't murdered anyone!"

"That's not for us to decide. You killed a man named Chaim, and we were paid to bring you here."

"Chaim was my friend. I never would have killed him. But I did witness his murder by a man named Zuriel."

The stocky man barked in laughter. "Zuriel? He's the man who hired us to bring you in."

"He wants to lay his guilt on my back!"

"Then prove your innocence before the judge. Like I said, this is none of our business."

Asaph looked for a way out of the house, but there was only one door, and it was blocked by the taller man. Asaph glanced at the kitchen to his left. Various vases and bowls were lined up on a counter, while the wooden table was spread with all kinds of fruits. The stocky man poured water in a cup and handed it to him.

"Thirsty?"

"Very." Asaph drank deeply while thoughts unspooled in his mind. Then he felt an unworldly calmness come down on him, very much out of character. He sensed that instead of fighting back, he needed to find a way to connect with his two captors.

"Were you there when the powerful sound struck the city?" Asaph asked.

While the tall man remained in the doorway as a guard, the stocky man picked up an apple and pulled up a chair. "I was. What do you think that was all about?"

"The *Ruach*. The breath of God."

The stocky man bit into his apple with a loud crunching sound. "The breath of God? You mean his spirit? The Scriptures talk about *Ruach Elohim* hovering over the waters when the world was created."

This man was learned for a bounty hunter. "That's right," Asaph said. "I believe the sound of the wind today may have been the very same Spirit.

What else would explain the disciples' ability to suddenly speak in different languages?"

"Is that what was going on? I remember hearing the sound of many languages, but to be honest we were more intent on apprehending you."

"A shoot will come up from the stump of Jesse; from his roots a Branch will bear fruit," Asaph said, quoting from the prophet Isaiah.

"The Spirit of the Lord will rest on him," the captor said, continuing the passage. "The Spirit of wisdom and of understanding, the Spirit of counsel and of might, the Spirit of the knowledge and fear of the Lord."

"Yes! You know your Scripture well. And this is the Spirit that came upon the followers of Jesus today. Jesus said he was going to send his Holy Spirit."

The stocky captor tossed an apple to Asaph and smiled. "Spoken like a true believer."

Asaph rubbed the apple in his hands, polishing it. "Have you heard the stories about Jesus?"

"You mean a resurrected Jesus walking the streets? Who hasn't? But I find the stories hard to swallow." As if to underscore his words, the captor began to cough and choke on a slice of apple. He poured a cup of water and drank it down in several big gulps. "Sorry, sorry, went down the wrong way."

When his captor regained his composure, Asaph continued. "The stories are true."

"Did you see the resurrected Jesus?"

"No, but many of my friends saw him."

"And you believe them?"

"I do. Were you in Jerusalem when Jesus was crucified?"

"I was."

"Then how do you explain the sudden darkness? The earthquake when he died."

"I admit it could be the Lord's disfavor with his people. But that's much different than saying it proves that Jesus rose to life."

Asaph crunched into his apple and leaned back on the bench. He still couldn't believe how supernaturally calm he felt in this predicament. Normally, his mind and heart would be racing.

"Jesus was betrayed for silver," Asaph said. "He died because one of his disciples betrayed him for a bag of money. You are doing the same thing to me."

The captor hurled his apple core against the wall. "You are an accused murderer, and you must be brought to trial! I am just doing my job!"

Asaph tried to backtrack because it's not a good idea to offend your captor. "You're right, you're right, what you're doing isn't the same as someone betraying a friend. I'm just saying that the outcome could be the same. An innocent man might be punished. I am that innocent man."

"The judge will sort it out."

With calm restored, Asaph returned to the words of Isaiah. "When Isaiah talked about the root of Jesse, he was referring to Jesus."

The captor laughed. "Jesus? What are you talking about?"

"Jesus is descended from Jesse. He is the root of Jesse, the Branch. The Messiah."

"Many have claimed to be the Messiah. What makes Jesus any different?"

"The resurrection."

"If it happened."

"Believe me, it did."

"But the Messiah—"

Just then, a presence filled the doorway, and the captor cut short their theological discussion. It was Zuriel, Asaph's childhood nemesis.

"Excellent work, Pharez and Abner," said Zuriel.

The stocky captor—Pharez—leaned in close to Asaph and whispered, "Don't worry. If you are innocent, the Lord will see to it that you go free."

"You failed to tie his hands as I asked," Zuriel said, moving in closer. Asaph noticed he had a knife in his hand.

"It didn't seem necessary," said Pharez. "He isn't going anywhere."

"Tie his hands and leave him to me."

When Pharez didn't budge, the other captor—Abner—grabbed a piece of rope hanging on a hook and lashed Asaph's hands together behind his back. Abner tied the knots tightly, the rope biting into his skin. Pharez must've seen the discomfort in Asaph's face because he leaned down and began to loosen the knot.

Zuriel waved his knife. "Leave the knot as it is, Pharez! Your job is finished. Leave me alone with the prisoner."

Pharez's eyes flicked in Asaph's direction. A sympathetic glance.

"Leave!"

Abner slapped Pharez on the shoulder. "Let's go."

Pharez didn't move, at least initially. He stared at Zuriel, clearly suspicious of the man's true motives. When Abner plucked at his arm, Pharez finally shrugged and exited, leaving Asaph at the mercy of Zuriel.

Zuriel turned to face Asaph, his blade flashing in the morning light.

Keturah

"Fellow Jews and all of you who live in Jerusalem, let me explain this to you; listen carefully to what I say," said Peter, the leader of Jesus's disciples. Peter stood on an overturned wooden box as Keturah and the crowd pressed close to him. He raised his hands and called for quiet. His voice boomed.

"These people are not drunk, as you suppose. It's only nine in the morning."

A titter of laughter rippled through the crowd. Peter knew what everyone had been thinking—what Keturah had also been thinking. When the disciples came hurtling out of the house, laughing and bubbling with excitement, then babbling in foreign languages, they seemed to be in an altered state, as if they had downed ten too many cups of wine.

"No!" shouted Peter. "This is what was spoken by the prophet Joel: 'In the last days, God says, I will pour out my Spirit on all people. Your sons and daughters will prophesy, your young men will see visions, your old men will dream dreams. Even on my servants, both men and women, I will pour out my Spirit in those days, and they will prophesy. I will show wonders in the heavens above and signs on the earth below, blood and fire and billows of smoke. The sun will be turned to darkness and the moon to blood before the coming of the great and glorious day of the Lord. And everyone who calls on the name of the Lord will be saved.'"

God will pour out his Spirit, even on servants? Even on women?

Keturah had spent much of her life as a lowly servant. And now the Lord was promising to pour out his Spirit on her? Jesus had always been unusually open to woman followers, but now he was promising to pour out his Spirit on them. On *her.* On Babette too, the baby in her arms.

Keturah felt a warmth pass over her face, then a tingling sensation rose from her foot, shivered up her spine, and reached her head. For a moment, it almost felt as if her entire body were growing, elongating, reaching into the clouds, extending her senses skyward. It scared her but also excited her. Keturah's feet were still planted on the ground, but it felt as if her head had risen to Heaven. Eternity filled her up like water rising from a well and spilling onto parched land.

Then she panicked. She was enjoying the experience, but she suddenly felt as if she were losing control of herself. So, she reclaimed her autonomy, fortified her willpower, and was suddenly earthbound once again.

Peter was still speaking. His words were still ringing.

"God has raised this Jesus to life, and we are all witnesses of it! Exalted to the right hand of God, he has received from the Father the promised Holy Spirit and has poured out what you now see and hear. For David did not ascend to heaven, and yet he said, 'The Lord said to my lord: Sit at my right hand until I make your enemies a footstool for your feet.' Therefore let all Israel be assured of this: God had made this Jesus, whom you crucified, both Lord and Messiah!"

Eliana clutched Keturah's sleeve. "Did you hear? Jesus is not just Messiah. He is *Lord!*"

Then Eliana raised her arms, closed her eyes, and sang these words: "The Lord will extend your mighty scepter from Zion, saying, 'Rule in the midst of your enemies!' Arrayed in holy splendor, your young men will come to you like dew from the morning's womb."

That was exactly how Keturah felt—like dew from the morning's womb. She was fragile and small and fleeting. Her life, all lives, appear mysteriously in the morning and are gone with startling suddenness by evening. But Keturah was no longer afraid of the fleeting nature of life. Jesus had defeated death, he had opened the breach in the wall, and he invited her to follow him.

"Have you seen Asaph?" came Sveshtari's voice from behind.

Keturah's otherworldly thoughts were suddenly brought back to earth by his intruding voice. Eliana had also been taken out of the Spirit, and she said, "I thought you were with Asaph."

"I was," said Sveshtari, rushing up to them. "But in this crowd and chaos, we became separated. I was hoping you saw him."

"You were supposed to be watching over him!" Keturah said to Sveshtari, jostling Babette in her arms.

"I was!"

"Then find him!" Eliana said.

"I'll help," said Keturah, putting a hand on Eliana's shoulder. Keturah didn't often have senses that operated beyond taste, sight, smell, touch, and hearing, but something was tugging on her, telling her that Asaph was in trouble.

Asaph

"Why did you kill Chaim?" Asaph asked bluntly.

Zuriel gave him a backhanded slap across the face, nearly knocking him off the bench.

Asaph rubbed his cheek. "That's not an answer."

This time, Zuriel switched the knife to his left hand and punched Asaph in the face with his right. It was like being struck on the bridge of the nose with a rock. Blood streamed from his nose until he tasted it on his lips.

"I didn't kill Chaim," Zuriel said.

"I was there. I know what I saw."

Zuriel put his blade to Asaph's neck and leaned in so close that Asaph could smell the onions on his breath. Again, Asaph marveled at how calm he felt.

"Are you going to kill me next?" Asaph asked.

"Give me one reason why I shouldn't?"

"Because the Lord says, 'Depart from me, men of bloodshed.'"

Zuriel's eyes revealed a flicker of fear.

"Since when have you become a pompous priest, throwing Scripture in my face? It's not the Asaph I've known all my life."

"That's because you've never really known me. Besides, my life has been transformed. I freely admit that when I was a tax collector, I was crooked. I treated people badly. I treated *you* badly."

Asaph could see the shock in Zuriel's face. Surely, Zuriel had never forgotten the day Asaph tormented him by fabricating imaginary taxes at the gate leading into Jericho.

"I am sorry for what I did to you," Asaph repeated.

Zuriel didn't respond.

"If my behavior contributed in any way to what you have become, then I ask the Lord for forgiveness."

"What have I become?" Zuriel said, finally recovering his tongue—and his anger.

"You tell me."

"No. I'm asking *you*." Zuriel aimed the tip of his knife between Asaph's eyes. "What have I become?"

Asaph didn't want to answer with the blade so close to his face. But he did. "You're a man of bloodshed. You tried to kill me on the day Jesus was crucified. Then you came in the night to murder me, didn't you? You might've succeeded if Eliana hadn't interrupted you."

Again, no response from Zuriel. Asaph knew he had hit the mark.

"And now you've come to finish what you failed to do two other times." Asaph closed his eyes, anticipating the blade sinking into his forehead.

Nothing happened. When Asaph opened his eyes, the knife was still there, shaking in Zuriel's unsteady hand. Then shadows filled the doorway, backlit by the sun.

"You forgot to pay us," came Pharez's voice. Zuriel whirled around, switching the knife back to his right hand.

Instantly, Pharez's eyes went to the blood streaming from Asaph's nose.

"What's this all about, Zuriel?"

"None of your business!"

"He's right," said Abner, entering the room just behind Pharez. "It's none of our business."

"The Lord makes it my business," Pharez said. "Zuriel, you said Asaph was wanted for murder. But I'm beginning to think it's you who is the murderer—as he said."

Zuriel didn't hesitate for a heartbeat. He charged at Pharez, knife at the ready. But Pharez grabbed a clay pot from a nearby table and hurled it into Zuriel's face. The man had a powerful arm, and the pot cracked upon impact. As Zuriel staggered backward, Pharez grabbed the wrist of Zuriel's knife hand and drove him backward against the kitchen table. Then Pharez head-butted Zuriel, knocking him out cold.

Abner stood off to the side watching calmly, as if he could care less if Pharez and Zuriel beat each other into oblivion. Once Zuriel was unconscious, Abner pulled out his knife and cut the moneybag from Zuriel's prone body.

"Here's our gold," Abner said, tossing the bag on the table. "Let's split it."

"Take it all yourself," Pharez said. "I want no part of this."

Abner's face lit up. "Whatever you say." In a moment, he was gone, and so was the bag of money.

Still panting, Pharez looked over at Asaph, as if to say, "What have you gotten me into?"

"Thank you, Pharez. I tell you the truth when I say that Zuriel is the murderer. And he would have killed me if you hadn't returned when you did. So, thank you."

"You better be right." Pharez pulled out a knife and cut Asaph's bonds.

"The Lord watches over the way of the righteous," Asaph said, quoting one of the Psalms of David.

"But the way of the wicked leads to destruction," added Pharez.

The two men fled the scene, but not until Pharez had pried the knife from Zuriel's hand.

Nekoda

"They must be stopped," said Bildad, one of Nekoda's fellow Sadducees on the Jewish high court, the Sanhedrin. A group of five Sadducee priests, Nekoda included, had gathered in Solomon's Porch on the Temple Mount to discuss the latest events in the city. A steady rain came down, a welcome blessing for the growers. A low and extended rumble shook the heavens.

"Followers of the Way claim the Holy Spirit descended on them, making it possible for them to speak many languages," said Javan. "The most ridiculous thing I have ever heard."

Nekoda was silent, still thinking about his brother Chaim's death. He wondered whether Asaph was really the culprit. He had just been visited by Pharez, one of the men given the job of bringing in Asaph. Pharez told him that Zuriel tried to execute Asaph on the spot and then attacked him. Pharez had doubts about Zuriel's sanity—and innocence.

"Nekoda, I'm asking you a question," came the voice of Javan.

Nekoda looked up and noticed that the other four priests all had eyes on him. "Sorry. What was your question?"

"We said that since your brother had been a follower of Jesus, we wondered if you had any ideas where these heretics are most vulnerable," said Bildad. "If we arrested their leaders, would that put an end to this movement?"

Nekoda shook his head. Their question irritated him. "Go ahead and arrest their leaders. You'll only make the movement stronger."

"But some claim that this Jesus is the Son of God," said Bildad. "We can't let blasphemy go unpunished."

"How do you know it's not true?" Nekoda said, giving in to the urge to bait his fellow priests. "I was at the Temple when the curtain was ripped in half, from top to bottom, at the moment of Jesus's death. How do you explain that?"

The other four priests stared at him in shock. Nekoda couldn't believe he had just uttered those words. But he found, deep within, a strong urge to defend his brother and his brother's beliefs.

"Do you believe Jesus of Nazareth is the Son of Man—the one spoken of by the prophet Daniel?" Bildad asked him.

Nekoda was treading on dangerous ground. "I don't believe it, but I do believe we should let the movement rise or fall on its own merit. If it is not of God, the movement of Jesus will perish, as has happened to one false Messiah after another. If God is on our side, what is there to fear?"

"You don't care about the people who are being deceived every day by Peter and the other disciples of Jesus?" asked Nathan. "You don't care about the Truth?"

"Of course I care about the Truth. But you can't force the Truth on people. I know that to be true. I couldn't force the Truth on my brother."

"It appears to me that you're allowing your feelings about your brother to cloud your judgment, Nekoda."

"No! For once, I'm allowing my feelings about Chaim to *clear up* my vision. I was blind about him. Chaim was as innocent as a dove."

"Doves make good sacrifices at the Temple," said Javan.

Nekoda grabbed Javan by the robe and shoved him against one of the pillars in Solomon's court.

"My brother's death served no purpose!" Nekoda placed his face close to Javan's. Bildad tried to peel him off Javan, but Nekoda gave Bildad a stiff-arm to the chest.

"Nekoda, think of who you are!" Javan shouted.

"I *am* thinking of who I am! I am the brother of Chaim, an innocent man killed for no good reason. It's about time I thought of myself as his brother."

Nekoda loosened his hold on Javan, who straightened his clothing and tried to regain his dignity.

"I will overlook this for now, Nekoda, seeing how emotional you are about your brother's death," Javan said. "But tread carefully. I could make trouble for you with the high priest. You said some very questionable things."

"Questionable, yes," said Nekoda. "These are matters we should be asking questions about! For instance, what happened to the body of Jesus of Nazareth?"

"It was stolen by his disciples," Nathan said.

"With Roman guards standing at the tomb?"

"Maybe they were paid off."

"The soldiers weren't that stupid. They have been executed for letting Jesus's body disappear. They knew the punishment. They knew that if they let Jesus's body be taken, they were as good as dead."

"Are you saying you believe Jesus is alive?" asked Bildad.

"I'm not saying that. But I am asking the question. What happened to the body? We must at least be asking the questions."

"I think your brother's death is loosening your hold on reality, Nekoda. Believing that Jesus is alive will not resurrect your brother," said Nathan.

Nekoda was tempted to attack Nathan for those words, but he was suddenly too weary to care. Too tired to do anything.

"Nekoda, go home and sleep off whatever is ailing you," Bildad commanded. "Then sit down with another priest and try to pray through the grief that is unraveling your mind. Your behavior—your *misbehavior*—won't be tolerated for much longer."

With a dismissive wave of his hand, Nekoda wandered off. He left the cover of the colonnade and strode into the rain, which had intensified. Let it rain, let it thunder. He really didn't care if a bolt of lightning roasted him on the spot.

3.

THE BOOK OF ACTS, CHAPTER 3

Asaph

ASAPH DIDN'T KNOW WHY he was so nervous as he made his way to the house where Eliana and her father had been living for the past week.

He had known Eliana since they were children, racing each other through the streets of their small village in the Judean hills not far from Jerusalem. But they had been through so much since those days; he was still afraid of what she might do or say when he knocked on her door. It didn't help that he was also shaken by the encounter with Zuriel the day before.

Eliana's father, Judah, had asked if Asaph wanted to delay this ritual to give him time to recover. But Asaph was a wanted man, and every day of freedom was precious. He wanted to do this as soon as possible.

Eliana and her father, Judah, had switched residences to the home of a family headed by Lucas, son of Tobit. They lived near the Pool of Siloam, the very place where Rufus had nearly killed Sveshtari—and where Zuriel had nearly killed Asaph on the day Jesus was crucified. Zuriel had known Asaph since childhood, and the hostility between the two men had only grown with every passing year.

Asaph carried a betrothal cup and wine, as well as a pouch containing the bride price. Normally, a groom would be accompanied by his father, but Asaph's father was long since dead. Asaph came to the gate leading into the courtyard of the Lucas household, and he stopped to offer up a prayer. When he heard footsteps behind him, alarms went off in his mind, and he whirled around to see a servant hurrying along with a sack of grain over his shoulder. Asaph was understandably jumpy. He slipped inside the protection of the outer courtyard without any further delay.

As he approached the door of the modest home, he prayed that Eliana's father would answer his knock. Although the father was the one answering the door, everything depended on the woman's consent. If the woman told her father not to answer the door, there would be no marriage. If she told her father to open the door, then her answer was yes, and they would be betrothed.

His future hinged on an open door.

Asaph and Judah had already drafted a marriage contract, the *ketubah*, which included family histories of the bride and groom, the story of how the bride and groom met, and both of their responsibilities in marriage. Asaph was amazed they were able to keep their story brief. Their story could fill a dozen scrolls.

Asaph stepped before the heavy, wooden door and knocked.

No answer. He had hoped that Judah would throw open the door only moments after he rapped on the wood. But no response. He knocked again. Nothing. No answer. His stomach clenched.

He was sure this was the right day and the right hour. He and Judah had carefully set it all up. Should he dare knock again? He didn't want to create a scene. Was Eliana having second thoughts? Did she decide that they were much too old to marry? He felt like a fool standing there with a betrothal cup and a jar of wine. If anyone spotted him . . .

"Who are you?"

Asaph turned to see a young boy and girl, no more than ten years old, approach him through the gate. He gasped at the sight because the boy and girl reminded him so much of himself and Eliana at the very same age.

"I am here to pay a visit to a woman named Eliana."

"There is no Eliana in this house," said the boy, folding his arms and giving him a fierce stare.

"She is a guest in the Lucas house," Asaph said.

The girl began giggling, but the boy didn't let go of his judgmental gaze. He pointed a finger at the house next door, beyond the stone wall. "*That* is the Lucas house. This is the house of Zubulun." He spoke the words as if to say, "How can you be so stupid?" Hadn't this boy's parents taught him to respect his elders?

The girl's giggle became a full-blown laugh.

Asaph sensed his face going red. He hurried away, leaving the laughter behind.

This time, as he approached the door of the correct house, he spotted Judah peeking out the window. And this time, when he knocked on the door, it opened before he had barely finished knocking.

"Enter, Asaph, my daughter has been waiting for you." Judah grinned as he said this. He stood next to Rabbi Mordecai, who had agreed to seal their covenant.

Then Eliana appeared in the doorway of a room at the back of the house. Her hair, which showed some signs of graying, was long and braided and spilled down the front of her aqua-colored tunic. Her belt was a fine, off-white cloth with brown stripes to match the brown of her headdress. She was dressed in her finest clothes; but most distinctive was the flowered gauze muslin veil. Like most Hebrew women, she preserved the face veil for the most special occasions.

Through the translucent veil, he could see that Eliana was smiling, trying to contain a laugh.

"You saw me go to the wrong house, didn't you?" Asaph asked.

"We did," said Eliana. "But it was a long and roundabout journey that finally brought us together—so going to the wrong house is the perfect picture of our relationship the past forty years."

"True. Our ancestors wandered for forty years in the desert."

"But they ultimately found the Promised Land."

"And you're my Promised Land," Asaph said, taking her by the hand.

"And you are my Joshua."

Rabbi Mordecai blessed the cup of the covenant, which would take them from betrothal through the final wedding ceremony at a later date.

"Blessed are you, Lord our God, Master of the Universe, who has sanctified us with his commandments, and commanded us regarding forbidden unions, and who forbad betrothed women to us, and permitted to us those married to us by *hupah* and *kiddushin*. Praised are you, Lord, who sanctifies His people Israel with *huppah* and *kiddushin*."

The rabbi handed the cup of wine to Asaph, who drank deeply and then passed it to Eliana. She lifted her veil and drank, sharing in the wine, sharing in the blood, entering into the covenant. Then Asaph produced the ring, which was solid and circular and strong, as their relationship should be. He slipped it onto Eliana's finger, saying, "Behold, by this ring you are consecrated to me as my wife according to the laws of Moses and Israel."

Their wedding day—and the consummation of their marriage—still lay in the future, but Asaph and Eliana were betrothed this day; they had entered into *erusin*. They were committed for life. They were in covenant together.

The two little children who once raced side by side through the streets of their village had run off in different directions as adults. But now they were together again, side by side. Now, whenever and wherever they ran, they would run together.

Keturah

Keturah never failed to be staggered by the Temple in Jerusalem—the largest and most magnificent structure she had ever laid eyes upon, even dwarfing Herod's palace in Machaerus, where she once served as a slave.

The Temple Mount was a massive rectangle that took worshippers deeper and deeper into the sacred center. The outermost part was the Court of Gentiles, which led into the Court of Women, then into the Court of Israelites (limited to Jewish men), and then into the Court of Priests, where the daily sacrifices were made. From there, the way was only toward more holiness, because next was the Temple itself with the Holy Place followed by the Holy of Holies, which could only be entered by the high priest once a year.

Keturah was only allowed to enter the Temple grounds as far as the Court of Women, but even that provided a view that seemed like something out of paradise. Everywhere she looked, she saw splendor. Four great lampstands, rising high above the ground on pillars, burned night and day. Ladders with hundreds of rungs led up the sides of the lampstands so men could keep them burning. At one end of the Court of Women was the magnificent Nicanor Gate, an enormous double-door that looked like it had been sized for giants. It was made of Corinthian copper that flashed in the sunlight like gold. At the other end of the Court of Women was a smaller but equally stunning door that allowed people to enter from the Court of Gentiles. No wonder it was called the Beautiful Gate.

Keturah, with Eliana by her side, watched as the disciples approached the entrance to the Court of Women, with hundreds of people following in their wake. The disciples had been creating a stir ever since the Spirit of the Lord came upon them, and hundreds of people were becoming converts every day. But the disciples were playing with fire. How long would Roman and Jewish authorities allow the Jesus movement to grow unimpeded?

"I am thinking of going to Nekoda and speaking to him on Asaph's behalf," Eliana told Keturah as they approached the disciples near the entrance of the Beautiful Gate.

"What does Asaph think of that?" Keturah said.

"I haven't told him, but I don't think he would approve."

Keturah stopped in her tracks. She was stunned. "Eliana, you are betrothed now. Don't you think he deserves to know?"

"Someone must tell Nekoda that Asaph is innocent; someone must tell him that Zuriel is the one who killed his brother. Asaph cannot do it because he will be arrested on the spot if he dared to approach Nekoda."

"It's too dangerous for you to do it as well."

Keturah saw two dangers. The first would come from Nekoda, who might apprehend Eliana to draw Asaph out of hiding. But the other threat would be to Eliana and Asaph's relationship. Operating behind your betrothed's back is not a good way to begin a marriage.

But Keturah didn't speak these fears. As they approached the Beautiful Gate, they saw that the disciples had stopped to talk to a lame man seated on the ground. She had seen this man many times, sitting near the gate, asking for alms.

Peter and John stopped directly in front of this man and were saying something to him. Keturah and Eliana squeezed through the crowd, moving within hearing range. The lame man looked around at the crowd, which suddenly encircled him. From the expression on his face, he looked intimidated by this level of attention.

"Look at us," Peter said to the lame man, who kept glancing from face to face, probably wondering which people were most likely to give him money. Eventually, the man focused his attention on Peter.

"I have no silver or gold," Peter said as the poor man's expression changed from eagerness to anger. "But what I have I give you."

Suddenly, the man's look of anger transformed to puzzlement. If Peter didn't have silver or gold, what good could he be?

"In the name of Jesus Christ of Nazareth, rise up and walk."

Then Peter took the man's right hand. The man looked confused, even afraid. He started to withdraw his hand, but Peter held on, as firmly as the fisherman once gripped his nets along the Sea of Galilee.

Slowly, steadily, Peter raised the lame man to his feet. The man looked like a newborn colt, unsteady on his legs, which had been unused since birth. For a horse, walking came on the first day after birth. For this man, was he finally going to get his legs after thirty or more years?

The man held on to Peter on one side and John on the other, his legs wobbling and buckling. It was obvious the man didn't want to let go of either disciple, but his legs straightened and strengthened right in front of everyone's eyes.

John tried to release him, but the man wouldn't let go. He clung to John more fiercely, but John gently peeled away his hand. The man shifted his free hand to Peter until he was holding on to the big fisherman with both hands.

Then Peter also let go, carefully removing the man's hands, which clutched at his robe. The man stood on his own, swaying like a tree in a heavy wind. He held out both hands for balance, but he was standing! The man glanced around, his shining gaze bouncing from face to face to face.

Then he lifted one leg and set it down. Then the other leg, as if testing them out.

He began to walk, keeping his eyes riveted to his feet as if he might collapse into a heap if he didn't keep staring at them.

The crowd, which watched in stunned silence, began to buzz.

"Praise the Lord in heaven!"

"Praise Jesus!"

Praise Jesus? Was Jesus present at this healing? When Peter had healed this man, he said "In the name of Jesus of Nazareth." Could the very name of Jesus unleash this much power? Keturah had seen power coming from the hands of Jesus before; she had also seen power in his words. Could there also be power in his name?

The healed man leaped. Not a big jump. Just a small leap, almost a skip, and he stumbled into the crowd, only to be caught by two men. They righted him, and he skipped again, then twirled on his newborn legs.

Someone said, "I'll race you to Solomon's Portico!" Then the man, lame from birth, began to run—slowly and awkwardly at first, then faster and faster. Peter and John ran alongside, and so did Eliana and Keturah.

Keturah was utterly astonished.

Eliana

Eliana could not contain her laughter as she ran alongside the healed man, nearly shoulder to shoulder. With every stride, his feet seemed to gain more strength, more power, as he moved swiftly toward Solomon's Portico. When he reached the colonnade, the man stopped to lean over, hands on knees, to catch his breath. His legs may have strengthened, but his lungs were obviously not used to the strain. He laughed between gasps, and the crowd pressed in on him, some patting him on the back.

When he straightened up, Peter wrapped him in a big-bear embrace, and the man broke down in tears. Then John put an arm around him and blessed him, while Peter turned to the crowd and began to speak.

"You Israelites, why do you wonder at this, or why do you stare at us, as though by our own power or piety we had made him walk? The God of Abraham, the God of Isaac, and the God of Jacob, the God of our ancestors has glorified his servant Jesus, whom you handed over and rejected in the presence of Pilate, though he had decided to release him."

Peter paused to stride up several stairs where he could be better seen. His words were a stinging rebuke to the authorities.

"But you rejected the Holy and Righteous One and asked to have a murderer given to you, and you killed the Author of Life, whom God raised from the dead. To this we are witnesses. And by faith in his name, his name itself has made this man strong, whom you see and know; and the faith that is through Jesus has given him this perfect health in the presence of all of you."

Peter had just described Jesus as the Author of Life. If there was any doubt about whether the disciples thought Jesus to be divine, this removed them. The very name of Jesus contained power, something you couldn't even say about Moses or Isaac or Jacob. Eliana felt a stirring once again, a shiver up her back. She found herself praying out loud.

Peter softened his next words, telling the crowd that he knew they had acted in ignorance when they handed Jesus over to be killed. He also said that the Messiah's suffering was foretold by the prophets, and he called on the people to repent.

Many did, hundreds of them. They crowded around Peter, begging to be forgiven. It struck Eliana that these people were no different than the lame beggar asking for alms; but instead of begging for money, they were begging for something far more precious.

Sometime during Peter's preaching, Eliana felt a nudge to leave and go directly to see Nekoda before she lost the nerve. She broke away from the crowd as the words of Peter carried across the Temple Mount. She was alarmed when Keturah joined her.

"You told me that what I'm doing is dangerous," Eliana said. "Please don't put yourself in harm's way for my sake."

"I'm not going to allow you to appear before Nekoda alone," Keturah said. "He is more likely to listen if there are two of us."

"I wouldn't be so sure. We are only women in his eyes, and I'm not sure the testimony of *two* women is much different than one."

"It can't hurt."

Eliana shrugged. She hoped Keturah was right. They moved on, heading toward the Upper City of Jerusalem, where the wealthy and powerful were concentrated like bristling bees.

Nekoda

Nekoda reclined in the courtyard of his home, reading a scroll of the Torah, when his servant girl, Chloe, ushered Zuriel and Abner into his presence. Zuriel and Abner had promised that they would track down Asaph and bring him in, but Zuriel came to him with the look of failure on his face, not to mention a nasty bruise on his forehead.

But Nekoda didn't need to look at Zuriel's face to know he had failed in his mission to capture Asaph. Pharez had already come by and told Nekoda what had happened. It wasn't a pretty picture.

Nekoda did not rise to greet Zuriel and Abner. He also did not invite them to take a seat. Abner, a tall, imposing figure, stood several steps behind Zuriel with his arms crossed. Nekoda couldn't read Abner's face.

The man maintained a cold stare and didn't say a word. It was all part of his intimidation ploy.

"That's a nasty mark on your forehead," Nekoda said to Zuriel.

Zuriel put a hand to his forehead, acting as if he barely knew the bump was there. "It was nothing. Just hit my head on a low doorframe."

"Ah," said Nekoda. Zuriel had started with a lie. Nekoda knew that Pharez, not a doorframe, had given him the bruise. "Did you have any success in tracking down Asaph?"

"Yes, Pharez and Abner found him, but before I got there, Asaph had already given them the slip. But don't blame them. Asaph is a slippery fellow."

"Is that so?" Nekoda was curious how far Zuriel would go with his fabrications. "You mean you never saw Asaph yourself?"

"Not at all. Like I said, by the time I got to the house, Asaph had already escaped."

"How?"

"He overpowered Pharez before he could bind him with rope."

Nekoda glanced at Abner. "Are you saying that Asaph overpowered Abner as well? That must have taken some uncanny strength."

"Abner had gone off to make water. So, it was only Pharez."

Abner's stoic look did not crack as Zuriel revealed this embarrassing bit of information.

"Abner, why didn't you wait until the prisoner was bound before leaving Pharez alone with him?"

"Pharez told Abner he had the matter under control," Zuriel said, answering for Abner. "Pharez gravely underestimated Asaph."

Zuriel sounded more and more confident in his lies. But before he could get too comfortable with his deceptions, Nekoda produced a knife from his sleeves. It was Zuriel's knife, taken from him by Pharez.

"Do you recognize this?"

Zuriel's mouth dropped open and beads of sweat dotted his forehead like pearls. Zuriel pretended to study the knife from a distance. "Who does it belong to?"

"It's yours, of course. So says Pharez."

"Then Pharez lies. I've never seen that knife before."

Zuriel spoke confidently. Nekoda might have even believed him under different circumstances. Nekoda laid the knife flat on his left palm.

"Funny. I've seen the handle on this knife before. I saw it in your possession," Nekoda said.

"That can't be! Maybe you saw something similar, but that isn't my knife." Zuriel turned to Abner. "Is that your knife?"

Abner slowly shook his head no.

"If this isn't your blade, then show me your knife." Nekoda took great pleasure in tormenting Zuriel.

"I don't have it with me just now."

"I've never known you to be anywhere without your knife," Nekoda said, offering him the blade.

"Then you don't know me." He could see that Zuriel wanted to leave, to escape this line of questioning. "But if you insist on giving me a new knife, I'll gladly take it," Zuriel said, snatching it from Nekoda's hand.

"You have a penchant for lying, don't you?" Nekoda said. "Did you also lie to me about who really killed my brother?"

Zuriel came to attention, presenting his angriest expression. He was quick on his feet, transitioning between emotions. Nekoda will give him that.

"You dare accuse me of killing your brother!"

"Not me. Pharez thinks you did it. He told me you were also preparing to kill Asaph when he stopped you. He said he knocked you out cold, and then he took your knife."

"I say it again. He's lying to cover up the mistakes he made in letting Asaph escape."

"And I say *you're* lying. I say you tried to kill Asaph because he knows you killed my brother."

A cold blankness came over Zuriel's face, as if he were slowly turning to stone. Scripture talks about people hardening their hearts. It almost appeared that Zuriel was hardening his entire being.

At that moment, Nekoda knew he was guilty.

Eliana

"What are you going to say to Nekoda when you see him?" Keturah asked Eliana as they moved past several sellers of fine fabric. The shops were significantly more lavish in the Upper City of Jerusalem, where government and Sadducee leaders lived. Most of the homes in this wealthy section of the city were two stories, built in Roman villa style with a central courtyard. Some even had multiple ritual baths, or *mikvehs*.

"I am going to tell Nekoda the truth—that Asaph is innocent of his brother's blood," Eliana said. "And I'm going to tell him that Asaph saw Zuriel murder Chaim. It was Asaph who comforted his brother when he was passing from this life. I'm going to tell him the truth."

"What if he asks why you, rather than Asaph, are delivering this news?"

"Again, I will tell him the truth. Asaph is hesitant to come in person because he knows he would be arrested. I'll also point out that Asaph doesn't know I'm doing this on his behalf."

"I hope Nekoda sees that you are being courageous, rather than deceptive by acting behind Asaph's back."

"It's worth taking a chance."

They neared Nekoda's home, one of those fine, two-story homes encircled by a brick wall. But as they approached the gate leading into the courtyard, they heard the raised voices of men. Then the gate was flung open, so fiercely and suddenly that it nearly slammed Eliana in the face. Rushing out of the courtyard was none other than Zuriel of all people! He was flanked by a tall tree of a man.

Zuriel came to a sudden stop. He and Eliana stood a short distance apart, staring at each other in shock.

Keturah placed a hand on Eliana's shoulder, as if to say, "Let's go," but Eliana didn't budge. She still wanted to talk with Nekoda, but Zuriel and the tall man blocked her way. As she made a move to step around them, she saw something dangerous flicker in Zuriel's eyes. In that instant, she knew what he was thinking, and she tried to backtrack.

"Grab the other one!" Zuriel told the tall man as he latched onto Eliana's arm and pulled her into the road.

"Stop it, you're hurting me!" Eliana shouted. She hoped Nekoda could hear their shouts.

Then Zuriel did the unthinkable. He drew out a knife and put it to her neck so that she felt steel against her skin. Immediately, her mind flew back to the day, as a little girl, when she was abducted by men who had invaded the sheepfold near Bethlehem. They too had put a blade to her throat as they took her away, treating her as their plaything until finally selling her into slavery.

Eliana nearly collapsed on the spot.

In the corner of her eyes, she saw the tall man chase down Keturah, who didn't get far before he grabbed her from behind. Keturah started to scream, but the man clamped a large hand over her mouth and pulled her head back so severely that Eliana was afraid he might snap her neck.

The narrow street was empty of people. There was no one to witness what was happening. Soon, the big man also had a knife out, and he held it at Keturah's back. Zuriel shifted his position so that he too put his blade against Eliana's back. When she started to call out, the knife went in just enough to cut through Eliana's clothes and prick her skin.

After that, she stayed silent as the men pushed them forward, whisking them away from Nekoda's home.

Sveshtari

The afternoon was wearing thin, and still no sign of either Keturah or Eliana.

Sveshtari and Asaph had gone to the houses where Eliana and Keturah were staying, as well as to the Upper Room where the followers of Jesus regularly met. But no one reported seeing the two women.

Sveshtari and Asaph then headed for the home of Joanna, the wealthy follower of the Way. Keturah had once served as Joanna's servant in Herod Antipas's palace, well before any of them met Jesus.

"Have Keturah and Eliana been here today?" Sveshtari asked, even before they had a chance to be seated at a table in Joanna's house. An abundance of fruit was piled in the center of the table, and servants busily poured cups of wine.

"I haven't seen either of them," Joanna said. "How long have they been missing?"

"Eliana has been gone since the fourth hour," Asaph said. Mid-morning.

"The same with Keturah," said Sveshtari.

"They didn't leave word with anyone about where they were going?"

Asaph shook his head, and Sveshtari said, "No."

"That seems strange."

"It's especially unusual for Keturah," Sveshtari noted. "The wet nurse said she expected Keturah back by the sixth hour."

"It's still not quite dark, so there could be an innocent explanation," Joanna said. "Could we take some time to pray?"

Sveshtari didn't want to waste any time praying; he wanted to use every available moment of daylight to keep hunting for Eliana and Keturah. But when Asaph agreed, Sveshtari didn't feel he could say no. So, Asaph and Joanna both prayed for Keturah and Eliana's safety, while Sveshtari squirmed in silence.

No sooner had they finished their "Amens" than Joanna had another visitor. It was Sveshtari's friend, Abel, a man who seemed to have connections in every corner of Jericho and Jerusalem. Sveshtari had sent him out on the streets a couple of hours earlier to hunt for the women.

Sveshtari rose from his chair. "Do you have word on Eliana and Keturah?"

Abel didn't answer immediately. He diverted his eyes and shuffled his feet. His silence didn't bode well.

"What happened?" Asaph asked. "Are they hurt?"

"They're being held captive."

Rage came over Sveshtari like a scorching wind. "Where are they? Who did this?"

"I don't know who's holding them," Abel said. "I was given a message about their abduction by a man named Abner."

"Abner! He was one of the men who captured me!" Asaph said.

"Is he holding the women? I'll kill him." Sveshtari drew out his sword. He was itching to use it.

"Abner said he was just delivering the message for the man holding Eliana and Keturah."

"Zuriel was the one who hired Abner and Pharez to capture me," Asaph said. "Is Zuriel holding the women?"

Abel shrugged. "Like I said, I don't know. But Abner says that if Asaph turns himself in to the guards at the Temple, the women will be released. If you don't, they will die."

Sveshtari closed his eyes. He visualized running his sword through Zuriel's gut. He could barely stand still.

"Abner says he will meet you at the Temple, and he will bring the women. If he sees you turning yourself in to the Temple guards, he will release them."

"When are we to meet them there?" Asaph asked.

"Before sunset. He wants you to present yourself to the guard stationed near the gate leading into the Court of Women. Eliana and Keturah will then be freed."

"How can we be assured this will happen?" Sveshtari demanded, pointing his sword at Abel.

Abel held out his hands and backpedaled. "Easy, Sveshtari. I'm just the messenger."

"The person making this demand has to be Zuriel," Asaph said. "Who else would want me to turn myself in?"

"Nekoda does," Abel said.

"But this doesn't seem like something Nekoda would do."

"You're right," said Abel.

"I agree. It must be Zuriel," Sveshtari said. "And Zuriel has to die."

"Not until we get Keturah and Eliana back."

"Of course. Then he dies. As painfully as possible."

Sveshtari knew that followers of the Way would be shocked by the ferocity of his feelings, but right now the words of Jesus were the furthest things from his mind.

4.

The Book of Acts, Chapter 4

Eliana

Once Eliana and Keturah had been taken outside the city walls, out of sight from other people, Zuriel blindfolded them and led them deeper into the hills. Eliana tried to keep track of the direction they were moving, but after the tenth turn, she was completely lost.

She had no idea where they were until they were led inside what she assumed to be a cave. Eliana felt a sudden coolness and a darkening of the light. The echo of their movements bounced off walls. She tried to nudge up her blindfold just enough to get a peek at their surroundings, but the cloth had been tied so tightly that she couldn't push it up without drawing attention.

When the blindfolds were finally removed, Eliana's hunch was confirmed. She found herself staring at the inside of a cave—an inner room of some sort. She couldn't see the entrance of the cave, but light still found its way into this room; therefore, they couldn't be too deep in the earth. Eliana and Keturah lowered themselves to the cold stone floor and put their backs against the wall.

Holding an oil lamp in his hands, Zuriel looked down on the two women. "I don't want to hurt you."

"You have a funny way of demonstrating that," Eliana said.

"I only seek justice for Chaim's death," he added.

"You have an even funnier way of showing that."

"Once I learn that Asaph has turned himself in to the Temple guards, then you will go free."

"But Asaph is innocent, and you know it. You know he didn't kill Chaim," Eliana said.

"You weren't there when it happened. I was there, and I saw him kill Nekoda's brother."

It's true that she wasn't there to witness the killing. When Chaim was being murdered on the streets of Jerusalem, Eliana was at Golgotha, witnessing a different murder—the execution of her Lord, Jesus the Messiah.

"Asaph would never harm Chaim," she said. "They were friends. Do you really think I'm going to believe your account of what happened to Chaim over Asaph's word?"

"It doesn't matter what you or I believe. It matters what the court system will believe. And I think there is a good chance that Asaph will be sentenced to death by stoning."

Eliana looked away, unable to maintain eye contact with Zuriel.

After an uneasy silence, she said, "What is it about you and stones, Zuriel? As children, you tried to get Asaph to hurl rocks at me. Now, as an adult, you're trying to get those who stand in judgment to hurl stones at Asaph."

"I'm sorry for what I did to you as a child," Zuriel said softly. Surprisingly, he sounded sincere.

"If you're truly sorry, then do not do this to my betrothed."

Zuriel started at these words. "You and Asaph are betrothed?"

"We are."

"But why would you want to become betrothed to a man who would kill to win you as a wife?" he asked.

"What are you talking about?"

"Chaim was a rival suitor of yours. Asaph is murdering the competition."

Eliana was horrified by the thought. Zuriel was very good at lying.

"You were never a witness to Chaim's death, Eliana," Zuriel continued. "All you have is his word that he didn't kill Chaim."

"His word is true."

"He is a tax collector," Zuriel said. "Tax collectors are practiced liars; they never change their core deceitfulness."

"He *was* a tax collector. He follows the Way now. He follows Jesus, and Jesus can change anyone. Even a tax collector. Even a demon-possessed woman like me."

"You want to believe he's changed, Eliana. He blinded you to the truth."

Eliana looked over at Keturah, who had remained quiet throughout this entire exchange. Keturah stared into space, not turning to meet Eliana's eyes. Zuriel's lies built upon each other, constructing an edifice of deceit. He spoke so calmly, so reasonably, that quiet doubts were planted.

"Let Asaph be taken to trial," Zuriel said. "If he's innocent, he has nothing to fear."

That statement broke the spell, and Eliana snapped her head in Zuriel's direction. "Jesus was innocent and look what happened to him when he was taken to trial."

"Jesus was *not* innocent. He claimed to be the Son of the Most High. He deserved to die."

"And yet he lives."

Keturah finally came out of her daze and glared at Zuriel. "She's right. Jesus lives. I saw him. He stood as close to me as you are right now."

Zuriel burst out laughing. "You were seeing things."

"If I was, then what about the other 500 along the Sea of Galilee? We all saw him—and listened to him."

"Mass delusion."

"Follow Jesus, Zuriel," Eliana suddenly said, feeling a stirring in her heart. "You can still undo all you've done if you profess to follow the Way. Let Jesus bring peace to your troubled heart." Eliana felt a power growing within her, like a rising bonfire. Then the words poured out. "Our Lord is betrothed to his people. We are united in him, and so can you be, if you only choose. Choose, Zuriel! My garment is gold, and I am presented to my Lord, my betrothed, without spot, without wrinkle. Pure. Clean. Redeemed in his eyes. Choose it, choose it now, Zuriel, before it's too late!"

By this time, Eliana was speaking so loudly and urgently that even Keturah stared at her in perplexed wonder. When she finished, Zuriel gaped at her without saying anything. Did any of her words hit their mark?

Ultimately, it was Keturah who broke the silence. "You've made a big mistake, Zuriel."

Zuriel smiled. "And what mistake is that?"

"You abducted the betrothed of Asaph and the betrothed of Sveshtari."

"Are you saying that you too are betrothed?"

"I am betrothed to Sveshtari, and he is not someone to tangle with. He will hunt you. He will kill you."

Eliana couldn't tell if her own words had any impact on Zuriel, but Keturah's words surely did. Zuriel was visibly shaken. She could see it.

"I'm not afraid," Zuriel finally said.

That was a lie. Eliana could see it in his eyes.

Then Zuriel turned and left the two women alone. He took his lamp with him, leaving them in the dark.

Sveshtari

Asaph, Sveshtari, and Abel began their search for the women at Nekoda's house in the upper city. Nekoda was the only other person, besides Zuriel, motivated enough to capture the women and use them as leverage to get Asaph to turn himself in.

Sveshtari told Asaph he shouldn't go with them to Nekoda's house, since the priest was hunting him and wanted him arrested. Asaph needed to steer clear of the priest's house, but he wouldn't see reason. Even when they told him to stay outside the gates of Nekoda's house, Asaph followed them into the courtyard. They found Nekoda in his courtyard, eating a simple meal of pomegranates and bread slathered with carob honey.

"We were told that the women were headed in the direction of your house," Sveshtari said.

"I never saw them. If they were coming this way, then they didn't make it. Only Zuriel came here today."

"Zuriel? He came here?"

"Yes, and I told him I was becoming more and more suspicious that he was behind my brother's murder. He wasn't happy to hear that." Nekoda turned his eyes on Asaph as he said this.

"So, you believe my innocence?" Asaph said.

"I didn't say that. But my suspicions about Zuriel are growing."

"For good reason. I saw him murder your brother. Zuriel stabbed him when Chaim tried to block his pursuit of Sveshtari."

"That's one version of the story."

"The true version."

"If the women were heading to your house, Nekoda, maybe Zuriel intercepted them and captured them," Abel said.

"That's a good possibility," Sveshtari said, turning toward Nekoda. "Do you know where Zuriel might try to hide the women?"

"I'm sorry I don't. But he's probably holding them somewhere outside the city. In a cave somewhere?"

"There are a lot of caves," Abel said. "Which one?"

Nekoda shrugged. "No idea."

"But you must have some hint. You hired Zuriel to capture Asaph, so you've been in contact with him."

"No. He was in contact with me. He was the one who volunteered to track down Asaph."

Nekoda shifted his gaze toward Sveshtari. "Is it true what Asaph says about Zuriel nearly capturing you on the day Jesus was crucified?" he asked, changing the subject.

"Yes, I fled from Zuriel and Rufus not long after you parted from them. They spotted me at the Temple Mount, and I fled from the Temple and into the sewer leading south toward the Pool of Siloam. I didn't see them again until we fought at the Pool of Siloam."

"But I saw," said Asaph. "Chaim tried to stop them from pursuing Sveshtari into the sewer, and he lost his life doing so."

Nekoda nodded and stared into space, absorbing their account. Then he looked back at Sveshtari and said, "I pray you find your women. Even if Zuriel is innocent of my brother's blood, he has no right to hold those two women as hostages."

"His actions point to his guilt," Abel said. "Why would an innocent man go to such lengths to have Asaph arrested?"

"He claims to want justice for my brother."

"A lie," said Asaph.

"You may be correct. But I need other witnesses to step forward before I believe your side of the story."

"Let us go," said Sveshtari, turning on his heels. "We're running out of light."

"And I need to turn myself in to the guard at the Temple," Asaph said. "It's our only option right now."

"There are always more options than you think," said Sveshtari as the three men began to run toward the Temple. The evening sun lit up the white stone with the fire of its dying light.

Asaph

Asaph rushed up the Monumental Staircase, an impressive set of stairs that alternated between long and short steps as it led up to the southern entrance of the Temple Mount. Sveshtari flanked him on his right and Abel on his left. At the top of the stairs, the trio pushed their way through the Double Gate, which was packed with people. Something was stirring inside the Temple grounds, with voices booming from the direction of Solomon's Porch.

Asaph was still planning to turn himself in to the Temple guard, despite the protests of Sveshtari and Abel. He wanted to do it alone, but Sveshtari and Abel weren't having it. They would go with him, no matter the risk.

Sveshtari was still being pursued by Roman authorities, but he argued that the Temple guards posed no risk to him. Temple guards were stationed at twenty-one points around the grounds, but these Levite police wouldn't know Sveshtari by sight, thankfully. Besides, Abel was on friendly terms with several of the guards, so Asaph hoped that would prevent any trouble.

Once Asaph turned himself in to the guards and the women were freed, he was confident that Sveshtari and Abel would eventually track down Zuriel and make him pay for what he had done. Asaph knew this desire for revenge went against everything that Jesus taught about forgiveness and mercy. But surely Jesus didn't expect them to let somebody like Zuriel get away with using innocent women as blackmail. "Vengeance is mine," says the Lord. But sometimes the Lord needed a little help in carrying out retribution.

Passing through the Huldah Gates, they emerged into the Court of Gentiles, the enormous outer court that encircled the Temple. Here, they found Peter and John preaching to people at Solomon's Porch, which ran along the eastern side of the court. The disciples, who had healed a man at the Beautiful Gate this very morning, were still going strong. The other disciples mixed in with the crowd, talking in earnest with anyone who would listen.

The topic: Jesus of Nazareth, of course.

"Stay back!" Abel snapped at Sveshtari and Asaph as they neared Solomon's Porch. Up ahead, several members of the Jewish ruling council, the Sanhedrin, headed toward Peter and John, along with a half dozen Temple guards. There was a good chance that some of these Sanhedrin priests—members of the Sadducee party—knew Asaph and Sveshtari by sight.

Asaph couldn't hear what the priests were saying to Peter and John, but judging by the flailing arms and heated expressions, it couldn't be good. When the Temple guards seized the two disciples by their arms, the crowd erupted. The noise became deafening. The crowd surged forward until Asaph was nearly lifted off his feet. He lost track of Sveshtari and Abel, who were carried away by the currents of the moving mass of people.

Asaph managed to turn himself around, and he fought his way in the opposite direction of Solomon's Porch, away from the heart of the tumult, fighting against the tide of humanity. He was buffeted by shouting people, their faces twisted by rage. The anger of the crowd was directed toward the Temple guards, who had arrested Peter and John.

The Temple authorities had finally made their move against the disciples by arresting the two leaders. It was inevitable, Asaph thought, because thousands of people had asked to be baptized into the Way during the past couple of days alone.

He never would have believed it, but Jesus was becoming more of a threat to the Jewish and Roman leaders *after* his crucifixion than before. When past "Messiahs" had arisen, the movement died when the Messiah died. But the Way was growing like a wild vine; this alone was evidence to Asaph that Jesus had risen. He was alive, and his vine was still growing and spreading throughout Jerusalem. Now, the authorities were trying to kill the movement by hauling Peter and John to prison. But those disciples were just two shoots. Rip them out of the ground, and the plant would continue to thrive. Asaph was sure. The root of Jesse was alive and well.

Asaph couldn't locate Sveshtari and Abel as evening shadows spread across the Temple Mount. Abner had commanded him to turn himself in at the gate leading from the Court of Gentiles to the Court of Women, deeper into the beating heart of the Temple Mount. Now that he had separated from his friends, Asaph would be able to turn himself in alone. It was better that way. Less risk to his friends.

Asaph made his way toward the Court of Women, fighting through the crowd, which still hadn't settled down after the arrest of the disciples. The Court of Women was huge, able to contain up to 6,000 worshippers. But Abner promised he would be positioned near the gate, along with Eliana and Keturah and the Temple guards. It would be an even exchange.

As darkness settled on the Temple, he hoped he would be able to see Abner. The enormous lamps, positioned in each of the four corners of the

Court of Women, blazed away like small suns. Even from outside of the court, he could see the glow as the lamps threw light into the air.

The Court of Women was surrounded on all sides by a wall with two golden doors—the Beautiful Gate where the healing had taken place this morning. As Asaph passed through the gate, he spun around, searching, but there was no sign of Abner, Eliana, or Keturah. He saw two Temple guards at the gate, but that was standard.

"Asaph!"

A voice erupted from the colonnade running along the edges of the Court of Women. Abner's voice came from the shadows amidst the rows of pillars. No sign of the women, though. No sign of the Temple guards.

"Abner, is that you?"

Abner emerged from the shadows and stood at the very edge of the colonnade.

"Where are Keturah and Eliana?" Asaph asked.

"Behind me, in the dark."

"And the Temple guards?"

"They are holding on to the women, ready to release them when you come."

"I want to see the women first."

Abner smiled. "Come near and you will."

Everything was telling Asaph to stay back, to be ready to run. Nevertheless, he inched forward, as if being drawn forward by a rope.

Keturah

Keturah's eyes had adjusted to the dark; she could see the shadow-draped figure of Eliana as she moved across the cave to their only exit out of this subterranean room. Eliana turned back toward Keturah and motioned her forward. When Keturah reached her side, Eliana pointed.

Keturah peered ahead and could see that the entrance to the cave was not too far away. The sun was setting, and the diminishing light shot flares of red and orange into the cave's opening. They could also see the shadows of three men; it was hard to distinguish them, but the one in the middle appeared to be Zuriel.

Eliana began to pray audibly, but silently, at Keturah's side. As she did, Eliana stepped into the wider space. Keturah followed, wondering what Eliana thought she was doing. There was no way they could get past three men. One of the three figures spotted them instantly.

"Where do you think you're going?" the man shouted—an unfamiliar voice. "Get back inside!"

Keturah stopped, but Eliana kept walking forward. Slowly. She didn't make any move to run.

"Get back in that room! Now!"

Then, without warning, Eliana began to speak in a loud voice. In another language! Keturah had no idea that Eliana could speak any languages except Aramaic, Hebrew, and maybe a little Greek. This was none of those.

But one of the men recognized it. "You speak Palmyrene?" the man said. "Where are you from, woman?"

Without stemming the flow of words coming from her mouth, Eliana's language suddenly seemed to shift again. Keturah still didn't know what she was saying, but the language sounded different.

"Now she's speaking Safaitic," the man said, turning to Zuriel and the third abductor. "I'm very impressed. She is a learned woman."

"The other day, the followers of the Way suddenly started speaking different languages," said the third man.

"It's simple trickery," spat Zuriel.

"I was there," the second man insisted. "I heard them. It was very bizarre. Maybe that's what's happening here."

Then Eliana shifted languages once again, and this time Keturah recognized the words. She was speaking Middle Persian. Surely, she would have known by now if Eliana had been taught all these languages. So how was she doing this? Had she been touched by the same Spirit that had given the disciples the power to speak different languages?

"She has special powers from God," said the second man with awe in his voice.

"You're easily impressed, Uzziah," said Zuriel. "So what if she can speak other languages!" All three men clustered closely around Eliana, as if trying to figure out if the languages were truly coming from her mouth, or whether it was a trick.

Keturah saw her chance. The men were focused solely on Eliana. Was this Eliana's idea all along—to draw their attention, to create an opening for Keturah to run?

"Will the Lord punish us for taking this woman prisoner? She has been touched by God," said the one called Uzziah.

"She's a follower of the Way, and they are anathema to the Lord!" Zuriel gave Uzziah a shove. "Just do what I tell you!"

Zuriel made another move to shove Uzziah. But when he shot out his hand, Uzziah slapped it away. As Zuriel drew his dagger, the third man stepped between them. Keturah saw her opportunity. She would never have a better chance.

"I say it again: This woman is touched by the Lord," said Uzziah.

"She's touched by a demon!" Zuriel shouted. "She was once possessed by spirits, and I think she has been again."

"I'm touched by the Holy Spirit!" Eliana declared in Aramaic, then in Hebrew, and then in several other languages. "I'm touched by the Holy Spirit! I'm touched by the Holy Spirit!"

As Keturah prepared to run, a wondrous thing occurred. A tongue of fire appeared on Eliana's head like a crown. A small flicker of fire. The flame didn't seem to burn; in fact, Eliana didn't even appear to know it was there. But the men backpedaled, their mouths agape.

This was her best chance. Tearing her eyes away from Eliana's flame, she darted for the entrance of the cave, where the sun was setting. She rushed into the cool, open air, hearing bellows of anger erupt from behind. As she ran, one of her shoes fell off, but she didn't slow down, even across brambles. From a distance, she could still hear Eliana praying, loudly and boldly in one language after another. There was power in her words, and Keturah prayed that the same power would carry her feet.

Asaph

As Asaph moved toward Abner, faces emerged from the darkness of the pillars. Two Temple guards. But no women.

Asaph came to a sudden halt. "Where are Eliana and Keturah?"

Abner grinned. "Who?"

"You promised to release the women. Where are they?"

"Don't worry. When we send word that you've turned yourself in, they will be released."

This was a setup. Asaph whirled around to flee and ran headlong into another Temple guard, who came from behind. Slamming a forearm against the guard's chest, Asaph broke loose but slipped as he darted to his right.

If he could make it through the Beautiful Gate, he had a chance of getting away. But two more guards stood at the gate, and they had spotted the commotion. One of them moved in Asaph's direction, so he shifted course. There were four gates leading out of the Court of Women, but guards were posted at each of them. He sprinted toward the southern gate in the hopes that the guard there had not been alerted.

Slowing down, Asaph mixed in with the mass of people exiting through the southern gate, and he heard the guards shout at people to get out of the way. He kept his head down and pressed forward.

"Apprehend that man!" bellowed one of the guards from behind.

"What man?" yelled the Temple guard at the southern gate.

"The one who girded his loins!"

Asaph had completely forgotten that he had tucked his tunic into his belt for easy movement. No other man in the crowd had done so. Frantically, he pulled out the material that had been tucked into his belt, but it was too late. He had been spotted by the guard at the southern gate.

He whirled around, seeking an escape route, but the guards had him hemmed in. He had nowhere to go, other than to prison.

Keturah

Keturah could hear them on the move, not far behind, gaining on her, clambering over rocks. She prayed that the darkness would cloak her as she fled northward across the rolling hills. As she ran, she looked for caves she might duck into. She scrambled up a slope, which slowed her down, but at least it took her off the narrow path that wound between the hills rising and falling on all sides. She heard wild dogs in the distance and the murmur of life coming from the city to her right.

Keturah reached a ledge, pausing to catch her breath and check where her pursuers might be. The darkness became thicker by the moment, and it was difficult to see anyone moving on the path below. She listened for the sound of steps but heard nothing. Pulling her legs up to her chest, she pressed her back against the rock behind her. It was safest to stay here where she could look down on any threats. If she wasn't moving, she wouldn't be making noise. And if she wasn't making noise, it was going to be difficult for them to track her in the blackness.

She heard the clink of rocks hitting rocks. It came from below, on the narrow passage that weaved among the hills. Someone was down there, but she couldn't make out the person. If she couldn't see them, then they couldn't see her. She hoped. Then she saw a black form shifting around below—a patch of darkness moving against an inky background. It was one of the men. He moved slowly, methodically. Most likely, Zuriel had sent out at least one of the men to track her while he remained behind to prevent Eliana from escaping.

She called on the Holy Spirit to help her. She was only a God-fearer, not a full follower of the Way, but she prayed that the Spirit didn't play favorites. The power she had seen in the disciples and in Eliana could not be denied. Eliana had always been in touch with the unseen world. When Keturah first met her friend on the road leading north from Machaerus, Eliana was tormented by evil spirits—spirits later cast from her by Jesus's disciples on the east side of the Sea of Galilee. Now, Eliana had opened the door to the Spirit of God. A Holy Spirit, the disciples called him. He was a person, the way they talked. The Spirit moved like fire and wind, but he wasn't an impersonal power like the forces of nature. He was living, he responded to prayer, he communicated, and he comforted, the disciples said. Some even called him a Counselor.

She needed this Spirit right now, for she saw another shifting shadow on the path below. Two men were just below her.

"Any sign of her?" asked Uzziah.

"We can't let her get back to the city and warn Sveshtari. He'll kill us all."

"Don't worry. She won't get that far."

"Why did we let Zuriel draw us into this? No amount of money is worth facing a man like Sveshtari."

"When we catch her, we'll kill her. And then we'll leave Zuriel alone with the other one. We'll leave the city. We'll fly to safety, but first we find the younger one, the pretty one."

"Maybe she climbed up one of these hills."

Keturah stifled a gasp. She groped in the dark for a rock. Something large enough to kill a man.

Holy Spirit, she prayed, *help me*. One of the men sounded like he was moving up the slope.

Sveshtari

When Sveshtari and Abel finally tracked down Asaph, he was being led out of the Court of Women by three Temple guards. The man, Abner, was nowhere to be seen, and neither were the women. Wasn't that the agreement? Asaph would turn himself in, and Keturah and Eliana would go free?

Sveshtari and Abel followed in the wake of the Temple guards who hauled Asaph out the southern gates of the Temple Mount and down the Monumental Stairs. They were taking Asaph to the prison inside the Sanhedrin building—Herodian Hall—just south of the bridge leading from the Kiponos Gate. People teemed in front of the door of the jail because, ironically, Peter and John were being released just as Asaph was being brought into the jail. Sveshtari watched as Asaph passed the two disciples and spoke to them. Peter reached out and touched Asaph on the shoulder as they passed each other, going in different directions.

Then Asaph disappeared through the prison gate, and he was gone.

"Do you see the women anywhere?" Abel asked.

"No!" Sveshtari snapped. In such a crowd, it would be extremely difficult to find Keturah and Eliana, especially in the darkness. He felt the urge to make someone bleed. Abel must have sensed his thoughts.

"Don't do anything stupid," he said. "Going into the prison and killing the Temple guards won't free Keturah. We need to locate Abner. We need to force him to tell us where the women are being held."

Sveshtari agreed. If they located Abner, he could make that man writhe until he revealed where Zuriel and the women were located. But it was going to be difficult to find Abner in this madhouse. There were too many faces.

Keturah

Keturah heard Eliana shouting from back in the cave, her voice carrying through the darkness with a disembodied eeriness. She shouted something in a foreign language, and it was heightened by the amphitheater of these hills.

Uzziah, the man scrambling up the side of the hill, paused.

"What is going on with that woman?" he asked the other shadow, who remained on the path below.

"As I said, she seems to be touched by a spirit of some sort," said the other.

"Or simply touched in the head."

The other man didn't answer immediately. Eliana had gone silent as well, but then her voice returned, a torrent of unintelligible syllables. *Where was she getting these words from?* Keturah wondered. It was as if she were drawing language out of a deep well.

"Maybe we should call it a day," said the man on the path. "I'm tired."

"What about Zuriel?"

"He hasn't paid us a single coin yet."

"And Abner?"

"We'll tell him that Zuriel became unreasonable, so we quit. Abner has low regard for Zuriel. He won't be surprised."

As Eliana continued to speak in unknown languages, Keturah heard Zuriel cursing and telling her to shut up.

"She's going to wake the dead," said the man on the path below.

"There are plenty of graves around here. Wasn't Jesus buried nearby?"

"They say he's walking around, alive again."

"Another reason we need to get out of here."

"I'm with you."

Keturah watched as the shadow moved back down the hill, joining his partner on the path below. Then they both moved off, away from the sounds of Eliana and Zuriel. Keturah waited as long as possible before she dared to move a muscle. Her right calf began to cramp before she finally stood up and stretched. The wind picked up in intensity, carrying all sorts of wild sounds in the air. Mostly jackals. Short bursts of deep-throated cries. Some sounds were dog-like, but others almost sounded like the screaming of a large bird of prey.

Normally, jackals won't attack humans, but they had been known to go after a child. She hoped she wouldn't encounter one on the way back to Jerusalem.

Eliana

Eliana tried to dash out of the cave, but Zuriel caught her easily, wrapping his arms around her waist from behind and lifting her off her feet. He laughed as he squeezed her. Eliana put up a fight but soon gave up when she realized it was useless. Instead, she went limp as he carried her back into the cave.

There was still no sign of the other two men who had gone off in search of Keturah. Eliana hoped that was a good sign. She was surprised that her plan had even worked—distracting the men and giving Keturah the opportunity to escape. To be honest, however, the plan wasn't really her idea. When those foreign languages burst out of her mouth, it probably surprised her more than it did the men.

"When did you learn to speak these languages?" Zuriel asked after hauling her deeper into the cave. "And how did you get a tongue of flame to dance on your head?"

A tongue of flame? Eliana was taken aback. "What flame?"

"You didn't know? A flame danced on your hair, but it didn't burn."

"I didn't feel it. I didn't even know it was there."

"And the languages?"

"I didn't know those languages."

"So, you're just making up sounds?"

"They're not made up. When I speak the words, I instinctively know their meaning."

Zuriel stepped closer, crowding her. Eliana backed up until her body came against the cave wall behind her. Then she slid down onto the cave floor to stay out of range of any attempts to molest her. With the other men gone, she didn't trust that Zuriel wouldn't try to take advantage.

"What did the words you were speaking mean?"

"They were words of judgment. Words of Isaiah."

Zuriel's eyes widened, almost imperceptibly.

Then Eliana spoke the words that had come to her in another language, only this time she spoke in a language he would understand—Aramaic.

"Woe to those who draw sin along with cords of deceit, and wickedness as with cart ropes. Woe to those who call evil good and good evil, who put darkness for light and light for darkness, who put bitter for sweet and sweet for bitter. Woe to those who are wise in their own eyes and clever in their own sight."

Zuriel smiled. "Are those words aimed at me?"

Eliana smiled back. "You tell me."

"If anyone is wise in his own eyes and clever in his own sight, it's your betrothed, Asaph. He robbed people as a tax collector. He robbed *me*."

"I know. But he has been cleansed of his past deeds. The prophet Isaiah also said, 'Though your sins are like scarlet, they shall be as white as snow; though they are red as crimson, they shall be like wool. If you are willing and obedient, you will eat the good things of the land; but if you resist and rebel, you will be devoured by the sword.'"

"The only way Asaph can be cleansed of his past deeds is by paying a price. He killed Chaim. His blood must be spilled."

"Blood *has* been spilled," said Eliana. "The blood of Jesus, the Lamb of God. Besides, you know and I know that Asaph did not kill Chaim."

"Not true. He killed Chaim, and he must be punished by stone."

"There you go with talk of rocks again." Then Eliana stared Zuriel directly in the eyes and added, "Do not resist and rebel against the Lord, Zuriel. If you do, you will be devoured by the sword."

"Does that woman ever stop preaching?" came a voice from behind Zuriel, a voice from the entrance of the cave. It was Abner. His presence ended their conversation just as she thought she was making progress with Zuriel.

"How did it go at the Temple?" Zuriel asked Abner.

"Asaph turned himself in to the Temple guards. He is now in prison."

Eliana felt a strange burning in her chest. Then she began speaking once more in an unknown language. And as the words spilled out, she knew their meaning. It was Isaiah again.

"The oppressor will come to an end, and destruction will cease; the aggressor will vanish from the land. In love a throne will be established; in faithfulness a man will sit on it—one from the house of David—one who in judging seeks justice and speeds the cause of righteousness."

Abner laughed. A hard bark.

"Don't look so intimidated by her babble, Zuriel," he said. "It's all nonsense." Abner glanced around, then added, "So where is the other woman? And where is Uzziah and Yoram?"

"They went in search of the other woman."

Abner exploded. "And why are they searching for the other woman? Did she get out of the cave?"

"She fled, yes."

"You had three men watching two women! Tell me how in the world one of them could slip out of the cave!"

"I don't have to explain anything. I'm in charge here."

"Yes, you are in charge. And that means you're responsible for the woman getting away."

Abner moved in on Zuriel, cornering him, but Zuriel stood his ground.

"Don't worry. They will find her," Zuriel said.

"But I still don't know how—"

"I *said* they will find her."

"And if she gets away, she'll lead her man back here," Abner continued, not letting go of his complaints. "Do you know what Sveshtari is capable of doing if he finds us?"

"We'll be long gone before he gets here."

Abner motioned toward Eliana. "Then kill her and let's go."

Eliana tried not to look horrified. She maintained a stolid expression, but she sensed herself crumbling inside. She looked at Zuriel.

"You are not in charge," Zuriel said. "You don't tell me what to do."

"Then it's time I was put in charge." Abner drew his sword.

Eliana thought he intended to kill her, but Abner charged Zuriel instead. Zuriel pulled out his short sword before Abner could strike. Abner thrust his sword, but Zuriel parried the lunge.

As the two men fought, Eliana stepped slowly to the side, edging closer to the cave opening.

"Where do you think you're going?" Abner said, momentarily distracted by Eliana's movements.

Wrong choice. When Abner glanced at her over his shoulder, Zuriel made his move, driving his sword into the man's side. Abner let out a roar.

Eliana didn't wait around to find out what happened next. She took off running, into the darkness.

Keturah

By the time Keturah stumbled to Joanna's residence in the city, a feverish ache throbbed in her legs. She was exhausted, nauseated, sore, and light-headed. She had lost her right sandal when fleeing, and her right foot was torn by nettles.

She used what little strength remained to pound on the door leading into Joanna's courtyard, but no one answered. It was late at night, but not so late that there wouldn't be anyone awake. Where were they? She began to weep as she pounded again on the door.

"Joanna!" she called out. "*Domina*!"

A light sprang up, but it came from the house across the narrow street. A neighbor peeked out her head and hissed, "Go away, beggar! Can't you see that people are sleeping?"

Keturah leaned her head against the door and struck it feebly, one, two, three more times. Hearing sound from the street, she glanced up and spotted two figures moving toward her in the darkness. They might be thieves, or they might be Zuriel's men, come to recapture her.

"Joanna!" she shouted.

"Quiet!" hollered the neighbor.

"Joanna, help!"

As the two men hurried toward her, Keturah looked around for anything she could use as a weapon.

"Woman, are you hurt?" said one of the men. It sounded like a sincere question, but you never knew. Keturah said nothing.

"Why are you pounding on Joanna's door at this time of night?" asked the other.

"Because she has no care for the peace of other people!" shouted the neighbor, leaning out the window.

"Still your tongue," said the first man. "Can't you see this woman is injured?"

"Do you know Joanna?" Keturah asked. "I was once her servant."

"Everyone who follows Jesus knows Joanna," said the second man.

"You follow Jesus?" Keturah was relieved to hear it. If they were telling the truth, she was in safe hands.

"We do. Do you know his teaching?"

"I do. And I too follow him."

Keturah was surprised to hear herself say that. She described herself as a God-fearer, but she had never claimed to be a follower of Jesus. She admired him, but given the circumstances, she decided it would be best to align herself with these two men. Her saviors.

Just then, the door began to rattle, and it opened before them. Joanna stood framed in the doorway, holding an oil lamp in her left hand.

"Keturah! Daughter, I am so happy to see you back! Are you all right?" Joanna put an arm around Keturah's waist and drew her through the gate. The two men hesitated, then followed.

"Thank you, Jason. Thank you, Michael," she said to the men. "Please enter and partake of refreshments for your trouble."

"It was no trouble," said one of the men, but they entered regardless. They were not going to turn away fresh fruit or wine.

"We've been worried sick about you," Joanna said, ushering Keturah into her home. "You're burning up, daughter, so we must get you into bed."

As the wife of the man who ran Herod's household, Joanna knew something about snapping commands. She mobilized her servants with speed and efficiency that would impress a general.

In moments, Keturah was stretched out on a bed as one of the servant women inspected the bottom of Keturah's right foot and treated her cuts with a soothing balm. Another servant dabbed her forehead with a cool rag.

"Rest, daughter," Joanna said. She stood in the doorframe, making sure that Keturah's needs were being met. In the background, Keturah could see the two men sitting at a table, eating and drinking.

Her stomach still churned, but the nausea began to subside as the tension left her body. The oil on her foot felt smooth and cool, and her mind began to swim. Then exhaustion flowed over her, carrying her away into darkness.

Nekoda: The Next Morning

Nekoda entered Herodian Hall through a double doorway. Herodian Hall, the building where the Sanhedrin met, butted up against a bridge extending out from the western wall of the Temple Mount. Inside, the Sanhedrin sat in a semi-circle, with thirty-five members on one side and thirty-five on the other, and the high priest seated in the middle. Morning sun poured through the high windows.

At the back of the enormous, rock-hewn room were benches where students watched the supreme court in action. Nekoda remembered the days, so long ago, when he sat on one of those benches, watching the proceedings and craving a time when he could take his place among the Sanhedrin.

Today, he had a place among the supreme court, but he no longer felt the same excitement or even pride. Today, his depression was deepening. He had betrayed his brother; he had been the cause of Chaim's death. And now two of his brother's friends—two disciples—had been hauled before the court. Peter and John.

The Sanhedrin had also brought in the man whom the disciples had healed at the Beautiful Gate. The man stood tall before the court; only one day ago, he had been incapable of standing anywhere.

Nekoda looked on with growing nausea.

One of the priests stood and began the questioning. "You healed a man at the Gate called Beautiful yesterday morning. By what power or what name did you do this?"

The one who answered was Peter, the big fisherman. He was a rugged sort, dressed plainly. His tunic was torn in a couple of places, and his beard was thick and unkempt. A wild man, from the looks of it. But he spoke eloquently for a Galilean.

"Rulers and elders of the people! If we are being called to account today for an act of kindness shown to a man who was lame and are being asked how he was healed, then know this, you and all the people of Israel: It is by the name of Jesus Christ of Nazareth, whom you crucified but whom God raised from the dead, that this man stands before you healed." As he spoke, Peter motioned toward the healed man, who looked confused and overwhelmed by the attention being heaped upon him.

The court erupted. Most of the Sanhedrin stood and shouted their protests, but Nekoda remained slumped on the stone bench.

Peter had just announced that he healed the man in the name of Jesus Christ. Names carry power. Names reflect the core of a person's being. Through the power of naming, you can bring order out of chaos. Naming separates one person from another; it brings organization. Just as God separated light from darkness, water from land, he gave his people the power to separate one animal from another through the power of naming. But to *heal* in someone's name? That could only be done in the name of the Lord. That power is reserved for the Creator alone.

And yet . . . Peter said he had healed in the name of Jesus Christ. He had separated the man from his suffering and the sickness from the man's body. And he had done it in the name of Jesus of Nazareth. The assembly was scandalized.

"Jesus is the stone you builders rejected, which has become the cornerstone!" Peter continued when calm had been restored. "Salvation is found in no one else, for there is no other name under heaven given to mankind by which we must be saved!"

Again, the assembly burst with righteous fury. Peter had taken his blasphemy a step further. First, the fisherman said he healed in Jesus's name. Now, he said that this name brought salvation. Nekoda knew he too should be outraged; he too should be standing on his feet, shaking his fist. But he felt no energy, no outrage. His brother had embraced these same things about Jesus. He would not shame his brother's memory by protesting the very things that Chaim believed. He would remain silent. Nekoda never listened to Chaim when his brother had breath; the least he could do is listen to these disciples and try to understand why Chaim could believe such things.

The high priest ordered Peter, John, and the healed man out of the room so the Sanhedrin could discuss the matter in private.

"What are we going to do with these men?" declared Reuben, a tall, reed-thin priest who stood in their midst.

"Everyone living in Jerusalem knows they have performed a notable sign, and we cannot deny it," said another. "But to stop this thing from spreading any further among the people, we must warn them to speak no longer to anyone in this name."

This name.

The priest was afraid to say the name out loud. He would only say: This name.

Jesus.

Nekoda felt a stirring, a sense he should say something. But what? Should he say that his brother, Chaim, claimed to have seen many healings in the name of Jesus of Nazareth? They would laugh him out of the room. Or worse yet, throw him out of the Sanhedrin. Nekoda had once laughed at Chaim. But he saw the healing that occurred the morning before with his own eyes. And he knew the man who had been healed was no fake. He had been at the Beautiful Gate asking for alms for years.

Lost in his dismal musings, Nekoda heard little of what was being discussed. He didn't come back to attention until they called Peter and John back into the room.

"You shall not speak or teach at all in the name of Jesus!" the high priest declared.

But Peter responded, "Which is right in God's eyes: to listen to you, or to him? You be the judges! As for us, we cannot help speaking about what we have seen and heard."

Nekoda smiled to himself. Peter, this uncouth Galilean, had them there. When faced with obeying God or obeying human dictates, the Torah was clear. Obey God. The man beside him noticed the smile on his face and scowled.

More threats followed, but Peter and John continued to insist that they couldn't stop themselves from speaking, from being witnesses to God's marvels. Around and around and around they went; it was like getting tangled in fishing line. But the Sanhedrin, in all its power, knew they could not use their full strength in this situation. All the people in the city were praising God for what had happened the previous morning in front of the Beautiful Gate. Could they really punish the people who made that healing happen?

They had no choice. They released Peter and John. They let the two fish off their hook and tossed them back to the masses.

5.

The Book of Acts, Chapter 5

Keturah

When Keturah awoke, her nausea was gone. But when she started to sit up, the wooziness returned. As she shook the cobwebs from her mind, she also became aware of the aches throughout her body. She had a fever, and she dropped back onto the mattress, sweating.

Closing her eyes, she heard movement in the room. Then voices.

"She's awake!" Sveshtari said.

"She needs to rest," came Eliana's voice. *Eliana?* She was back? She was freed by Zuriel?

Keturah opened her eyes and tried to sit up once again. The room began to spin, and Eliana whirled before her eyes. Her friend took her gently by the shoulders and lowered her onto the bed.

"Rest, Keturah."

Keturah tried to smile, to show her happiness at Eliana's release. Then she groaned and lay back down, the room slanting like the deck of a ship as dream images flooded upon her. She saw herself underwater, diving deep through crystal clear water. There were fish all about her, and then a net coming down upon her head. She became tangled in the cords of the net, which filled with fish, and she felt herself being drawn up to the surface.

Beams of light broke through the water, and she saw the fluttering images of men above the water, fishermen hauling in the net. Then the net tore open, and Keturah kicked free and swam deeper and deeper. But the water remained clear even as she reached the very bottom. And when she looked around, she saw no signs of life. Not a single fish or creature of the deep. Just miles and miles of submerged emptiness. She was alone at the bottom of the sea.

Eliana

With Keturah asleep and in good hands, Eliana rushed through the busy streets of Jerusalem with Sveshtari and Abel, who were barely able to keep pace with her. They had asked her to lead them to the cave where she and Keturah were kept prisoner, but Eliana's priority was Asaph. She carried a sack of food for Asaph because if friends and family don't provide food, prisoners go hungry.

Eliana noticed that the city seemed more crowded than normal, and there was an unusually large number of sick people. Several hobbled along with crutches, a couple of people had bandaged arms, another was being carried on a stretcher, and several blind men were being led by the arm.

"It's the disciples," said Abel. "Word is spreading about the healings, and the afflicted are swarming from towns all around Jerusalem."

"It's like Jesus all over again, except the healing is coming from his disciples," said Sveshtari.

Eliana shook her head. "It's not the disciples doing the healing. It's the Holy Spirit."

Sveshtari shrugged and exchanged glances with Abel.

Up ahead, the bright white walls of the Temple Mount loomed, and the closer they got to the Temple, the more crowded it became. They passed by a string of stalls where a man suddenly blocked her way and tried to get her to stop and look at his carpets. Sveshtari gave the man a stiff arm to the chest, sending him staggering back several steps.

"That was a little rough, wasn't it?" Eliana said.

"If you pause for even a moment, they'll latch onto you like leeches. You want to see Asaph, don't you?"

Suddenly, a young man tried to snatch the bag of food from Eliana's hands, but this time it was Abel's quick reflexes that saved the day. Before the man could yank the sack away, Abel's hands were on his wrist, twisting. When the man let out a screech, Abel released him.

"Don't tell me that was a little rough too," said Abel.

"Definitely not too rough," Eliana said. "He was trying to take Asaph's food."

As they rounded a corner, Eliana couldn't believe what she saw. Sick people, lying on beds and mats, lined the street. There had to be dozens of them. It was like walking upon a battlefield with the injured laid out in a row.

One old man grabbed the hem of Sveshtari's robe. "Please ask the disciples to come look at us. Please ask them to heal us!"

Sveshtari snapped the robe out of the man's grip.

"Even if they could walk past us, that's all we ask!" another man shouted. "If Peter's shadow touches me, I will be healed!"

"Can you believe that?" Abel asked.

"I can," said Eliana. After the events since Pentecost, none of this surprised her.

At last, they reached Herodian Hall, which sat on the southern side of the Temple Mount, just to the west of the Monumental Staircase.

"Don't go any closer, Sveshtari," Eliana said. "The Temple guards may not be Romans, but they probably know who you are. You'll put yourself at risk if you get too close to them."

Sveshtari grunted, but it was hard to tell if that was an agreement or not.

"We'll be at Solomon's Porch, looking for the disciples," Abel said to Eliana. "When you're done visiting Asaph, you can find us there. Just look for Peter's shadow, and I'll be under it."

"Not at all funny," she said, breaking away and heading for the prison with her sack of food still intact. She was anxious to see, with her own eyes, that they hadn't harmed a single hair on Asaph's head.

Sveshtari

Sveshtari hoped that Eliana would be quick about her business with Asaph so they could head beyond the city walls and try to find the cave where the women had been held. He knew he should be thinking about Asaph's predicament in prison, but he was anxious to find Zuriel—and to carry out his own form of rough justice. Besides, if Abner was as badly injured as Eliana described, he might still be in the cave, barely alive. Sveshtari would make him talk.

The Court of Gentiles on the Temple Mount was a madhouse as Sveshtari and Abel finally worked their way up the stairs and through the Huldah Gates. Sveshtari stood a head taller than most people, and he could see the disciples working their way through the crowd, laying hands on people and praying. While some of the disciples did the praying, other disciples acted as bodyguards of sorts, keeping the crowd from crushing them from all sides. But they weren't doing a very good job.

"Why aren't more men helping to control the crowd?" Sveshtari said. "There aren't enough disciples to both pray and handle crowd control, so they need more hands."

"After the earlier arrest of the disciples, many people are probably afraid of getting in trouble with Temple authorities," Abel said. "So, they're letting the disciples do all the work."

"Cowards. I'll show them how it's done."

The former bodyguard worked his way through the crowd. He didn't shove people aside roughly, but he was firm as he moved people out of his path. He had to lift one small man off his feet, coming at him from behind and clamping hands on the man's arms. The man, caught unawares, let out a yelp as Sveshtari moved him aside.

"Make way," said Sveshtari.

"Wait your turn!" somebody barked, but Sveshtari turned on him with an intimidating presence.

"I'm not here for healing. I'm here to give the men some space to work."

Abel, a much smaller man, followed in Sveshtari's wake, and he too echoed those commands. "Give them space. Give them space. They can only pray for one person at a time!"

Eventually, Sveshtari sidled up beside one of the disciples—Matthew Levi. Matthew had his hands on a man's eyes, praying fervently. He had to be loud to make himself heard above the din. But as he prayed, other sick people pressed in from behind. Several reached out and touched Matthew, and one man even tried to yank the disciple backwards. Sveshtari latched onto the man's hand, squeezed firmly, and removed it from Matthew's shoulder.

"Give him space!"

"Who are you? You aren't a disciple!"

"I'm the one telling you not to disturb the disciple when he's praying for someone else!"

Sveshtari had a way of rising on the soles of his feet and broadening his shoulders when he boomed a command. He could be fearsome, even without his armor. The man shrank back into the crowd, and so did several others.

Sveshtari extended his arms. He had an eagle-wide wingspan, and his sleeves drew back, revealing the thickness of his forearms. The disciples needed a little muscle on their side if they hoped to pray for these people without being crushed, and it didn't hurt to display his strength to the crowd.

Sveshtari noticed that Abel had approached another disciple, Simon the Zealot, and he too tried to provide the same kind of protection. But Abel's wingspan was more sparrow than eagle, and his presence was not nearly as intimidating. Still, at least he was trying to help, and he had some success in keeping people from pressing too closely.

Once Sveshtari had his space staked out, with his arms extended, holding people back like a human wall, he began to pick up what was happening with the prayers. Some of the people came away from the prayer shouting praises to the high heavens, leaping up and down. But Sveshtari couldn't tell if it was all an act or whether healings were taking place. When Matthew approached a man with a tumor bulging underneath his left eye, Sveshtari thought, *This is going to be interesting*.

Matthew placed both hands on the tumor and began rebuking *ha-satan*, the accuser, in Jesus's name. Sveshtari knew what it was like to be pursued by an accuser, for he had more than his share of human adversaries. So, the idea of a spiritual accuser made sense to him.

A woman tried to catch Sveshtari unaware and slip beneath his outstretched arm. As Sveshtari made a move to snag her, Matthew turned toward him and said, "Let the woman come to me."

This surprised Sveshtari because he knew how strict Hebrews could be when it came to contact between unmarried men and women. Besides, this woman was cutting in line. Sveshtari was about to say something when he realized that the man with the tumor was standing there, beaming and extending his arms to the sky. The side of the man's face was smooth and reborn. The tumor? Gone! But how? Something like that doesn't just fly off a person's face.

Stunned, Sveshtari forgot to do his job for a few moments, and the crowd took advantage, surging forward. But he soon recovered and brought the people back under control.

The prayers and healings went on for the longest time, but Sveshtari didn't weary. In fact, he was energized by the excitement boiling all around him.

As the day progressed, the noise of the crowd suddenly became deafening, and the people began to draw back. He glanced over his shoulder and saw Temple guards, dozens of them, pushing through the crowd. The sight of their bronze, Thracian-style helmets jolted Sveshtari, a Thracian by birth. Each soldier wore a bronze muscle cuirass, a sturdy breastplate and backplate. Also: a red tunic, red mantle, and even red boots, and a sizable, oval shield with a bronze rim. All very threatening.

Leading the way was the high priest wearing a thickly padded blue cap with a gold band at the brow. His robe was also blue, with gold tassels around the hem, tiny bells, and miniature, golden pomegranates. His small cape was embroidered in bands of gold, purple, scarlet, and blue, with two gold shoulder brooches inset with sardonyx. Very splendid.

The finery and weaponry, not to mention the authority of the man's office, was all it took to clear a path through the crowded portico. People scattered. To their credit, the disciples stood their ground, and so did Sveshtari.

Abel tugged at Sveshtari's robe. "Shall we leave?"

"We will not. We stay with the disciples. Never retreat from a battle."

Then the Temple guards went to work, laying heavy hands on the disciples. When two soldiers clamped down on Sveshtari, his first instinct was to use his fists. But one look from Matthew stayed his hand. He felt a surge of hatred for these guards—fellow Thracians who were doing the job that Sveshtari had done not so long ago. He wanted to display his strength. But when Matthew put a hand on his shoulder, calmness draped over him like a cloak. What was it about these disciples? He also felt a strengthening of his spine and a cooling of his anger.

Sveshtari and Abel were caught up in the day's catch. The soldiers shoved them along, herding them in the direction of Herodian Hall—and the prison inside. Asaph was about to get company.

Eliana

The prison smelled of sweat, but by the time Eliana had finished delivering food to Asaph, she was accustomed to the odor. Eventually, the Temple guard told her she had to clear out because they were bringing in fresh prisoners. Eliana wished she could give Asaph something as simple as a squeeze of her hands, but she was not allowed to get close enough to him.

Back in the light, Eliana tried to control her emotions. Seeing Asaph imprisoned reminded her too much of Jesus. She had followed Jesus's trial and crucifixion every bloody step of the way, and she knew what it was like to be at the complete mercy of the Temple and Roman systems of justice.

The same helpless feeling came over her now, draining her of energy. Trying to halt the wheels of justice was like stepping in front of a chariot at full tilt and stopping those wheels.

When she left the prison, she was in for another shock. Horrified, she stood aside for the arrival of the next batch of prisoners. The disciples, all twelve of them, were being herded into the prison. The authorities had tried to squash the followers of the Way by murdering Jesus; what was stopping them from killing all twelve disciples?

"Sveshtari! Abel!"

The names flew from Eliana's tongue when she saw her two friends also being pushed toward the prison entrance. This had to be some mistake. They weren't disciples! She tried to latch onto Sveshtari's sleeve and pull him out of the line, but a Temple guard used the butt end of his spear to crack her on the wrist, knocking her hand free.

"Leave us be, Eliana," Sveshtari said. She knew Sveshtari, and she could see that he was itching for an excuse to attack these guards. Doing so would be suicide, even for Sveshtari, so she decided to pull back. She didn't want to give him any reason to defend her.

"There must be some mistake," she pleaded to one of the guards, but he was not about to answer a woman.

Keturah was going to be devastated when she found out that Sveshtari had been swept up in the dragnet. Sveshtari was a fugitive. And if the Temple authorities hand him to the Romans, it won't go well. The priests had handed Jesus over to the Romans and look how that turned out.

Eliana watched her friends as they were marched through the prison doors and swallowed by the system.

"I can pray for you, sister," came a voice to her right.

She turned to see an old man, at least twenty years her senior. He was bald, except for tufts of gray hair perched above his large ears. He had a round face with age spots scattered like small islands across his forehead and the top of his head. His left eye was clouded and partially closed, and she wondered if he had lost sight in it. His face was weathered, with a thin, short-cropped, gray beard. But he looked kindly. Grandfatherly.

He also looked vaguely familiar, probably because he had attended many of the Upper Room prayer meetings. She knew many of the followers of the Way by name, but not this one. Their numbers had been multiplying day by day, as rapidly as the fish and loaves had been multiplied by Jesus. She couldn't keep up with the flood of new faces and names.

"Yes, please pray for me, brother," she said, trying not to break down in tears in front him. "My betrothed, Asaph, has been arrested, as have two of my friends—Sveshtari and Abel."

"I will pray, Sister Eliana," the old man said.

She blinked in surprise. "You know my name?"

The old man seemed suddenly startled, as if he had said too much.

"I do. Doesn't everyone know who Eliana is?"

Eliana didn't know how to respond. She had been following Jesus for a long time now, but she never imagined she had reached the point where "everyone" knew her name. She studied this man even more closely. Yes, there was something very familiar about him, buried deep beneath his wrinkles and mask of age.

Then it struck her with the suddenness of a rockslide. She nearly buckled beneath the revelation. It couldn't be! She felt a wave of nausea as the memories struck her, throbbing in her head.

"Is it you?" she said, barely above a whisper.

The old man seemed similarly pained. A red blush crossed his face, and he diverted his eyes in shame. He had reason to feel shame, for what this man had done was pure evil. And he had the nerve to ask to pray for her?

She was tempted to spit in his face. If she had a knife in her hands, there was no telling what she would do.

"Are you Moshe?" she asked.

"Moshe is dead," he said with disgust. "I am a new man. A new creature. My name is Hosea because God is my salvation."

Moshe . . . Hosea . . . whoever this man was, he was no follower of Jesus. He couldn't possibly be! This man was one of the brigands who had abducted Eliana in Bethlehem so many years ago when she was just ten years old. He was one of the men who had stolen her youth, stolen her innocence, and stolen her joy. After tormenting her for most of a year, he and his fellow bandits had sold her into slavery, sending her to hell for nearly thirty years.

And he dared to ask if he could pray for her?

She began shaking uncontrollably, her mind buzzing with evil intentions. If her dog, Lavi, had been beside her, she would have commanded him to tear this man to pieces.

"You know me, don't you?" the old man said on the verge of tears. He bowed his head. "After what I did to you, I know I do not deserve forgiveness. But I am a follower of Jesus now. Does that mean anything?"

Eliana didn't respond. She did the only thing she could think to do to save herself and save this man. She turned and ran, praying that the ground would open and swallow them both.

Keturah

Something was terribly wrong. The moment Eliana dragged herself through the door of the communal compound, Keturah could sense it.

Keturah was watching Babette try to roll from her stomach to her back when Eliana trudged into the room. Her friend had never looked this defeated.

"What happened?" Keturah asked. "Is Asaph all right? Are you feeling ill?"

Eliana slumped into a chair. Her gaze was vacant.

"Oh Eliana," Keturah said, scooping up Babette and rushing to her friend's side. Babette cooed and smiled, but Eliana didn't even look at her. "What's happened to Asaph? Please tell me."

Staring at her sandals, Eliana muttered, "Sveshtari and Abel have also been arrested. They too are in prison."

"What? That can't be right? Did the Romans capture them?"

Eliana didn't answer. This wasn't like her. Even when Asaph had been arrested, she still had fight in her. But now? It's like she had been beaten into the dirt.

"Eliana, you're scaring me! Are Sveshtari and Abel in the hands of the Romans?"

Finally, her friend shook her head. "The Temple guards arrested them. They're in prison with Asaph."

"Do the Romans know he's been taken?"

"Not yet. I don't think so."

"That's something," Keturah said, pacing the room. "What can we do? We must do something!"

Again, no response. Not a word. It was like talking to a stone wall. Quietly, Eliana began to weep. Again, Keturah rushed to her side, with Babette nestled in her right arm. She used her free hand to take Eliana's. Her fingers were ice cold. On a hot day like this?

"You must be ill," Keturah said, bringing Eliana to her feet. Everything about Eliana's manner spoke despair. She tried to stir some warmth in

Eliana by reciting a psalm she had recently memorized. "Deep calls to deep in the roar of your waterfalls. All your waves and breakers have swept over me."

Still nothing. Then Eliana muttered, "My bones suffer mortal agony as my foes taunt me."

Keturah waited for her to finish the psalm, but her friend was quiet.

"Complete the psalm, Eliana. Please, complete the words."

Silence. So, Keturah finished the psalm for her: "Why, my soul, are you downcast? Why so disturbed within me? Put your hope in God, for I will yet praise him, my Savior and my God."

Eliana still wouldn't respond, wouldn't look at Keturah. She wouldn't even look at Babette, who reached out and began playing with Eliana's hair. Her friend loved it when Babette did that. "Put your hope in God," Keturah urged.

Eliana raised her head, as if she had to use all her strength to do it. "How?" she said. "Today, I have seen the devil."

"You need to see the disciples. You need to see Peter," Keturah said, beginning to panic. How could she, a God-fearer, help her friend deal with this kind of spiritual sickness? Eliana needed counsel from one of the disciples. Someone who knew Jesus. Someone who would know what to do.

"Peter is also in prison. *All* the disciples are in prison."

What had happened on the Temple Mount? Was this the beginning of the tribulation that Jesus spoke about? Jesus had told his disciples, just before he died, that they would be seized and persecuted. They would be put in prison and brought before kings and governors, all on account of the name of Jesus.

Asaph

Asaph wasn't sure what was more shocking. Was it seeing his friends hauled into prison, along with the disciples? Or was it the prayers being said, and the songs being sung from behind bars?

The disciples were herded into several cells. Abel was placed in Asaph's cell, but Sveshtari was shoved into a cell farther down the dim-lit hall. As the soldiers chained them together, the disciple Nathanael began to pray for the Temple guards. One of the guards was clearly shaken by the prayer.

The soldiers hurried through their tasks, connecting the string of chains and locking them in, trying not to make eye contact with the man praying for them. No sooner had the guards taken their positions than Peter began belting out songs, despite not having the most polished of voices. Even when the others joined in the singing, Peter's voice stood out like a sore thumb. But the real miracle was that they were singing at all in this dark pit.

Until the disciples arrived, Asaph had been slouching in a corner of his cell for much of the time, feeling sorry for himself. The only light that had entered the prison all day was when Eliana came to him with food. He was amazed by her strength and courage—a flame that never seemed to go out. He wished he had just a portion of her faith.

Now, the light in this prison seemed to grow brighter with the presence of the disciples. It was naturally a dark, dank place. The only sunlight that slipped in came like a thief through a single, barred window on the other side of the enormous room. The floor was brick, but it was slick with dampness and who knows what else. Asaph's cell included a hole in the floor for all to use as nature saw fit. The ceiling was low, barely rising above his head when he stood, and the outer wall leaned in, as if close to collapsing. It was quite a contrast to the splendor of the nearby Temple Mount.

Asaph leaned back against the wall, the feeling of cold stone beneath his head, and joined the singing. He was chained to John, who was chained to James, who was chained to Abel, who was chained to Thomas. All were singing.

"We cried to the Lord in our trouble, and he saved us from our distress. He brought us out of darkness, the utter darkness, and broke away our chains! Let us give thanks to the Lord for his unfailing love and his wonderful deeds for mankind, for he breaks down gates of bronze and cuts through bars of iron."

The more Asaph sang, the more he almost believed it.

Sveshtari

Sveshtari was getting a headache, and he wondered if he should ask one of these disciples for prayer. He had seen the wonders they perform, so one little headache should be an easy healing for a miracle worker. But Sveshtari thought it might be selfish, asking them to use their power for something so petty. They should be using it on things like tumors—or escaping from prison.

"How did you manage to remove that man's tumor?" Sveshtari asked, leaning toward Matthew, who shared his cell. There was a lull in the singing, a welcome relief from Peter's singing voice.

"Which tumor?" Matthew asked.

Which tumor? How many had he healed?

"The man had a tumor beneath his left eye. You took it away."

"I did nothing of the kind. The Lord heals, not me."

"But he heals *through* you."

Matthew shrugged. "He uses all of us. He can use *you*."

Sveshtari looked away, embarrassed by the very idea. After spending a year with the disciples, immersed in miracles, Sveshtari still felt uneasy with the supernatural. He was accustomed to gods who used their powers mostly for mischief. He was more comfortable with swords honed by man than swords of the spirit.

Then Peter started singing again. Somebody should use their spiritual powers to heal his singing voice. Perhaps the guards will release them without trial, just to rid the prison of Peter's vocal horrors.

"But I pray to you, Lord,
in the time of your favor;
in your great love, O God,
answer me with your sure salvation.
Rescue me from the mire;
do not let me sink;
deliver me from those who hate me,
from the deep waters.
Do not let the floodwaters engulf me
or the depths swallow me up
or the pit close its mouth over me!"

When evening fell, the singing had subsided. So had Sveshtari's headache. He spent much of the time talking with Matthew, who was once a tax collector. It's too bad that Asaph, also a former tax collector, didn't share this cell with Matthew because the two men could have swapped a lot of stories.

It had been an exhausting and eventful day, so it wasn't long before sleep began tugging on Sveshtari's eyelids. He was sitting on the cold prison floor, with his back against the wall, when he slid into slumber.

He didn't know how much time had elapsed before Matthew nudged him awake.

"Sveshtari, Sveshtari," Matthew whispered. "Wake up."

Sveshtari instinctively reached for his belt, where he normally carried a weapon. But of course, he found nothing. It was dangerous for people to wake him up prematurely. Matthew was lucky he was without a weapon.

Matthew had a big grin, visible even in the shadows. "It's time to leave."

Time to leave? That doesn't sound good. Where would the Temple guards be taking them at this time of night?

Being visited by soldiers in the dead of night is never a good thing. He thought specifically about John the Baptist, who lost his head during one such visit.

However, as his surroundings slowly came into focus, Sveshtari realized he had been unshackled. But who had removed his chains? He saw no sign of Temple guards. Instead, an extremely tall man stood at the door of the prison cell, which had swung wide open. He couldn't see what was happening beyond the door of his cell, but he could hear many people shuffling about, murmuring.

But who was the man standing at the door? He wasn't dressed like a guard, and Sveshtari hadn't seen him among the prisoners. He would have noticed someone so tall. Sveshtari was taller than average, but this man dwarfed even him.

Everyone was beaming as they filed silently out of the cells. Sveshtari suddenly broke into a grin when he spotted two Temple guards slouched against the wall, eyes closed. At first, he thought they might be dead. But as he passed by, he heard labored breathing coming from one of them. Sleeping on guard duty could be punishable by death.

"Who is the man who opened our cells?" Sveshtari whispered when he was reunited with Abel and Asaph.

"Who is he?" Abel said, repeating the question as if he couldn't believe Sveshtari's ignorance. "He's an angel, of course."

Sveshtari glanced at Asaph to see if he agreed with this wild idea. Asaph nodded. "Abel is right—I think. What else could he be?"

As the prisoners shuffled toward the exit, they must have passed a half dozen more Temple guards, all sound asleep. Either this visitor had supernatural powers befitting an angel, or else he had somehow drugged the soldiers.

Just as they were about to exit the prison complex, the angel, or whoever he was, stopped and turned.

"Go, stand in the Temple courts," he said to the disciples, "and tell the people all about this new life."

The disciples were visibly excited by this command. They reminded Sveshtari of soldiers getting ready for battle. But Sveshtari still didn't understand this form of weaponless warfare. The angel was telling them to return to the Temple and start preaching once again—open defiance against the powers.

He couldn't imagine doing such a thing without a sword strapped to his side.

"We need to let the women know what became of us," Sveshtari said to Asaph and Abel as they reemerged into the open air of the brisk Jerusalem night. "Then I need to get back to sleep. I'm exhausted."

"How can you sleep on a night like this?" Abel asked, backpedaling in front of Sveshtari as they walked.

"I don't know. Maybe I'm asleep right now and all this is a dream."

Keturah

Keturah was buried in sleep, with Babette nestled by her side, when raucous sounds erupted from below in Joanna and Chuza's house. She was sure the authorities had come to arrest them.

She scooped up Babette, who awoke with a cry, adding to the confusion and chaos. She calculated how she could escape the house without being seen when she suddenly heard laughter. Whatever was happening downstairs was a source of joy, not fear. She berated herself for waking up Babette, who kept on crying. The nursemaid, who also slept in the room, was already awake and lifting the child from her hands.

"Not to worry, *Domina*," said Ruth.

Keturah still could not get used to being addressed as *Domina*, a term often used by slaves toward their masters and mistresses. Keturah used to address Joanna as *Domina*.

"I will feed Babette, and that will put her back to sleep," Ruth said. "Go down and join the celebration."

"Celebration? What's happening?"

"Can't you hear the voices?" Ruth asked, gently rocking Babette, who began to settle down. "Can't you hear the voice of your betrothed?"

With Babette now quiet, she listened. It sounded as if a wedding feast was going on downstairs. Then, amid the laughter and clamor, she heard the voice of Sveshtari. But how? Why would he have been released from prison in the middle of the night?

Throwing on a cloak and sandals, Keturah raced down the twisting stone stairs leading to the first floor. The room below was filled with light because servants had lit more than a dozen oil lamps. Sveshtari, standing at the foot of the stairs, turned to face her, and Keturah threw herself into his arms. As he swung her around, she burst out laughing.

When her feet touched the ground again, she looked around. The room was filled with all twelve disciples, plus Abel and Asaph.

"Where is Eliana?" Asaph asked, his face glowing, his eyes like torches.

"She must still be asleep. I will rouse her. But first . . . how . . . why did they set you free?"

"They didn't set us free," said Abel. "The Lord did. An *angel* did!"

"An angel? How do you know it was an angel? What did he look like?"

Abel started to answer, but the disciple Matthew pulled him into a dance circle. Several disciples had begun to move slowly in a circle, while several women sang. Initially, the disciples danced individually, snapping fingers, clapping in rhythm, raising their feet, and slapping their ankles. Spinning, twirling. Their hands danced almost as much as their feet. They raised their arms in praise, swaying right, swaying left, their entire body bending back and forth like palm trees in the wind.

Eventually, they linked hands and continued to move in a circle, an unbroken band, and they danced around and around, increasing speed with every circuit until they seemed to be on the verge of lifting off the ground like the spinning wheels in Ezekiel's vision.

Then Asaph broke away from the circle dance and looked toward the staircase. Keturah turned to see Eliana moving down the stairs—slowly. She was sure the celebration would lift Eliana out of the mire that had trapped her earlier in the day. The sight of Asaph certainly helped. Eliana smiled for the first time since she had returned from the Temple Mount; but she didn't rush down the stairs and throw herself in Asaph's arms as Keturah would have guessed.

Something was seriously wrong.

Eliana maintained her smile and picked up her pace as she trudged down the stairs. Then she slipped gently into Asaph's outstretched arms and began to sob. Asaph probably assumed they were tears of joy, but Keturah knew her friend better than him. The tears contained some joy. But there was an element of grief as well.

When the dancing was over, the entire household of Joanna gathered around, including her husband Chuza. Joanna's husband still ran the household of Herod, so he kept his distance from the disciples and his wife's eccentric belief in Jesus. Keturah wondered what he would make of all the disciples in his room in the middle of the night, claiming that an angel had released them from prison. Jesus and the Way were a source of tension between Chuza and Joanna, but to his credit, he didn't try to drive the disciples out of his house this night. She hoped he wouldn't get into trouble with Herod if news leaked out.

Then Peter began to talk, telling everyone about the remarkable events. He described how the angel suddenly appeared in the prison and how their chains shattered in the angel's hands as he gently ran his finger across the iron rings. Then the angel opened the door of each cell because, as one of the psalms says, the Lord can break down gates of bronze and even cut through bars of iron.

"It's all true," Sveshtari whispered in Keturah's ear. "I have never seen anything like it. Never."

And Keturah had never seen Sveshtari like this. He was normally so reserved, so skeptical. But now? He could barely sit still. His enthusiasm scared her just a little.

Then Peter said that the angel gave them all an order. "Go, stand in the Temple courts, and tell the people the full message of this new life."

Go, stand in the Temple courts? Keturah was shocked. What good was it for this angel to release the men from prison if it meant sending them right back to the Temple to be arrested again?

Keturah looked at Eliana, who was working hard to smile at Asaph and share in his joy. In the past, Eliana never had to work at being joyful—at least not since the day she was delivered from that demon. A shiver shot down Keturah's spine, and she looked around, half-expecting to see a demon trying to break into this celebration, tormenting Eliana. But she saw only happy faces. Nothing could put a damper on the disciples' exultation. Peter began singing, and even his squawking voice could not ruin the mood.

Then it was more dancing as the men joined hands, creating a circle—a string of links forged by the fires of the Holy Spirit.

Eliana

Eliana tried her best to put on a brave face, but Asaph saw through her in an instant.

"What's wrong?" he asked when they finally had a chance to be alone. The disciples had dispersed for the night, and Asaph and Eliana were left alone in Joanna's courtyard. "I would think you'd be happy I'm free."

Eliana took his hand. "Of course I'm happy! I am overjoyed!"

"It doesn't appear that way."

"It's been a difficult couple of days."

Asaph ran his fingers across the back of her hand. "I only ask because it is uncharacteristic of you. When you came to visit me in the prison yesterday, I marveled at your courage and your strength."

"Just because I am sad doesn't mean I am without strength," she said, deflecting his observation. But she had to admit there was truth to his words. Yesterday, she did feel strong. But this night . . . Her strength was depleted, leaving her vulnerable. Unprotected.

But she would not admit this to Asaph. The last thing she wanted was to spoil his happy moment. What's more, the last thing she wanted to do was to tell him about the man, Hosea, and how he had reentered her life like a slumbering disease, come back again.

"Pray for me, Asaph," she said.

"I will. I have." He kissed her on the side of her face. "I wish you could have been there to experience it, Eliana." Then, realizing what he had just said, he added, "I mean I don't wish you were in prison; I wish you could have been there for our release. If I had any doubts about Jesus and the Way, they are banished."

"That makes me happy." Then tears broke through her resistance, and she began to sob again. Asaph wrapped an arm around her, and she laid her head on his shoulder. "Lord be my protector," she whispered.

"He is," Asaph whispered in her ear. "I sense that the angel who came to us this night is present right now, looking after you. Looking after *us*."

"I pray you are right." She closed her eyes and buried her face in his chest. Strangely, his clothes carried the scent of spices; she would have thought that he'd still be carrying the scent of prison.

"There are angels all around us," he whispered.

"I believe that." But as she responded, she noticed movement in the darkness, the flit of a fast-moving shadow. Immediately, her mind returned to the night when she was almost killed by the attacker who had infiltrated their compound. Had the attacker returned? She let out a gasp.

"What's wrong?" Asaph asked.

"You don't see?" Eliana asked.

"See what? Do you see an angel?"

"I do. Don't you?"

Asaph followed her gaze and turned his head toward the darkness. "I don't. But as long as you can see the angel, that is the important thing."

However, it soon became clear that this wasn't an angel of God. The shadow moved into the faint light of the courtyard fire. There, standing before her, was Calev—the demon who had tormented her for so many years. The demon who had been banished from her life.

Calev had returned.

Nekoda

This was ridiculous! Standing before the Sanhedrin, in Herodian Hall once again, were the Twelve. How the twelve men wound up there was bizarre. Nekoda wasn't sure what to make of it.

Earlier this day, the high priest had demanded that the twelve leaders of the Way be hauled from the prison and brought before them. But when the captain of the Temple guard reached the prison, he was shocked to discover that the prison cells were empty! The guards were still at their posts, as if nothing untoward had happened. But when they opened the cells one by one, the prisoners were clean gone. It was like some incredible magician's trick.

What's more, word reached them that the Twelve were back at the Temple Mount, back at Solomon's Portico, preaching to the throngs. Somehow, the leaders of the Way had escaped, but the fools didn't flee Jerusalem, as any sane person might have. They went right back to the Temple and started preaching again! Nekoda wasn't sure whether he should admire their courage or laugh at their stupidity.

Even more ridiculous, word had spread that an angel had led them out of their prison cells. Nekoda had heard excuses before from Temple guards who had failed in their jobs, but this one was beyond the pale.

Angels!

Nekoda thought it was much more likely that the apostles had connections with some of the Temple guards, who found a way to spring them in the night. Or maybe someone on the Sanhedrin, a secret sympathizer, had arranged for their release. But angels?

When the high priest heard about the mysterious prison break, he ordered the captain and his lieutenants back to Solomon's Colonnade to apprehend the men once again, but he told them not to use a show of force. Wise thinking. The Twelve's popularity had grown exponentially overnight, and any use of force could trigger an uprising.

Fortunately, the apostles gave themselves up willingly—again, making Nekoda question their sanity. Now, the Twelve stood before the Sanhedrin in a *déjà vu* display. It was almost comical, but none of the priests were laughing.

Caiaphas, the high priest, glared at them. "We gave you strict orders not to teach in this name."

This name. As before, Caiaphas seemed almost afraid to utter the man's name out loud. *Jesus.* Nekoda thought it made it look as if Caiaphas was terrified of the name.

Caiaphas continued. "We ordered you not to teach in this name, and yet you have filled Jerusalem with your teaching and are determined to make us guilty of this man's blood."

Peter repeated the argument he had used the last time he appeared before them. "We must obey God rather than men! The God of our fathers raised Jesus from the dead—whom you had killed by hanging him on a tree. God exalted him to his own right hand as Prince and Savior that he might give repentance and forgiveness of sins to Israel. We are witnesses of these things, and so is the Holy Spirit, whom God has given to those who obey him."

Peter's words flew at them like arrows, one after another, and the entire body of the Sanhedrin surged to its feet, most of them shouting and shaking their fists. Nekoda shot to his feet because it was expected, although he didn't have the heart to shout. But he had to admit there was much in that brief speech to offend. Peter said Jesus was exalted to God's right hand—the seat of honor. He was a Prince! A Savior even! Jesus gives repentance and forgiveness! But only the Lord Almighty can do that. And what was all of this about the Holy Spirit?

"Put them to death!" someone shouted from behind Nekoda.

"Yes! Death to blasphemers!"

Another *déjà vu* moment. Nekoda felt as if he had been transported back to the day when the same threats were being hurled at Jesus of Nazareth on this very same spot.

He noticed that the voices shouting for the blood of these men were all Sadducee priests such as himself. The Pharisee members of the Sanhedrin, a minority on the court, did not call for the death penalty—and a death penalty could not be declared without the support of the Pharisees. The Pharisees were the party of the people, much more popular than the wealthier Sadducees. Nekoda hated to admit this, but it was true. He and his fellow Sadducees were unfairly labeled as elitist, just because they had larger homes and finer clothes.

When the shouts and threats had dwindled, the prisoners were escorted from the room so debate could ensue. After several Sadducees had spoken, all advocating death by stoning, one of the Pharisees finally rose to his feet. It was Gamaliel the Elder, of course. He carried the most respect among the Pharisees. The masses loved him, and even Nekoda felt a large measure of respect for him. Gamaliel the Elder was the grandson of the great Hillel, a rabbi with moderate views of the Law. Gamaliel took after his grandfather in many ways.

"Men of Israel, consider carefully what you intend to do to these men," Gamaliel said in calm, even tones. "Some time ago, Theudas appeared, claimed to be somebody, and about 400 men rallied to him. He was killed, all his followers were dispersed, and it all came to nothing."

All true. Theudas was a flash of fire that burned hotly and briefly.

"After him, Judas the Galilean appeared in the days of the census and led a band of people in revolt. He too was killed, and all his followers were scattered."

Again, all true. Judas the Galilean led a revolt against the census, which was conducted to impose taxes on the Lord's chosen people. He urged Jews not to participate in the census, and he and his followers even burned the homes of some of those who gave in to Roman rulers.

"Therefore," Gamaliel continued, methodically, "in the present case I advise you: Leave these men alone! Let them go! For if their purpose or activity is of human origin, it will fail. But if it is from God, you will not be able to stop these men; you will only find yourselves fighting against God."

Gamaliel adjusted his robes and calmly sat. The entire body of Sanhedrin sat in stunned silence. Although people around him shifted uncomfortably, and some even muttered, no protests were made out loud. Gamaliel had made it clear that the Pharisees would not support the killing of the leaders of the Way with stones.

But the Twelve could still suffer in other ways. When the men were brought back before the Sanhedrin, the high priest declared that they would be flogged before being let go. They might not have to pay with their lives, but they would still pay with their blood.

Asaph

Asaph couldn't look; the sound was bad enough. The whip-crack, the slap of leather against skin, the grunts of human misery. The apostles were being whipped, one by one, with the standard forty lashes minus one. The "minus one" had been added as an extra precaution so that the person doing the whipping didn't accidentally exceed the maximum number of stripes.

"Let us leave here," Asaph urged Eliana, who stood at his side, her eyes wide open.

"Never," she said.

Eliana had done the same thing when Jesus was flogged and then crucified. She vowed to keep her eyes open and would not turn away throughout the entire ordeal. She wanted to be a witness to what happened to Jesus, every step of the way. If she couldn't share in Jesus's suffering physically, she told Asaph not long ago, she wanted to share in it spiritually and emotionally by watching it to the bitter end.

So, it didn't surprise him that she wouldn't leave until all twelve disciples had been flogged.

When the whip-cracks stopped, Asaph lifted his head and looked. The authorities were done with Thomas, whose back was streaked by fiery stripes. But the man had his arms raised to heaven, and he was praising God.

"I sought the Lord, and he answered me; he delivered me from all my fears," Thomas declared as he walked to where the rest of the Twelve awaited him. "Those who look to him are radiant; their faces are never covered with shame. The angel of the Lord encamps around those who fear him, and he delivers them!"

"It's true," Asaph whispered to Eliana. "The angel of the Lord encamps around those who fear him."

Although it seemed dream-like, Asaph would never forget being delivered from prison by that angelic being. But despite the power of that visitation, he didn't know if he could come away from a flogging with praise on his lips, as Thomas was doing.

The next apostle stepped forward: John. His back was bared, and he was inspected to make sure he was physically fit enough to handle the thirty-nine lashes. Most of the apostles looked in good shape, so he assumed that most, if not all, of them would be given the maximum. During the flogging, if a person looked like he couldn't survive another blow, sometimes the remainder of the flogging was postponed for another day. But Asaph didn't expect that with these men. They came away singing!

John bowed to the ground, with his back exposed, and the punisher stood above him on a stone, gripping the whip. Asaph closed his eyes, and the cracks began. One. Two. Three. Four. Five. Six. On the seventh, John began to make a sound. A grunt, followed by muttered prayers. Asaph couldn't make out the words, but with each crack John's voice rose in volume. He realized that John was praying in another language.

"Are you sure you want to stay and watch this?" Asaph asked Eliana once again, hoping she would suggest leaving.

She didn't answer. Her gaze was fixed, her eyes pools of tears.

Something odd had happened to Eliana between the time she came to him in the prison and now. She was quieter than normal. Nervous. Restless. When he had asked her about it earlier in the day, she snapped at him.

It was easy to see that a darkness had come over her. Keturah told Asaph that she had not seen Eliana like this since before she had been delivered from an unclean spirit.

The whip-cracks went on and on and on and on—two-thirds of the strikes on John's back and one-third on the chest. Asaph wanted to plug his ears, but he couldn't be seen as weak. If these men could endure the feel of the whip, he would endure the awful sound of it.

Soon, it was over for John, and Asaph opened his eyes. John wobbled on his feet, and one of the other apostles had to catch him. But John was smiling—or at least trying to smile—as he collapsed in the arms of Matthias. Asaph had to wonder what Matthias, the newest disciple, must be thinking. Was he regretting his new position among the Twelve?

Matthias, with his back bared, was the next to approach the whipping ground. He smiled at the man holding the bloody whip and said a few words to him. A blessing perhaps? A word of forgiveness? Whatever he said, the man holding the whip didn't look pleased.

Then Matthias bowed to the ground, offering his back to his tormentor, as a sacrifice to the Lord.

6.

The Book of Acts, Chapter 6

Eliana: Month of Tammuz (Late June), 30 A.D.

The Upper Room overflowed, and Eliana stood in the back away from the commotion. As the number of believers appeared to double every day, the room was no longer large enough to hold everyone who came to worship daily. The room was deafening as people talked and prayed, while the Twelve worked to sort out the most recent controversy. Hellenist widows complained that they were being overlooked when it came to the daily distribution of food among the fellowship. Hebrew widows were getting preferential treatment.

Eliana was friends with a couple of Greek-speaking, Hellenist widows, so she was aware of the problem. Some of her Hebrew friends said it was a simple communication breakdown with the Greek-speaking widows, but her Hellenist friends thought it was more than that. Wealthy members contributed much of the food and money to be distributed, and the wealthiest believers tended to be Hebrews. The Hellenists thought the wealthy Hebrews were more concerned about their own.

It was a mess. But at least the Twelve were committed to putting things right. At this moment, they were in the process of appointing Hellenist leaders whose job would be to make sure all the widows and other poor were taken care of.

"Are those the ones they've chosen?" Eliana asked Asaph. He had drifted to the front of the Upper Room, closer to the Twelve, and had come back to report.

"They've narrowed it down to seven leaders."

Peter called for quiet. As the hum of the room died down, he introduced the gathering to the seven new Hellenist leaders: Stephen, Philip, Prochorus, Nicanor, Timon, Parmenas, and Nicolaus. Eliana knew Philip, Nicanor, Timon, and Nicolaus, but not the others.

The Twelve clustered around the seven new leaders, laying on hands, and they prayed over one leader at a time. Eliana closed her eyes and descended into prayer; she felt herself dropping deep into her thoughts and meditations. As the world whisked away, she saw herself in a dark cave, not unlike the one where Zuriel had kept her captive, not unlike the one where she and her family hid from the Romans when they were on the run, not unlike the one where she had seen Jesus as a baby—and not unlike the one where Jesus had been buried.

It seemed as if her entire life had been one cave after another. Places of refuge, places of new birth, places of imprisonment, and places of death. She saw herself walking through this cave as it sloped downward. A winged creature flitted over her head, but she could only hear it, not see it. The air was damp, and she heard rushing water coming from somewhere to her right.

Then a figure emerged from the darkness, as if a shadow had peeled off the cave wall. Eliana froze. She tried to turn and run, but her legs were leaden.

The figure standing in front of her had the shape of a man. But it was not human. It was Calev, the demon who had once tormented her. She had only seen a visible form of him twice—just before Peter had cast him out of her and then again a few days ago. Calev took slow steps in her direction.

"Hello, Eliana, I have come to reconcile with you."

"In the name of Jesus Christ, stay back!"

At the mention of Jesus's name, Calev halted. Did the name stop him in his tracks?

"In the name of Jesus, stay back. In the name of Jesus, stay back. In the name of Jesus, stay back . . ."

"I have a gift for you," Calev said, and she watched in horror as he reached down and picked up a container. It was dark in the cave, so she could barely make out what he held in his hands. It seemed to be a basket with a lead covering. There was something alive inside this basket. An animal? Another demon? Whatever it was, Eliana didn't want it. She tried to turn and run, but she couldn't lift her feet; they had become rooted to the ground.

"In the name of Jesus Christ, free me. In the name of Jesus Christ, free me. In the name . . ."

"Eliana!"

This time, it was Asaph's voice she heard, and she suddenly found him gently massaging her right shoulder. She sucked in a breath, as if she had been underwater, drowning, and had suddenly come up for air. She found herself back in the Upper Room, surrounded by Asaph, Keturah, and several people. One of them, strangely enough, was one of the Hellenists who had just been appointed as one of the new leaders.

"This is Stephen," Asaph said. "He asked if he could pray for you, Eliana. You were unconscious and seemed to be in trouble. He has come to help."

Eliana looked into Stephen's eyes, which were dark brown with the hint of a half-moon shadow beneath them. Gentle eyes. His hair was black and slightly curled, his beard equally black and short-cropped.

"Thank you," Eliana said. "Please. Yes, please pray."

Then another face came into view, just over Stephen's right shoulder, and Eliana felt as if she were back in that cave. This time, she wasn't looking at Calev. She was looking at the man who called himself Hosea. But to Eliana, he would always be Moshe, one of the men who had abducted her as a child.

Eliana's heart raced. It felt as if her heart had become the creature in the basket, trying to break out. It began beating wildly, and she started shaking.

"What is that man doing here?" she asked.

When Hosea heard those words and saw her face, he backed up several steps. Both Stephen and Asaph turned to look at who or what had struck terror in Eliana. They seemed perplexed because Hosea was just a scruffy old man with lopsided eyes, who looked just as terrified as Eliana.

"I . . . I just . . . just came to see if I could help," Hosea said. Even his voice was weak, cracked by age. But if Asaph had known this man when he was younger, he would realize why Eliana choked with terror. Once again, she had a hard time breathing. She gulped and gasped.

She had to get away. She couldn't look at that man's face for one moment longer. Her heart was trying to break out; it seemed to be hurling itself against her chest from the inside. Eliana took off running. She was out the door of the Upper Room in two heartbeats. Then she took the stairs two at a time down to the street below.

"Eliana!"

She heard Asaph's voice calling from behind, but she didn't stop, didn't turn. This time, her feet were not stone, and her legs were not rooted to the ground. They were flying, carrying her who knows where.

Asaph

Asaph and Eliana used to race each other through the streets of their village as children. Back then, they would run neck and neck along the twisting pathways. But on this day, Eliana was running at a speed he had never seen from an older woman. She flew through the crowd, weaving in and out of people like a fast-dodging bird, avoiding one obstacle after another. Asaph's pursuit was much clumsier, and he had to stop several times to fight his way through a knot of men standing at the various shops, bickering over prices. He couldn't keep up, and Eliana was quickly gone from sight.

He headed toward the Temple Mount but finding her in the mob would be next to impossible. He tried anyway, mystified by her behavior over the past few days. What was it about that pitiful old man that had spooked her?

After looking for her fruitlessly at the Temple Mount, Asaph wound his way back to Joanna's home in the Upper City—the place where Eliana was staying.

"Have you seen Eliana?" he asked when he reached the courtyard, where Joanna was feeding several followers of the Way. Feeding and housing followers of Jesus had become a full-time job for her. Helping her was Eliana's father, Judah.

"She burst into the house, looking as if she had seen a demon," said Judah.

"Maybe she has. Where is she?"

"In her room. I was giving her time to be alone. Don't you think it best if you do the same?"

"I don't know any more. Have you noticed how strangely Eliana has been behaving the past couple of days?"

"How could I not?" Judah said. "But she won't tell anyone what's bothering her."

"I must go to her."

Judah led him upstairs to Eliana's room and knocked gently. "Eliana. Eliana! Asaph is here. He's come to comfort you."

No response.

"Eliana. I am opening the door," Judah said. "Is that all right?"

Still no answer.

For a moment, Asaph feared that Eliana had done something terrible to herself. He had never seen Eliana during the time when she had been possessed by a demon, but he had heard stories.

When Judah swung open the door, they found Eliana sitting in front of the window, hugging herself, as if for warmth. But it was a hot day. How could she be chilled?

"I will leave you two alone." Judah left the door ajar as he departed.

Asaph approached from Eliana's right side, where he could get a good look at her. Her eyes flashed in his direction, but only for a moment. Then she returned to staring out the window. She closed her eyes. A tear slipped from her right eye, trailing down her cheek.

Pulling up a chair, Asaph sat, afraid to break the silence.

"Who is that man?" he asked gently. "Why are you so upset by a harmless old man?"

Eliana's eyes lit with fire, and she turned on him in anger. "He's not harmless!"

Asaph had touched a wound. "I'm sorry. I didn't know. He's not harmless. I believe you. But how has he harmed you?"

"If you knew, you would not marry me." Eliana spoke barely above a whisper. But at least she was talking.

"Nothing could prevent me from marrying you, Eliana. It's what I have wanted since we were children."

"Was I ever really a child? I can't remember ever being a child. I can only remember . . ."

Asaph was confused. How could Eliana act as if she had forgotten their time as children?

"We had good times together as children," he said. "Racing through the streets, trying to see who could reach the village gate first. You often won those races."

Eliana's eyes flicked in his direction once again. He was hoping for a glimmer of a smile over these fond memories. But nothing. Then it was back to staring out the window.

"We also climbed trees. Don't you remember those days?"

Still staring out the window, she said in a stilted, dead tone, "Our favorite tree became cursed."

She was right. The tree they most loved was used to crucify one of Eliana's neighbors. Asaph had witnessed it, and he would never forget the crucifixion. From that day forth, he never climbed the tree ever again. He never even touched it. As for Eliana . . . Her family had disappeared into the night, like evening mist, never to return.

"I am as cursed as that tree," Eliana said. "I am just as tainted. Like that tree, you would never want to touch me if . . ."

She turned toward him and stared.

"If what, Eliana?"

She took a deep breath, trying to contain a sob.

"I am cursed," she said. "I am unclean."

Asaph reached out and put his hand on hers, to show that she was not unclean to him. She yanked her hand away.

"You are washed by the Living Water of Jesus of Nazareth," he said. "You know it is true."

"I thought it was true. Until . . ."

He waited for her to finish her thought, but silence returned.

"Until you met that man?" he said. "Who is he, Eliana?"

Eliana shook her head as more tears squeezed beneath her closed eyelids.

Then Asaph knew. The awareness came over him like a swiftly moving shadow. He was almost afraid to ask the next question.

"Was he one of the men?" Asaph didn't complete the thought. He didn't say, "One of the men who abducted you. One of the men who abused you."

Eliana gave a nod, the slightest of nods.

At first, Asaph's mind went blank at this news, as if all his thoughts of comfort had been erased in an instant. In their place came an army of unwelcome thoughts, invading his mind. His thoughts bristled with anger and hatred. He felt the fury of vengeance rise from his core. As he stood to his feet, his chair fell backward with a bang.

"I am going to kill the man," he said. Then he turned and barged from the room. He began running, almost as fast as Eliana had run earlier in the day.

Sveshtari

Sveshtari and Abel entered the courtyard of Joanna's house, expecting an evening of fine food. They had been scouring the city for Zuriel, but the man seemed to have disappeared. This didn't surprise Sveshtari. They had lost their window of opportunity to find him when they were arrested. Zuriel was probably long gone if he knew what was best for him.

As they strolled into the courtyard, they entered a madhouse. They found Eliana in tears, being restrained by two female servants, while Judah and Joanna tried to calm her down.

"I'm so glad to see the two of you," Joanna said when she spotted Sveshtari and Abel. "We need your help."

"What's happening here?" Sveshtari said. "Eliana, what's wrong?"

Eliana shook loose of the two servants. "Asaph is going to kill him! You must stop him!"

Sveshtari hadn't seen Eliana like this since the night she tried to drown herself in the Sea of the Galilee—the same night he had plunged into the water to save her and was nearly drowned as well.

"Who is Asaph going to kill?" Abel asked.

"Hosea! He's going to murder Hosea! You must stop him!"

Abel looked at Sveshtari. "Who's Hosea?"

"Just go! Find Asaph!"

"They're going, Eliana. Don't you worry. They're going," said Joanna. She motioned for Sveshtari and Abel to walk beside her as she escorted them back into the Jerusalem streets. So much for a night of food and relaxation.

"Who is this Hosea?" Abel asked again.

"He is an old man, a follower of the Way," Joanna said.

"And why in the world would Asaph want to murder a follower of the Way?" asked Sveshtari.

"Because he was one of the brigands who abducted Eliana as a child."

Sveshtari came to a halt. He turned to face Joanna directly, stunned by the news. "And she recognized him after all of these years?"

"The man came to her, seeking her forgiveness."

Sveshtari didn't say what he was thinking. He not only couldn't blame Asaph for wanting to kill the man; he wanted to help him do it.

"You two must stop Asaph before he does something that will land him in prison—or stoned to death. That will kill Eliana."

"True," said Sveshtari. He was lost in thought, still thinking about the audacity of this man to ask for forgiveness.

Abel tugged on his sleeve. "Joanna is right. We must hurry!"

Reluctantly, Sveshtari followed Abel into the night. Abel rushed ahead, stopping every so often to urge Sveshtari along. Truth be told, Sveshtari was in no hurry to stop Asaph from killing this man. How could any human being expect someone like Eliana to forgive such an atrocity? The only thing that could set things right was the shedding of blood—and it couldn't be the substitutionary blood of a lamb. Sveshtari sought the real blood of the guilty party.

Sveshtari had once witnessed the sacrifice of several bulls to Mars Ultor—Mars the Avenger. The god Mars went by a host of names, but Mars Ultor had a special place in Sveshtari's pagan past. His father brought him to Rome, to the Temple of Mars Ultor, to witness the sacrifice of a bull to the god; he was mesmerized and astounded that this mighty beast, a raging bull, could be transformed into a bleeding mountain of dead flesh. That is what the god of Vengeance was about—transforming life into death. But these followers of the Way constantly talked about transforming death into life.

He pictured that bleeding bull suddenly coming to life and rising to its legs once again. In real life, it never happened. The bull remained as dead as stone. But imagine if it had risen back to its feet!

Despite his boyhood education in the ways of retribution, Sveshtari grudgingly admitted that it was wise to stop Asaph from carrying out his own act of vengeance. Asaph was in enough trouble already, facing the false accusation that he murdered Nekoda's brother, Chaim. The last thing he needed was to add a real murder to his name.

"Asaph probably went to the Upper Room to find the old man," Abel said, still trying to hurry him along. Abel was shorter, but his legs were in perpetual motion.

As they neared the house where the disciples gathered, they heard the sounds of worship. This house was the heart of the movement, and like any good heart, it kept up a regular beat of music and prayer. The first floor was where believers came to receive apportionments of food, and it was bustling with noise and movement. Several men and women were handing out bundles of food to outstretched hands, mostly grains and fruit, but there was no sign of either Asaph or the old man.

Abel nudged Sveshtari's shoulder. "Upstairs." Then he bounded up the stairs, two at a time. Sveshtari trudged close behind. In the Upper Room, they found clusters of people seated on cushions in small groups—praying. On one side of the room were the men, and on the other side were the women.

"Look. Over there." Abel nudged him again and pointed. Asaph stood in a corner, set apart from the people. He leaned against a wall, partially cloaked in shadow, and he had his eyes on a circle of believers in prayer.

"Which one is the old man, do you think?" Sveshtari asked.

"It must be the one with the droopy eye. The man is old, and he keeps glancing at Asaph with a look of fear."

"That's the man?" The old man looked more pitiful than Sveshtari had imagined. Rotund, soft, mostly bald. Where would the pleasure be in wreaking vengeance on such a creature? It would be more like squashing a bug than bringing down a bull.

Abel, fast-moving as always, darted across the room before Sveshtari could take two steps in Asaph's direction.

"Eliana is worried about you." Abel spoke softly so he wouldn't disturb the people wrapped in prayer.

"She has nothing to worry about," Asaph said, his voice rising. Abel motioned for him to keep his voice softer. "I am going to confront her demon for her. I will make him pay for what he has done."

Sveshtari glanced at the old man. "That's a pitiful-looking demon, if you ask me. He's not worth your energy."

"Demons take many shapes. Evil can come wrapped in pitiful forms."

"Listen to yourself," Abel said. "You're calling a follower of Jesus a demon."

"What would you call a man who abducted a child and destroyed her childhood? What would you call a man who did that to my betrothed?"

"I would call him a man in sore need of salvation."

"It would be a crime to save such a man from eternal punishment. He stole Eliana's childhood," Asaph said.

Sveshtari agreed.

"Was it a crime that Jesus saved me from eternal punishment?" Abel asked. "I too stole many things from many people."

"You never stole a young girl's life."

"True. But I stole many other things of great value. I lied and cheated. But I am made new. It's the same with Sveshtari here. He killed. He stole people's lives. But he too can be redeemed."

Sveshtari noted that Abel had said "he *can* be redeemed." Didn't Abel believe he was already redeemed? He wanted to protest, but they needed to keep the focus on Asaph.

Abel did not let up. "Sveshtari killed Keturah's father, and yet she came to forgive him. She even agreed to become betrothed to him."

Sveshtari felt his defenses rise like a wall of shields. "Now hold on, Abel. That was my duty as a soldier, as a bodyguard in Herod's palace.

I stopped Keturah's father from assassinating Herod. That's completely different than a brigand abducting a young girl and selling her into slavery."

"I don't think Keturah would look at it that way."

Sveshtari didn't answer. He wanted to lash back at this little thief. Abel had a way of slipping into his mind and creating havoc, like an intruder overturning tables and chairs and breaking vases.

But . . .

Something told Sveshtari that Abel was right. Sveshtari had begged Keturah for more than a year to forgive him for what he had done. So, he knew what it was like to be desperate for absolution. Could this old man be seeking the very same thing?

Once again, he balked at the comparison. Whenever he kills, he does it to defend others. When he killed Keturah's father, he did it to defend Herod, which was his job. When he killed the Roman soldiers on Mount Arbel, he did it to defend the Zealot freedom fighters. That's a world away from abducting a girl and having your way with her.

As Abel continued to talk Asaph out of shedding blood, the nearest prayer group ended their time together and people began to disband. To Sveshtari's horror, the old man approached. He stepped directly in front of Asaph, who looked confused and bitter. The old man said nothing, but his lower lip began to quiver. Tears pooled in his eyes.

Sveshtari rolled his eyes. The man was so pitiful. So weak. These were not the blazing eyes of a bull. These were the helpless eyes of a lamb—and lambs were born to be killed.

Sveshtari had never thought before about the differences between the sacrifices of the Hebrews and the sacrifices of the Romans. The Jews primarily sacrificed lambs and pigeons—helpless creatures, weak creatures. But in the cult of Mars, bulls were sacrificed. Powerful creatures, fiery and furious. This old man may have been a bull in his youth, when he committed unspeakable crimes. But now, in his old age, he had been reduced to that of a helpless creature.

Still, the old man didn't speak. He didn't try to defend himself, as Sveshtari was so quick to do when Abel got under his skin. He didn't try to explain away his crimes. He just stood there as the tears continued to build in his eyes.

Then the man fell. He didn't collapse as if in a faint. There was volition in his movement. But his collapse was sudden and startling. The old man lay prostrate on the floor, his legs fully extended and his arms stretching to both sides.

He made the shape of a cross on the floor.

By now, the man was sobbing. Other believers in the room couldn't help but notice what was happening, and they gathered around. A couple of men crouched, laid hands on the back of the prostrate man, and began to pray. Others seemed to sense that Asaph was the other half of this tug of war between two spirits, and they too laid hands on him and began to pray for him. Abel joined in the prayer, but Sveshtari just stood there, unsure what to do or say. He had spent a lot of time among followers of the Way, and he considered himself a God-fearer, but he couldn't get used to these open expressions of prayer and worship.

He looked at Asaph, who had also begun to weep. Such weakness! Sveshtari's father used to beat him at the slightest sign of tears, but these men were displaying their grief openly. Without shame!

Sveshtari looked down at the prostrate man, whose back vibrated with tremors as his weeping intensified. Then more men gathered around, laying on hands, praying simultaneously in different languages. Sveshtari felt a weakness in his own legs, and he realized that he too was beginning to weep. But he wasn't weeping for Asaph or for this old man, beaten down by the horrors of his past. He realized he was shedding tears for himself, for the blood he had shed.

Then it hit him, in a flash of understanding. He had never wept about killing Keturah's father. He had asked for forgiveness, again and again and again. But he had never wept. Until now.

Suddenly, Sveshtari's legs gave out, as if an enemy in battle had cut his legs out from beneath him. He collapsed to the floor. All his strength was taken from him in an instant. Without thought, without choice almost, he lay flat on the floor, his arms extended to both sides. The same position as the old man.

Sveshtari had become the bull, drained of life, drained of blood. He felt as if he had died alongside the old man, the bull next to the lamb, and both wracked by tears. He felt hands being laid on his back. He heard prayers all around in multiple languages, some speaking, some singing. And it occurred to him that everything in his life had converged on this single moment in time. All of time became concentrated into a sharpened tip, like a spear, and it pinned him to the ground.

He felt himself dying, but it wasn't a bad thing. He felt his old self spilling out on the floor like blood from the holy wound in Jesus's side. This was the mystery that eluded him for so long. He realized, for the first time in his life, that this was the only way he could ever be truly alive. He had to die. He had to be pinned to the ground by remorse and repentance. His tears flowed like blood.

Keturah

Sveshtari had changed in some strange way. Keturah saw it the moment he and Abel stepped into Joanna's home with Asaph in tow. Also entering alongside them was one of the new leaders of the Way—one of the Greek speakers. Stephen was his name.

"Is everything all right?" Keturah said, sliding beside Sveshtari and slipping her hand in his. His eyes were reddened, as if he had been weeping. But Sveshtari never wept. She had never even seen so much as a single tear in all her days with him.

"We got to Asaph before he could do anything foolish." Sveshtari drew her toward the courtyard. "We must talk."

"But I should be with Eliana."

"She is in good hands."

As they moved into the courtyard, Keturah looked back to see Asaph and Eliana deep in conversation with Stephen. Away from the light of the house, in the darkness of the courtyard, Keturah became conscious of a strong scent, a beautiful scent, hanging in the air. Joanna's courtyard thrived with white lilies, a tall flower that bowed its head, as if in humility. Sveshtari also lowered his head and started to speak, then hesitated. He seemed afraid to talk, so she began.

"What happened? I can see that something has happened, Sveshtari."

"I told you. We prevented Asaph from doing anything stupid."

"No. I mean what happened to *you*?"

His head drooped even more. As her eyes adjusted to the dark, she could see his pain.

"Something happened to you. What was it?"

"This old man, the man who sought Eliana's forgiveness . . . He was knocked to the floor."

"By Asaph? By you?"

"By the Holy Spirit, I think."

By the Holy Spirit? This didn't sound like Sveshtari talking. Something definitely was different.

Sveshtari heaved a sigh. "The same Spirit knocked me off of my feet."

Keturah gasped. Not only had she never seen Sveshtari weep, but she can't recall ever seeing him knocked down by anyone. He was as strong and immovable as a bull.

"I was pinned to the floor, like a crucified man being nailed to a cross," he said.

Keturah winced at the image. She wrapped her arms around him tightly. "Were you afraid?"

"It was frightening, but at the same time . . . There was a strange release. It felt like the day I escaped from the Fortress of Machaerus and gave up my life as a bodyguard."

Sveshtari and Keturah kissed, then returned to a silent embrace.

"Like an apple tree among the trees of the forest is my beloved among the young men," Keturah said. "I delight to sit in his shade, and his fruit is sweet to my taste. Let him lead me to the banquet hall, and let his banner over me be love."

"That is from the Hebrew Scriptures," Sveshtari said.

"Yes. You're getting better at recognizing Scripture."

Again, Sveshtari sighed. "There's one other thing, Keturah." Again, she could hear a hint of fear in his words.

"Yes?"

"I shed tears this evening."

"I could see that."

"It was that obvious?"

"I know you."

"But it's more than that, Keturah. I shed tears of remorse."

Keturah pulled away and looked him in the eyes. She had never seen such sadness in his face before.

"I shed tears of remorse for the things I have done . . ." Another deep sigh. "I shed tears for your father."

Now Keturah was weeping. There was sadness in her weeping, but there was also the fragrance of joy. Sveshtari had begged for her forgiveness for many months, and she had reluctantly given it to him. But this was the first time she felt deep sorrow in his words of repentance. This was no act, just to get her to love him. If anything, he was taking a big risk bringing up the topic of her father when she had already forgiven him.

Sveshtari let go of Keturah and put a hand to his eyes. He sat down on a bench beside the bed of flowers. She sat next to him and rested her head on his shoulder. She felt his shoulders quake.

"See! The winter is past; the rains are over and gone," she said, once again reciting Scripture. "Flowers appear on the earth; the season of singing has come."

She paused and breathed in the scent of evening. Then she raised Sveshtari's head, lifting his chin, and they kissed once again. This time, she spoke no Scripture, but she let the words of the Lord flow through her mind like a spring of Living Water.

My beloved has gone down to his garden, to the beds of spices, to browse in the gardens and to gather lilies. I am my beloved's and my beloved is mine; he browses among the lilies.

Eliana

Stephen's words stunned Eliana.

"Jesus is calling you out of exile," he said.

Stephen and Eliana sat across from each other at Joanna's table. Asaph sat on one side of Eliana and Joanna on the other, like guardian angels.

She had been expecting Stephen to tell her she needed to learn to forgive Hosea. But he didn't say anything of the sort. He said nothing about Hosea being a believer, a brother in Christ even, and that she needed to be reconciled to him. Instead, Stephen said she had been in exile.

"Why? What do you mean I'm being called out of exile?"

Stephen leaned over the table and spoke softly. "Your heart is still in exile. When you were abducted by evil men, they carried you to a far-off land, and a piece of your heart remains there still, trapped in exile."

"But Jesus transformed me. He saved me."

"He has. I know of your story."

Stephen knows my story, Eliana thought. She didn't know she had such notoriety.

"But the Spirit is telling me that although Jesus brought you out of exile, a piece of you still remains in bondage in Babylon."

"By the rivers of Babylon we sat and wept when we remembered Zion," Eliana said, reciting the Psalm that spoke of the people of Israel being forced into exile in the strange land of Babylon.

"When you were taken as a child, you were brought to a foreign and frightening land, just as the Israelites were taken into exile in Babylon," Stephen said.

That much was true. When her abductors were done with her, they sold her into slavery in Egypt—her Babylon, her place of exile. At that time, she thought that Cavel was her only protector. She didn't realize that Cavel, a demon, was her captor.

"There on the poplars we hung our harps, for there our captors asked us for songs, our tormentors demanded songs of joy," Stephen said, completing the words of the Psalm. "The tormentors said, 'Sing us one of the songs of Zion!' But how can we sing the songs of the Lord while in a foreign land?"

Eliana nodded. She knew the story well. When Israel went into exile in Babylon, the people who had captured them and killed their children demanded that they pick up their harps and sing songs of joy! It was like rubbing salt in a wound.

"Jesus does not ask you to sing songs of joy when you're in torment," Stephen said. "He's not asking you to embrace Hosea in joy, as if the actions of that man's past don't matter. But he is asking you to break free of your captor once and for all. He's asking you to come out of exile, sister Eliana. Do you remember those words of hope when Israel came out of exile? 'Love and faithfulness meet together; righteousness and peace kiss each other.'"

Righteousness and peace kiss each other? She had heard those words before, but she was at a loss for what they meant. Righteousness demands that Hosea pay for his crime. Righteousness punishes the wicked. But how can righteousness and peace kiss each other? How can they be reconciled?

"Let me pray for you." Stephen rose to his feet and extended his arms before her. Asaph placed a hand on one shoulder, and Joanna took Eliana's hand, enclosing it in both of hers.

Then the prayer began.

"Do not hand over the life of your dove to wild beasts," Stephen said. "Do not hand over the life of your daughter Eliana, your dove, to the demon of hatred. Do not forget the lives of your afflicted people forever. Have regard for your covenant, because haunts of violence fill the dark places of the land."

As he spoke, Eliana fell deep within herself, deep into the same cave she had seen before. The same haunt of violence. The same dark places.

"Turn your steps toward these everlasting ruins, all this destruction the enemy has brought on the sanctuary," Stephen continued.

Was Eliana the sanctuary he spoke about? Was she in ruins?

"But you, Lord, are our King from long ago," Stephen said. "You bring salvation on the earth. You split open the sea by your power. You broke the heads of the monster in the waters. You crushed the heads of Leviathan and gave it as food to the creatures of the desert. Crush the head of Satan. Crush it, Lord!"

As Eliana became wrapped in these words, she saw Cavel once again before her; he appeared in the cave of her consciousness, carrying the same basket, and once again something was trying to break out of the container.

"Remove the presence of evil from sister Eliana's life!" Stephen said. "Take this evil to the farthest reaches of the land!"

As Stephen spoke those words, Cavel began to struggle over the basket—a large basket, an *ephah*, used to measure out flour for sin offerings. She could not see who he was struggling with in the dark, but it was a winged creature of some sort. She heard the rustle of wings, saw flashes of movement, and felt flutters of energy. Then the lead cover on the basket flew open and out tumbled an idol. It was a wooden carving of Asherah, the pagan goddess of fertility, the mother of Baal. She was often represented by trees and was worshipped at Asherah poles.

As Eliana looked on in stunned horror, the goddess began to grow and rise from the ground like a fast-growing tree, extending branches to all sides, filling the cave with tentacles of wood, reaching out for Eliana. Even more shocking, she realized that this tree, this Asherah pole, was the very same tree that she and Asaph once climbed as children.

They loved that tree until it became cursed on the day her neighbor was crucified upon it. But what was the meaning of the tree? Jesus was killed on a tree of sorts. And on that tree, all our sins were placed. She sensed that this tree in her vision, this Asherah pole, had been poisoned by sin. It had become a tree of death, not a tree of life, and this tree began growing within her on the day she was abducted by Hosea and those other men.

"Tear down the altars of Baal and Asherah in our sister's heart," Stephen said, as if he could see into her spirit, as if he were witnessing the very same vision. "There is only one throne and one God to sit on that throne. Burn away the idols that remain in her heart, Lord Jesus Christ!"

With those words, Eliana felt an intense heat within the cave of her vision, and the floor of the cavern cracked open, flames leaping out like arms. Then the Asherah tree, the Asherah idol, burst into an inferno of hissing wood. She could see that Cavel was also in the midst of the fire, trying to save the idol, trying to put out the flames. But the tree began to crack, and sparks flew out from the center of the fire, then spun around and around in an ever-intensifying vortex. The flames wrapped the entire tree, as if in chains, and she could still see the face of the goddess imprinted on the bark of the tree, screaming as the tree was thoroughly and utterly consumed.

When it was over, what remained of the tree was a pile of ash, which was lifted into the air and swirled in circles, slowly filling up the basket, the *ephah*. Cavel was also gone, and Eliana sensed that he too had been consumed by the flames; all that remained was the ash in the basket. Then two women appeared, both with wings, and they took hold of opposite ends of the basket and rose up into the air.

Then Eliana found herself back in Joanna's house, back at the table, with Asaph and Joanna flanking her on both sides and Stephen staring at her intently.

"Where are they taking the basket?" she asked Stephen, as if he would have any notion of what had happened in her vision.

"To Babylon," he said. "Your sin has been taken back to the place of your exile. You are free. You have come out of exile. You are home."

Asaph: Three Months Later, Month of Tishri (Late September), 30 A.D.

An old man stood in the darkness with a twisted ram's horn to his lips, and the sound of the shofar carried through the night. He began with an urgent, staccato sound, followed by a long, extended blast. This was the call: The bridegroom was returning.

For Asaph, it was as surprising as it was exciting. Asaph didn't know the day that he, the bridegroom, would be going forth to claim his bride. Traditionally, that decision would have been his father's. But his father was long lost to the world, so Eliana's father, Judah, made the decision for them.

Tonight was that night—the long-awaited union of Asaph and Eliana. It had been a long, strange journey. Typically, a Hebrew bride would be between the ages of twelve to eighteen years old, while the groom would be between fourteen and twenty-four. Both Asaph and Eliana were in their forties.

The father of the groom usually selected a bride for his son—or sometimes the pairing was made by the matchmaker. But Asaph and Eliana, friends from childhood, had found each other in their later years. Nothing in life had been ordinary for them. So, despite their age and lack of an extended family, they were determined to seal the covenant of their commitment in the traditional way. That meant blowing the shofar to announce the return of the bridegroom to collect his bride and bring her to their new home.

Asaph was surrounded by men carrying torches, lighting up the night as they paraded through Jerusalem toward the home of Joanna, where Eliana was still living. The night was smoky and warm and intoxicating.

Strange, though . . . Asaph recalled what had happened to Jesus on the night of his betrayal, when men with torches also paraded through the night. But instead of sealing a marriage with a kiss of commitment, Jesus's death was sealed with the kiss of betrayal. The arrest of Jesus in the Garden of Gethsemane was a twisted distortion of the marriage ceremony, a betrayal of covenant love.

But Asaph would dwell no more on that terrible night. Today was about joy and eternal commitment. He adjusted the gold crown, like that of a king, that he wore as the bridegroom, the *chatan*. Once more, the sound of the shofar carried across the rooftops of Jerusalem as their procession streamed through the narrow, desolate streets, a river of Living Light moving steadily toward Eliana. The words of Scripture, which he had memorized, also streamed through his mind.

You are a garden locked up, my sister, my bride; you are a spring enclosed, a sealed foundation. Your plants are an orchard of pomegranates with choice fruits, with henna and nard, nard and saffron, calamus and cinnamon, with every kind of incense tree, with myrrh and aloes, and all the finest spices. You are a garden foundation, a well of flowing water streaming down from Lebanon.

Eliana

Keturah draped a golden necklace around Eliana's neck and placed golden rounds on her head, befitting a queen. Eliana's clothes were multicolored, beautifully embroidered, the finest she had ever worn, and golden bracelets jangled on her wrists.

Eliana was veiled, viewing the world from behind a shimmering strip of fabric. Veils conceal what is holy, and Eliana felt a holiness she never would have imagined in her former life. She had already gone through purification in the waters of the *mikveh*, and she had been scented with perfumes. All senses were at work in her purification—sight, sound, touch, and smell.

I bathed you with water and washed the blood from you and put ointments on you, said the words of Ezekiel, speaking of Israel as a bride being prepared for Yahweh. *I clothed you with an embroidered dress and put sandals of fine leather on you. I dressed you in fine linen and covered you with costly garments. I adorned you with jewelry: I put bracelets on your arms and a necklace around your neck, and I put a ring on your nose, earrings on your ears and a beautiful crown on your head. So you were adorned with gold and silver; your clothes were of fine linen and costly fabric and embroidered cloth. Your food was honey, olive oil and the finest flour. You became very beautiful and rose to be a queen.*

Eliana felt like a queen, from her head to her feet, but she knew it was all the Lord's doing. She had once been a lost soul, homeless and hungry and dressed in rags, and the Lord had clothed her with salvation and placed on her head the crown of life.

Asaph's "two witnesses"—Sveshtari and Abel—had already come to Joanna's house to announce that Eliana's bridegroom was coming. This set everything in motion. All the preparation was now coming to fruition.

Jesus had described John the Baptist as "the friend of the bridegroom," for he had announced Jesus's arrival as the Messiah. Jesus the groom asks us to be ready. And by the time that Eliana heard the shofar in the night, she was ready in all respects.

"We are ready to go forth and meet the procession," said Keturah. She carried an oil lamp, which cast a soft glow that danced against the walls. Keturah slipped out of the room with the other attendants—ten lights in all. With Eliana in their midst, the ten attendants went into the streets, lamps in hand, to meet the bridegroom's procession. In the darkness and with the veil concealing so much, Eliana had to rely on the steady direction of Keturah on one side, Joanna on the other.

Eliana, with the veil down, could see a stream of light coming toward her. As the bride and her attendants converged with the bridegroom and his friends, so did the lights they carried. The two rivers of light became one river to carry the bridegroom and the bride, the king and the queen, back to the house that Asaph had prepared. She could not make out the people all around her, but she saw dozens of lights dancing about, like stars. She had always been a stargazer as a child, painting the constellations in the night sky with her pointed finger. Now, the stars had come down to her to celebrate this day.

Eliana was led into the *aperion*, the bridal carriage in which she would be carried by four strong men. She felt herself lifted, which is what the wedding ceremony, the *nissuin*, was all about. She was raised up and carried, as if on a cloud, and she savored the gentle swaying of the *aperion*, as singing erupted on all sides. Would this be what it felt like when she was carried to the King of all Creation on her last day on earth? Would the stars come down to greet her, and would she be carried on a cloud?

At last, they reached the home that Asaph had prepared—a home that would be their own. She hadn't had a permanent home since the day her family fled the Romans. She had been on the run ever since, but now they had a place to rest and start a family, Lord willing. She was beyond the normal age of childbearing, but who knows? Sarah was much older than her when she had Isaac.

To represent the heavens, under which their union takes place, four men unfurled a canopy, the *huppah*. Each corner of the canopy was held up by the branch of a cedar tree. Their new house would be a covering, a *huppah*, protecting them from the outside elements of both weather and demons. It would provide shade by day and a refuge from storms.

Eliana's father led her beneath the *huppah* and gave her to Asaph. Behind the veil, she could not distinguish Asaph, but she knew his touch. All her senses were raised to high levels. Then Asaph lifted her veil to partake of the cup of wine, the cup of praise, while seven blessings were spoken over them.

"Blessed are you, Adonai our God, Ruler of the universe, Creator of the fruit of the vine.

"Blessed are you, Adonai, our God, Ruler of the universe, who has created everything for your glory.

"Blessed are you, Adonai, our God, Ruler of the universe, Creator of Man."

It was true. God had created man and woman, a perpetual fabric woven together like the beautiful clothes she was wearing this day. The seven blessings continued to unfurl, word by word, each one leaping to be heard.

"Blessed are you, Adonai, King of the universe, who has created joy and gladness, bridegroom and bride, mirth and exultation, pleasure and delight, love, brotherhood, peace, and fellowship. Soon may there be heard in the cities of Judah and in the streets of Jerusalem, the voice of joy and gladness, the voice of the bridegroom and the voice of the bride, the jubilant voice of bridegrooms from their canopies, and of youths from their feasts of song. Blessed art Thou, Adonai, who makes the bridegroom to rejoice with the bride!"

After this seventh blessing, Asaph and Eliana drank of the cup, and the taste was fruity and ripe. No longer would Eliana be called Desolate. No longer would she be called Deserted. Her name would be Hephzibah, or "my delight is in her."

For the next seven days, there would be feasting and food and mirth and exultation. But for this night, there would be consummation, as Asaph took her by the hand and led her to their new home, their new covering, their new canopy.

As he did, Eliana was transported once again to the days of their youth when they ran through the streets of their village and climbed trees. The cursed tree at the edge of their Eden had been burned away, and now they were prepared to grow a new tree, a solid and sturdy tree, with many branches and an abundance of fruit.

Asaph clasped the oil lamp in his left hand, and her hand in his right. He set the lamp on the table—their only light—and they faced each other. Then he reached out and removed the gold rounds from her head. His clothes also smelled of sweet perfumes. Eliana and Asaph kissed once. Then twice. Then a third time, and she tasted honey.

Until the day broke and the shadows fled, Eliana would bound among the mountain of myrrh and the hills of incense.

Nekoda: One and a Half Years Later, Month of Nisan (Early April), 32 A.D.

Nekoda heard raised voices, angry voices, and the sound of shattering pottery as he approached his home in the Upper City of Jerusalem. He hurried through the gate and threw open the door of the house, only to find his two sons wrestling on top of the mosaic floor. Hiram, his older boy at eighteen, was sitting on top of Ezra, his sixteen-year-old, and he pummeled him with both fists.

Nekoda was a widower, so the only woman in the household was his mother, who tried to separate her two grandchildren. When Hiram nearly struck his grandmother by accident, Nekoda exploded. He looped an arm around Hiram's neck and pulled. He was so enraged that he didn't stop to think for a moment about what he was doing. He dragged Hiram off Ezra, his arm tightening around his son's neck. Even Ezra seemed alarmed at his fury.

Nekoda tossed Hiram to the side like a rag. His son, gasping for air, stared up at him with pure hatred. But Nekoda spoke before his son could spit out a single word.

"It's one thing if you two boys are going to fight, but you very nearly struck your grandmother!"

Hiram glanced at his grandmother, as if checking to see if she showed any mark of violence. "I apologize, grandmother."

Hiram rubbed his neck. Ezra looked at Hiram as if in sympathy for the bruising from his father.

"Are you all right, brother?" Ezra asked, even though he was the one who had been bloodied. Ezra's nose bled, and a black bruise was already forming around his eyes. And yet he was asking if Hiram was all right? What was wrong with him?

"Get away from me!" Hiram shouted. "Father, your son is being poisoned by the followers of the Way, and yet you do nothing! You are a member of the Sanhedrin! Do something! Do something for a change!"

What Hiram said was true. For the past two months, Ezra had been hanging around Solomon's Portico, listening to Jesus's disciples preach. Nekoda forbade him from mingling with followers of the Way, but he suspected that Ezra was doing it on the sly.

"I saw Ezra at Solomon's Portico only last week, listening to Peter preach," Hiram said, confirming Nekoda's suspicions. However, Nekoda didn't like it that Hiram saw himself as his brother's keeper; he didn't like it that Hiram had no qualms about reporting on his brother's behavior.

Hiram had been consorting with the followers of Saul of Tarsus, and Nekoda wasn't sure he liked that any more than Ezra listening to followers of the Way. Saul was a Pharisee in the strictest sense, and his passion for purity was ferocious. Saul prowled the Temple courts, arguing with followers of the Way, making threats, and looking for infractions against the Law among fellow Jews. Nekoda's old friend, Jeremiel, had been equally obsessed with the minutia of the Law, but Jeremiel had a tender spirit. Saul was a lion, looking for offenders to devour with his righteous anger.

"Aren't you going to rebuke your son for disobeying your command to stay away from Peter and the Way followers?" Hiram said, glaring at his father.

"It's not your job to monitor your brother's every movement," Nekoda snapped back.

"Yes, it's *your* job. Do it!"

Nekoda had to control himself to keep from slapping Hiram. Instead, he growled, "Honor thy father. Or have you forgotten one of the most important of laws?"

He could see that this hit Hiram is his most vulnerable spot—the Law. "I do honor you," he finally said, a bit subdued. "Perhaps I could have worded my statement in a less threatening manner. But you need to know that Ezra has been disobeying your command to stay away from the disciples."

Ezra just stood there, not defending himself, not saying a word. Nekoda wished he had some of the fire of Hiram. But both sons had drifted to extremes. One too aggressive, the other too passive. Didn't they know that the best politicians were not hot or cold?

"Ezra, we need to talk about this—but not now and not in front of Hiram."

"Yes, Abba."

"In the meantime, I do not want to see any more fighting between the two of you. You are brothers, and I don't want you to wind up as Cain and Abel or even Jacob and Esau. Be more like Moses and Aaron."

"The followers of the Way insult Moses," Hiram said, still not letting go of his fury.

"How are they doing this?" Nekoda asked his oldest son. "I sincerely want to know."

"They heal on the Sabbath. They show disdain for the Law. And disdain for the Law is the same as disdain for Moses. They need to be held accountable."

Hiram was reciting the words of Saul of Tarsus, who wanted the Sanhedrin to crack down harder on the followers of Jesus. He was under the man's spell, and that was just as bad as Ezra falling under the spell of Peter the apostle.

Maybe worse.

Sveshtari

Sveshtari positioned his chisel at the cutting edge of a hefty piece of limestone, knocking it with firm whacks of his wooden mallet. Chips of stone shot into the air, along with little puffs of dust, as his chisel worked along the edge, biting away at the stone.

Sveshtari was making an ossuary to hold the bones of the deceased. For over a year now, he had been laboring as a *tecton*, a craftsman who worked in both stone and wood, much the way that Jesus did. Sveshtari had traded his sword for a chisel, and it was an entirely satisfying existence.

Stonecutting would be a noble trade to pass on to his son when his boy was old enough to wield a chisel and mallet. But it would be many years before that would be possible. His son, Asher, was not even six months old.

Keturah was in the courtyard of their home, nursing the child. Sveshtari could hear her voice intermingled with that of Eliana. The two friends were always together, always chattering.

A couple of months after Eliana and Asaph had gone through the *nissuin*, the wedding ceremony, Sveshtari and Keturah sealed their marriage contract. Although he and Keturah were God-fearers and not full Hebrew converts, they went through many of the same Hebrew marriage rituals.

However, they did not observe other Hebrew rituals, most notably circumcision for their son. Sveshtari still could not see the reasoning behind such a barbaric desecration of a boy. Keturah had asked him if they could circumcise Asher, probably due to Eliana's influence, but he was adamant. No son of his would undergo this ritual.

Now, Keturah was expecting another child—the third including Babette, their foundling. Babette was two years old, and she was talking up a storm. As Sveshtari's mallet beat out the rhythm of his work, he could hear Babette babbling and laughing with the two women.

Eliana and Keturah had become even closer over the past two years, if that were possible, because they shared the most remarkable of life's experiences. Both were expecting children at roughly the same time. When Asaph and Eliana announced the coming of their first child, there was both astonishment and joy throughout the growing community of the followers of the Way.

"Sarah was much older than me! And Elizabeth was about my age when she had John," Eliana constantly reminded people whenever they marveled at her condition. Nevertheless, having a first child at her age was still highly unusual.

Every night, as they spoke their prayers before sleep, Keturah would pray for Eliana. Before Asher was born, Keturah had lost two babies in the womb. For Eliana, this might be her only chance at a child, so Keturah prayed constantly that Eliana and Asaph's child would make it into this world, squalling and very much alive.

Sveshtari continued to chip away at the limestone, dust flying. The irony wasn't lost on him that he was creating a different kind of womb. This ossuary for bones was a womb for the dead as they awaited arrival in a new and more glorious life. Plenty of Hebrews still dismissed the notion of life after death, but Jesus had shattered that idea. Sveshtari prayed for the man or woman whose bones would wind up in this ossuary. He prayed it would be a temporary vessel, like the cave that held Jesus's body before he rose to life.

"Sveshtari! Sveshtari, come quickly!"

The voice was that of Abel, and it reached Sveshtari's ears moments before the little thief came dashing into view. He still thought of him as the "little thief," even though Abel had taken on a respectable trade, selling pottery in the markets outside the Temple. Abel had also married a young woman named Hannah, and they wasted no time in starting a family.

Sveshtari set aside his chisel and mallet and wiped the stone dust from his fingers. "What's wrong?"

"Come quickly! There is trouble at the Temple!"

Sveshtari grabbed his knife; he no longer carried a sword, but he kept a knife close, especially in these troubled times.

"What's happened now?" he said, hurrying alongside Abel. As usual, his friend wanted him to run, but Sveshtari would not humiliate himself that way. He would walk fast. But run? No.

"It's Saul of Tarsus and the Hebrews from the Synagogue of the Freedmen."

Sveshtari assumed as much. The Synagogue of the Freedmen in Jerusalem was made up of former Hebrew slaves and their descendants—*libertinoi*. They had been voicing strong opposition to the followers of Jesus, accusing them of blasphemy against God and Moses. At times, the hostility bordered on violence, but the followers of the Way were committed to non-violence.

Sveshtari wasn't as enthusiastic about the idea of not fighting back. He had his knife. Just in case . . .

Abel, even with his shorter legs, bounded up the Monumental Staircase two at a time, like a mountain goat, urging Sveshtari along. When they swung into view of Solomon's Colonnade, where the disciples never ceased to preach, they found a sight that was becoming routine—Temple guards using their spears to keep back the crowd. They had a prisoner in their midst, and Sveshtari was not surprised to see who it was: Stephen.

Over the past two years, Sveshtari had developed a fondness for this fearless man. Stephen was the one who finally brought Eliana out of her depression, and it was his prayers that brought Sveshtari to his knees.

"This is an outrage!" came a familiar voice to their right. It was Hosea, the man who had caused such grief for Eliana. Ever since the day that Stephen prayed for Eliana, she and Hosea had found peace. Initially, Sveshtari thought this was unnatural. But now, after two years, he recognized it for what it was. A miracle.

"What's happening?" Hosea asked Sveshtari, slipping beside him.

"Nothing new," Sveshtari said, watching as the guards whisked Stephen away toward the meeting place of the Sanhedrin. The angry crowd followed, and people jostled against Sveshtari. He pushed back. "They'll just interrogate him, warn him not to preach about Jesus, and maybe flog him. But they'll release him."

Even as he said this, Sveshtari was nagged by doubts. For some reason, this arrest seemed different than all the others.

Nekoda

Nekoda was tired of the theatrics. He was tired of the constant tension and conflict, broiling all around him. He was tired of people like Saul of Tarsus, a small man who was always seething about something. He was tired of the bickering between his hot-headed son and meek-minded son.

Nekoda tried not to look bored as yet another one of Jesus's disciples was hauled before the court. No matter how many times they brought various disciples before the Sanhedrin, it always ended the same. The men were lashed and released, and then they went straight back to the Temple and began preaching about Jesus again. If anything, this constant persecution was only growing the number of Jesus followers, not tamping down the movement. In that respect, maybe his son Hiram was correct. Maybe they needed to wield a firmer hand over followers of the Way.

As Stephen stood before them, several members of the Sanhedrin stood up and hurled accusations.

"This man has made threats against our very Temple!" shouted Matthias, a Pharisee. "He said that not a single stone of the Temple would be left standing on another! We cannot stand by while threats are made against the holiest spot on earth!"

Nekoda sighed. The same argument was made against Jesus, who allegedly said similar things about the Temple being torn down, and about a new Temple, not made with human hands, rising in its place in three days. Whenever threats were made against the Temple, the Romans allowed the Sanhedrin the freedom to carry out their own punishment. But the accusation didn't work against Jesus, and they had to rely on Roman complicity to kill the Nazarene. What made Matthias think the accusation would work against Stephen?

"This man is also leading an attack on Moses!" added another Pharisee. "By attacking the Law, he attacks Moses!"

That sounded exactly like his son Hiram speaking—and Saul of Tarsus. An attack on the Temple and Moses's Law was an assault on the two strongest foundations of their faith. Nekoda wondered if this line of prosecution might get them somewhere, when all else had failed.

For two years, they had been listening to followers of the Way preach in the Temple precincts, stirring up trouble. For two years, there had been no letup in the bickering, pitting Jew against Jew, son against son.

Perhaps, Nekoda thought, he let his affection for his brother, Chaim, influence his attitude toward the Way. Maybe he was too tolerant of this movement, which was tearing apart families like his. Maybe if he hadn't been so accommodating to these false beliefs, his son Ezra would not have been taken in.

Witnesses came forward, one after another, speaking against Stephen, accusing him of wanting to tear down the Temple. When one of the witnesses stepped in front of the court, Nekoda shot to his feet. The witness was Zuriel, the man he still believed to have murdered his brother. For two years, he hadn't been able to prove a thing, so this man walked freely. Even worse, Zuriel had aligned himself with Saul of Tarsus, gaining a cloak of protection. And now he stood before the court, hurling his own accusations at Stephen.

"I too heard Stephen say that he wanted to destroy the Temple!" Zuriel shouted, pointing at the disciple. "In fact, he wants to tear down the Holy of Holies!"

Tear down the Holy of Holies? This was a new one to Nekoda. A wave of indignation rippled through the court. Then Stephen turned and scanned the faces of the Sanhedrin. Nekoda couldn't help but see the same look that his son Ezra gave to his brother Hiram, even after being pummeled.

His face did not show a trace of anger or hatred or disgust. Stephen's face almost glowed.

7.

THE BOOK OF ACTS, CHAPTER 7

NEKODA

"ARE THESE CHARGES TRUE?" asked the high priest.

Silence. At last, the entire room hushed to hear Stephen's response. This was the pivotal point of the trial. Stephen scanned the Sanhedrin—a semi-circle of men, all eyes on him.

Then he began to speak of Abraham. At first it seemed that Stephen was avoiding the question: "Are these charges true?" What does Abraham have to do with the case against him? But this line of speaking was not unusual for many Hebrew teachers. Their speeches often wandered every bit as much as Abraham wandered when he left his home country to discover the land that Yahweh had promised. Abraham finally settled down, and Nekoda hoped that Stephen's speech would also finally settle down and find a home as well.

But he didn't. Next, he talked about Joseph, another wanderer—although this patriarch's wandering was not by choice. Joseph was sold into slavery by his eleven brothers and wound up in Pharaoh's prison in Egypt. But, like Abraham, his wanderings also led to a final, settled place. Joseph wound up as Pharaoh's right-hand man, and his wise decisions saved the country—and his own family—from starvation.

Still, Stephen wasn't done. He next talked about Moses. Another wanderer. Another pilgrim of God. After fleeing from Egypt, Moses wound up in Midian, where he found a wife and spoke to a burning bush. Then, upon the Lord's command, he returned to Egypt and led the Israelites out of slavery, leaving miracle after miracle in his wake. Moses and the Israelites continued to wander, this time through the wilderness, until they wound up at Yahweh's destination—the Promised Land.

Was Stephen done after talking about these wanderers? Not at all. He went on to speak of the Tabernacle, as it wandered across the land in the hands of Joshua and King David. The Tabernacle was a portable home for the Lord, the forerunner of the more permanent first Temple, built by Solomon. The Temple was the House of God. Did that mean no more wandering?

"However, the Most High does not live in houses made by human hands!" Stephen said. This, at last, brought everyone in the Sanhedrin to attention. One Sadducee priest, who had been nodding asleep, popped his eyes open.

"As the prophet says," Stephen continued, "'Heaven is my throne, and the earth is my footstool. What kind of house will you build for me?' says the Lord. 'Or where will my resting place be?'"

Nekoda knew that passage from the prophet Isaiah. He couldn't argue with the legitimacy of Isaiah, but what was Stephen trying to say by hurling that passage at them? Was he trying to say they were wrong to build a Temple as a House of God?

It's true that God cannot be nailed down to one location, but that did not justify an attack on the Temple. Then Stephen erupted. "You stiff-necked people!" he shouted, using the same words that Yahweh had hurled at the stubborn Israelites during the time of Moses. "Your hearts and ears are still uncircumcised!"

Stephen's accusers became ever more agitated. Nekoda gazed at the visitors' section and saw Saul of Tarsus pacing the floor and glaring. Stephen treaded on dangerous ground by saying that their hearts and ears were uncircumcised. The prophets often used this phrase to say that certain people were unable to hear the Truth of the Lord, unable to draw the Word of God into their hearts.

How dare he?

But Stephen was not done. "You are just like your ancestors! You always resist the Holy Spirit! Was there ever a prophet your ancestors did not persecute? They even killed those who predicted the coming of the Righteous One. And now you have betrayed and murdered him—you who have received the Law that was given through angels but have not obeyed it!"

This was too much for Nekoda. Stephen, this arrogant little man, was telling all the Sanhedrin they were no better than the people of old who killed the prophets. In fact, in Stephen's eyes, they were worse! They killed Jesus, whom he called the Righteous One. The Messiah.

Nekoda sensed that this was much different than any of the other trials of the disciples over the past two years. Stephen had struck at the heart of their faith by accusing them of murdering God and his prophets! The entire Sanhedrin as a body leaped to their feet. A couple of men held back Saul of Tarsus, who seemed to want to tear Stephen apart with his bare hands. But there was no stopping the members of the Sanhedrin who came down from their seats and pressed in toward Stephen.

A couple of Sanhedrin—Gamaliel was one of them—tried to hold back the crowd, but it was as futile as holding back a wave. The angry priests converged on Stephen, and several people grabbed him by the arms and began to haul him toward the door. The place was so loud that Nekoda couldn't make out what people were shouting.

Stephen was trapped in the center of the wrath, and he appeared to be staring up toward the ceiling. He was shouting something, but Nekoda had no idea what he was saying. His face continued to be lit up, and Nekoda looked around to see where the light was streaming from, since it was a grey day, with low-hanging clouds and very little light pouring through the windows.

A Temple guard grabbed the back of Stephen's clothing and lifted him up, carrying him forward. The crowd surged toward the door in a stream of anger and self-righteous judgment.

This was not going to end well.

Sveshtari

Sveshtari backpedaled to get out of the path of the crowd pouring out of the Court of the Sanhedrin, while Abel and Asaph leaped to the side. They spotted Stephen, clasped in chains and caught in the violent vortex of the mob, while fists and shouts of anger rained down on him.

"I think they mean to kill him," said Abel, and Sveshtari had to agree. If the Sanhedrin were going to flog him, they would have it done in an orderly, but brutal, manner. This was pure frenzy.

Sveshtari drew his knife, and Asaph pushed his hand down. "Put that away! Do you want to get yourself killed as well?"

"We can't stand by and do nothing!"

"We can pray for a miracle," said Asaph, but that seemed so weak and useless in comparison to making someone bleed. The three of them followed the mob as it streamed north in the direction of the Damascus Gate. Sveshtari could already see men picking up rocks as they hurried along. Sveshtari also picked up a rock. Perhaps in the chaos, he could hurl it at the skull of one of these crazed priests.

Asaph

Up ahead loomed the Damascus Gate, a formidable passage through the northern wall of Jerusalem. It was also called the Lion's Gate, for the image of devouring lions strolled across the stone of the arched entrance. Asaph recalled that he once dreamed of wielding the power of a lion in the political arena. But he had seen what lions do to innocent people. They shred people to pieces.

This mob had become as blood-crazed as any lion that tasted human blood. When Sveshtari picked up a rock, Asaph tried to tell him not to do anything foolish. If he hurled the rock at a priest, this mob would turn on him next, and even Sveshtari was not strong enough to fend off an entire pride of lions.

Stephen was shoved to the ground, as men on all sides tossed off their cloaks and laid them at the feet of the Pharisee named Saul. They wanted to free their arms so they could hurl their rocks with deadly speed and accuracy.

Asaph suddenly spotted Zuriel standing to the right of Saul. Asaph hadn't encountered him in a long time, but the sight of his sneer was enough to boil his blood. Maybe Sveshtari had the right idea after all. So, Asaph snatched up a rock the size of a melon.

"Now you're thinking," said Sveshtari. "We can take out a couple of these men, and no one would know who threw the stones once the rocks start flying."

"Let me have Zuriel," Asaph said.

"Zuriel?" Sveshtari scanned the mob. "Where? I'll help you crush that man!"

"You two are mad!" Abel said. "Zuriel is standing next to Saul of Tarsus. You will be spotted, and then Saul will make you the next targets!"

He was right, but Asaph wouldn't put his rock down. He kept his eyes on Zuriel as the man bent over and picked up a rock. Zuriel exchanged smiles with Saul, who nodded his approval. Then Zuriel strode forward, and the rocks began to fly toward Stephen.

The air filled with soaring stones. From all sides, the rocks thumped against defenseless human flesh. Most of the rocks pummeled Stephen's torso, but one of the rocks struck him in the side of the skull with a sickening crack. Blood gushed from the wound, covering Stephen in a red mask.

With glazed eyes, Stephen staggered, and for a moment the rocks let up. He gazed at the sky and pointed, barely able to maintain his balance. "Look!" he declared, "I see heaven open and the Son of Man standing at the right hand of God!"

The Son of Man was *standing?* Usually, Jesus *sat* at the right hand of God. Was he standing as a tribute to Stephen?

This enraged the crowd even more, and the rocks began to fly once again. Stephen stumbled toward the wall of the Lion's Gate, holding up his arm as a shield. Two more rocks caught him directly in the face, one crushing his nose, the other opening a large gash above his right eye. Still, the man stayed on his feet and kept trying to speak. Stephen wiped the blood out of his eyes and held his arms to the sky. Another flurry of rocks came at him like a hailstorm, battering him over and over.

He collapsed to the ground in a heap. But even after he fell, the rocks kept coming. Where were all these stones coming from? Jerusalem was a city of stone, but Asaph didn't realize there were so many just lying about. Stephen's face was barely visible amidst his blood-soaked tunic. Relentless, the rocks kept coming to make sure the man would not rise again.

Asaph snapped. Tossing aside his rock, he shoved through the crowd, heading straight for Zuriel who was bent over, scouring the ground and searching for a fresh stone. Roaring, Asaph threw himself on Zuriel's back and brought the surprised man tumbling to the ground headfirst. Asaph began to pummel Zuriel, his fists out of his control. His fists were not as lethal as rocks, but he was going to ensure that Zuriel also bled on this day.

Asaph felt men trying to pull him off Zuriel, and he lashed out wildly. He struck a couple of the men, and he thought one of them might have been Saul of Tarsus. Zuriel managed to squirm out of his clutches and jump to his feet. Asaph's punches had mostly landed on the back of Zuriel's head, not a very good choice of targets to make a man bleed.

Zuriel grinned. "I thought you were a follower of the Way, Asaph. I thought you were a man of peace. But some things never change, do they? You claim that Jesus changed you, but you're no different than the bully of a boy I knew when I was young."

Asaph panted, and he felt many eyes on him, including the lightning eyes of Saul. He suddenly realized how vulnerable he was. He had put himself in terrible danger, and Eliana would be furious. Asaph and Eliana had a child on the way. How could he put himself in such peril just to land a few innocuous punches on his enemy?

When a man tried to grab him, Sveshtari latched onto the guy's arm and nearly twisted it out of its socket. When another man lunged for Asaph, Sveshtari used a perfectly aimed and intensely powerful punch to the man's throat to send him staggering and gasping for air. After that, people gave them space as Sveshtari took hold of Asaph on one side, while Abel grabbed his other arm. They hauled Asaph away, but they hadn't gone far before a Temple guard stepped into their path. The soldier drew his sword.

Sveshtari

In his peripheral vision, Sveshtari noticed a man hawking ornate blankets from a stall. Quickly, he snatched a large blanket from the hands of the startled street-seller and charged forward, wrapping it around the Temple guard's sword and head-butting him. Because the soldier was wearing a helmet, he aimed his head at the man's exposed nose and struck it like a battering ram. Then he twisted the man's sword hand, which was still wrapped in the blanket, disarming the guard. Hurling the blanket back to the furious street-seller, he emerged with the soldier's sword in his hand and barreled forward. Seeing the flashing steel, people scattered out of his path.

The streets were packed, but Sveshtari cleared a path, careful not to shove any women or children. He wasn't gentle with the men, sometimes giving them a stiff arm that sent them staggering and stumbling backward into a cart of fruit and figs. He sensed Abel and Asaph right behind, following the pathway that he was clearing.

By the time he had gone beyond the Temple Mount district, the streets began to clear, and the trio stopped to catch their breath and look around. No sign of Temple guards in pursuit. Sveshtari looked down at his right hand, which still clutched the guard's sword.

"That guard is going want his blade back," Abel noted.

"If he finds me," said Sveshtari. "You see any sign of Temple guards?"

"None," said Asaph. "But Zuriel knows who we are. Do you think he knows where we live?"

"He may not, but he certainly knows where the disciples can be found, and he knows we might be found there as well," said Abel.

"For now, we steer clear of the Upper Room," said Sveshtari.

"Agreed," said Abel.

Then the trio pressed forward. The distant sounds of chaos at the Lion's Gate could still be heard. The image of Stephen, with the side of his face crushed and his body in a crumpled heap, stuck with Sveshtari as he began to move at a rapid clip. This time, even Abel had to hurry to keep up with him.

Nekoda

Nekoda's sons were tearing at each other's throats once again.

Hiram and Ezra stood in the middle of the courtyard of his home, screaming. As Nekoda moved toward them, intending to step between, Ezra let fire at his brother: "You murdered an innocent man!"

Hiram moved two steps closer. "Stephen was not an innocent man!" The brothers were nearly nose to nose. "He accused us of killing the Messiah, of murdering the Lord's Righteous One!"

"And you proved his case by killing another one of the Lord's prophets!"

"Stephen was no prophet. He was a blasphemer!"

Nekoda pushed his two sons apart.

"Look!" Ezra said, pointing at his older brother. "Look at his clothes! They are stained with the blood of an innocent man!"

Hiram stared at his tunic, as if unaware until now that his clothes were splattered with blood in a few places. Nekoda had been horrified to see his oldest son hurl stones at Stephen, but he blamed Saul for what Hiram had become.

"I will not hear any more of this," Hiram said, heading for the door of their home.

"Where do you think you are going?" Nekoda said. "The streets have become dangerous."

"Dangerous for the followers of the Way! Not for me!"

After Hiram left, slamming the gate on his way out, Nekoda looked at his younger son, who continued to shake with fury. Or was it fear? Would the authorities see Ezra as one of the followers of the Way? Was he in sudden peril? Nekoda assured himself that his position on the Sanhedrin would keep Ezra safe from the wolves.

"I must go too." Ezra headed for the door.

Nekoda blocked his way and put both hands on Ezra's shoulders. "Stay here. It's too dangerous. Someone might accuse you of being a sympathizer of the Way."

"I am more than a sympathizer, Abba. After today, I am a *follower* of Jesus of Nazareth! I must go to be with my family at a time like this!"

"*I* am your family!"

Nekoda tried to embrace his son, but Ezra broke past him. The next moment, his youngest son was also gone. Nekoda slumped into a chair and ran his fingers across his scalp. He was losing both of his sons, one to Saul of Tarsus and the other to Peter and John. One had joined a pack of wolves, while the other had joined a flock of sheep. One had already killed in judgment, while the other was in mortal danger.

Nekoda's thoughts went to his dead brother, for Ezra reminded him so much of Chaim. Then he began to weep.

ELIANA

Four months into her pregnancy, Eliana still experienced waves of nausea. But this irritant seemed minor on this night in Jerusalem.

Saul of Tarsus had been unleashed. Word had gone out that he was planning to descend on the suspected meeting places and homes of disciples and other followers of the Way. Therefore, Asaph and Sveshtari brought Keturah and Eliana to Joanna's home, where they would have a wall of protection, thanks to Joanna's marriage to Chuza, the head of Herod's household. Saul and the Temple guards wouldn't dare violate these premises.

With Keturah and Eliana secure, the four men—Sveshtari, Asaph, Abel, and Eliana's father—slipped away to help the more vulnerable members of their community. Sveshtari brought out his old sword, and so did Asaph. Eliana told them the disciples did not advocate armed resistance, but they would not listen. They had already forgotten those words of Jesus.

Eliana understood their rage. She did. She was devastated by the news of Stephen's public murder. But she wasn't going to let the persecution of her people give her permission to go against the teaching of her Lord and advocate for the sword.

Eliana, Keturah, and Joanna huddled before a fire, watching the smoky dance of flames. The night was windy and warm, and they hadn't felt a drop of rain for over a month. The city was a tinderbox in more ways than one.

"Let us pray," said Joanna. She closed her eyes and held up her hands. "My help comes from the Lord, the Maker of heaven and earth. He will not let your foot slip—he who watches over you will not slumber; indeed, he who watches over Israel will neither slumber nor sleep. The Lord watches over you—the Lord is your shade at your right hand; the sun will not harm you by day, nor the moon by night."

No sooner had Joanna finished praying this Psalm than they heard the first screams in the night. Saul was on the move.

8.

The Book of Acts, Chapter 8

Nekoda: Month of Iyyar (Early May), 32 A.D.

NEKODA RUSHED TOWARD THE sound of upheaval coming from the vicinity of the Upper Room. It was early evening, and an orange haze had settled on much of Jerusalem as a dust storm carried airborne sand from the desert. Men and women covered their mouths with cloths to filter out the blowing sand.

Was this a sign of the Lord's displeasure over the death of Stephen? Was the very ground lifting into the air and blowing away in protest? Nekoda's robe snapped in the wind as a gust stopped him in his tracks.

Despite the haze, the house of the Upper Room loomed ahead. It was mobbed by people, and the swirling orange mist made the scene other-worldly. It appeared that Temple guards had broken through the front door of the house and were hauling out believers. Even women! He couldn't believe the soldiers were laying hands on women!

Most of the people did not resist, but one man tried to break free; he was clubbed in the side of the head and went down in a heap.

A tall man, Nekoda shoved his way closer to the action and spotted Saul of Tarsus. Of course, Saul would be found at the core of the commotion. Lately, he seemed to be wherever there was unrest. Saul snapped commands, sending Temple guards into motion. The guards had arrested and released the disciples many times before, but this was on a larger scale. The net was wider, and it seemed to be as undiscerning as a dragnet, hauling in everyone from the Upper Room.

Word of Stephen's execution had spread and so had the fear of an uprising. Was this Saul's way of snuffing out rebellion before it could begin?

Then Nekoda spotted his son Hiram. He stood to Saul's right, pointing out various people. Was he identifying followers of the Way? It certainly appeared that way. Hiram seemed to be enjoying himself, relishing his proximity to power.

So far, Nekoda hadn't seen his younger son, Ezra. He was afraid Ezra might've been in the Upper Room when the guards descended. But no sooner had this thought flitted through his mind than he spotted Ezra working his way through the crowd. Ezra was moving away from the house of the Upper Room, which was good. *Move, move, move,* Nekoda urged with his thoughts. *Get as far away from Saul as possible.*

Then Ezra suddenly stopped. He turned. He looked directly at his brother. No! He should be fleeing. Nekoda tried to fight his way through the crowd to intercept his younger son, but a bruiser of a man turned and gave him a shove.

"Lay your hands off me! I am a member of the Sanhedrin!"

That only riled the man even more, and he latched onto his arm. "You're one of the Sanhedrin? You killed Stephen today!"

"No, I did not do that," Nekoda said, casting a glance in the direction of his sons. Ezra was moving closer to Hiram! Was he going to confront his older brother? He couldn't allow that to happen, but this man had a firm grip on his arm.

"Listen, I am sorry for bumping into you, but I must get through this crowd. It's important!"

The man seemed to take pleasure in his desperation. "Why? Are you anxious to help with the arrests?"

"No, it's my sons . . ."

Frantic, Nekoda watched as Ezra moved within an arm's length of his brother. Hiram had his back to Ezra and hadn't yet noticed him. Hiram was too busy lavishing his attention on Saul. Nekoda tried to shake loose from the bruiser, but the man held on tighter and laughed.

Nekoda continued to gaze past the big man. Ezra stood directly behind Hiram, staring at the back of his brother's head. "Turn around and run, turn and run!" Nekoda shouted, which only confused the man holding on to him.

"Turn and run? Is that a threat?"

"No, it's . . ."

Nekoda could see that Ezra had spoken, and Hiram wheeled around to face his brother. Then the two brothers began to argue, and Saul of Tarsus took notice. Nekoda had no idea what they were saying to each other, but he could imagine.

When a Temple guard laid hands on Ezra, Nekoda could stand it no longer. He broke loose from the man, tore his robe, and let out an anguished cry. This startled the big man so much that the guy backpedaled and stepped out of his way.

But it was too late. The guards had taken his youngest son. Ezra was now in the clutches of Saul.

Eliana

Eliana left the protection of Joanna's home to carry food to some of the widows who followed Jesus. Asaph would be furious if he knew what she was doing, especially with her expecting their first child. Under normal circumstances, these widows would show up at homes where food was distributed every day. But these were not normal circumstances. Hundreds had been arrested, and the jails filled with followers of Jesus. Even women were being taken. Even widows!

As a result, many of the widows hunkered down in their homes, praying to the Lord that their loyalty to Jesus would not bring the Temple guard to their door. The Jesus followers of Jerusalem were under siege, and Eliana was doing her part to make sure the widows didn't go hungry.

The sandstorm provided some measure of cover as she hurried from one house to another. But the intensity of the storm fluctuated. When she spotted three Temple guards moving along the street in her direction, she put her head down and pressed forward, a basket of food in her right hand. She prayed they would not stop to ask if she was a follower of Jesus. If they did, she couldn't deny it. She *wouldn't* deny it—not like Peter did on the day of Jesus's trial. Since Jesus's resurrection, Peter had acted with uncommon courage, so she tried not to judge him too harshly for his behavior that night. But Eliana vowed she would not deny Jesus. Never.

Eyes down, she was within an arm's length of the soldiers. A gust kicked up a fresh flurry of airborne sand, and she pulled the cloth more tightly across her face.

"Stop right there," said one of the soldiers.

Eliana pretended she didn't hear.

"You! Woman! Stop!"

Slowly, Eliana turned to face the three soldiers. They wore bronze helmets with red tunics and red mantles. One of them had drawn his sword.

"Would you care for any fruit?" Eliana lifted her basket into view.

"You read my mind," said one of the guards in a friendly enough tone.

Two of the guards reached into the basket and selected apples, while the third one—the one with the sword drawn—stood two paces back and glowered. She smiled in his direction, but his expression did not crack. She was terrified that he was going to ask: Are you a follower of Jesus?

Do not deny it, she thought. *Never deny it.*

Just when she thought the third soldier was about to speak up, one of the other guards reached into the basket, plucked out a third apple, and tossed it to him. He barely reacted in time to catch it.

"Never turn down an apple," said the jovial soldier. "It's not forbidden fruit."

"Shalom," said Eliana, bowing her head and making a move to go.

"Wait!" said the jovial soldier, before she could take two steps away.

She turned. *Do not deny it. Do not deny my Lord.*

"Shalom," said the soldier, giving her a parting grin. Then the three soldiers turned away and strolled into the veil of dust.

Offering praise for her deliverance—and for apples—Eliana picked up her pace until she found the last house on her list to visit. It was a small home in the Lower City, where a poor family of three shared a cramped space with two widows. She left them with round loaves of freshly baked bread, along with a tantalizing mixture of dates, honey, walnuts, almonds, apples, and cinnamon.

After blessing the food, Eliana made her farewells and ducked through the low doorway into the alleyway. In the distance, she heard a scream, and she wondered if Saul was continuing his house-to-house search for followers of the Way. The sooner she returned to Joanna's home, the better. She wanted to get back before Asaph returned to find her gone. She wouldn't hear the end of it.

Hurrying up the alleyway, she paused before reaching a perpendicular street, which normally was busy. But ever since the arrests began, the streets were quiet. She tried to keep to the twisting hidden paths through the city, but every so often she had to cross a wider street.

When she emerged from the alley into the street, she sensed movement to her right. To her horror, it was a soldier. And not just any soldier. It was the very one who had glowered at her. The other two guards were gone.

"I followed you," said the guard. "You are bringing food to followers of the Way."

"I bring food to widows. The Torah tells us to feed the widows and orphans. Do you not believe the Torah?"

She immediately regretted her choice of words. The last thing she wanted was to irritate this man.

"Of course I believe in feeding widows and orphans! But I also believe in purifying our streets of blasphemers."

The guard took a step closer. She held her ground and smiled. Her heart was beating wildly, but she managed to conceal the nervousness in her voice.

"I am pleased that you approve of my ministry to the poor among us," she said. "Shalom."

She made a move to cross the street, but the guard put a hand on her shoulder.

"I wanted to ask you before, so let me ask it now," he said. "Are you a follower of Jesus?"

Eliana now understood the panic that must have howled in Peter's ears the night he denied Jesus. Three times he said he did not even know the Messiah. It would be so easy to lie, she thought. Just tell the guard what he wants to hear and then return home and offer your confession to the Lord. Jesus would understand.

But then . . . she remembered the look on Jesus's face after the big fisherman denied him for a third time. She remembered hearing the cock crow, and she remembered seeing the pain in Peter's eyes. It was much worse than the pain in his eyes when he was recently flogged.

"I believe that Jesus is the Anointed One. Jesus has risen from the dead, and He enfolds me in His grace."

There. The words were spoken. She was prepared to go to prison. But was she prepared to die like Stephen?

"What seems to be the problem?" came a voice from the midst of the dust storm. A man's voice. A familiar voice.

The soldier lifted his hand from Eliana's shoulder and drew out his sword. Stepping out of the haze was Hosea!

"Who are you?" the soldier demanded.

"I am a follower of the Anointed One, who gives me rightful access to the tree of life."

What is Hosea doing?

"And who is the Anointed One in your eyes?" asked the guard.

Hosea gave Eliana a gentle nod. Was he telling her to run?

"I asked you," the soldier repeated. "Who is the Anointed One in your eyes?"

Hosea locked eyes with the guard. "Jesus of Nazareth, of course. I have seen him resurrected."

As he spoke, Hosea began to backpedal, drawing the guard farther away from Eliana. Once again, he nodded at Eliana. He wanted her to run. But she couldn't just desert him!

"You would much prefer to arrest a man than a woman, would you not?" Hosea said, backpedaling even faster.

"I prefer to arrest both of you."

Then Hosea turned and jogged just out of reach of the soldier. "You have to catch me first."

"That will not be a problem." The guard was fast, but amazingly Hosea was even quicker, dancing out of his reach. Barely.

Eliana felt so helpless. She had stood by while they crucified her Lord. She had stood by when they beat Stephen to a bloody pulp. She had stood by when they flogged the disciples. She was tired of standing by and getting trampled beneath the boots of the authorities.

But Hosea's sacrifice should not be in vain. She owed him that much. He urged her with his eyes. He *pleaded* with his eyes. So, she obeyed, turning and taking off running. As if the very elements were urging her forward, a gust of wind struck her in the back and propelled her forward, faster and faster, until she disappeared into an alley and lost herself in the maze of Jerusalem.

Asaph

Asaph leaped from his seat the moment that Eliana arrived at Joanna's house and rushed into the dining hall. He was prepared to bark at her and ask what she was thinking by venturing into the streets. But he could see that she was shaken, so he held his fire as she melted into his arms.

"What's happened?" he asked.

"It's Hosea. He's been arrested."

"I see." It wasn't much of a response, but Asaph had a difficult time feeling torn apart by the news. He understood that Hosea was a brother in Christ, but he couldn't get himself to feel anything for the man.

Eliana, on the other hand, offered what seemed to be a supernatural spirit of forgiveness to her former captor. In return, Hosea became protective of Eliana in an almost fatherly way, which was still difficult for Asaph to accept.

At that moment, Eliana's father appeared, bringing Eliana a cup of water. He had slowed down considerably in the two years since Jesus's death and resurrection. Her dog, Lavi, limped along by Judah's feet, also showing his age and a bad right hip.

"Sit, Eliana," Judah said. "Tell us what happened."

Eliana found a chair and took a deep drink of the water. Her hands were still shaking. When she set down the cup, Asaph took one of her hands and cupped it in his to bring the shaking under control. Then Eliana unraveled the story of how she had visited several widows, only to encounter a hostile Temple guard on the way back. If Hosea hadn't intervened, she would be sitting in a Jerusalem jail at this moment.

"I will pray for Hosea," said her abba. Like Eliana, Judah had reconciled with Hosea. This, too, was shocking because when Judah first learned that Hosea had become a follower, he had an even greater desire to kill Hosea than Asaph.

Asaph bowed his head. "I underestimated the man. I'm sorry he's been taken."

"He was arrested for my sake." Eliana was on the verge of tears.

"It's his way of redemption," her abba said. "For what he did to you in the past."

Eliana motioned with her hand. "But that sin has already been washed away. He didn't have to do anything more! All our sins were nailed to the cross when Jesus died—including what Hosea did to me as a girl."

Asaph flinched. How could his wife think this way? Her words lined up with Jesus's admonition to forgive our enemies, but it was too much for Asaph. It seemed unnatural to forgive such a thing.

"You're right. He didn't have to sacrifice himself." Judah put a hand on his daughter's shoulder. "But he willingly did it. He welcomed the opportunity to suffer for the cause of Jesus—and for you. Knowing Hosea, he was more than willing to suffer shame for the Name."

Suffer shame for the Name. That's precisely what Peter had said after he had been arrested the second time—and then flogged. The name was Jesus, and the suffering was cleansing, Peter said. The disciples and others seemed to have a supernatural power that allowed them to rejoice in suffering. Asaph prayed for the same power, but the thought of pain struck him with trepidation.

"We are part of a fellowship of suffering," Judah added. "Nevertheless, it's time our fellowship scattered like seeds. I think it's time for all of you to consider leaving Jerusalem."

Eliana snapped to attention. "How can I think of leaving when Hosea has just been arrested for my sake?"

Over the past week, many followers of the Way had been slipping out of the city. Asaph had to admit that the thought crossed his mind that they too should leave. He was pleased to hear Judah voice his opinion.

"Hosea sacrificed himself for a reason," Asaph said. "He sacrificed himself so you and our child would be safe."

"And the safest place for your child would be outside of Jerusalem," Judah added. "As far away from Saul and the Temple guards as you can get."

Eliana shook her head. "I can't just leave those who are suffering and imprisoned. I can't leave you, Abba. And what of those who have died?"

Stephen may have been the first martyr in Jerusalem, but there were others.

"Think of your unborn child, Eliana," Judah said.

Eliana flinched and stood up abruptly. "I am protective of the child."

Judah took her hand. "I know you are. That's why I think you know what you must do. Keturah and Sveshtari should do the same. All of you should leave the first chance you have."

"But we are safe within these walls."

Asaph scratched his beard. "For now. But the walls of Joanna's house will not keep away the Temple guards forever. Besides, look what happened tonight. If you're arrested, our unborn child will also be put in prison."

Eliana stared into space. "But that would mean leaving the city where Jesus died and was resurrected."

"The Holy Spirit will go where we go," Asaph said. "And Judah, you must come with us as well."

"But I'll just slow you down. I don't move as fast as I once did."

"If I go, you must go with us," Eliana said to her abba. Asaph could see she wasn't going to budge on that.

Sitting back down, Eliana put her face in her hands and began to sob. Both Asaph and Judah wrapped their arms around her and let her pour out her grief. Then Eliana slid to her knees and touched her forehead to the floor.

"From on high he sent fire, sent it down into my bones," she moaned. "He spread a net for my feet and turned me back. He made me desolate, faint all the day long."

These words of Lamentations were first applied to the people of Judah after Jerusalem and the former Temple were destroyed. But the words were just as fitting for Eliana and Asaph because Jerusalem was once again falling to pieces all around them. The buildings still stood, but the authorities were attempting to tear down the new Temple, which is Jesus Christ.

Asaph and Judah knelt beside Eliana, with their arms still wrapped around her prostrate body. Judah picked up on the stream of Lamentations.

"Arise, cry out in the night, as the watches of the night begin," he said. "Pour out your heart like water in the presence of the Lord. Lift up your hands to him for the lives of your children."

The darkness closed in on them as Eliana, Asaph, and Judah continued to pray and lament and weep into the evening. Judah got up at one point to light a couple of candles. But then the praying continued, with heads bowed to the floor, words pouring out.

Eliana tapped her chest with a gentle rhythm. "All our enemies have opened their mouths wide against us. We have suffered terror and pitfalls, ruin and destruction. Streams of tears flow from my eyes because my people are destroyed."

Fitting words, Asaph thought. Saul was trying to destroy their people. Utterly and completely. Saul would not rest until every follower of Jesus was behind bars or buried beneath the ground.

For that reason, they had no choice. They had to leave Jerusalem.

Nekoda

"You need to end this obsession with Jesus of Nazareth," said Nekoda as he hustled Ezra away from the prison, where he had been held for a day. Ezra had been imprisoned in the Sanhedrin's jail, one of several jails in Jerusalem. With Saul on the march, the prisons were filling up fast.

"If you're arrested again, I am not sure I can use my influence to get you out again," he added.

"I didn't ask you to get me out." Spoken like a true martyr.

"If you're not going to care about your own safety, then somebody must."

"I am grateful for your help, Abba. I truly am. But I cannot deny my devotion to the Messiah."

Nekoda shook his head. "A Messiah who died the death of a common criminal."

"A *resurrected* Messiah."

Nekoda didn't want to argue with his youngest son. He was tired of disputes, especially with followers of Jesus. He had had his fill of the disciples' preaching at Solomon's Colonnade, as well as the constant speeches being made by Peter and other disciples before the Sanhedrin.

"If somebody asks if you are a follower of Jesus, just tell them you are the son of a member of the Sanhedrin," Nekoda suggested. "You don't have to deny Jesus. Simply deflect their question with your father's position of power. They will back off."

"I will answer honestly."

"But this answer is true. You *are* the son of a member of the Sanhedrin."

"They will press me further. I will be honest."

"But they might not press the question if they know who you are. Who *I* am." Nekoda came to a halt at a street corner and turned to face Ezra. "If you will not hide your allegiance to Jesus, then at least leave Jerusalem. For my sake."

Ezra looked down at his sandals and sighed.

"What about your friend Abel?" Nekoda asked. "He is a resourceful man. He can get you out of Jerusalem."

Ezra raised his head and looked Nekoda in the eyes. "You never taught me to run from battles before."

"If it's a battle you cannot win, then retreat can be strategic. It doesn't mean you're giving up. If anything, you can spread Jesus's message to a wider audience if you leave Jerusalem."

Nekoda truly believed this line of reasoning. When Jews were sent into exile, they spread into far-reaching communities. He didn't like the idea that the message of Jesus might spread beyond Jerusalem. But if it kept his youngest son alive, then so be it. Besides, didn't Gamaliel say that if this movement is not of God, it will wither on the vine?

"Don't give your brother what he wants," Nekoda added.

"What do you mean?"

"He would like nothing better than for you to be imprisoned for years. And he and Saul would like nothing more than for the followers of Jesus to remain in Jerusalem. If they stay in the city, that makes it all the easier for the Way to be contained. If you leave the city, that makes Saul's job so much harder."

Ezra stroked his chin. He had the makings of a beard, but his whiskers were scraggly and sparse. "I must be honest, Abba. You make good points."

Nekoda broke into a smile and draped an arm around Ezra's shoulder. "Of course I make good points. As much as I disagree with the disciples' mission, I do believe that if you leave Jerusalem, you will help to spread their teaching. I'm willing to admit this because I care more about your survival than I do the suppression of the Way."

"I will give it thought, father."

"Don't take too much time. When your brother hears that you have been released, he may bring Saul to our doorstep to question you about your beliefs. You must act before he can."

"I will act soon," said Ezra, and Nekoda felt a tremendous weight taken off his chest. But he wouldn't rest until he saw Ezra leave this city and get as far away as possible from his brother, Hiram.

Keturah

The two wagons were almost ready. It was still dark as Keturah and Eliana hurriedly baked bread for the journey from Jerusalem. They needed as much bread as possible for the road, so they baked through the night, kneading the dough and slapping it against the hot exterior of a jar oven.

Some of their bread was unleavened because they didn't have time to wait for it to rise. They were like the Israelites of old who fled from Egypt with unleavened bread because there was no time to spare for the leavening.

The families of Keturah and Sveshtari, Eliana and Asaph, and Abel and Ḥannah were preparing to leave with a caravan of Jesus followers, led by Philip, one of the newly appointed elders. Eliana also convinced her father to go with them.

Over the past few days, followers of the Way had been slipping out of the city to avoid prison. But the twelve disciples decided to stay in Jerusalem because they saw it as their duty.

Meanwhile, persecution continued to spread across the city. Saul's men were intent on stamping out every spark of the Way.

The unleavened bread wasn't the only Passover reminder for Keturah. On Passover, Jews had a ritual in which they removed every trace of chametz they could find in their house. "Chametz," or leaven, was a symbol of sin, and even a small amount could taint the whole. So, they searched for every morsel of leaven in the house to be rid of it.

"To Saul and his people, we have become the leaven that must be eradicated," Keturah told Eliana. "We are the Passover chametz."

Eliana stuffed several loaves of bread in a sack and loaded it on the wagon. "I never thought about it that way. But you're right. In Saul's mind, even a small number of Jesus followers can taint the entire city. So, he's trying to destroy us all."

"Are you ready?" Asaph appeared with a basket of fruit and loaded it into the wagon.

"We are ready." Keturah placed both of her hands on her belly, which was beginning to swell with new life. So far, she had been spared the morning sickness that had afflicted Eliana. "I hope the movement of the wagon doesn't cause us to go into early labor. Are we being foolish heading out onto the road at a time like this?"

Crouching, Eliana playfully tugged on the stick locked in her dog's jaws. "The risk to us—and to our unborn children—is much greater if we stay in Jerusalem. Perhaps we will someday be able to observe our escape with the same symbolic foods that we eat at the Passover seder."

"Yes. We will have bitter herbs to remember our own enslavement to sin," said Keturah.

"And we will have salt water, which symbolizes the tears we shed when afflictions strike," added Eliana, tossing the stick for Lavi to fetch.

Keturah smiled, for their wordplay was beginning to feel like a game. "And we will have charoset to represent the mortar of the new faith we are building."

In the Hebrew tradition, charoset—a mixture of apples, nuts, wine, and cinnamon—represented the mortar used for the bricks that the Israelites were forced to make while enslaved.

"And we will have the roasted egg, the symbol of new life," added Eliana, putting a hand gently on Keturah's life-enriched belly. Then Keturah put a hand on Eliana's stomach as well, sharing a moment, the same as happened so long ago between Elizabeth, the mother of John the Baptist, and Mary, the mother of Jesus.

"Don't they also say that Israelites are like eggs?" Keturah said with a wink. "The hotter things get for them, the tougher they get."

"May it be the same for followers of the Way," said Eliana.

Nekoda

Nekoda was shocked by what he saw. His oldest son, Hiram, hauled a woman from her home, while Saul's enforcers pounced on others in the house. He had always taught his sons to respect women, but Hiram was yanking on the woman's arm so hard that she let out a scream.

"The Lord forgive you, for you know not what you do!" the woman shouted. Jesus reportedly spoke similar words from the cross.

Hiram shook the woman with both hands. "I know exactly what I do. I am running a spear through the heart of this blasphemous movement!"

As Nekoda rushed forward, he prayed that his son spoke metaphorically when he said he was "running a spear through the heart" of the Jesus movement.

"Hiram, let go of her! I did not raise you to treat women with such disregard!"

Hiram kept hold of the woman's arm as he whirled around to face his father. "Mind your own business, Abba. You raised me to fight for the purity of our faith, and this movement must be killed in its cradle!"

"Why is everything about 'killing' and 'driving spears through hearts'? Rabbi Gamaliel said that if the Jesus movement is not of God, it will die a natural death."

Hiram spit to the side. "Gamaliel is a fool!"

"Please, teacher, force your son to release me. I am not harming anyone." The woman looked to be in her forties—with tears streaking her dusty face.

Hiram flinched when Nekoda put a hand on his shoulder. "This is not the way, my son."

"This woman claims that Jesus is the Messiah. *Jesus!* He died on a cross, and the Word of the Lord says that a hanged man is cursed by God."

Nekoda couldn't argue with that. The ancient Jewish philosophers believed there would be a time of chaos followed by a time of the Law followed by an age of the Messiah. The Spirit of the Lord shall rest upon the Messiah, said Isaiah. But how can the Spirit of the Lord rest upon a man crucified before all eyes?

"But Jesus did not die on a tree," the woman said. "He rose! He rose to life!"

Hiram struck the woman across her face with the back of his hand.

"You go too far!" Nekoda shouted, locking his arms around Hiram's waist and pulling him backward.

The woman broke away and sprinted down the street.

Seeing her escape, Hiram drove his elbow into Nekoda's stomach, causing him to release his hold. Staggering backward, Nekoda tried to catch his breath. He gasped, trying to suck in air, and lowered himself to the ground. He gripped his mid-section.

Hiram started to take off for the woman, but he stopped when he saw his father on the ground, gasping for breath. After casting one last glance at the woman as she rounded a corner, Hiram strode back to Nekoda.

"Are you all right, Abba?" His voice almost sounded gentle.

"I am fine, Hiram. I am too old for wrestling with my sons."

Hiram stared at him, and Nekoda could see a trace of tears in the corner of his eyes. Hiram blinked the tears away and held out his hand.

"I am sorry, Abba."

"Peace be with you." Nekoda took his hand and rose to his feet as his breath returned. Again, he put a hand on Hiram's shoulder, and this time his son did not flinch. "You burn too hot, my son."

"You can never burn too hot when you are on fire for the Lord."

But was Hiram truly on fire for the Lord? Or was he burning with fire from another realm?

"Shalom, Abba," said Hiram before running off to join his compatriots. Were they hunting for more Way followers?

"Shalom," Nekoda said, weary beyond belief as he watched his son disappear down the street.

"Shalom" meant so much more than "peace." It meant being whole in body, mind, and spirit. It meant you are complete in God. But Hiram was not whole. His mind and spirit had been given to another power. He had given himself to chaos—and to the spirit of Saul, the conductor of this chaos.

"I'm definitely getting too old for this," Nekoda repeated as he limped off after his son.

Eliana

Eliana stared at the looming walls of Jerusalem, which were draped in shadow as their small caravan slipped from the city after dark.

They passed through the Golden Gate on the eastern wall of the city—the same gate where Jesus entered Jerusalem. That day seemed a lifetime away.

Jesus had entered the city while seated on a donkey—the same way Eliana and Keturah were leaving the city, with their men walking beside them.

Jesus had entered through the Eastern Gate, the gate of mercy, as a humble king, just as the prophet Zechariah said: "Rejoice greatly, Daughter Zion! Shout, Daughter Jerusalem! See, your king comes to you, righteous and victorious, lowly and riding on a donkey, on a colt, the foal of a donkey."

Zechariah had directed his message at the "Daughter of Jerusalem," which was how Eliana thought of herself. Walking just ahead of them were four other daughters of Jerusalem. They also happened to be the daughters of Philip, the deacon leading their contingent north.

This Philip was not to be confused with the disciple Philip. This Philip was a soft-spoken man who carried a quiet authority. He was a good listener, which also made him an effective evangelist. Philip said the secret to evangelism was listening for fifty of every sixty minutes and talking for ten.

His two oldest daughters, Hermione and Eutychis, walked in their father's footsteps, for people said they were prophetesses. Perhaps the two younger daughters would also someday become prophetesses, but they were still very young.

Two-year-old Babette, another daughter of Jerusalem, rode with Keturah, who cradled baby Asher in her arms. Eliana had difficulty getting comfortable on a donkey while straining under the weight of her unborn baby. She understood what Jesus's mother, Mary, must have felt while riding the donkey to Bethlehem.

The group remained quiet as they passed by the army of tombs on the eastern side of Jerusalem. Many faithful Jews were buried here with their feet facing the city. That way, when the end of time arrived, they could simply stand up in their graves, and they would be facing the Holy City.

The people in their caravan were warned not to speak a word until they were safely beyond the city. No sense drawing attention to themselves.

When they eventually put the city behind them, several of the men lit lamps and began to whisper—a signal that absolute quiet was no longer required.

"Why are we traveling to Samaria?" Keturah whispered to Eliana. "I thought you people hate Samaritans."

Eliana stifled a laugh. "*You people?* Aren't you a part of my people now? Aren't you part of the Way?"

"I mean the Jews. I thought Jews went out of their way to avoid Samaria."

"That is not the way of Jesus. He carried his message to Samaritans and even Greeks, so Philip is doing the same." After a pause, she added, "Besides, the Jews who are trying to arrest us will be less likely to follow us into Samaria."

"That's a good enough reason for me."

Sveshtari shot a stern look at Keturah and put a finger to his lips, signaling her to lower her voice. They were out of the city but still a long way from safety. They could not breathe easily until day broke and they had crossed into Samaria.

Sveshtari: Sebaste

Sveshtari felt the heat of hostile stares as they entered the Samaritan city of Sebaste. The city, rebuilt by Herod the Great, was sprawling and wealthy. Sveshtari admired its defensive structures, such as its large citadel and strong walls. The city was perched on a hill, making it easy to defend.

As they moved into the central city square, with its impressive columns, people continued to eye them with suspicion. It was clear that the citizens of Sebaste had also built internal defenses—high walls within their spirits and minds to keep out foreigners.

Sveshtari put a hand on the hilt of his sword.

"You need not use your sword." Philip put a hand on his shoulder.

"The people here are cutting us with their glares. They need to know that my weapon can also cut."

"A sword will not make them any more welcoming. You'll make them feel even more threatened."

Philip didn't say it as a rebuke. He had a way of speaking these things without the ring of judgment. Sveshtari eased his hand away from his sword.

As a crowd gathered, a man emerged from one of the buildings on the edge of the marketplace, striding out with authority. He carried a snake, whose head rose into the air and darted in all directions, tongue flickering from its mouth. Several people from the crowd gathered around the man, adding to the menace. This man was more than a snake charmer. He clearly had a way of also charming his community.

Sveshtari's hand returned to the hilt of his sword. Philip cast a warning glance at him and faced the snake-handler squarely.

"Shalom! I bring words of peace to the people of Sebaste."

"If you bring words of peace, why does your friend have his hand on his sword?"

Philip smiled. "You needn't worry about my friend any more than I need to worry about the snake coiled in your hands."

"And how do you know you have nothing to fear from me or my little friend here?"

Philip took several steps closer. "Why should I fear the serpent? Scripture tells us that one will come to crush the head of the serpent, and I am here to tell you that this person has come."

The snake-handler laughed, and his sidekicks joined in.

Philip ignored the mocking laughter and continued. "Yahweh told the serpent in the garden, 'And I will put enmity between you and the woman, and between your offspring and hers.' This offspring will crush the head of the serpent, even as the serpent strikes his heel."

"And do you claim to be the one who crushes the head of the serpent?" asked the man. "I sincerely doubt it."

Philip extended his arms to the side. "I do not claim to be the one who has crushed the head of the serpent, but I speak in his name. I speak in the name of Jesus of Nazareth!"

Jesus's name brought stunned silence.

"We have heard of this Jesus," said a man from the crowd, eventually breaking the silence. "They say he was crucified. It doesn't sound to me like he crushed the head of a serpent. It sounds like *he* was crushed."

"When Jesus was crucified, the serpent struck his heel," Philip said. "But the serpent's head was crushed when Jesus rose from the dead three days later."

"That is a lie," said another man. "No one can rise from the dead."

"Jesus became the curse by dying on the tree. And by becoming the curse, he crushed the curse. He freed us all from death!"

By this time, the townspeople had completely encircled them. Sveshtari stayed close to Keturah, prepared to kill anyone who dared touch a hair on her head. But Philip didn't seem the least intimidated.

"Jesus also frees us from our infirmities." Philip's eyes moved to a woman to his left who leaned on a crutch. Then he turned and nodded at Eliana. She dismounted from her donkey, aided by Asaph.

"What are you doing?" Asaph whispered to Eliana.

"Crushing the head of the serpent." She seemed to know exactly what Philip was asking. Eliana approached the woman with the crutch. "May I lay hands upon you, sister?"

The woman glanced around, looking for an answer among the crowd. No one said a word, so the woman shrugged and said, "Fine."

As Eliana placed both hands on her shoulders, Philip raised his hands, palms outward, and began to pray aloud.

"Lord Almighty, look down on this woman with pity. She has been bitten by the serpent of disease. She has been hobbled by the curse. But you came to undo the curse. You came to crush the head of the devil. You came to heal."

Eliana also began to pray, but in a foreign tongue.

Philip kept both hands raised, about a hand's-breadth from the woman's face, as he spoke.

"Praise the Lord, my soul, and forget not all his benefits—who forgives all your sins and heals all your diseases, who redeems your life from the pit and crowns you with love and compassion, who satisfies your desires with good things so that your youth is renewed like the eagle's. Praise the Lord, all his works everywhere in his dominion. Everywhere is his dominion. Everyone exists in his dominion. Every sickness is under his dominion. In the name of Jesus, lift our sister from the pit and crown her with compassion."

Tears pooled in the woman's eyes. No one said a word. A dog barked in the distance—the only sound amid the sanctified silence.

Then the woman dropped her crutch, and it fell against a stone with a clatter.

Eliana released her hands and stepped back. She motioned for the woman to walk forward to meet her.

The woman's eyes lit up like bonfires. She took three steps toward Eliana, who continued to backpedal. Four more steps. Then five.

The woman turned toward the crowd, eyes blazing. "I am healed! The Lord has crowned me with His compassion!"

The change in the crowd was instantaneous. Malice melted away, and several women clustered around the one who was healed. Eyes once filled with suspicion were suddenly transformed into eyes full of wonder.

Sveshtari cast a look at the snake-handler. Even the snake-handler's mouth hung open. Sveshtari smiled. He had disarmed enemies before, snatching weapons from their hands before they could react. But this was the first time that Sveshtari had seen someone disarm a person using only words. Philip had done it. He had caught the snake-handler off guard. He had crushed the serpent's head with only a word.

Asaph

Asaph led Eliana atop her donkey along the trail on a blue-sky day with only a touch of a breeze. Eliana insisted on traveling to the Jordan River, a day's journey to the east of Sebaste, because Philip was leading a group of people who asked to be baptized. She wasn't going to miss it, pregnancy or not.

Asaph darted his eyes at Simon, the snake charmer who had joined the caravan—minus the serpent. Simon Magus, a magician, told Philip that he too sought to be baptized, but Asaph had his suspicions. So did Abel, who was making this trip because he had not yet been baptized. Keturah, not feeling well, remained back in Sebaste with Sveshtari, Judah, and Abel's wife, Hannah.

"What do you make of Simon Magus?" Asaph asked Abel.

Abel was a thief and con man in his earlier life. So, if anyone could discern a trickster, it was him.

"I have my doubts about him."

"Did you tell your doubts to Philip?"

"I did."

"And?"

"As you can see, Simon is among our number today. Philip said he talked to the sorcerer and decided he was sincere in his transformation, in his desire to be baptized."

"If Simon has given up the darkness, then we should welcome him," said Eliana. She had been quietly listening. "God turns darkness into light."

Asaph wiped the sweat from his brow. "But I still sense darkness clinging to this man."

"That's the purpose of baptism. To wash that darkness away."

"But I fear that Simon is more impressed by Philip's miracles than he is drawn to Jesus," Abel argued.

The healing of the lame woman was only the first of many signs and wonders that amazed the people of Sebaste. Philip had been chosen by the disciples to distribute food among the widows of Jerusalem. But he was proving to also be an effective evangelist and wonder worker.

Asaph nodded. "Simon loves a good miracle. People in the city told me that Simon once claimed he could levitate."

Abel laughed. "The only thing he could magically lift are gold coins from the pockets of gullible people."

"You two are ones to talk," said Eliana. "A former tax collector and a former thief."

Asaph was not put off by his wife's rebuke. "Maybe that's why we are suspicious. We know what it's like to be poisoned by mammon."

"And we know what it takes to get that poison out of your system," Abel added.

"I pray you are wrong about Simon."

Asaph smiled. "Truthfully, I pray we are wrong as well."

At last, they reached the banks of the Jordan—a modest river that snaked south from the Sea of Galilee until it emptied into the Dead Sea. Two seas—one alive with an abundance of fish and one dead from an abundance of salt. The Jordan River was the link between the two seas, a link between two worlds, a link between life and death. It was only fitting that so many baptisms were performed in this waterway.

Asaph had been at the Jordan River long ago when John the Baptist baptized Jesus. At the time, he scoffed at John, and he didn't even know who Jesus was. Perhaps he should not scoff at Simon Magus. Maybe he should trust Philip's judgment.

Philip waded into the water as they collected on the bank. About fifty people made the short trip—forty of whom were going to be baptized.

"It's about time you're doing this," Asaph said teasingly to Abel.

"I know, I know."

"Why did you put off your baptism?"

"Besides the fact that I can't swim and I'm afraid of water?"

"You will be fine in God's hands," said Eliana as Asaph helped her down from the donkey.

Abel grinned. "I have confidence in God's hands. It's Philip's hands I'm afraid of."

Asaph nudged him on the shoulder. "The water is not deep. I don't think you could drown if you tried."

"I also don't care for snakes." Abel nodded knowingly. "What if there are snakes in this water?"

Abel was referring to the time when Asaph had been bitten on the lip by a water snake in the Jordan River.

"Remember," said Eliana, "Philip is doing the work of the man who crushed the head of snakes."

"And water snakes are not that common, despite my own run-in with one," added Asaph.

Philip motioned for the crowd to settle down. Then he began to preach.

"Today, you will pass through the water, like Noah, like Jonah, like Moses, like Elijah. Noah survived the deep waters in the ark, while Jonah was rescued from dark waters by a great fish. Moses survived the dangerous waters of the Nile in his small basket, and he led the people of Israel through the waters of the Red Sea. Elijah crossed the water after striking it with his cloak."

Holding up his hands, Philip paused before saying, "Today is your time to make a crossing. It is your time to cross from death to life, from sin to forgiveness. You stand on the shore of repentance, and you walk into deep waters, where you will rise again!"

"I thought you said the water isn't deep," Abel whispered to Asaph.

"It's a metaphor, Abel. The water is only up to Philip's waist."

As Philip began to baptize the people, one by one, Abel moved toward the back of the line. He was a courageous man in so many ways, but Asaph could see his ambivalence. Abel kept looking around, studying the surface of the Jordan River—probably checking for water snakes.

Being a short man, the water rose much higher on Abel when he finally reached Philip. Philip put one hand behind Abel's back and the other behind his head. Then he declared, "I baptize you in the name of the Father and the Son and the Holy Spirit."

Lowering Abel backward into the water, he held him there for a couple of seconds. It must have felt like eternity to Abel.

When their friend emerged from the water, he sputtered and smiled and gave Philip a bear hug.

"Amen!" Abel raised both arms and stared into the sky.

Simon Magus stood even farther back in the line, but not at the tail end. Asaph said a silent prayer, rebuking himself for the doubts still buzzing in his mind. Simon appeared to be sincere, so why was he being judgmental?

When Simon was lowered and then raised from the water, he shouted, "Shalom, shalom!" Then he did a little jump in the water.

Was he trying to levitate? Was he trying to create a baptismal scene that no one would ever forget? Again, Asaph rebuked his thoughts. Perhaps Simon was simply jumping for joy.

"Amen!" Asaph shouted, trying to act enthusiastic. But it was an act. A performance. He still didn't trust Simon Magus.

Keturah: Four Months Later, Month of Elul (Early September), 32 A.D.

Keturah felt enormous. At her eighth month, her belly was like a miniature mountain. Eliana was at roughly the same stage, yet her belly was not nearly as large. They were quite the pair as they strolled through the market of Sebaste, accompanied by Asaph. He had volunteered to carry whatever food they purchased because of the strain it might put on their backs.

Asaph pointed them in the direction of Jewish vendors. But he grudgingly accepted the buying of figs from a Samaritan man.

"I still do not understand what Jews have against the Samaritans," Keturah said to Eliana as they left the market. "They seem nice to me."

Asaph answered before Eliana had a chance to speak. "Samaritans are compromisers. When the Assyrians sent our people into exile long ago, some intermarried with Gentiles. They became unclean. They became Samaritans."

Eliana cocked her head. "But, husband, Jesus spoke of the Good Samaritan."

After a pause, Asaph shrugged. "He did. But that doesn't mean it is proper to worship alongside these people. I will purchase food from them because Jesus did. But I will not worship with them because they sacrifice at the wrong temple."

"You mean their temple on Mount Gerizim?" asked Keturah.

"Yes. Our Temple in Jerusalem is at the center of the universe."

"But that doesn't mean we should shun Samaritans," Eliana insisted. "Jesus talked with a Samaritan woman at a well."

Keturah was afraid she had triggered an argument. "I'm sorry I brought this up."

Asaph linked arms with Eliana. "Don't be, Keturah. Eliana is correct, as always. Jesus did speak with Samaritans. He traveled through their land—and Philip clearly agrees that Samaritans are worth reaching and teaching. That's why we're here."

"Asaph knows when I am right." Eliana squeezed his arm.

"Which is all the time," Asaph said, laughing.

Keturah smiled. She was astounded that Asaph could joke about Eliana being correct "all the time." Most men would not say such a thing, even in jest. She doubted that Sveshtari could joke about something like that.

She also pondered how women had something in common with Samaritans. They were lesser. Why else did some rabbis thank God for not making them a woman?

"Ohh." Keturah paused to catch her breath as pain shot across her lower back. There were times when she wished God had not made her a woman, and this was one of them. But such thoughts were fleeting. Whenever the aches subsided, and she felt the presence of life inside her, she thanked the Lord for the gift of growing her child within her.

Eliana put an arm around her shoulders. "Are you all right? Let us sit."

"Just for a moment," Keturah said. "I will be fine."

She and Keturah found large stones on which to rest. The pain soon began to ebb.

"I know the psalms say that children are like arrows in a quiver," Keturah said. "But sometimes it feels as if the arrows are digging into my back."

"I understand exactly."

Keturah took a deep breath. "But your pregnancy seems so much less difficult than mine."

"I had considerable morning sickness," Eliana reminded her.

"Yes, but once that subsided, you seem to be handling your time with less suffering."

"I think I am just good at hiding my pains. When I was young, hiding pain was a matter of survival."

Keturah nodded. When Eliana was young, held captive by men, pain was a constant companion. "I too should never complain."

"Complain when you need to. Never feel you cannot tell me everything." Eliana took her hand. "If I had a friend like you when I was young, I would've been pouring out my complaints night and day. That is what sisters are for."

Keturah nodded, but she still felt weak in comparison to Eliana.

"You created my inmost being; you knit me together in my mother's womb," she said, speaking one of the psalms that Eliana had taught her.

"I praise you because I am fearfully and wonderfully made," Eliana added, continuing the psalm. "Your eyes saw my unformed body; all the days ordained for me were written in your book before one of them came to be."

"Thank you for those prayers," Keturah said. With the sharp stabs of pain gone, she rose slowly to her feet. Then they headed back to the home where they were staying.

Keturah was ready for this baby to be born. She was ready to reach the summit of the mountain.

Asaph

Asaph was weary, for everything was happening too fast. Philip's ministry in Sebaste continued to draw Samaritans to the movement in staggering numbers. Samaritans!

Asaph also couldn't keep up with Abel, who was energized by everything happening around them. Asaph and Abel were on their way to a home where Peter was set to address the followers of the Way. Word had reached Jerusalem about Philip's mission to the Samaritans. So, Peter and John traveled to Sebaste to see with their own eyes what was happening.

"Do you think Peter will disapprove?" Abel asked Asaph as they made their way through the city. "I think Jesus's message needs to reach every living person, including Samaritans!"

Asaph nodded but said nothing. He knew he should welcome these new believers, but it was hard to think of Samaritans as fellow travelers along the Way. Jesus calls for uncompromising devotion, but these people were compromisers!

Abel had a dance in his step this morning. He faced Asaph while walking backward and talking non-stop.

"I want everyone to experience what I felt at the Jordan River!" Abel said, accidentally bumping into a man behind him. "Sorry," he said, turning around and walking face forward.

Ever since his baptism, Abel had been overwhelmed by excitement. He couldn't literally levitate, as Simon Magus claimed to do, but he behaved as if he did. Abel was walking on air as they headed to see Peter, the disciple who walked on water.

"I pray that Peter approves of what Philip is doing in this city," Asaph said, but did he really mean it? Unclean Samaritans were joining their ranks each day.

"You don't say that with much conviction." Abel nudged him on the shoulder and smiled.

Asaph ran a hand across his head. "Just tired I guess."

Tired of Abel's eternal energy.

At last, they reached the home of a wealthy man in the center of Sebaste. Asaph and Abel passed through a door in an outer wall and entered a crowded courtyard, open to the sky. People found places to sit wherever they could. Some sat on the stairs leading to the second story of the house. But most sat on the ground because the few benches were already filled. Others stood in the colonnade off to their right.

Peter and John were already talking from a raised platform in the center of the courtyard. Seated on the ground in front of the two disciples was Simon Magus. Leave it to Simon to claim a prominent place close to Peter and John.

"We did not follow cleverly devised stories when we told you about the coming of our Lord Jesus Christ in power, but we were eyewitnesses of his majesty!" Peter declared to the people. "Jesus received honor and glory from God the Father when the voice came to him saying, 'This is my Son, whom I love; with him I am well pleased.' We ourselves heard this voice that came from heaven when we were with him on the sacred mountain!"

"He's referring to the transfiguration, isn't he?" Abel whispered.

Asaph nodded. During the transfiguration on a mountaintop, Jesus had appeared to the disciples alongside Moses and Elijah! Moses represented the Law, while Elijah represented the Prophets, and both had glory-filled encounters with God on the top of mountains.

Samaritans and Jews fought over vying mountaintops—one on Mount Gerizim and the other on the Temple Mount in Jerusalem. In the transfiguration, Jesus declared his Kingship on a new mountain—a place where the Law and Prophets come together. But was it a place where Samaritans and Jews can come together?

"We also have the prophetic message as something completely reliable, and you will do well to pay attention to it," Peter continued, stepping down from the platform and walking among the crowd. "This message is a light shining in a dark place, until the day dawns and the morning star rises in your hearts!"

Without warning, Abel shot to his feet. "That day has dawned! The morning star has risen in my heart!"

Peter cast his gaze in Abel's direction and pointed to the sky. "But the day of the Lord will come like a thief. The heavens will disappear with a roar; the elements will be destroyed by fire, and the earth and everything in it will be laid bare!"

"Amen! The day of the Lord will come like a thief!" shouted Abel. As a one-time thief, he knew something about stealth and surprise.

What happened next began with soft prayers, a murmuring among the people, bubbling up with patient momentum.

"See, I lay a stone in Zion, a chosen and precious cornerstone," Peter said. "The one who trusts in him will never be put to shame!"

Is Jesus the cornerstone he talks about?

"To you who believe, this stone is precious. The stone the builders rejected has become the cornerstone!"

But where does this cornerstone belong? What is it building? Does it belong to a new Temple? Is Jesus the new Temple, replacing the ones where Samaritans and Jews worshipped?

"Once you were not a people, but now you are the people of God!" Peter continued. "Once you had not received mercy, but now you have received mercy!"

We are the people of God? Was Peter saying that the people in this room, Samaritan and Jew, were one people? This was a revolution and a revelation beyond imagination. This was impossible. The two rival Temples were becoming one Temple, a living Temple, a holy Temple, a Temple of the living God, ruled by the One King.

Peter extended his arms like Moses on Sinai. "Declare the praises of him who called you out of darkness into his wonderful light!"

That's all it took for the courtyard to explode with praise. If there had been a roof on this courtyard, it would have been blown halfway across the city. Prayers blazed across the gathering as Peter and John moved among the believers, laying hands on them.

Asaph stood, taking it all in, unsure what to do or say until John appeared before him.

"May I pray for you?" John asked.

Asaph nodded. Then he felt John's hand rest on his right shoulder. Any hesitation was gone. Any fear was gone. Any skepticism was gone.

"A time is coming when we will worship the Father neither on this mountain nor in Jerusalem!" Asaph prayed. "A time is coming!"

"That time is here," said John. "God's worshipers must worship in the Spirit and in truth. The time is here!"

Suddenly, Asaph fell to the ground as if God hurled a slingshot stone from the depths of the Heavens. When he got back to his feet, he felt like he was floating in the air. Not literally floating like Simon Magus claimed. This was more than a magician's trick. He had been lifted by the hand of his King.

The glory of the Lord was a consuming fire, and Asaph's heart was hot within him.

The fire was spreading, and no human could stand in its way.

Eliana

Eliana saw the change in Asaph immediately. He had always held something back in his passion for Jesus. He had been raised on the Law, a solid and inflexible set of standards. But he always had trouble with the more amorphous Spirit. He held back, afraid to give up his will to the Spirit of God.

But not today. Not after hearing Peter speak.

"On the way back to the house, I talked to a half dozen people about how Jesus heals," Asaph said, unable to sit down. He paced the main room of their house, while Eliana looked on, amazed. "I came to get you because Peter and John are performing wonders! You must come and see!"

"I am willing." Eliana held out her hand, and Asaph nearly yanked her to her feet.

"Hurry! I don't want us to miss a moment!"

Keturah was just leaving the kitchen when Asaph passed by, dragging Eliana behind.

Eliana cast a knowing look at Keturah as they rushed past. "Asaph wants to show me what Peter and John are doing! Come join us!"

"But I'm watching Babette."

"Bring her along!" Asaph shouted as they exited the house.

"Careful, Asaph. I can't move as fast as you with the life I'm carrying."

Asaph finally came to a stop and stared at Eliana's life-filled belly. "I'm sorry. In the excitement, I forgot."

What could be happening that would make him forget she was with child?

On the way to the house where Peter and John ministered, Asaph called out to everyone he passed. "Come! The disciples of Jesus are performing miracles!"

By the time they reached the house, about a dozen other people were following in their wake.

Asaph was right. Something dramatic was going on in the courtyard. Prayers and praise rose from just beyond the walls surrounding the house. Entering the courtyard, Eliana came across a scene that reminded her of what had happened in the Upper Room in Jerusalem when the Holy Spirit roared like a wind. Everywhere she turned, people were either on their knees, standing with arms raised, or completely prone on the ground.

Peter stood by the stone stairs leading to the second floor. People pressed around him as he laid hands on them, one at a time. Simon Magus stood beside Peter, intently studying what the disciple did and what he said.

"I feel as if I never knew how to properly pray until today," Asaph said as he weaved through the crowd with Eliana in tow. She had prayed for this change in Asaph for a long time. But now that her prayer was answered, she was a little frightened by his transformation.

When they reached Peter's side, the disciple had his hands on a man's shoulder and prayed, "By his wounds you have been healed. Return to the Shepherd and Overseer of your souls."

Then he turned to another man, laid on hands, and said, "By his wounds you have been healed. Return to the Shepherd and Overseer of your souls."

"Are those the words?" asked Simon Magus, who studied every movement that Peter made. "If I speak those words, will I have your power?"

Peter turned to Simon Magus, furrowing his brow. "It is not *my* power. It is the power of the Holy Spirit."

"But how do I get it?" the magician asked.

"Get what?"

"The power of the Holy Spirit. If I speak those words, will I receive the power?"

Peter sighed. Eliana could tell he was trying to restrain his frustration. "Simon, it is not about the words. It's about the *Spirit*!"

"But what's your secret?" Simon Magus would not let it go.

"There is no secret."

The magician dug into his robes and pulled out a sack of coins. Then he reached into the sack, coins clinking, and he pulled out several silver bits of money. Eliana stared in shock.

Simon Magus held out the pieces of silver to a dumfounded Peter. "Give me this ability, so that everyone on whom I lay my hands may receive the Holy Spirit. I'll pay you."

Peter stared at the coins in Simon's outstretched hand. The confusion on his face slowly transformed to irritation—then anger.

"May your money perish with you because you thought you could buy the gift of God with money!"

Peter slapped the magician's hand, sending the coins flying across the courtyard. Eliana was nearly struck by one as it flew past her eyes.

"You have no part or share in this ministry because your heart is not right before God!" Peter bellowed. The people who had been praying all around suddenly stopped, turned, and stared.

Simon Magus's face reddened, as if the disciple had slapped his face rather than his hand. "But—"

"Repent of this wickedness and pray to the Lord in the hope that he may forgive you for having such a thought in your heart! For I see that you are full of gall and wormwood and captive to sin."

Simon wilted before the onslaught of words. The man had seen the power of the Holy Spirit and determined that the power was in Peter's hands. So, he took several steps backward, as if fearing that Peter was going to strike him dead—or cloak his body in leprosy.

"Pray to the Lord for me so that nothing you have said may happen to me," the magician whimpered, turning away and scurrying for the exit.

Eliana wanted to stop Simon. She wanted to explain that the Holy Spirit is a gift, not something you can purchase. She wanted to tell him that although all power belongs to God, He is not an Almighty Magician. He is our Father.

But Simon whisked past her before she could work up the courage. He stopped to pick up one of the coins, and people in the crowd handed him a couple of the other pieces of silver. Then he rushed for the door like a man with a lion hot on his tail.

9.

The Book of Acts, Chapter 9

Eliana

Eliana dreamt about being on the Sea of Galilee with Jesus—sitting in the back of the boat while he calmly tossed a dragnet over the right side of the vessel. It was just Jesus and her. The sky was deep blue, and the breeze was soft and warm. She leaned back and closed her eyes when she was suddenly yanked back into reality.

She awakened to the sound of rushing water.

Eliana sat bolt upright, breathing heavily. It was the dead of night, and the house was shrouded in darkness. She was drowsy and confused until it dawned on her that their bed was wet.

Her water had broken.

"Asaph," she said, giving him a nudge. "Wake up, Asaph."

Groggily, Asaph sat up, a shadow in the darkness. "What's happened?"

"It's my time. The baby."

Those words woke him up instantly. Asaph leaped out of bed and threw on his cloak. "I will send for the midwife."

Eliana responded with a moan as her body clenched with pain. When Asaph rushed back to her side, Eliana motioned with her hands. "Go! Hurry!"

Everything began happening with speed and urgency. After her next wave of pain, the midwife and several other women hurried into the room, taking charge. Keturah was among them, rushing to her side.

"You are strong," Keturah said, sitting next to her on the bed. "You have nothing to fear."

Eliana wished she could believe that.

Asaph was gone, banished to the courtyard. Keturah massaged Eliana's back, while another woman mixed wine with powdered ivory and prayed for unseen assistance from the angels who attend to births.

"Let me help you," said Maya, the midwife, gently bringing Eliana to her feet. Maya helped her onto the birthing stool, which she had brought along. The birthing stool had a U-shaped opening for the baby's arrival, as well as firm back supports and a place for her feet. Maya placed a pillow below the stool to cushion the baby's arrival.

With another contraction, Eliana's belly hardened like stone. Pain shot across her lower back, and she tried to breathe in rhythm. When the pain eventually faded, like a wave receding into the ocean, Eliana began to pray.

"May the Lord answer me in my distress, may the name of the God of Jacob protect me. May he . . ."

Eliana's psalm was interrupted by another bolt of fire in her back, wrapping around her stomach. As pain flared, she tried to focus her mind on soothing memories. Her mind flashed back to the day she held another newborn in her arms—the baby Jesus. She was just ten years old at the time, playing in the hills of Bethlehem, when she encountered Mary, Joseph, and the child. Mary was just a young girl when she gave birth. She must have been terrified.

Eliana had witnessed and helped with many births since that day, so she knew what was coming. But that didn't lessen the pain or the fear. She had experience with age, but her age also brought great danger. Was she a fool to marry and be with child at such an age? She had witnessed two mothers die in childbirth.

"I am ready to give my life," she whispered to God.

Her words also reached Keturah. "The Lord is with you," Keturah said. "Have faith that he will carry you and your baby through this voyage."

A voyage. Eliana liked that image. Is that why she had dreamed of being on the Sea of Galilee when the birth pains struck? The disciples often told stories of Jesus on the sea—calming the storm and walking across water. She needed Jesus to calm the storm inside her body. She needed him to quiet the fears that washed over her.

She prayed once again, but the words that came from her mouth were not her native language. The Holy Spirit came over her with authority. While the contractions took control of her body, the Holy One took control of her spirit. She was at the mercy of God and his angels.

Keturah dabbed her forehead with a soothing sea sponge, while another woman put a cup of water to her lips. Then Eliana cried as a fierce pain hit her full force. The pains came faster and stronger. The storm was intensifying.

As another pain clenched her body, she shouted the next words of her prayer. "Then they cried out to the Lord in their trouble, and he brought them out of their distress!"

When the wave of pain had flowed away, her voice calmed. "He stilled the storm to a whisper; the waves of the sea were hushed, and he guided them to their desired haven."

"You speak the truth," said Maya as she massaged Eliana's back muscles. "The Lord will guide you to your desired haven."

But the storm was not over. Another pain, this one stronger than the last, slammed into her, and she nearly fell from the stool. The women helped her maintain her position as they soothed her with prayers of encouragement and supportive hands.

The night was endless.

KETURAH

It was daylight when Eliana began to push. Eliana was clearly exhausted, drenched with sweat and in tremendous pain. But she hadn't lost complete control, despite her groans and growls.

Keturah had been by her friend's side since the beginning of labor, although she took several breaks to sit or lie down. The midwife insisted upon it, considering that Keturah was also due soon.

Keturah couldn't help but picture herself in the same position in the coming weeks. Soon, she too would be on the birthing chair, pushing a new life into this world. She knew a lot of women didn't survive, so the chances that both she and Eliana could beat the odds was daunting.

"Rags! We need more clean rags!" Maya snapped, and Keturah dashed to grab some from the stack.

As Keturah handed the rags to Maya, she saw the blood. Had Eliana torn? Some bleeding was normal, but how much? Keturah had only been present at one other delivery, and she didn't remember this much blood.

"Don't just stand there!" Maya shouted at Keturah. "Pray!"

Keturah felt lightheaded and found a chair. She began to tremble at the thought of losing her greatest friend. One of the other women put a hand on her shoulder.

"Maya told me to offer her apology. She didn't mean to snap at you, especially in your condition." The woman sighed. "But it would be good if we prayed."

Keturah was still getting used to praying out loud to the Hebrew God. She didn't have much Scripture memorized, not like Eliana. So, she bowed her head and kept her words silent and simple.

Please, Lord. Save Eliana. Save the baby.

Asaph

It was nearly the sixth hour—midday—and Asaph wondered if something had gone terribly wrong. No one had brought him an update, which was a bad sign. If the delivery had been progressing smoothly, he would have received news.

It angered him to be kept in the dark.

Asaph spent much of his time pacing, but when the sun reached its zenith, he and his father-in-law stood facing Jerusalem, and together they said the midday prayer—the *minhah.*

"I will exalt you, my God the King," Asaph said. "I will praise your name for ever and ever. Every day I will praise you and extol your name for ever and ever."

Asaph continued with the psalm, occasionally opening his eyes in the hopes that his prayer would be instantly answered, and the midwife would emerge from the house with glowing eyes and a healthy baby in her arms.

When no one came out of the house, he was tempted to barge in and see for himself what had happened. But he was too afraid of what he might see. He sat down, his legs aching, while Judah took a seat next to him.

Asaph tried to smile. "Tell me something to take my mind to other places. What has happened with Simon Magus?"

"I fear he might be losing his mind."

"He did seem stricken by the curse that Peter put on him."

"It goes deeper than that. I heard that Simon Magus vows to have himself buried for three days to prove he too can rise from the dead."

Asaph's eyes went wide. "Do you really think he would try that?"

"If the rumors about him are true, I doubt he would risk it. He strikes me as a fraud."

Asaph picked up a handful of sand and moved it from one hand to the other. "I don't know. He could be in touch with dark powers. I could not believe my ears when he offered to buy the power of the Holy Spirit from Peter."

"To him, money speaks louder than prayer."

Asaph let the sand sift through his fingers, then brushed his hands together. "I wish *my* prayers were louder. I have been praying without ceasing and still . . ." Asaph nodded toward the door of the house. "I also wish my wife were louder. I haven't heard her screams for some time now. I fear it when things get too quiet."

"Then let me pray with you." Judah placed a hand on Asaph's shoulder. But no sooner had he done that than there was movement in the doorway. The midwife, Maya, emerged with Keturah at her side. Were they smiling? Were their faces shining?

They weren't. But maybe they were just tired. They had to be exhausted. Then Keturah looked in Asaph's direction and gave him a blossoming smile. Maya, always the serious one, still didn't smile. But Asaph cherished her words.

"You have a girl, Asaph."

Asaph shot to his feet. "And Eliana?"

"She lost a lot of blood. But she survived."

Asaph dropped to his knees and pressed his face to the ground. He felt Judah's hands on his back as they gave thanks.

"Come," said Maya. "Your wife and child are waiting."

Rising to his feet, Asaph brushed sand from his clothing and followed the women into the house. He crossed the threshold into a new life. He had become an abba.

Nekoda: Jerusalem, One Year Later, Month of Ab (Late August), 33 A.D.

The sun was just casting light on the horizon when Nekoda found his son Ezra at the stables behind their house in Upper Jerusalem. He was strapping supplies to one of their donkeys. From the look of it, he was preparing for a journey of many days.

"Are you fleeing, my son? Are you in danger?"

"I am not. I'm much safer than my brothers and sisters of the Way."

Nekoda cringed to think that Ezra thought more of his "brothers" in the Way than of his real brother, Hiram. "If you are safe, then why are you fleeing?"

"Who says I am fleeing?" Ezra tied a sack of bread to the saddle.

"Your donkey says it all. Has your brother threatened you? Please, my son, be honest with me. I have no intention of stopping you because I want you to remain safe and far away from Saul. He continues to fill the jails with the followers of Jesus."

"Evidently, the jails in Jerusalem must be at capacity because Saul is turning his wrath on Damascus."

"Damascus?"

"Yes, he has been given authorization to arrest the followers of Jesus in Damascus."

"Has the Way spread that far north?"

"Does that surprise you? Damascus is not so very far from Galilee, where Jesus began his ministry."

As Ezra mounted his donkey, Nekoda held on to the reins. "But if Saul is turning his focus from Jerusalem to Damascus, why are you leaving?"

"I must warn my brothers and sisters in Damascus. I will have at least a one-day head start on Saul and his followers. Please. Hand me the reins."

But Nekoda would not step away. He was stunned to realize that his son was not fleeing from danger. He was riding directly into trouble.

"Don't go, Ezra. This is not your fight."

"It is clearly my fight. The Lord told me not to be afraid, even though I'm surrounded by briers and thorns, and I live among scorpions."

"I can try to convince Saul not to carry his persecution to Damascus."

"I am sorry, Abba, but we both know that Saul will not listen to you."

"I can at least convince your brother not to go to Damascus in Saul's company."

Ezra sighed. "You have as much chance of stopping my brother as you do of stopping me."

Nekoda stared into Ezra's eyes as the truth sank in. He let the reins drop from his hands and patted the neck of the donkey.

"Be safe, my son." He bowed his head, ashamed by his lack of authority over his two boys. They were men now—wild donkeys, the both of them.

He stepped aside. As Nekoda raised his head, he found himself staring at the extended hand of his son.

They clasped hands. Then Nekoda kissed the back of Ezra's hand and sent him on his way. He prayed Ezra would reach Damascus before the scorpions struck.

Nekoda hurried to the home of Boaz in the Lower City because that was where any expedition north would begin. As expected, he found his oldest son, Hiram, meeting under an olive tree just outside Boaz's compound. A large group of men had gathered, and Saul stood at the center.

Ezra appeared to be correct. Saul and his companions were preparing for a trek somewhere. Nekoda kept his distance, crouching beneath the shade of a nearby tree and observing. When the men disbanded, Nekoda waited until Hiram had broken off from the group. He stepped into line with his son.

"Where is Saul bound for?"

Hiram stared straight ahead as he answered. "Who said he's leaving Jerusalem?"

"I hear things."

"From my brother?"

"I am on the Sanhedrin. I have my sources."

Hiram paused to pick up a stone and fling it at a tree. "Yes. We are leaving. I will be gone for a couple of months at least, Abba."

"Where to?"

"I do not believe Saul would wish me to share that information."

"Even with your father? Is that how you honor me?"

"A father should not pressure his son to break a confidence."

Nekoda strived to rein in his anger. He took a breath before answering. "It matters not where you are going. I plan to join Saul's company on this trip, wherever it might be."

Hiram came to a sudden stop and pivoted to face his father directly. "You do not trust me? You think I need my abba to hold my hand?"

Nekoda didn't say that it was Saul he didn't trust. "As a member of the Sanhedrin, we need to be aware of what Saul is doing. Saul cannot prevent me from coming."

"Saul has the approval to . . ." Hiram didn't finish his sentence.

"To what? To arrest more followers of the Way?"

"Do you object to that?"

"I do not. But the Sanhedrin still needs to know what Saul is doing. So, I am going with the caravan."

Hiram put his hands on his hips and scowled. "You cannot stop Saul in his mission. The Way has spread beyond Jerusalem."

"It's spreading thanks to Saul. He's driving them out of the city with his persecution."

"It is not persecution. It is justice. This movement must be killed in its infancy."

"That's the Roman way—killing newborns."

Hiram rolled his eyes—another blatant sign of disrespect. "I am talking about a movement, not an actual baby."

"I know that. But killing believers in a newborn movement is as suspect as killing a newborn baby."

"You only say that because you have a son in the newborn movement."

As Hiram made a move to walk away, Nekoda grabbed his arm. "And you have a *brother* in the Way. Do you care nothing for Ezra?"

"I care that he is deceiving himself—and blaspheming the Lord. As a member of the Sanhedrin, don't you worry that your son blasphemes the Lord?"

Nekoda tightened his grip on Hiram's arm, trying to elicit a response. But Hiram stared back at him, as if his grip meant nothing. As if his opinion meant even less.

Nekoda released the pressure, shoving Hiram's arm aside. "So be it. But know this. I am traveling north with Saul's band."

"So be it." Hiram strode away, leaving Nekoda flatfooted and fuming.

The Road to Damascus: Four Days Later

Saul and his men closed in on Damascus as they traveled along the Great North Road. By nightfall, they should be in the city. Nekoda, riding on a donkey, stayed near the back of the line.

Saul had grudgingly accepted Nekoda's presence among the men because he couldn't say no to a representative of the Sanhedrin. Saul also may have tolerated his presence as a favor to Hiram. Nekoda doubted that his son told Saul that he did not want his father among them.

Damascus was a large city, heavily populated by Gentiles and tainted by Greek decadence. Herod the Great had built a new gymnasium in the city, where naked men wrestled and competed. Jews stayed well away from such places.

Damascus was dedicated to Dionysus, the god of wine and pleasure. Some also called him Bacchus, and he supposedly had the power to stir passions in people until they were caught up in an uncontrollable frenzy. Despite this reputation, Damascus had a sizable Jewish population in the thousands. And if Saul was right, it was also home to a growing number of Jesus followers.

Nekoda kept his eyes on Zuriel, a poisonous presence among the group. Zuriel, the man likely responsible for the death of Nekoda's brother, rode near the front of the pack, as close to Saul and the center of power as possible.

Nekoda kept his distance from Saul because the man frightened him. Saul was determined to stamp out every last spark of belief in Jesus. For Saul, the fires of Jewish belief must be safely contained in the Temple, where the Holy One dwelled.

Jesus, on the other hand, was a wildfire.

Ezra described Jesus as the new Temple—a blasphemous idea. The Temple was where heaven and earth touched. The Lord was present in the Temple's Holy of Holies, and no one had access to this sacred space, except for the High Priest, and even he could enter only one time per year.

And yet . . . on the day that Jesus was crucified, the curtain that separated ordinary men from the Holy of Holies was torn in half, from top to bottom, as if the Lord God had done it with his own hands. Nekoda had been making a sacrifice in the Temple when it happened, so he was a first-hand witness. The fabric of the cosmos had been torn. Nekoda couldn't get the sound of tearing fabric out of his mind, even to this day. No human could have ripped that curtain. It was so thick and massive that it could only be lifted by several hundred men.

As the sixth hour approached, Saul had the men assemble for midday prayers, the *minhah*.

"I will exalt you, my God the King," Saul prayed aloud when everyone was standing and facing Jerusalem. "I will praise your name for ever and ever. Every day I will praise you and extol your name for ever and ever."

The daily prayers were like ladders to heaven—rungs to the clouds. But like any ladder, the prayers had to be firmly planted in the ground. The ladder had to be stable. It had to be anchored by tradition.

As Saul continued to exalt the Lord, a brisk wind picked up from the west, stirring the soil and snapping at the folds of their clothing. Nekoda lowered his head to keep the stinging sand from flying into his eyes. Suddenly, an explosion burst before them, and a flash of light, as bright as twenty suns, enveloped the men.

In an instant, they were submerged in a sea of light, an otherworldly glow, as a blast of holy wind swept over them. Nekoda had no memory of falling to the ground, but he soon realized he was sprawled out on the dirt. So were the other men in the group.

He examined his arms for any sign of wounds and noticed that his skin had an unearthly glow. But he didn't seem to be hurt. The light enveloped them, but it had a core from which it streamed. He didn't dare look at it directly. That would be more dangerous than staring directly at the sun.

All the men shielded their eyes except for one—Saul. He stared directly into the blaze, which was like a burning cookpot, only a million times more intense. Abraham once saw a burning cookpot pass between the halves of sacrificial animals—a smoking symbol of the Lord passing before them. Was this burning brilliance a similar symbol of the Lord? Or was it the actual presence of God?

Next came a sound like the delayed thunder after a lightning strike. It was an extended rumbling sound, but Nekoda thought he heard faint words in the rumble. He strained to understand the words, but it was like trying to decipher a foreign language. Or was it all his imagination? People see images in the shapes of clouds. Maybe it was a trick of the ear, hearing words in the rumble of thunder.

But Saul also seemed to hear something. He rose from his knees and spoke to the light. "Who are you, Lord?" he shouted into the blaze. He spoke to a burning sky like Moses talking to a burning bush.

Then the light intensified, the holy core throbbed, and the thunderous speech rolled on and on and on. Vibrations passed through Nekoda's body, thrumming all around him, growing in intensity. He stopped his ears for fear that his eardrums would explode from the pressure.

The light surrounded him and pushed on him from all sides, like a thousand layers of ocean, crushing him. He stretched out on the ground, hoping it would relieve some of the pressure.

When Nekoda worked up the courage to raise his head, he saw Saul continuing to stare into the core. Even though Nekoda didn't look at the brightness directly, the indirect glow hurt his eyes, so he buried his head in his arms. Moments later, the light cut off in an instant as if God had snuffed a candle between two fingers.

Dazed, Nekoda worked his way to his feet. Most of the men seemed equally confused, staggering. But not all of them were dazed. Hiram looked around, hands on hips, as if he didn't understand what the commotion was about.

Nekoda rushed up to his son. "Did you see that? Did you feel that? Was this the Lord?"

Hiram furrowed his brow. "What are you talking about?"

"Did you see the light?"

Hiram pointed to the midday sun. "The only light I see is up there."

"But this light came to earth. Surely, you saw it. You too were thrown to the ground."

"Yes, I lost my balance. But it was just a brief earthquake, nothing more."

"And what about the thunder? You heard the thunder, right? There were words in the thunder."

Zuriel swaggered up to them. "Words in thunder? You have lost your mind, old man."

Nekoda turned to some of the other men—the ones with dazed expressions. "But you saw it, didn't you?" he asked one of them. The man slowly nodded.

The next to approach was Saul. He staggered toward them, his face aglow, continuing to radiate glory. His mouth was open, but no words came out. Most strange were his eyes. His pupils had faded, the color scorched away. And when Saul walked, he put his hands out to feel his way forward.

Nekoda gasped. Saul was blind.

Sveshtari

Sveshtari couldn't believe he had been talked into allowing this ritual to take place. When he first became a God-fearer, he vowed he would not get circumcised—and he had remained faithful to that oath. But eight days ago, Keturah gave birth to their fourth child—a beautiful baby boy. Today, the child, Ethan, was going to experience the *b'rit milah*. He was going to be circumcised.

As tradition would have it, the circumcision was taking place on the eighth day after the birth.

"God created the universe in seven days," Eliana had told him. "So, the eighth day signifies a new beginning, a new creation."

A small group had gathered in the local synagogue. Asaph and Eliana were there, along with their one-year-old girl, Eve, and their second child, a newborn boy, Jaren. Joanna was also there, as well as many people from the church. Abel would serve as the *sandak*, which meant he held Ethan during the ceremony. Sveshtari was grateful that the job didn't fall to the father because he didn't want to see the procedure up close.

"I am pleased you are allowing this," Abel said to Sveshtari as they gathered in the cool of the synagogue. "Maybe you'll be next." Abel constantly chided him for not getting circumcised when he became a God-fearer. "Circumcision is a sign of the covenant with God."

"Couldn't God use a different sign?" Sveshtari muttered. "A tattoo maybe?"

"To seal a covenant, blood must be shed." Abel adopted a serious tone. "When Jesus died on the cross, He suffered a spiritual circumcision. He was cut off from God. He shed his blood and sealed the New Covenant."

"I see," Sveshtari said half-heartedly, hoping to change the subject.

But Abel was fixated. "When Adam and Eve were driven from the Garden, an angel guarded the way back to the Tree of Life with a sword. They too were cut off. Therefore, to get back to the Tree of Life, we must pass under the sword. We must be circumcised."

As a former bodyguard, Sveshtari felt the slice of a blade many times. So, why was he so squeamish about the blade of circumcision? He had no response for Abel's words. He grunted and glanced toward the door, where the *mohel*, or circumciser, had just entered.

Keturah handed Ethan to Abel, and they gathered around a table where the delicate cutting would take place.

"Blessed be he who comes," said the *mohel*, a small Jewish Christian man, close to sixty years old. "We welcome all. We welcome Elijah."

The *mohel* cast his eyes toward an empty chair, which was reserved for the prophet Elijah. Taking the baby Ethan from Abel, the *mohel* placed him in the empty chair—on Elijah's lap presumably. Sveshtari's mind wandered until Abel sidled up to him and gave him a nudge.

"Sorry," Sveshtari said.

This was his moment to recite a reading over his new son. For one panic-stricken moment, his mind went blank. The words had flown from his mind like frightened birds. All eyes turned toward him. Then, slowly the words returned and roosted in his head.

"He will proclaim peace to the nations. His rule will extend from sea to sea and from the river to the ends of the earth," Sveshtari said slowly as each word settled on his tongue. "As for you, because of the blood of my covenant with you, I will free your prisoners from the waterless pit. Return to your fortress, you prisoners of hope. I will bend Judah as I bend my bow and make you like a warrior's sword."

Bows. Swords. These were words Sveshtari could understand. But he still didn't fully understand why covenants had to be sealed with blood. Was it because our blood was the most precious part of us?

Ethan was moved to the table, where the ritual was performed. Within minutes, the red-faced baby began crying. There wasn't a lot of blood, but enough that Sveshtari wondered if he had done the right thing by agreeing to this circumcision.

Quickly, it was finished. The blood was shed, and Ethan was welcomed into the Jewish family, despite having been born to former pagans who now followed a resurrected rabbi. A strange pedigree indeed.

Ethan continued to wail as he was handed back to Keturah. Sveshtari understood his pain. He'd be wailing too.

Nekoda: Damascus, Three Days Later

Nekoda knocked on doors for two days, hunting for his son Ezra among the Christ followers in Damascus. He hit dead end after dead end until he eventually showed up at the home of a man named Ananias—an older man with a shock of gray hair and an enormous beard.

"Ezra isn't in trouble, is he?" Ananias asked, standing in the doorway. His eyes assessed Nekoda from head to toe. Nekoda's clothing gave him away as someone of high standing—someone who might be on official business.

Nekoda smiled disarmingly. "I hope he's not in trouble. I am Ezra's abba."

Ananias brightened at the word "abba." He stepped aside and motioned for Nekoda to cross the threshold.

Nekoda touched the *mezuzah*, a small container affixed to the door containing a written prayer. Then he kissed his fingers and entered the dark interior of the house.

"Abba?" Ezra's voice came to him from the shadows.

"Ezra, I am so happy to find you at last!"

Nekoda extended his arms for an embrace, unsure whether Ezra would reciprocate. After a moment's hesitation, Ezra rose from his seat and wrapped his arms around his abba. It felt good.

Nekoda's older son, Hiram, had been distant for a long time. But he pulled away even further after the incident on the road to Damascus, which Hiram denied had anything to do with Jesus.

Nekoda prayed that his relationship with Ezra wouldn't suffer the same fate.

Ezra stepped back from the embrace. "What are you doing here? You haven't come to talk me into coming home to Jerusalem, have you?"

"Not at all. I came with your brother and Saul in a caravan."

Ezra started at those words. Nekoda should have realized that the name "Saul" would alter the atmosphere immediately. Ezra shuffled backward into the dark.

"Have you come to arrest us?"

Nekoda put up his hands. "No, no, absolutely not."

It pained Nekoda to hear the fear in his son's voice. He was never one to instill fear in his sons. Fear of the Lord, yes. But fear of their father, no.

Nekoda glanced at Ananias. "Strange things have been happening."

That was an understatement. Ever since what happened on the road to Damascus, Saul had changed. He had become observably depressed, silent and unwilling to eat or even drink water. This was so unlike the confident, brash Saul who had been terrorizing the Church.

Nekoda had also changed in these few days. He still didn't know what to make of what had happened on the road, but it had left him uneasy. Destabilized.

Ananias grabbed his walking stick from the corner and took Nekoda by the sleeve. "Take me to Saul before I lose my nerve."

Ezra rushed forward to block Ananias's path. "What are you talking about? You cannot go to Saul! It's too dangerous."

"I agree," said Nekoda, trying to show that his sympathies lay with them, not with Saul. "It may still be too dangerous to go near Saul."

Ananias banged his walking stick on the floor and smiled. "That's exactly what I told God when he spoke to me in a vision."

"A vision?" *Why is it that everyone except me is having visions and supernatural encounters?* Nekoda thought.

"The Lord told me to go to the house of Judas on Straight Street and ask for a man from Tarsus named Saul. This man, Saul, had a vision that told him I would come and place my hands on him to restore his sight."

He was right about the location. Saul was staying on Straight Street at Judas's home. And how did he know that Saul had been blinded? Perhaps the word had spread.

"Saul has been praying and fasting for the past three days," Nekoda said. "But I know nothing about him having a vision of you."

"Then take me to him right away. When the Lord commanded me to do this thing, I told him I was terrified. I didn't want to do it. But the Lord said Saul is his chosen instrument to proclaim his name to the Gentiles and their kings and to the people of Israel."

Gentiles? Saul is going to proclaim the message of Jesus to the Gentiles? That sounded preposterous. Nekoda couldn't imagine Saul proclaiming the name of Jesus to anyone, but especially not to Gentiles! Besides, since the incident on the Road to Damascus, Saul had been acting too depressed to preach. Nekoda wondered if he was overwhelmed with the knowledge that he had been persecuting innocent people.

"Please, take me to Saul before I change my mind." Ananias rushed outside into the light. It was a picture-perfect morning after a day of rain.

"If you insist." Nekoda hurried after him, followed close behind by Ezra.

"I beseech you to turn around," Ezra said, but there was no stopping Ananias. He used his walking stick to propel himself forward through the streets, passing Bab Sharqi, the Gate of the Sun, and turning left down Straight Street—the main east-west road through the heart of Damascus.

On the way to the house of Judas, Nekoda explained the strange happenings on the road to Damascus, and his story seemed to give confidence to Ananias. But Nekoda's son wasn't totally convinced.

"Ananias, what if it is a trap?" Ezra asked.

"Do you really believe your father would lead his son into a trap?"

Ezra shot a glance at his father. "Abba, you have always shown concern for my safety. Forgive me for my question."

"I have sometimes given you cause for suspicion, so I take responsibility for your doubts."

He spoke magnanimous words, but it still hurt to realize that he didn't have his son's complete trust.

At last, they reached the house of Judas on Straight Street. Ezra raised his hand to knock on the door. Then paused.

"Are you sure you want to do this?" he asked Ananias one more time.

"Of course I am not sure. But the Lord seemed quite sure of himself."

With a sigh of resignation, Ezra rapped on the door. They waited. No answer. Ezra knocked again. Finally, the door creaked on its hinges as a young man in his twenties opened it. "May I help you?"

"I am here to speak with Saul," said Ananias, gripping his walking stick with both hands.

"Is that you, Ananias?" called a voice from inside the house.

"It is!"

"He knows you?" Ezra whispered to the older man.

"He does now."

Ananias stepped into the home, where Saul sat in a corner. Saul had a narrow face and wide forehead. He was partially bald with a rim of hair at the back and a small peninsula of hair in the front. His pupils still had a washed-out appearance as he searched the room for the source of the voices. Then he smiled.

Nekoda had not seen many smiles from Saul until now.

Saul motioned for them to come closer. "I have been expecting you, Ananias. What took you so long?"

"The same thing that took you so long to obey God," Ananias responded.

Nekoda gasped. He waited for Saul to be insulted. However, Saul just grinned and nodded his head.

"Good response, my brother, good response. The Lord had to remove my vision before I could truly see."

"That is what it often takes," Ananias said. "The Lord had to hit me over the head before I could work up the nerve to come here."

"He hit you over the head, and he knocked me off my feet. Truly, we are brothers in Christ."

Nekoda's eyes went wide. Was Saul really calling himself a "brother in Christ?" The words that the Lord spoke to Saul on the road to Damascus must have been powerful to turn his heart and life completely around—to turn him from persecutor to penitent.

"May I place my hands on your shoulders and pray?" Ananias asked.

Saul nodded. "You may."

Ananias handed his staff to Nekoda and shuffled forward. He stood behind Saul and put both hands on his shoulders. Then he closed his eyes as silence descended. Nekoda waited for him to speak, but Ananias remained silent for what seemed like an eternity. Nekoda shifted the weight on his feet and opened his eyes briefly to see what was happening. Ananias still had one hand on Saul's shoulder, but he raised the other to the ceiling. Finally, he spoke.

"Brother Saul, the Lord Jesus, who appeared to you on the road as you were coming here, has sent me so that you may see again and be filled with the Holy Spirit."

Nekoda was confused. Ananias spoke to Saul, not to the Lord. Prayers should be directed toward God, but maybe he was just warming up before a long, eloquent prayer.

But Ananias never got to a long, eloquent prayer.

Saul leaped to his feet and rubbed his eyes. "I can see!"

In case Nekoda thought any of this could be an act, the pupils of Saul's eyes had regained full color.

Saul stared at his hands, then looked up. "I can see you, Nekoda!" Then he spotted Ezra standing in the background and said, "And this is one of your sons, is it not? I saw him back in Jerusalem, and now I see him again. *I see him!*"

"Praise God!" Ezra exclaimed.

Nekoda wasn't sure what to say or do. Just three days ago, Saul was a man to be feared. But after the incident on the road to Damascus, Saul had become vulnerable, depressed, and unwilling to eat or drink. Now, he suddenly burst with joy, rushing forward and wrapping Nekoda in a bear hug. Nekoda's head spun. Everything was changing so fast.

Then Saul wheeled around again and faced Ananias. "And you must be Ananias, my brother!" Saul wrapped him in an embrace. "Thank you for leading me out of darkness. It was like I spent three days in the grave. Then brightness and light."

"Sound familiar?" Ananias said.

Saul nodded vigorously. "Yes, yes, I see."

"I don't," Nekoda interjected. "What do you see?"

"Jesus was in the tomb for three days," Saul exclaimed. "Then he rose! He rose indeed! I was dead for three days, but now I live. I was blind, but now I see!"

Saul placed one hand on Nekoda's shoulder and another on Ananias's. Then he began to dance and sing, moving in a circle at ever-increasing speeds. He sang the words of Isaiah: "I will lead the blind by ways they have not known, along unfamiliar paths I will guide them; I will turn darkness into light before them and make the rough places smooth!"

Nekoda was out of breath when he finally came to a halt and Saul slapped them both on the back. "I'm hungry!" he shouted. "I haven't eaten in three days!"

Ananias put a hand on Saul's shoulder. "Then you must come to my home and share a meal, brother."

"Yes, yes, but first . . . !" Saul's eyes gleamed. "First, I must be baptized!"

Eliana

Eliana, Asaph, and Sveshtari lugged sacks of food from the Sebaste market, following a path that took them past the massive Roman theater. Keturah had stayed back to take care of the children.

Cheering erupted from inside the theater because today the gladiatorial games were taking place. Eliana shuddered to think about what was happening within those walls. If she had remembered, she would have suggested taking the long way home from the market, bypassing the theater.

As it began to spit rain, she prayed for a downpour that might drive away the spectators and end the games prematurely. The sky rumbled, but it was distant thunder, and the clouds held back their reserves, releasing no more than a brief drizzle.

"Teach me the Way of Jesus! I'm hungry for the words of the Messiah! Can anyone tell me about Jesus of Nazareth?"

Eliana was shocked to hear these words rising from her left. She snapped her head around and saw a middle-aged man dressed in rags kneeling in front of the Roman theater. Normally, she found people begging for food or money, but this man was begging for the words of Jesus. Extraordinary!

Eliana and Asaph came to a stop and exchanged a glance, while Sveshtari continued walking as if he hadn't heard the man's pleas.

"Do you truly want to hear about Jesus the Christ?" Asaph asked the man.

"What are you doing?" Sveshtari said, making his way back to them.

The man, whose eyes were raised to heaven, lowered his gaze and smiled. "Yes, I do want to hear! Can you tell me about Jesus? I heard there were followers of the Way in the city. Are you part of the Way?"

"We are," said Eliana.

"Then tell me about Jesus, and the truth will set me free!"

Eliana set down her sack. She was all prepared to give him the Gospel message when she sensed movement from her right. The man who was begging for the Gospel swung around to face two approaching men who strode with authority. The beggar pointed at Eliana, Asaph, and Sveshtari.

"They told me they are followers of Jesus! They're part of the Way!"

They had been set up. The man in rags was not begging for the Truth. He was fishing for followers of Jesus, and the two men walking toward them had the clear intention of arresting them. Had the Zealots moved their attacks from Jerusalem to other cities such as Sebaste?

Asaph took Eliana by the hand and pulled her in the opposite direction. But they came face to face with another man. Eliana gasped. It was Zuriel! What was he doing in Sebaste?

"Eliana? Asaph? I should've known you're the troublemakers in Sebaste." Zuriel tried to speak with firmness, but when he spotted Sveshtari, he was clearly intimidated.

"Arrest these disciples of Jesus," Zuriel snapped at the approaching Zealots. Three more thugs had arrived, but Eliana doubted that five men would be enough to handle Sveshtari. Zuriel backed up several steps because he wasn't about to get his hands dirty.

A crowd of onlookers gathered around them, sensing violence in the air.

"When someone strikes you on the right cheek, offer them the left," Zuriel said, reminding Sveshtari and Asaph not to think of fighting back.

Sveshtari and Asaph formed a protective wall in front of Eliana as they backed away from their attackers, which now numbered six. Behind them was a row of market stalls, including a booth that sold fishing nets and supplies. Eliana noticed Sveshtari's gaze move to the nets as they continued to back away from their attackers.

She guessed what he was thinking. Sveshtari no longer carried a sword, but he was good at improvising. Didn't gladiators use nets and tridents to fight in the arena?

As one of their attackers rushed forward, pulling out a knife, Sveshtari sprang into action. He snagged a fishing net and hurled it over his attacker in one seamless move.

While the attacker let out a curse, the man at the stall protested. "Hey! Leave my nets alone!"

But Sveshtari was just getting started. He grabbed another fishing net and hurled it over Zuriel. Both men were like flies caught in a web. Asaph contributed his part by pulling on the net that had Zuriel in its grip. Zuriel lost his footing and slammed to the ground.

Sveshtari knocked the legs out from under the other man caught in the net. Then he reached for a third net, this one large enough to toss over the heads of two more men. The crowd burst out laughing, while many people clapped their approval.

The remaining attackers melted into the crowd. They weren't about to be humiliated by becoming snared in a fishing net. Zuriel, still on the ground and thrashing, poured out a stream of curses. When Zuriel managed to rise to his knees, Sveshtari gave him a kick to the nose, and blood gushed.

That was unnecessary, Eliana thought, but said nothing.

While the shopkeeper worked to untangle the other men and recover his nets, Sveshtari grabbed the net containing Zuriel and dragged it across the square in front of the Roman Temple.

"This is better than anything we could've seen in the arena," said a man in the crowd, running alongside.

"You should be fighting in the amphitheater," said another observer as Sveshtari dragged a cursing Zuriel across the stone. "I'd pay good money to watch you fight."

Sveshtari handed the fishing net to a young man, who was more than happy to take Zuriel for a bumpy ride.

"Time to go," Sveshtari said, picking up his sack of food. Asaph and Eliana did the same, and they made their escape while their attackers struggled in the nets like animals in a trap.

Nekoda: Damascus

Saul had changed dramatically, but in some ways, he hadn't changed at all. He was still zealous. He was still a man of action. He still spoke his mind with the bluntness of a hammer. But he directed all his energy along a completely different course. He couldn't stop talking about Jesus Christ.

For months, Saul had been the greatest threat to the followers of Jesus. But now, in the blink of an eye, he had become a pilgrim along the Way, putting himself into harm's way by speaking about Jesus at the synagogue. *At the synagogue!*

The man didn't know the meaning of the word "tact."

"He's going to get himself killed," Nekoda told Ezra after one volatile scene at the synagogue. They sat at a dinner table, sharing wine, bread, and fruit.

"He's fearless." Ezra smiled, then popped a fig in his mouth.

"Maybe he needs a healthy helping of fear if he hopes to stay alive."

Ezra drizzled honey on his bread, then spread it with his knife. "If I said anything like that to him, he would rebuke me for standing in the path of the Lord's mission."

"Ah." Nekoda bit into his bread.

"Now that several days have gone by, what do you think?" Ezra asked.

Nekoda chewed slowly, methodically, trying to buy time for his response. He dabbed his mouth. "What do I think about what?" he responded, although he knew exactly what Ezra was asking.

"What do you think about Jesus now that you've witnessed two miracles? The Road to Damascus. Then Saul regaining his sight."

"Miracles are staggering to the mind, but I would not put my faith in them. The Law is a more solid foundation."

"I too don't think you should put your faith solely in miracles. Your faith must be in a person. The Christ. The Messiah."

"I am a member of the Sanhedrin, my son. I cannot be seen running after any prophet claiming to be the Messiah."

"But Jesus is not just any prophet. How many of those claiming to be Messiah rose from the dead? How many prophets appear to their enemies on the road and strike him blind—then heal him?"

"Food for thought," Nekoda said, still stalling.

Truth be told, he had been giving more thought to Jesus of Nazareth than he let on. Nekoda had always been taught to be deliberate. But Saul was a completely different animal. He was a rampaging bull—an animal that reversed directions in a heartbeat. Nekoda was more like a large ocean-going vessel. Turning around took time. Try to turn a large ship too sharply, and it might tip over and sink.

Nekoda was rescued from any further interrogation by a knock at the door.

"I will get it," he said, escaping from the clasp of Ezra's questions. He hurried to the door and opened it.

It was his oldest son.

"Saul is out of control," Hiram snapped, striding into the room without a word of greeting.

Ezra was on his feet immediately, meeting Hiram glare to glare. "It depends on what you mean by out of control. He's under the control of the Holy Spirit."

"A man in control does not mingle with Gentiles. A man like that deserves the spear of Phinehas!"

The spear of Phinehas? During the days of Moses, when Phinehas saw an Israelite consorting with a foreign woman, a Gentile, he drove a spear through both of them in one swift move. Was Hiram threatening to skewer Saul?

"How can you say that about Saul?" Nekoda asked. "Doesn't what happened on the road to Damascus give you any pause?"

"Saul claims he heard Jesus speak to him. But that is nonsense. He was deceived by the evil one, Abba."

Nekoda couldn't believe he was defending Saul. But something prodded him to speak. "Saul says the voice told him, 'I am Jesus, whom you are persecuting. Now get up and go into the city, and you will be told what you must do.'"

Hiram stepped within a handsbreadth of his father. "And you heard those words?"

"I heard what sounded like language intermingled with thunder. But I could not make out the precise words."

Hiram folded his arms across his chest. "Your fellow Sanhedrin in Jerusalem will be keen to know that you accept Saul's blasphemy."

Nekoda shook his head solemnly. "Son, you act rashly in making judgments about Saul," Nekoda said.

"Acting swiftly is not the same as acting rashly. Phinehas was swift in his judgment of that sinful Israelite, but he was not rash."

"You are not Phinehas," Ezra interjected.

"But I carry Phinehas's spear!"

Content to have the last word, Hiram exited the dwelling as rapidly as he entered. Nekoda's heart thumped double-time.

He turned to Ezra. "I believe that Hiram and the others mean to kill our friend Saul."

"It's a good thing Saul is planning to travel into Arabia," Ezra said.

Nekoda was stunned. His son, Ezra, was beginning to trust him! Why else would he divulge such information about Saul?

"Arabia? If he's trying to escape to safety, why choose Arabia?"

"He's not fleeing. He's running toward something."

"And what would that be?"

"He's running toward Mount Sinai!"

Mount Sinai was where Moses encountered Yahweh and received the Ten Commandments. It was also where Elijah encountered God in the small, still voice. Nekoda couldn't imagine what Saul was seeking on Sinai. But he was curious.

Nekoda had been planning to return to Jerusalem in a day or two. But how could he return to Jerusalem after all that had happened to him in Damascus? And more importantly, why had God chosen to place him in this unique position? Could he simply return to his old life in Jerusalem and reclaim his position of power and authority on the Sanhedrin?

Was God also drawing him to Sinai, the holy mountain? Was the Lord also trying to speak to him? Could he pass up this chance? For once in his life, should he take a risk?

SVESHTARI

Sveshtari hated the idea of leaving Sebaste. He wanted to stay and fight Zuriel and the Zealots. But he knew there was a time for strategic retreat, and Keturah convinced him this was it. So did Eliana. And Asaph. And Abel.

Abel, always the effective intelligence gatherer, discovered that Zuriel was assembling a formidable force to attack Sveshtari and their families. Zuriel had been thoroughly humiliated when Sveshtari dragged him past the amphitheater in a net. He was out for blood.

"We have to think about the children," Keturah said—an argument that Sveshtari couldn't dispute. So, as the afternoon sun blazed, their families slipped out of Sebaste. They had four routes from which to choose—east to the Jordan River, south to Jerusalem, north to Galilee, or west to Caesarea Maritima on the Great Sea.

They opted for the western route because many Jesus followers had gone in that direction. Among them was Philip, who took the road west from Jerusalem to Gaza.

Before departing, they prayed the *Shema*, the ancient Jewish prayer recited twice a day: *"Shema Israel, Adonai Eloheinu, Adonai echad."*

Hear, O Israel, the Lord our God, the Lord is one.

There was more to that prayer, which Sveshtari had memorized in its entirety. But the beginning line was emblazoned in every Jewish spirit.

"We say the Lord is one," Sveshtari said to Asaph and Abel as they led the donkeys down the hills of Samaria toward more level ground. "But how does Jesus fit into the *Shema*? If he is the Son of God, doesn't that make the Lord *Two*, not One?"

"The Lord is One, but he is also Three," said Asaph. "At least that's how Philip explained it to me."

"*Three*? How can you be both One and Three? And who is number Three?"

"The disciples refer to the Third Person by many names. The Holy Spirit. The Wonderful Counselor."

Sveshtari ran his hand along the donkey's muzzle. "People keep talking about this Holy Spirit, but what is it?"

"The Spirit is a *who*, not an *it*. He's not an impersonal force. He's a person. A Counselor. He is God's Spirit, and he speaks from within; he breathes on us, changing our hearts from stone to flesh."

"A breath? That makes it sound like a force, not a person."

"Only living people have breath," noted Abel. "Without breath, we are dead. Remember that day on Pentecost when the disciples began talking in other languages?"

"How could I forget?"

"That was the Holy Spirit in action."

"God the Father stands before us as our Creator," Asaph said. "Jesus is at our side as our Advocate, and the Spirit is within us as our Helper. But they are One. And they are all on our side."

Asaph, Sveshtari, and Abel went silent, each absorbing the words as they carefully stepped down the path strewn with rocks. Sveshtari's feet dislodged a rock that tumbled downhill, clinking along the way.

"I'm not sure I fully understand what you are saying, but I take comfort that we have Three on our side," Sveshtari said.

"Three who are One," Asaph added.

"When I see Peter next, I'll have questions."

"So will I," said Abel.

"As will I," added Asaph.

Soon, they were on level land, and the pathway west was much smoother.

Nekoda: Mt. Sinai, Eight Months Later, Month of Nisan (Early April), 34 A.D.

Nekoda wondered, for the hundredth time, if he had done the right thing by joining Ezra and the group of believers who followed Saul to Arabia. He had deserted his position in Jerusalem for this? He was trapped in a tent made of goat hair, listening to the wind roar and the sand beat against their dwelling.

This morning, they had set up camp at the foot of Mount Sinai. No sooner had Saul left to climb the mountain alone than a massive sandstorm swept in from the west.

It was one of the largest sandstorms Nekoda had ever witnessed. As the morning progressed, a massive wall of sand appeared on the horizon like an approaching army. The very earth was on the move, lifted from the ground and filling the air, spinning and rolling forward. Millions upon millions of sand particles came together like locusts, blotting out the sun.

"If Saul wanted a storm on Sinai, the same as Elijah, he got it!" Nekoda told Ezra. His mouth was covered to keep out any sand particles, so he had to shout to make himself heard—especially above the roar of the storm. "I pray he is safe."

Ezra extended his arms to the side. "The Lord didn't lead him to Sinai to die!"

It was too difficult to talk above the sound and the fury, so Nekoda prayed silently. As he did, he contemplated the strange things that Saul had been saying. He said that circumcision is "merely outward and physical" and that a person is not a Jew if he is only one outwardly.

Saul also talked about a "circumcision of the heart!" He said the Spirit circumcises our heart, cutting like a knife, drawing blood. We are not circumcised by the written Law, he said, but by the Spirit.

According to Saul, we are righteous through faith in Jesus, and it's available to all who believe. Even Gentiles! It was mind boggling. Had he signed on to follow a madman into the wilderness?

But whenever Nekoda kicked back at Saul's words, the image of his two sons appeared in his mind. Hiram was all Law, all judgment, all condemnation. Ezra, his youngest, was grace personified. When Nekoda put flesh on those ideas, when he saw them acted out by his two sons, he saw exactly what Saul was trying to say.

He also saw the difference in Saul. The old Saul was Law writ large with righteous fury. The old Saul was a sword that shed blood. But the new Saul was grace. He still carried a sword, but he wielded a sword of the Spirit that healed. It was an internal sword that cut away the sickness, more like a surgeon's knife.

Just yesterday, Saul explained that we are "more than conquerors through him who loved us." He said he is convinced that neither death nor life, neither angels nor demons, neither the present nor the future, nor any powers, neither height nor depth, nor anything else in all creation, will be able to separate us from the love of God that is in Christ Jesus our Lord.

If those words were true, then even a sandstorm couldn't blot out the Son of God. As if to answer his thoughts, the wall of the tent bulged inward, filled with a blast of heated air, then snapped back.

The sand beat against their shelter, but this thin skin, made by the hands of Saul, protected them from destruction.

Eliana: Joppa, the Coast of the Great Sea

Eliana noticed Keturah wincing as she bound sheaves of barley. Keturah was with child—her fifth. It was a hot afternoon with no breeze from the sea. Their dog, Lavi, rested in the sun in a nearby field.

"You should take a break," Eliana said. "Find some shade."

"What shade?"

Keturah was right. The nearest shade tree was a good distance away. Eliana thought Keturah should still try to get out of the sun, but she said nothing more about it.

After fleeing Sebaste, their families had settled in Joppa, northwest of Jerusalem on the Great Sea. It was an important seaport—the place where Jonah boarded a ship while fleeing from God's command to preach deliverance to the Ninevites, a non-Jewish people. Ironically, ever since the persecution of the Way began, the Gospel spread its deliverance message to non-Jews in Joppa at a surprising rate.

Eliana finished binding a sheaf of barley and tossed it on the pile. The Feast of the Firstfruits was one day away—a day in which Jews celebrated the beginning of the barley harvest. They presented the firstfruits of their harvest to the priest, who waved it as an offering to the Lord.

"Jesus rose from the dead on the Feast of Firstfruits," Eliana said, working on the next sheaf of barley.

Keturah smiled. "I have a feeling you're going to tell me there is a special meaning to that."

"You know me too well." Eliana scooped up an armload of barley. "One of the apostles said that by rising on the third day after the crucifixion, Jesus became our firstfruits of the resurrection. And we, his followers, are the remainder of the harvest."

"Which means . . .?"

"Which means we, too, will rise to eternal life."

"If I hadn't seen Jesus on the shore of Galilee, I would never believe we could rise from the dead," Keturah said, wiping her brow.

"Today, the day before the Feast of Firstfruits, we typically recite the words of Ezekiel: 'Dry bones, hear the word of the Lord! This is what the Sovereign Lord says to these bones: I will make breath enter you, and you will come to life. I will attach tendons to you and make flesh come upon you and cover you with skin; I will put breath in you, and you will come to life. Then you will know that I am the Lord.'"

"You're saying that Jesus will put flesh on our dry bones?"

"I am."

Keturah sighed and wiped her brow again.

"Please, rest," Eliana said. "I will take a break with you."

"Perhaps you are right."

With Eliana's help, Keturah rose groaning to her feet, and they wandered in the direction of the nearest tree.

"Come, Lavi!" On Eliana's command, their dog limped toward them and followed them across the dry field.

"You are my Ruth," Eliana said, linking arms with her friend.

"How so?"

"Ruth, a non-Jew, stayed faithful to Naomi when they traveled to Bethlehem. And you have always stayed faithful to me."

"Where you go, I will go, and where you stay, I will stay," Keturah said, quoting the words of Ruth to Naomi. "Your people will be my people and your God my God. Where you die, I will die, and there I will be buried."

Eliana crouched beneath the tree. "And where you and I both die, we will be resurrected."

Keturah removed her hat and fanned her face. "Our dry bones will leap."

"May we never be parted, my sister."

Lavi rested his head in Eliana's lap and closed his eyes as she scratched behind his ears.

Nekoda: Two Years Later, the Road Back to Damascus, Month of Sivan (Late May), 36 A.D.

Nekoda and Ezra set their wooden pegs in place and connected the four corners of the large tent. Then, after all the ropes were secured, they put the entrance poles in place, raising the large tent. When it was finished, the sloping skin of the tent blended in with the undulating landscape of sand.

Nekoda had spent all his life in luxury in the finest of two-story houses, complete with fountains and statuary. But now he was on the move, following in the footsteps of Saul, never stationary for more than a week. He and Ezra had become tent experts and could set up their dwelling faster than it took to cook a meal.

They had been using this tent for two years now, and it showed its wear. The edges were frayed, and the goatskin was getting thin. The beauty of goat hair was that when it was dry, it shrank, allowing small holes to form. This made it possible for the tent to breathe in the hot weather. Inside, it was remarkably cool.

When Nekoda first started living in one of these tents, he was sure that when it rained, these small holes would let in a torrent of water. But goat hair swells in the rain, naturally plugging the holes and making the tent completely waterproof in the rainy season.

It was as if the tent were alive, like a human body coping with fluctuations in weather.

"Have you decided what you're going to do when we return to Damascus?" Ezra asked his father when they settled into the shade of the tent, leaning on cushions.

"I have not. My friends back in Jerusalem probably assume I am dead."

"You *are* dead. Your old self died in the desert, did it not?"

"True. But I live again."

Tomorrow, they would be back in Damascus, the place where Nekoda's new life began—the place where Saul's new life also began.

"Maybe I should return to Jerusalem after we're back in Damascus," Nekoda said.

"Why return to Jerusalem if that old life has died?" Ezra asked.

"Perhaps I could help to spread the Good News among my friends."

"Herod Antipas could make that difficult."

Nekoda was shocked that his son, so bold for the faith, was counseling caution. Even more surprising, Nekoda found himself counseling boldness.

"We must take risks. Saul takes risks," Nekoda said.

"Saul is not my father. I do not worry about him like I do you."

Nekoda smiled. Ezra may be his youngest son, but he was the heir to his heart.

"You are correct about Herod, though," Nekoda said, adjusting his position on the cushion.

Herod Antipas was the one who had beheaded John the Baptist and been complicit in the crucifixion of Jesus. He could not be trusted. Herod made his headquarters in Caesarea Maritima, but he had a way of spreading his poison far and wide.

The next day, they took down the tent, rolled it up, and hefted the bulky skins onto the back of the prostrate camel. It was a three-man job, while a fourth man stood at the head of the camel with a rope, keeping the animal in position. Then they secured the load to the back of the camel, using one of the many knots Nekoda had learned over the past two years. He was a magician with rope, and his hands flew.

This was not the life he had expected two years ago, but he was content. More than content. He had found the true meaning of the word "shalom." He was complete in mind, body, and spirit. What would his brother, Chaim, think if he could see him now? Surely, he would beam.

For years, Nekoda had exercised the mind, but his body had gone soft, and his spirit had petrified like wood. But now . . . shalom.

Saul preached to the Nabateans in Arabia. He preached to the Jews he encountered on the road home. He preached to everyone in his path, Jew or Gentile. He preached to those who opened their hearts to his message and to those who stood against him.

In Damascus, he preached in the synagogue.

Nekoda sat among the men who had gathered to hear this odd preacher, who had just returned from Mount Sinai, the holiest of mountains. The room was packed with expectant souls, waiting to hear about the mountain where Moses received the Law.

As Saul spoke of the righteousness of God, given through faith in Jesus Christ, Nekoda kept his eyes on the men on all sides. He could see the moment when their eagerness became skepticism. Then anger.

Saul was undaunted. "There is no difference between Jew and Gentile, for all have sinned and fall short of the glory of God!"

Nekoda could sense the air being sucked out of the room as dozens of men took deep breaths in astonishment. Nekoda closed his eyes and prayed for Saul's safety.

"And all are justified freely by his grace through the redemption that came by Christ Jesus. God presented Christ as a sacrifice of atonement, through the shedding of his blood—to be received by faith."

As a priest in the Temple, Nekoda knew what it meant to sacrifice spotless lambs on the altar. He had sacrificed a lamb at the same moment that Jesus shed his blood on the cross. The darkness that descended and the earthquake that rocked Jerusalem when Jesus died were just the first signs that Nekoda witnessed. He wondered what had taken him so long to see what was right in front of his face?

Saul must have seen the stunned expressions in the synagogue crowd. But he kept plowing forward.

"For we maintain that a person is justified by faith apart from the works of the law. Or is God the God of Jews only? Is he not the God of Gentiles too? Yes, of Gentiles too, since there is only one God, who will justify the circumcised by faith and the uncircumcised through that same faith. Do we, then, nullify the law by this faith? Not at all! Rather, we uphold the law."

These were words of revolution. Nekoda feared for Saul's life—and for his own.

The Next Day

Nekoda sifted through fruit in the market of Damascus, not far from one of the gates of the city. He spotted a half dozen Nabatean soldiers standing guard at the gates. This was new. This was ominous.

"Why so many soldiers?" Nekoda asked the shopkeeper while examining the apples.

The shopkeeper cast a glance over his shoulder. "I wondered the same thing. I hear that the Nabatean ethnarch in the city looks to arrest a troublemaker."

"What troublemaker?"

"If I could guess, it's the man who has been preaching about the Son of God. He's got the city in an uproar. The ethnarch seeks only peace in Damascus."

Are my own people working with the Nabateans to trap Saul?

If this was true, then the irony wasn't lost on him. His fellow Jews were working with Gentiles to capture or kill a Jew who had the audacity to preach to Gentiles. It seemed as if the entire city wanted Saul dead or jailed.

Nekoda reported his news to the followers of the Way at the house of Judas on Straight Street—the same house where Saul had received his sight. But the news had already preceded him. Saul was in danger. While several men left to retrieve Saul, others discussed possible means of escape.

"This is the only way out of the city for Saul," said Seth, one of the local leaders of the Way. He pointed to a large basket on the floor.

"You want to hide Saul in that?" exclaimed another—Jesse.

"The gates are heavily guarded. It's the only way."

"But the guards will be checking any baskets you try to smuggle past them," Jesse said.

"I agree. That's why we plan to lower Saul from the city wall. Joab and Miriam have a dwelling in the city wall. We can lower him from their window."

Jesse's mouth dropped open. He looked around the room, perhaps waiting to see if anyone else would speak against this insane idea. "Hiding in a basket is a humiliating way to escape."

"Humble is a better word," Nekoda pointed out. "Besides, Saul will be in good company. Moses escaped in a basket."

"But Moses was a baby when they put his basket in the Nile. You are treating Saul like an infant."

"We are all babies in the faith," Ezra said. "If we must use a humble means of escape, so be it."

"He makes a good point," Nekoda said, gently.

Jesse started to protest when the door opened, and Saul strode in, flanked by the two men who had fetched him. Saul glanced from face to face.

"We know how to get you out of the city alive," Ezra said.

"How?"

Ezra pointed toward the basket on the floor. Saul's eyes landed on the basket and went wide. A proud man like Saul will probably never agree to being hidden in a basket, Nekoda thought.

As Saul continued to stare at the basket, he stroked his beard. Then his eyes lit up, and he looked at the men, one by one. When his eyes met Nekoda's, he laughed.

"Brilliant!"

Later the same day, Nekoda, Ezra, and Saul moved through the shadows as they made their way through Damascus, heading for the city wall under the cover of darkness. Jesse went ahead of them, making sure the way was free of guards, then signaling them to move forward. Another man had already delivered the basket to Joab and Miriam's home, built into the city wall.

Ezra, Nekoda, and Saul leapfrogged from building to building, scurrying into the open for only moments at a time. Jesse whistled his signal whenever the coast was clear.

Nekoda was surprised that Saul readily agreed to escape in the basket. The man had changed in so many ways. The old Saul would never agree to such a humiliating form of escape. But Saul said the Lord desires his people to be as wise as serpents. Nekoda wondered if Saul knew that Jesus had said a similar thing during his teaching.

Another whistle, another forward movement. Almost there now. Joab and Miriam's house was just around the corner.

When they rounded a building, the door of a nearby house was thrown open, and out strode two Nabatean guards with swords drawn and torches lighting the way. Nekoda glanced around for a place to hide, but they had already been spotted.

As the guards approached, Nekoda gathered his wits and stepped forward to meet them in the road, putting every bit of authority behind his voice. "What seems to be the problem?"

The two guards shoved their torches in his face, sizing him up, taking in his robes of power. "Who are you?" The first guard spoke with a measure of respect. There was a crack in his voice.

"I am a member of the Sanhedrin, and we are moving our prisoner."

"Your *prisoner?*" The second guard waved his torch at Saul. "This man looked like he was roaming freely through the streets."

Nekoda scowled. "Don't worry, we have it all under control."

"You haven't even bound his hands."

"That was not necessary. He goes willingly."

Nekoda had to admit that this was a strange system for moving a prisoner through the city. But it was the best he could come up with in the moment. He hoped the trappings of his office spoke louder than his reasoning.

"We are transporting the prisoner to his lodging for the night. Tomorrow morning, we will deliver him up to the ethnarch."

"Why not deliver him tonight?"

Nekoda rose up on his toes. "Do you want to be the ones who rouse the ethnarch from his bed? Besides, it is our custom to give the accused a final night of prayer and peace."

Now, he was making things up out of thin air. He prayed the Nabatean guards would assume it was a Jewish tradition.

"We can help you transport this man to the house," said one of the guards.

"Thank you. Your assistance is appreciated."

So, the small contingent completed the final stretch with Arabian guards at their sides. As they neared the house, one of the guards motioned toward the door. "Shall one of us stand guard inside and the other stand guard outside?"

Nekoda shook his head. "Surely, you know our Laws about foreigners crossing the thresholds of our homes."

He prayed the guards wouldn't take offense.

They didn't.

People throughout the Roman empire were accustomed to the tolerance given to the odd ways of the Jewish people. Jews were the only ones allowed to make sacrifices "for" the emperor, rather than make sacrifices "to" the emperor, as done by the rest of the populace.

The guards watched as Ezra and Nekoda directed Saul through the door of the home built into the city wall. Inside, they found Jesse, Miriam, Joab, and six others waiting for them.

"Upstairs," Joab whispered.

They rushed up the stone staircase to the room where Joab kept watch on the world outside the city. He was a watchman, whose job was to alert the city of approaching enemies or strangers. Setting on a nearby table in the upper room was a trumpet, used to warn the city.

A watchman sounds the trumpet when the enemy's sword comes against the city—a key part of a city's defense. But tonight, they were leading an *offensive* attack. They were releasing Saul into the world as an army of one.

Saul stepped into the basket. "Good thing I've been fasting for three days. I don't weigh as much as I did three days ago, so lowering me from the window will be much easier."

Nekoda smiled at Saul's light-hearted manner. Saul lay on his side in the basket in the position of an unborn baby.

"I'm ready to be re-born," he joked, aware of his position in the basket.

After closing the lid, Joab wrapped rope around the basket, using a four-point harness. Although Saul was a small man, it took several men, including Nekoda, to lift the basket to the windowsill.

After Joab made sure the coast was clear, they began to lower the basket, careful to be sure it made a soft landing on the ground below. Then Saul used his knife to cut a hole in the side of the basket, and he crawled out. He placed the cutaway back into the basket and motioned for the men to draw his escape capsule back up.

Finally, Saul stared up at them with arms outstretched, offering a last prayer—a silent prayer. Then he turned and scampered into the darkness like a thief in the night.

Nekoda worried about what the guards would say when Saul didn't exit the house in the morning. But he was confident he could find a way to blame the Arabian guards for Saul's disappearance.

"Thank you, Abba." Ezra wrapped him in a warm embrace.

Nekoda still couldn't believe he had crossed yet another line. He had gone from embracing the Way to actively abetting the escape of Saul.

There was no turning back—for Saul or for Nekoda.

10.

The Book of Acts, Chapter 10

Eliana: Joppa, Four Years Later, 40 A.D.

A war raged in the air—a war of scents. And the battleground was the atmosphere surrounding the home of Simon the Tanner.

It was a little past noon as Eliana carried a blue perfume juglet filled with her latest creation—an inexpensive scent made from sage and other secret ingredients, using olive oil as the carrier. She was delivering the perfume to Simon's wife, who could use all the beautiful aromas she had at her disposal to battle the odors of a tannery.

As Eliana exited the outskirts of Joppa, the smell of the tannery hit her, even from a distance. The Mishnah said a tannery should be located at least 50 cubits from the edge of town, on the east side. The smells generated by the ingredients used to convert animal skins to leather were powerful and foul. It's no surprise that a tannery was classified on the same level as a bathhouse or urinal. A tanner was often compared to a man with boils or someone who collects dog excrement.

Despite the reputation for uncleanliness, Simon the tanner ran a booming company as reflected in his opulent home. It was large enough to house Peter the apostle for the past several years.

Eliana and Asaph now had two children—Eve, almost eight years old, and Jaren, seven years old. They would have liked a larger family, but at their age, two children were two more blessings than they had ever envisioned.

Sveshtari and Keturah had four children over the past nine years, bringing their total to five, while Abel and his wife, Hannah, were expecting their sixth child.

As the tannery odors increased in potency, Eliana placed her sleeve, scented with cinnamon, near her nose.

"Shalom, shalom," said Simon the tanner's wife, Martha, as she met Eliana at the gate. "You couldn't have come at a better time with your perfume. The odors are especially strong today."

Eliana handed the perfume to Martha, who raised it to her nose and took a deep whiff.

"Pleasing is the fragrance of your perfumes; your name is like perfume poured out," Martha said, quoting Solomon's song. "Please. Won't you stay for breakfast?"

Eliana wanted to get away from the tannery as soon as she could, but she didn't want to be rude. Guests rarely lingered at Martha and Simon's house because of the smell, and Eliana didn't want to retreat at the first whiff.

"That would be lovely," she said.

"We can eat in the garden, where the flowers provide some relief."

When they reached the garden, they found Martha's husband, Simon, waiting for them at the table. A tray laden with fruit and bread was set in front of him.

"Before we eat, Eliana, I told Peter that I would bring him his meal," Martha said. "Would you like to join me?"

"I haven't talked to Peter in a long time. I would love it."

Eliana felt a close bond with the Rock, as some called him, because he had cast the devil from her so many years ago near the graveyard at Gergesa. Jesus was her Savior, but Peter had been her savior with a small "s."

"Where is Peter?" Eliana asked.

"On the roof praying." After setting down the juglet of perfume, Martha picked up the tray of food and headed for the staircase leading to the home's second floor and the roof above.

Eliana had always been impressed that Peter would live with the tanner—the epitome of uncleanliness. Their Jewish heritage taught them to shun uncleanliness whenever possible. So, for Peter to lodge with a tanner was miraculous.

When they reached the rooftop, they found Peter on his knees with his eyes firmly shut. A fly landed on his forehead, but the disciple didn't flinch. Impressive concentration.

"Is he asleep?" Eliana whispered.

Martha shrugged. She tried to be as quiet as possible as she laid the tray in front of Peter. As she did, the cup nearly toppled over, but she caught it in time. The movement created enough racket that Peter's eyes popped open.

Backing away, Martha blushed. "I am sorry, Peter, for interrupting you. I should have waited to deliver your food. I am very sorry."

Peter's eyes sharpened, and he smiled warmly. "Do not worry, Martha. I think it was the aroma of the fresh bread that drew me out of my prayer—not any noise you made."

He could smell fresh bread in this environment? That too is impressive.

"I was so hungry that I even had visions of food," Peter said before they could head back down the stairs. "But it was the strangest vision that I've ever had."

Eliana was intrigued. "What did you see?"

"I saw heaven opened and something like a large sheet being let down to earth by its four corners. It contained all kinds of four-footed animals, as well as reptiles and birds. Then a voice told me, 'Get up, Peter. Kill and eat.'"

"Four-footed animals? Reptiles and birds?"

"The most unclean of animals. That's why I told the Lord in my vision, 'Surely not! I have never eaten anything impure or unclean.'"

"What happened next?" Martha asked.

"The voice said, 'Do not call anything impure that God has made clean.' I saw the sheet being let down to earth three times! And each time, the Lord said not to call anything impure that he has made clean."

Maintaining ritual purity was a lifetime pursuit for any devout Jew. But Jesus constantly pushed the boundary by dining with unclean tax collectors and prostitutes. Peter obviously took this message to heart. Why else would he live with an unclean tanner?

Nevertheless, Eliana thought, this was a singularly strange dream. The Lord was asking him to eat at a feast of unclean food!

"Whatever the dream is telling you, the meal we bring you is clean and nourishing and flavorful," Eliana said.

"I am sure it is. Thank you both."

Eliana bowed and turned to descend the stairs. But she hadn't even reached the top stair before Peter halted them with a word.

"Hold on! I think three men are waiting for me at the gate of your house."

"What makes you say that?" Martha asked. "I didn't hear any noise at the gate."

"I didn't hear anything either. But the Spirit told me three people are seeking me."

"Let me go to the front gate to let them in," Eliana said. "You've got your hands full, Martha."

Eliana didn't wait for Martha's agreement. She scurried down the stairs, darted through the courtyard, passed through two more rooms, and finally reached the gate in the stone wall encircling the compound. At this distance, it would have been impossible for Peter to hear anything unless the guests were blowing horns. But Peter said the Spirit told him of their presence.

She had learned never to underestimate the Holy Spirit. Or Peter.

When she opened the gate, she shook her head in flabbergasted amazement. Three men stood on the other side, and one was just preparing to knock.

"Shalom," she said.

"Shalom," said the first man—a distinguished fellow who looked to be in his fifties, around Eliana's age. "We have come to see Peter."

"Welcome, my friends," came Peter's voice from behind. He approached, wiping his hands with a towel. "Come, share my table with me and my friends."

The three men bowed and shuffled into the courtyard, where Simon the tanner awaited. Martha went off to fetch more food and drink.

The youngest of the three men had a difficult time concealing his discomfort while breathing in the air. He scrunched his face as if he had swallowed something sour.

Peter watched the young man struggle for air and smiled. "I'm the one you're looking for. Why have you come?"

The oldest of the three was the spokesman. "We have come from Cornelius the centurion. He is a righteous and God-fearing man, who is respected by all the Jewish people. A holy angel told him to ask you to come to his house so that he could hear what you have to say."

"I would be happy to speak with Cornelius."

The surprises kept coming. Eliana was aware of Cornelius, a God-fearer who lived in Caesarea. But it was still unusual for a strict Jewish believer to cross the threshold of a Gentile's house. Eliana had no problem with it, of course. But Peter, as one of the leaders of the Way, encountered immense pressure to abide by all the Jewish purity laws.

Yet Peter didn't hesitate to accept their offer.

"It is too late to leave today," Peter added. "You are welcome to stay here, and we can head for Caesarea Maritima in the morning."

From the look on youngest man's face, Peter might have just as well invited him to spend the night setting up a tent on a dung heap.

"That is kind of you," said the oldest man. "We will leave in the morning then."

Eliana made her departure from Simon the tanner's house at the first appropriate opportunity after the meal was finished. Martha discreetly paid her for the perfume before Eliana said farewell and headed for home.

With every step from the tanner's home, the air became fresher. She sucked in deep breaths but could still catch whiffs of the tanner's chemicals embedded in her clothing. She put clothes washing on her schedule for the afternoon.

Asaph

Peter invited a half dozen men to join him on the trip to see Cornelius in Caesarea Maritima, with Asaph and Sveshtari among the number. Asaph wasn't certain why Peter wanted them to join him, but he welcomed the break from stonecutting for a few days.

The small band made the trip north from Joppa the next day—a two-day trip by foot. At fifty-five years of age, Asaph had less tolerance for walking eight hours in a day, and he struggled to keep pace with Sveshtari's brisk walk. Sveshtari may be in his thirties, but he remained as vigorous as ever. He had never given up the discipline of a soldier.

After the first day of walking, Asaph's big toe on his right foot developed a blister. By the time they set up camp, night had fallen, so they gathered around the fire for a meal. The night was cool, but the crackling flames made it bearable.

The next morning, after a simple breakfast, they were back on the road—another solid six hours of trudging. It was a clear blue day with the Great Sea stretched out to their left in all its glory. A cool breeze came in from the sea, providing welcome relief.

When they reached the city walls, the road cut through greenery. But before they reached the city gate, they had a preview of the city's opulence when they passed the Roman theatre, lounging just outside the walls. Caesarea was Herod the Great's pride and passion. Herod loved all things Roman, and his goal was to build a sparkling city on the sea that would rival anything in the Roman world—although on a smaller scale than Rome.

To drive home his groveling admiration for Rome, Herod the Great named the city after Caesar.

Asaph tried not to gawk as they passed through the city gates and saw the Temple of Augustus rising in the distance, perched on the edge of the harbor. The city bustled with activity as they moved through the forum and wound their way to the home of Cornelius, a centurion in charge of one hundred soldiers—at least in theory. Most often, centurions led roughly eighty men. Six "centuries" formed a cohort, and ten cohorts made a legion.

"Nice home. Cornelius must make a good living," Asaph whispered to Sveshtari.

"It's more remarkable that this centurion is a follower of Jesus of Nazareth," said Sveshtari.

"I've come to expect remarkable things almost every day."

A man emerged from the house and strode toward Peter. Surely, this had to be Cornelius. He wore ordinary Roman clothing with a distinctive and dramatic blood-red cloak draped down his back. When he reached Peter, this leader of men threw himself on the ground, prostrate.

"Stand up," Peter said urgently, obviously alarmed that anyone would bow before him, least of all a Roman centurion. "I am only a man myself."

Cornelius rose to his feet and turned toward the front door of his house. Everyone else, including Peter, stared at the door as if it were a portal into a new world. In some ways, it was.

Peter looked around. "You are well aware that it is against our law for a Jew to associate with or visit a Gentile."

When Peter paused, Asaph was afraid the visit would end with those blunt, inhospitable words. After an uncomfortable silence, Peter smiled and continued. "But God has shown me that I should not call anyone impure or unclean. So, when I was sent for, I came without raising any objection."

With those words, Peter stepped toward the door, and Cornelius's friends let out a collective sigh of relief. Being a tall man, Peter had to duck as he entered the centurion's home.

"May I ask why you sent for me?" Peter asked once everyone had settled onto cushions around the large table in the center of Cornelius's courtyard.

While servant women brought out fruit, bread, and water, Cornelius explained. "Three days ago, I was in my house praying at this hour, at three in the afternoon. Suddenly, a man in shining clothes stood before me and said, 'Cornelius, God has heard your prayer and remembered your gifts to the poor. Send to Joppa for Simon who is called Peter. He is a guest in the home of Simon the tanner, who lives by the sea.' So I sent for you immediately, and it was good of you to come. Now we are all here in the presence of God to listen to everything the Lord has commanded you to tell us."

Remarkable words spoken in a matter-of-fact way. Cornelius and Peter had been given complementary visions, and yet he described it as if it were as ordinary as biting into one of the apples on the table.

Sveshtari

Sveshtari was shocked when he was asked to join Asaph and the others on the trip to Caesarea. But now he understood why Peter invited him. Sveshtari was a God-fearer like Cornelius. Sveshtari was also a former soldier, tying him to Cornelius in multiple ways.

Since becoming a God-fearer, Sveshtari had gained a greater appreciation for the magnitude of changes that the Way brought to the land. The followers of Jesus broke down barriers between Jews and Samaritans, and now they were doing it between Jews and Gentiles.

Stepping across the threshold of Cornelius's house was a revolutionary act. However, the fire of this revolution was not a fire of destruction, as is often the case with revolutions. It was the fire of a forge where metals are melted and reshaped. It was the fire of creation, not annihilation. Jesus was reshaping a new way of relating to one another.

Still, Sveshtari felt strange sitting among these believers, operating on an equal basis. Out of habit from his time as a bodyguard, he glanced from person to person, continually assessing the safety of the situation. But all he saw were eager expressions as Peter began to speak.

"I now realize how true it is that God does not show favoritism but accepts from every nation the one who fears him and does what is right," Peter began. Again, revolutionary words.

Then he launched into the story of Jesus's ministry in Galilee, his baptism, his crucifixion, and his resurrection. The crowd was mesmerized.

"Jesus commanded us to preach to the people and to testify that he is the one whom God appointed as judge of the living and the dead," Peter declared. "All the prophets testify about him that everyone who believes in him receives forgiveness of sins through his name."

Everyone! That included Gentiles. And that included God-fearers like Cornelius and him.

As Peter continued to speak, Sveshtari suddenly sensed a force piercing his body like a sacred spear. He gasped so loud that the man next to him glanced over to make sure he was all right. Was it just him, or were others sensing the atmosphere in the courtyard? It was like those days when the temperature suddenly drops, and the wind stirs the trees. Everyone can sense it at once.

Sveshtari looked around and realized he wasn't alone in feeling this transformation. Several people closed their eyes and recited silent prayers. One man extended his hands into the air in surrender to the High God. The spiritual tension rose and rose. Souls were awakening. The Lord was being raised like a banner. Yahweh was exalted in their midst. Sveshtari could see the revelation and reflected glory in people's eyes. Even Peter must be sensing something because he stopped to glance around and smile.

Then the glory of God was unleashed into their midst. Several of Cornelius's friends began to pray in foreign languages, their tongues mingling. Sveshtari felt himself ascending the mountain of the Lord.

He began to pour out praises. "The Lord is strong and mighty, mighty in battle! Lift up your heads, you gates. Lift them up, you ancient doors, that the King of glory may come in!"

He began by speaking in Greek, the language of the Gentiles in the room. But then, with the suddenness of a clap, he realized he was no longer speaking Greek. He was speaking another language, a language completely foreign to his mind. And yet he strangely understood the words.

"Where can I go from your Spirit? Where can I flee from your presence? If I go up to the heavens, you are there; if I make my bed in the depths, you are there. If I rise on the wings of the dawn, if I settle on the far side of the sea, even there your hand will guide me, and your right hand will hold me fast."

The courtyard vanished from his senses. He saw himself settling on the far side of the Great Sea, carried by rushing wind and streams of light. Then he saw himself being shaped from the ground like a new Adam.

"For you created my inmost being! You knit me together in my mother's womb. I praise you because I am fearfully and wonderfully made. I was woven together in the depths of the earth. Your eyes saw my unformed body. All the days ordained for me were written in your book before one of them came to be!"

Sveshtari lost track of time. He was lifted—floating and flying. Words leaped from his tongue. In the Spirit, he watched as a Doe of the Dawn bounded into view, springing from the trees. Jesus was that doe, leaping into the world, unspoiled and unexpected. Jesus was the sun, rising at one end of the heavens. Jesus was a voice going out into all the earth, to the ends of the world. Jesus was the bridegroom coming out of his chamber. Jesus was the champion rejoicing to run his course.

Then, time gradually restarted, the praises dwindled, and the courtyard settled back to some kind of normalcy—like when a storm has passed.

Sveshtari opened his eyes and saw everything and everyone with fresh eyes. He had never felt so exalted and yet so humbled by the majesty of his King.

"Surely no one can stand in the way of their being baptized with water," Peter said, motioning to everyone in the room. "They have received the Holy Spirit just as we have."

Peter was referring to the Gentiles. He was referring to the God-fearers. He was referring to Sveshtari! So, they all marched to the shore of the Great Sea, where Gentile after Gentile was lowered beneath the waves.

Sveshtari was one of them. He recalled how he had once hidden beneath the waters of the *mikveh* to escape the men hunting him. But this time, it was the waters of baptism protecting him, saving him, rescuing him. He also recalled how he nearly drowned trying to rescue Eliana from deep waters, but Peter's strong arms had pulled him from the sea.

Once again, the fisherman's strong arms raised Sveshtari from the water. He pulled him from the depths and raised him to the heights.

"I will join you this evening. I need time to think," Sveshtari told Asaph after their time in Cornelius's home had ended.

Asaph put a hand on his shoulder. "You were baptized twice today, weren't you?"

"Yes. Once by fire. The second time by water."

"I am proud of you."

"Proud of me? But I did nothing. The Lord did it all."

"The Lord surely did. But you surrendered to him, and that is doing something."

"Shalom," said Sveshtari, clasping hands with his brother. "I will be back by dinner."

"Take your time. Savor this day."

Sveshtari walked to the shore of the Great Sea, near the hippodrome, where chariot racers would normally blaze around the oval track. But now it was deserted and silent. The sea was turquoise, a precious jewel far more beautiful than Herod's man-made structures jutting into the water.

He put a hand on the knife strapped to his waist. He had lived his life by the knife and the sword. He also assumed that one day, as Jesus said, he would die by the sword.

Sveshtari drew his *pugio* from the golden sheath. He ran his fingers across the flat side of the silver blade. It was smooth and cool to the touch. Unbuckling the sheath from his waist, Sveshtari slid the *pugio* back into its case. Then he flung it into the water, turned, and marched back to the city. He sensed a man following behind, so he turned right at the road near the Temple of Augustus, then made a quick left and another right. The presence continued to follow.

Even more disturbing, he sensed other figures encircling him. As he stopped to examine pottery in the marketplace, he sensed eyes from multiple sides. He had been chased by Herod Antipas's men for many years, but Antipas had been in the grave for a year now. Sveshtari thought he was beyond the reach of any king, except for the King of the Universe.

"That was not wise of you to dispose of your knife, Sveshtari."

The voice was familiar and unwelcome. Sveshtari set down the pottery and turned to see Zuriel. The man carried a *sicarii*, a curved blade—the dagger of choice among Zealots. If Sveshtari wanted to, he could disarm Zuriel in an instant. He had done it before with better trained men than Zuriel.

But Sveshtari had spotted other men with swords drawn. One from the right, one from the left, and a third in front of him. He had a wall at his back, behind the seller's tent. He was hemmed in from all sides.

Sveshtari had often fought successfully against such odds, but when six more men emerged from the crowd, all armed, Sveshtari realized the day was against him—especially considering he was unarmed.

"All who draw the sword will die by the sword," Sveshtari said, again quoting Jesus.

"And all who go around unarmed will die even sooner," Zuriel said. Then he motioned for one of the other men to bind Sveshtari's hands.

II.

The Book of Acts, Chapter 11

Keturah

Keturah and Eliana were putting food on the table when the men came rushing through the door. Asaph led the way, followed by Abel and the others. Keturah paused in her work, expecting Sveshtari to enter behind them any moment.

"Where's Sveshtari? What happened to Sveshtari?"

"He's probably feeding the animals," said Eliana as she poured cups of wine for the men. The house bustled with the energy of children—Eliana and Asaph's two children, Keturah and Sveshtari's five, and Abel and Hannah's six.

Keturah made a beeline for Asaph.

"Where is he?"

When Asaph didn't immediately respond with assurances, Keturah's mouth went dry and her heart raced.

Asaph motioned toward the table of children. "Eliana, will you watch the children while I talk with Keturah?"

Keturah's legs went weak.

"I can keep an eye on the children," Babette said to Eliana. Babette was ten and a half years old and wise beyond her years.

"Thank you, Babette," said Eliana, linking arms with Keturah to prop her up. They headed for the courtyard, away from the noise.

When they reached the well in the center of the courtyard, Keturah couldn't hold in her words any longer. "Where is Sveshtari?" she asked as she settled down on a bench. "Why didn't he return from Caesarea with you?"

Asaph still wouldn't make eye contact! What was he hiding?

"Sveshtari was captured by Zuriel and his men." He spoke softly, as if afraid to say such words aloud.

"Zuriel?" Eliana leaped to her feet. "I thought that jackal was out of our lives! What right does he have to arrest Sveshtari?"

"Zuriel is the head of a group of thieves and rebels. He also holds grudges. He remembers every slight in his life."

"You mean he has not forgotten what Sveshtari did to him in Sebaste?" Keturah asked.

"He'll never forget the humiliation."

"But why did you return home without freeing him from Zuriel?" Keturah's panic rapidly turned to anger. "If you had been the one captured, Sveshtari would not rest until he freed you."

"It is more complicated than that."

"How can it be more complicated?" Keturah's voice rose. Realizing the children might hear, she repeated her question more softly. "How can it be more complicated?"

"Sveshtari was sold to a *ludus*."

A *ludus*. A gladiator school.

"Then break him out."

"That takes planning. And time."

"If he's being forced into gladiator contests, he may not have time."

Asaph didn't argue that point.

Sveshtari: Caesarea Maritima

The gladiator trainer, Marius, glared at Sveshtari with a practiced intensity. Marius, his head completely shaved, had a thick neck and sizable biceps shown off by his leather vest.

Sveshtari was not impressed. He had seen better displays of masculine might during his training as a bodyguard and soldier.

"What god do you follow?" Marius said.

"The one true God of Israel and his son, Jesus Christ."

Marius's glare transformed into a dumfounded stare. "I have heard of fools who follow a fisherman from Galilee. You're one of them?"

That did not deserve a response. Sveshtari stared back at him.

Marius circled him like a tiger. He spit to the side to emphasize his disdain. "If you follow a fisherman, you shall be a fisherman. You shall be a *retiarius.*"

Marius smiled, probably figuring this assignment would be a punch to the gut for Sveshtari. The *retiarius* was the lowest of gladiators, entering the arena with the least amount of protection. He wore no helmet and no armor, except a *galerus*, a metal guard worn on one shoulder, and a *manica* that protected his left arm only. In addition to this minimal amount of armor, he would wear a light tunic.

The weapons of a *retiarius* were a fishing net, trident, and dagger—ironic choices since snaring Zuriel in a net landed him in this predicament. His opponent would be a *secutor*, a heavily armed gladiator who represented a fish. The *secutor's* armor displayed what looked like scales, and his helmet had a crest resembling a fin. He also carried a large shield and deadly *gladius* sword.

"The Lord is my shield," Sveshtari said, crossing his arms.

In a blur of motion, the instructor snapped his whip at Sveshtari, biting his shoulder and leaving a thin red line. Sveshtari barely moved a muscle.

Marius nodded and smiled. “You appear to have some training in pain control. You will need it. Dismissed.”

Giving a slight bow, Sveshtari turned and walked away from the teacher, looking to his right and his left for ways to break out of this cage. His shoulder stung like fire.

Eliana

Eliana volunteered to take care of Keturah’s brood while her friend traveled to Caesarea in the hopes of seeing her husband. For protection, Keturah would be accompanied by Asaph and Abel.

Eliana embraced Keturah. “I will pray for you three times a day.”

“Pray for Sveshtari as well. He will need it more than me.”

Then Eliana gave her a blessing for the road: “I lift up my eyes to the mountains—where does my help come from? My help comes from the Lord, the Maker of heaven and earth.”

When Keturah, Asaph, and Abel had left, Eliana returned to the house, where Babette stood in the door. Eliana marveled at Keturah’s oldest, who had been plucked from the ash heap as a baby. Babette had been discarded by the *pater familias*, but the Lord was her new *pater familias*. He would never discard a life as callously as a Roman father.

Babette was a serious young girl, old beyond her years. And as the oldest among the children, she was like a second mother. She was responsible, hard-working, and stoic like her father—even though Sveshtari was not her biological abba.

With her mother on the road to Caesarea, Babette looked more serious than ever.

"Will my ima come back?" she asked.

"Oh yes, Babette, oh yes, she will be back as soon as she can." Eliana rushed to Babette and wrapped her in a warm, motherly hug. She stroked Babette's long black hair. Babette wasn't crying. She rarely showed tears, but she had to be crumbling inside.

"What if they kill her? What if they kill my father?"

Eliana pulled away to look Babette in the eyes. "The Lord will protect her. The Lord will also protect your abba."

"Will he *promise* to protect them?"

It wasn't lost on Eliana that Babette's name meant "God's promise."

"We can ask him to do so, Babette." Then Eliana recited her second prayer of protection of the morning: "He will cover you with his feathers, and under his wings you will find refuge; his faithfulness will be your shield and rampart. You will not fear the terror of night, nor the arrow that flies by day, nor the pestilence that stalks in the darkness, nor the plague that destroys at midday."

"Thank you," Babette whispered, glancing back at the door of their house. On the other side of the door, the other children swarmed. Their voices—happy voices—increased in volume. Babette made a move for the door. "I must make sure they don't break anything."

Always the responsible one.

"I will help you, Babette." In more ways than one, Eliana would try her hardest to help this girl.

Eliana hadn't been there when Keturah found Babette, a squalling baby on a trash pile. But Keturah had described the scene many times. Babette was only a baby when Keturah saved her, but the sense of rejection, the sense of being discarded by her biological father, the sense of being no better than something you toss on a trash pile, must have become imprinted in some fashion. Now, the abduction of her adoptive father and departure of her mother must be bringing those feelings to the surface.

But Babette's stoicism and Eliana's words of comfort could go only so far. Babette needed the Lord's wings. His wings were holy and healing.

Eliana heard the breaking of pottery on the other side of the door. She rushed inside because Babette would need her help with the children. She couldn't do it alone.

Sveshtari

Sveshtari stood in the practice arena, holding the net in his left hand and the three-pronged trident in his right. The contrast in armor with his opponent was astonishing. Most of Sveshtari's body was fair game. But what he lacked in protection, he could make up for in agility.

It was ironic that Sveshtari had tossed away his dagger just before being captured and thrown into the life of a gladiator. He did not want to be a killer. He was tired of shedding blood, for he had been baptized in the blood of Jesus. But at least he wouldn't be expected to kill in a practice arena. Marius could not afford to see his men killed when it didn't count.

"Show me what you can do," Marius said. "And if you can't perform, don't worry. Your death will be swift."

Did Marius mean what he said, or was he trying to inject the fear of the gods in him? Was he willing to let him be killed in practice if he didn't perform? In this early test of his skills, maybe Sveshtari didn't have immunity after all. With that ominous thought rattling around in his brain, the contest began.

The *secutor* rushed at Sveshtari because he was at an advantage in close combat. A trident was useless unless you stood at a distance. But Sveshtari, nimble and unencumbered by armor, spun out of the way, danced around the disoriented *secutor*, and flung out his net.

The *secutor*, partially blind because of his helmet, thrashed in the net like a helpless fish. The fin-like crest on his helmet was designed to cut through netting, but Sveshtari was too quick for it to be put to use. He tightened the snare and yanked it, pulling the fighter off his feet. The gladiator hit the ground with a rattling thud. Sveshtari placed a foot on his chest and aimed his trident at his neck.

It was over in less than a minute.

Marius rushed in to break up the contest. He probably feared that Sveshtari might finish off one of his fighters, but he needn't worry. Sveshtari was done with killing.

The *secutor* fought his way out of the net and clambered awkwardly to his feet. Sveshtari couldn't see his face, but he could imagine a mixture of embarrassment and rage.

"You have obviously used a net before," Marius said. "Why didn't you tell me?"

"You never asked."

"Did you ever fight in the arena?"

"No, but I was always fascinated by the net-men when my father took me to witness gladiator spectacles growing up. I learned how to use the net while I trained as a Thracian soldier."

Marius smiled. "You were a Thracian soldier? Why didn't you say something sooner?"

Suddenly, Marius was Sveshtari's best friend, slapping an arm around his shoulder. "Can you show me your skills against two more of my *secutores*? Just to be certain this wasn't a fluke."

"Bring them on."

"And do not worry. They will be under orders not to kill you—although if you perform the way you just did, they may not get the chance to harm you."

Marius called out his next *secutor*, while Sveshtari readied for action. He hadn't expended too much energy in the first, brief battle. He had plenty of reserve.

Keturah

Keturah was horrified to learn that Sveshtari was one of the *damnati*—men who were forced to become gladiators for a crime they committed. But at least he was not a *damnati ad gladium*, which would've meant he was condemned to die in the arena.

Sveshtari was a *damnati ad ludos*, which meant he was given a fighting chance. Some *damnati ad ludos* even went on to become veterans—men who had survived one or more fights. The odds of being killed in the ring were roughly one in ten. Not the greatest of odds, but Keturah trusted in Sveshtari's survival skills. If anyone might be that "one in ten," it was her husband.

However, as a *damnati*, Sveshtari was locked up in a cell. Keturah had to run a gauntlet of stares as a slave escorted her to the cages. The gladiators stopped what they were doing to feast on her with their eyes. Every single one of them stared.

She passed through a courtyard and entered the section where the *damnati* were imprisoned. Men reached at her through the bars like ghouls. Finally, she reached Sveshtari's cell, which he shared with a variety of unpleasant creatures.

"Keturah," Sveshtari hissed. "What are you doing here?"

"I had to see with my own eyes if it was true—that you had been arrested and forced into the arena."

"Is this your mistress, net-man?" came a voice from one of the men sharing the cell.

"Mind your own business," Sveshtari snarled. Then he turned back to Keturah. "You have seen me, so please go back to Joppa, where you are safe."

"I had to make sure you were alive."

"He's alive—for now!" came the same voice.

Sveshtari pounced, slamming the man against the cold, wet wall. "*You* may not be alive for much longer if you don't keep your mouth shut!"

"I'm just having a little fun." The man put up his hands in surrender and smiled. Then he turned to Keturah and said, "Your consort, Sveshtari, is proving quite good with the net, so you needn't worry about him."

"He is my *husband*," Keturah corrected. Sweat slickened her forehead as she turned her gaze on Sveshtari. "You are a net-man? But that is a dangerous role."

"As he said, I am good with the net. I will survive." Then he whispered, "And I will leave this life and return to you."

"But how? You are condemned for life."

"I have managed before. I will again. So, please return to Joppa."

"I will. Soon."

"Soon? But who is taking care of the children?"

"Eliana and Hannah. The children are in good hands." She studied the jail conditions. There were several buckets for human waste, but otherwise the cell was relatively clean. The *lanista* knew the value of a gladiator and had incentive to keep them healthy.

"Who came with you to Caesarea? Who is your covering?"

"Asaph and Abel."

Sveshtari let out a soft growl.

"But do not blame them for my being here. It was my decision. If they had not agreed to chaperone me, I would have come alone."

"Then give them my thanks."

Keturah could tell that Sveshtari was humiliated to be seen in a prison. She hoped her presence would not distract him from his primary job—staying alive.

"Time is almost up," said the slave, who stood at a distance, observing their interaction.

Sveshtari reached through the bars to take Keturah's hands. "Stay safe."

"Stay alive."

"Though an army besiege me, my heart will not fear," Sveshtari answered. "Though war break out against me, even then I will be confident."

"I love you, Sveshtari."

"I love you."

Once, Keturah had been prepared to kill this man—to drive a knife into his chest. Now, she stared into the abyss of separation.

The slave drew her away. Her last image of Sveshtari was of him staring back at her, his hands clutching the bars as if he wanted to yank them apart like Samson.

Sveshtari

The animals went first. Two elephants strode into the arena to lead off the *pompa*, the parade to begin the day of bloodletting. Then came three ostriches strutting across the sand. Two tigers followed, rolled out in cages, and they clawed at the bars as they snarled.

Jugglers played with fire, while a pair of clowns ran around the arena. One of them pretended to get his head stuck in the tiger's cage, while the other one tried to pull him out. The clown's head was yanked out of the cage just in time before the animal could remove it from his shoulders. Then the two clowns fell backward into a heap and began to argue and fight with wooden swords.

At last, Sveshtari and the other gladiators strode into the arena, and the crowd rose to its feet as one and roared. Caesarea's arena was nothing like what you would find in Rome, but it was packed, and the sound was all-encompassing. The gladiators held up their swords and bellowed cries of triumph. Sveshtari did not. He wasn't a performing animal—or a clown. He was determined to maintain his dignity.

As Sveshtari and the other gladiators filed out of sight, slaves used miniature catapults to fire wooden balls into the frenzied crowd. Spectators fought over the balls, which carried inscriptions on them, indicating what prize the person had just won. The prizes ranged from a broken sandal to a new house.

Sveshtari was scheduled for the fourth fight of the morning. While he waited in the wings, he heard the shouts of "*Iugala! Iugala!* Kill! Kill!" Peering out on the arena, he saw the losing gladiator on his knees, waiting for the sword to be driven through his bent neck.

After the body had been dragged away and the bloody sand raked, it was time. Sveshtari strode into the arena with his net, trident, and knife. Unlike his opponent, he had no helmet, so the crowd could look him in the eyes.

"Galilean! Galilean!" the crowd chanted. The *lanista* had given him that name as a title of mockery, but Sveshtari embraced it. He held up his trident in salute, and the crowd roared their approval.

Keturah

"Are you sure you want to see this?" Abel asked.

"I am sure." Keturah was determined to watch. They sat near the top rows of the arena, giving them a good view of the gladiators. If Sveshtari were killed, she wanted to be there, to experience it with him. If she couldn't be by his side, this would have to do.

"Does Sveshtari know you are here?" Asaph asked.

"I left him with the impression I was returning to Joppa. I was afraid he'd try to discourage me from coming."

"He surely would have," said Abel.

"I also didn't want my presence to be a distraction. He needs complete focus to live."

"After his combat, we shall leave for Joppa." Asaph spoke as if this plan was non-negotiable.

Keturah nodded her agreement. She didn't tell him that if Sveshtari survived, she planned to take her children and move to Caesarea. She couldn't bear the distance between them, especially when his life hung in the balance.

"My father was not a faithful Jew, so he often took me to see gladiators," Abel said to Asaph. "I take it you never went to the games."

Asaph shook his head. "Not true. When I was a tax collector, I emulated all things Roman, so I went to the games as often as I could. But since becoming a follower of Jesus, I have come to see the pointless cruelty."

"But there *is* a point to it," Keturah interjected

Asaph and Abel stared at her as if they couldn't believe her words.

"People seek blood. It satisfies a deep craving to make others bleed." Keturah knew this intimately. At one time, she craved the idea of making

Sveshtari bleed for his sins against her. "But Jesus shed his blood for us, so we no longer have a need to make others bleed."

"You speak truth," said Abel. "Jesus was our gladiator, dying in an arena as big as the world."

"When Jesus died, Eliana was determined to be a witness to his crucifixion. So, I am determined to be a witness to Sveshtari's fate in the arena."

Keturah was going to say "Sveshtari's crucifixion," but she didn't want to even speak the word. Keturah wasn't ready for Sveshtari to be taken from her, especially in such a bloody way.

Suddenly, the crowd rose in unison. The fight was about to begin.

Sveshtari

The *secutor* didn't go after Sveshtari from the opening signal of the battle as his other opponents had done in the practice arena. Word must have gotten around that Sveshtari dominated his opponents when they tried to attack him from the get-go. He would nimbly dodge their attacks and tangle them in his net within the first few minutes.

So, this *secutor* held back, biding his time, short sword in his right hand.

A good *retiarius* could hurl a net with accuracy from a long distance—and Sveshtari had confidence he could do that. But that approach gave his opponent time to react to the net flying through the air. Therefore, Sveshtari would wait for the *secutor* to come to him. *Secutor* meant "the chaser," so he would wait for the chase to begin.

Sveshtari had only one try with his net. Once the net was thrown, it couldn't be retrieved and used a second time. He didn't want to squander his one opportunity.

Sveshtari also didn't want to be too predictable, so he went on the offensive. Using his long trident, he jabbed the *secutor* in the helmet, stunning him momentarily. He made a move to go for his helmet a second time, but the *secutor* raised his shield to deflect the stab—just as Sveshtari hoped he would.

The second jab to the helmet was a feint. Quickly, Sveshtari lowered his trident and swiped behind the ankle of the secutor's front foot, tripping him up. The gladiator fell backward, slamming into the ground. The next second, he was hopelessly tangled in the net, and Sveshtari had his foot on the man's sword hand. He placed his trident at the exposed spot of his neck.

The crowd roared, "Galilean! Galilean!"

As the chant swept over him, Sveshtari prayed that the crowd would chant, "*Mitte, mitte!* Let him go! Let him go!" He didn't want to kill this man. He didn't want to kill *anyone*. He had washed his hands of blood.

His heart sank when they began to bellow, "Kill! Kill! Kill!"

"Lord, help me," he said aloud.

While keeping the trident at the defeated man's neck, he kicked away the *secutor's* sword.

"Kill! Kill! Kill!"

The crowd was waiting. The people had paid good money to see blood spilled. Who knew what the *lanista* would do to him if he didn't finish off his victim.

Even the victim was waiting. He had stopped thrashing in the net and stared up at Sveshtari, waiting for the verdict. Sveshtari could not see the man's entire face, but he could see his eyes. The eyes did not plead for him to spare his life. They were direct and unblinking. Challenging him. Daring him to defy the crowd.

Suddenly, a wind rose up in the arena. It came out of the west as abruptly as the windstorms on the Sea of Galilee. The wind began slowly with a gentle tugging on the robes of spectators. But moment by moment, it picked up velocity, and the crowd looked at the sky for signs of an imminent dust storm. Then the soil of the arena began to move, rising into the air. Levitating.

Sveshtari kept his trident aimed at his victim's neck as he too looked around at the flying dust. The air took on a yellowish tint. Then, on the far side of the arena, the dust began to take the shape of a dust devil—a miniature column of swirling dust. The crowd went silent. They must've been wondering, *Was this the work of the gods?*

The dust devil moved across the arena in the direction of Sveshtari as if it were another one of his opponents. The very soil of the arena was challenging Sveshtari to combat. Sveshtari removed his foot from his defeated opponent's chest. Then he picked up his opponent's sword and marched directly for the dust devil. The spinning column of soil expanded in size, threatening him as any gladiator would.

What do I do? Sveshtari wondered. *How do I fight a dust devil? How do I fight any sort of devil?*

Sveshtari knew he had to do something. The crowd was expecting it. He glanced around at the audience. The people were pointing, and some were standing, craning their necks.

Do something! *Anything!*

The dust devil came at him with increased speed. So, Sveshtari did what came naturally when attacked. He slashed at the personified wind. To his shock, the dust devil collapsed like a fallen man. The wind continued, but the dust devil vanished just as quickly as it had appeared.

The crowd exploded. "Galilean! Galilean! Galilean!"

Stunned, Sveshtari saluted the crowd, tossed aside the sword, and exited the arena to the everlasting chant of his name.

Keturah

"Did you see that?" Keturah shouted to Asaph and Abel. "The Lord sent a mighty wind!"

It was true. The Lord had fashioned an opponent out of the dust, a sparring partner, and Sveshtari had cut it down to the delight of the crowd.

Keturah stepped into the aisle and hurried down the stone steps. She hoped to catch Sveshtari's eye before he disappeared into the bowels of the hippodrome. But by the time she reached the arena level, Sveshtari had already saluted the crowd, cast aside his sword, and marched out of sight.

She paused to take in the sights and sounds. People were still on their feet, applauding what they had seen. She heard the word "miracle" spoken at least three times.

"Did you see that?" she cried again when Asaph and Abel appeared at her side.

"How could we not?" Abel said. "The wind came out of nowhere, and now it's gone."

"Come," Asaph said, drawing her toward the exit. "You're going to get crushed by the crowd, Keturah. It's time to leave."

With such divine protection, Keturah suddenly had confidence that Sveshtari might survive in the arena. Some gladiators lived to see old age. And after seeing the miracle, Keturah had faith that her husband might just be one of them.

Sveshtari

When Sveshtari exited the arena, the *secutor*, the man whose life he had spared, was waiting for him. The *secutor* removed his helmet, his eyes full of surprise.

"How did you do that? How did you conjure a dust devil?"

Sveshtari grinned. "I did nothing of the kind. The Lord gave me another opponent to kill because he did not wish for me to kill you."

Other gladiators pressed in close to hear the two opponents talk.

"At first, I thought you were a coward when you hesitated to kill me. I was almost tempted to do the job for you. But then that wind . . . "

Another gladiator spoke up. "I was in Jerusalem when the sound of a powerful wind roared through the streets, and the followers of the Way began to speak in foreign languages. Can you speak in other languages, Galilean?"

Sveshtari shrugged. "Only when the Spirit speaks through me."

Then two soldiers took knees before Sveshtari as if he were a god. Sveshtari was taken aback and a bit afraid. Would the Lord strike him down for inspiring such idolatry? He pulled one of them back to his feet.

"Do not worship a mere mortal. Those who run after other gods will suffer."

By this time, the *lanista*, Marius, had fought his way through the men packed around Sveshtari.

"That was remarkable, Galilean." Marius gripped both of Sveshtari's shoulders and shook him in celebration. His eyes gleamed. "Can you do it again?"

"You should ask whether God will do it again. I cannot speak for the Almighty."

Marius slapped an arm around his shoulder, while others formed a path through the crowd. "I must confess that you infuriated me when you hesitated to kill your defeated opponent. I was already thinking of ways to have you killed in the arena as punishment. I was leaning toward using tigers. But then . . . "

Marius stopped to look him in the eyes. "But then that wind! That power! People will be talking about you for weeks! People will flock to see your next fight!"

Marius broke into laughter. Already, the trainer was probably calculating how much money Sveshtari could make for him.

"Showing mercy could be the thing that sets you apart, Sveshtari. It will sell tickets."

"Mercy is what I was taught by Jesus of Nazareth."

"That's good! Normally, the crowd hates a merciful gladiator. But you! After word gets out about the miracle, I think they might accept it from you! They might even come to expect it."

"Blessed are the merciful, for they shall obtain mercy."

"What a great line! In your next fight, shout those words. Do it!"

Sveshtari couldn't believe his ears. He was being asked to preach the Gospel in the arena? Although Marius probably didn't know he was quoting Jesus, he was being asked to bring the words of the Prince of Peace into the most blood-soaked building in the Empire.

That was the true miracle.

The *lanista* slapped his shoulder. "But, of course, Sveshtari, you will have to win before you can show mercy. If you ever lose, you're a dead man."

Sveshtari understood, but he had no fear. The Lord knew what to do with dead men.

Nekoda: Jerusalem, Eight Months Later, Month of Iyyar (Early May) 41 A.D.

Nekoda couldn't put it off forever. It had to happen eventually. He returned to Jerusalem for the first time in eight years.

People in Jerusalem had heard about his conversion, thanks to his older son, Hiram, who spread the news far and wide. If a son could disown a father, Hiram would have done it long ago.

"What do you think Hiram told people to explain my conversion?" Nekoda asked Ezra as they approached the Damascus Gate on the northwestern side of Jerusalem.

"I fear he has told people you have gone mad."

Two towers flanked the gate on either side. One tower had been rebuilt, but the one on the east side of the gate was crumbling and in dire need of repair. For Nekoda, the two towers were picture-perfect representations of his relationships with his two sons. One relationship was healthy and strong. The other was crumbling to dust. He wondered if it was beyond repair.

After passing through the Damascus Gate, they were immersed in a bustling marketplace. Memories flooded back, some good but many bad. The last time he lived in Jerusalem, he was a powerful person. He was a persecutor—or at least he sided with the persecutors.

Now, he might very well become the target of persecution by the new ruler of Judea—Herod Agrippa I, the grandson of Herod the Great. When Gaius, also known as Caligula, became the Roman emperor, he gave his friend Agrippa the tetrarchies once ruled by Philip and Lysanias. Then, three years ago, Agrippa was handed the tetrarchy of Herod Antipas, his uncle who had been sent into exile.

Agrippa carried the name "Herod," and nothing good ever came from someone with that name. Even in Damascus, Nekoda had heard stories of fresh persecutions breaking out against the followers of Jesus in Jerusalem.

So why walk back into a hornet's nest? Nekoda asked himself that question every step along the road to Jerusalem. He still had extended family in the city, and he wanted to tell them about his conversion to their faces.

"Is it worth the risk?" Ezra asked as their donkeys plodded down an empty street.

"If Saul can be bold in the name of Jesus, so can I."

After Saul escaped from Damascus, the apostle had returned to Jerusalem straightaway, causing a stir. In fact, when he first tried to join the disciples, they were terrified of him. They thought it was a trick. But Barnabas smoothed the path, much the way that Ananias did for Saul in Damascus.

"I have to hand it to Saul," said Ezra. "When he returned to Jerusalem, he preached so courageously that many wanted to kill him. To protect him, the believers sent Saul to Caesarea and put him on a ship to Tarsus. If you are threatened, I hope you will be willing to leave the city."

"We shall see."

Dismounting from their donkeys, Nekoda and Ezra moved into the wealthier Upper City. His older son had taken over his home years ago, so he thought he would start there.

"You have a lot of nerve showing your face in Jerusalem." These harsh words erupted from his right. He recognized the voice immediately. It was Obed, one of the most prominent Sadducees in the city.

"Shalom to you, my friend."

"Shalom? You, a traitor to our people, dare to say shalom to me?"

Obed stood only an arm's length away. He was shorter and older than Nekoda—not a formidable figure. But, like a small dog trying to act twice its size, Obed struck an aggressive pose, both hands clenched.

"Peace, brother," Nekoda said, extending his right hand like an olive branch. "Why do you call me a traitor to our people?"

Obed waved his hands in anger. "You follow the blasphemers!"

Nekoda folded his arms across his chest. "Which ones?"

"The followers of the Nazarene! Peter! James! And Saul!"

"Why wouldn't I follow Saul? I was on the road to Damascus when he had his vision of Jesus Christ."

"Those are false words!"

Ezra had stood by quietly, but no longer. "You cannot silence the Gospel of Jesus," he said. "If you try to quiet us, the stones will cry out."

By this time, a small crowd had clustered around them, like schoolchildren hoping for a fight.

Obed eyed the stones scattered at his feet. "The stones will cry out all right. They will cry out as we hurl them against your skull."

"Like you did to Stephen?" Ezra asked.

"Yes, *exactly* as we did to Stephen!"

Another man tried to act as peacemaker, stepping in front of Obed and holding him back by placing his hands against his chest. But Obed wasn't done. He pointed at Nekoda, then moved his finger toward Ezra.

"Do you dare claim that Jesus Christ rose from the dead?"

"I believe it because the tomb was empty," Nekoda said. "I believe it because the living Christ appeared to us on the road to Damascus. I believe it because I saw the bright light! What else could explain Saul's sudden transformation? I was there! He was changed in an instant."

"You lie!"

Ezra tossed up his hands in dismissal. "Let us leave, Abba. This man is a fool."

"I warn you: Do not return to your home, Nekoda!" Obed shouted as the father and son kept moving down the street. "Your family has disowned you!"

As they made their way uphill along the street, a stranger slipped beside them. *What now?* Nekoda thought.

"Shalom, Nekoda and Ezra."

"Do we know you?" Nekoda asked.

"No, but Saul told us about you. When I heard your name being shouted by that man, I realized the Lord had put me in your path."

Nekoda and Ezra stopped to hear more. "Do you follow the Way?"

"Yes. My name is Shelach, and that man tells the truth. I do not think you will be welcome in your old home. But if you follow me, I can take you where you are welcome—and safe."

"Show us the way."

Shelach motioned them forward and turned left onto a narrow, dusty street. "Peter has just returned from Caesarea. You are not going to believe what happened to him there."

"After all I've experienced, I will believe it," Nekoda said. "Lead on."

As they followed Shelach, Nekoda couldn't shake the sense that people in the shops they passed were glaring at them and muttering. Word of their arrival was spreading, reaching the ears of friends and foes.

Judging by the expressions on people's faces, he counted more foes than friends.

Shelach led them to a large home, owned by one of the wealthier followers of Jesus. When they entered, they were greeted by welcoming expressions—a far cry from the greetings they had received in the streets. Nekoda felt safe, like coming in from a storm. However, as he approached the courtyard, he sensed a growing tension within this home. Many people were crowded into the courtyard with Peter standing in the center. Nekoda and Ezra seemed to have arrived in the middle of a heated discussion.

"You went into the house of uncircumcised men and ate with them," one of the men said to Peter. He wasn't openly angry, but there was a tightness in his voice.

This is intriguing, Nekoda thought as he and Ezra found their seats. After being around Saul for so long, he was used to crossing the Gentile/Jew barrier. Saul had taken the Gospel to everyone, Samaritan and Gentile alike. But Peter? Had he done the same?

As Peter began to explain himself, Nekoda noticed a couple of Sadducees slip into the house and stand toward the back of the courtyard. They tried to remain inconspicuous, but heads turned and spotted them. Even Peter seemed to notice.

Nevertheless, the apostle proceeded with his story.

"I was in the city of Joppa praying, and in a trance, I saw a vision. I saw something like a large sheet being let down from heaven by its four corners, and it came down to where I was," Peter said. "I looked into it and saw four-footed animals of the earth, wild beasts, reptiles and birds. Then I heard a voice telling me, 'Get up, Peter. Kill and eat.'"

Several people gasped.

Peter smiled. "That is exactly how I responded. I replied to the voice, 'Surely not, Lord! Nothing impure or unclean has ever entered my mouth.' The voice spoke from heaven a second time, 'Do not call anything impure that God has made clean.' This happened three times, and then it was all pulled up to heaven again."

"How do you know it was the voice of the Lord?" one person asked.

"Because right then three men who had been sent to me from Caesarea stopped at the house where I was staying. The Spirit told me to have no hesitation about going with them. Six brothers also went with me, and we entered the man's house. He told us how he had seen an angel appear in his house and say, 'Send to Joppa for Simon who is called Peter. He will bring you a message through which you and all your household will be saved.'

"As I began to speak, the Holy Spirit came on them as he had come on us at the beginning. Then I remembered what the Lord had said: 'John baptized with water, but you will be baptized with the Holy Spirit.' So if God gave them the same gift he gave us who believed in the Lord Jesus Christ, who was I to think that I could stand in God's way?"

The crowd went stone-cold quiet as they soaked in these words, absorbing their revolutionary meaning. The followers of Jesus in Jerusalem clearly didn't have the same open attitude about taking the Gospel to the unclean Gentiles. Several leaders began to challenge Peter. But their words faded from Nekoda's attention, for he was experiencing something odd and terrifying. A surge of energy rose from his feet, flashing up his spine like lightning. He felt the urge to pray out loud. Initially, he tried to hold back, but the desire to speak grew and burned. Suddenly, he began to speak aloud the words of Isaiah.

"Listen to me, you islands; hear this, you distant nations: Before I was born the Lord called me; from my mother's womb he has spoken my name. He made my mouth like a sharpened sword, in the shadow of his hand he hid me; he made me into a polished arrow and concealed me in his quiver!"

The men arguing with Peter went quiet as heads turned in his direction. Anyone who understood Isaiah knew those words spoke of the Messiah. The Chosen One was the polished arrow in God's quiver, fired into the world like a flaming arrow.

The words of Isaiah continued to flow—words about the Messiah, words about Jesus.

"I will also make you a light for the Gentiles, that my salvation may reach to the ends of the earth!"

A light for the Gentiles?

How could people hear those words from Isaiah and not realize the Lord's Master Plan? God chose the Jews as his people, but that was just a seed, just a beginning. The Lord wanted the tree to extend its branches to every corner of the world, providing shade to the entire world, not just to the Jews. Everyone, Jews and Gentiles, were called back to the Tree of Life, which grew in the soil of Eden. Jesus was the Second Adam. He was our second chance. He was bringing salvation to all who believe!

Those words, Isaiah's words, were like a bursting dam. The people in the courtyard, men and women, began to sing and pray and rejoice. A couple of men even danced in the corner. Then the wind picked up, entering the courtyard door and spinning the dust and flapping the fabric of their robes.

A woman began to sing words of Isaiah: "I say to the captives, 'Come out,' and to those in darkness, 'Be free!' They will feed beside the roads and find pasture on every barren hill. They will neither hunger nor thirst, nor will the desert heat or the sun beat down on them. He who has compassion on them will guide them and lead them beside springs of water."

"Shout for joy, you heavens," Ezra sang, putting an arm around his father's shoulder and raising his other hand. "Rejoice, you earth; burst into song, you mountains!"

Nekoda didn't know how long they sang and prayed. It seemed like it had been only a moment, but judging by the angle of the sun, it had lasted a long time. When the praying and singing finally trickled to an end, Nekoda noticed that the two Sadducees were gone. They were probably reporting back to the authorities and alerting Herod Agrippa about what they had witnessed.

Agrippa would not sit idly by as the Holy Spirit turned the city upside down. He would draw his sword. His judgment would be swift and severe.

12.

The Book of Acts, Chapter 12

Eliana: Caesarea Maritima, Three Years Later, Month of Tammuz (Late June), 44 A.D.

It made Eliana sick entering the hippodrome in Caesarea Maritima, but she did it for her friend. Keturah had been by Eliana's side every bloody step of the way through the scourging and crucifixion of Jesus, even though Keturah didn't believe in the Messiah at the time. The least Eliana could do was be with Keturah as she suffered through the dangers that Sveshtari faced in the gladiator arena.

Three years ago, Asaph and Eliana had moved their family from Joppa to Caesarea to be with Keturah and her children. Sveshtari had survived four years as a gladiator—an incredible feat. He had also earned a massive following as the Galilean. The whirlwind that appeared during his first fight in the arena was just one of several miracles that punctuated his performances.

Whenever these miracles occurred, Keturah said the Holy Spirit was behind them, and Eliana believed it. It seemed as if every believer she knew had been touched by the Spirit at some point.

"How can you go to these games?" a neighbor asked one morning while Eliana was preparing to join Keturah at the arena.

"How can I not? Keturah is my friend."

"The Talmud says that anyone who attends the games is a shedder of blood."

Eliana had heard this argument many times. If you attend the games, you are responsible for what happens in the arena.

She knew her answer by heart. "But Rabbi Nathan says we are allowed to go to the games to lend our voices to save lives."

Whenever a gladiator is defeated, it's often the volume of the crowd's voices that determines whether he will live or die. Eliana and Keturah shouted in favor of life, but they usually didn't get their way. They were drowned out by those who sought blood, not mercy. Whenever that happened, it brought back memories of how they shouted for Jesus to be freed, while most of the crowd called for his crucifixion.

"Good morning, Keturah," Eliana said as she and Asaph entered her friend's home, which was next door to their house in Caesarea. They brought along their children because Babette would be in charge of watching them. She was already becoming a tall beauty at the age of fourteen.

"Morning," Keturah said. "But I wouldn't call it 'good.'"

Eliana nodded. "You are right. There is nothing good about this morning."

Keturah made it clear that she didn't want to talk as they trudged toward Herod's hippodrome, a magnificent U-shaped structure built on the edge of the aqua-blue Great Sea. Caesarea was the gemstone city of Herod the Great, grandfather of the current King Agrippa I.

Herod the Great was long dead. But in his day, he once tried to hold gladiatorial games in Jerusalem, and the Jewish population would not stand for it. So, he settled for Roman-style spectacles in Caesarea on the edge of the most beautiful water in the world. The proximity between beauty and death was unnerving.

They entered through the north gate and walked into a wall of noise. The hippodrome could seat 10,000, and the place was already at capacity. Many came early for the chariot races, which were run in the long, oval-shaped arena. The hippodrome doubled as a fighting ground for gladiators.

The sky was as blue as the water, a picture-perfect setting for some of the ugliest violence you could imagine. A slight breeze picked up the light brown dust, but Eliana saw no signs of the whirlwind.

The stadium was always packed on days when Sveshtari the Galilean fought. People came looking for a miracle.

So did Keturah, Eliana, and Asaph.

Nekoda: Jerusalem

James, the brother of John, was in fine form. The room in Benjamin's house was packed with people standing along the walls, sitting on the floor, and gathered on benches and cushions. Nekoda and Ezra sat along the back wall, absorbing the words of the apostle.

James retold the story about the day he and his brother, John, had the audacity to storm up to Jesus and demand, "We want you to do for us whatever we ask."

James shook his head, as if he couldn't believe the nerve of his younger self. He and John treated Jesus like a magician who granted wishes sight unseen.

James continued, relating how he and John said to Jesus, "Let one of us sit at your right and the other at your left in your glory." He put both hands over his face as if hiding the blush of embarrassment. Then, uncovering his face, he told the group he had learned since that day that God's kingdom was upside down. In the Kingdom of God, the servant rules, the Lamb is King, and the repentant sinner sits in glory.

Ezra leaned in close to his father. "Saul also talked about glory—an eternal weight of glory. Do you remember?"

Nekoda nodded, recalling their time with Saul. Saul said our tribulations were light in comparison to the eternal weight of glory. Our glory was something solid, something tangible, something with weight, something that lasts. But our tribulations were like chaff that blew away in the slightest breeze.

Before the Spirit rushed through Nekoda's life, every slight, every wrong that someone committed against him weighed him down like the heavy packs that Roman soldiers sometimes forced Jews to carry for a mile. And when his brother, Chaim, was murdered, he became perpetually angry, seething, and resentful. But now those loads had dissolved to dust and blown away in the wind.

But James wasn't done with his confession. He also retold the story about how Jesus once led them through a town of Samaritans, where the people rejected his message. In anger, James and John had said, "Lord, do you want us to tell fire to come down from heaven and consume them?"

Back then, James and John—the Sons of Thunder—wanted Jesus to bring down the fire of judgment on Samaritans like an avenging army burning cities in its path. But today, James called for God to bring down a different fire—the fire of the Holy Spirit. This fire purified instead of punished. It consumed our sins instead of consuming cities.

As James led them into prayer, Nekoda closed his eyes and asked God for the weight of glory to fall on his shoulders, replacing the fears that still burdened him. He wasn't far into his prayer when a commotion at the back of the room jolted him back to the visible realm. Soldiers pushed their way into the room, shouldering men and women out of the way.

James stopped talking and held up a hand to calm the believers. "What is your purpose in entering this room with force?"

The lead officer drew out his sword. "Are you James, the disciple of Jesus of Nazareth?"

"I am," James said without hesitation.

"Come with me. We are under orders from King Agrippa to take you into custody."

"Why?" Nekoda rushed toward the front of the room. "What has he been accused of?"

One of the other soldiers, sword drawn, stepped into Nekoda's path. "And who are you?"

"I am a former member of the Sanhedrin, the highest Jewish court. I demand a reason for his arrest."

"A 'former' member?" the soldier said. "'Former' doesn't entitle you to a reason. It doesn't entitle you to anything."

"Do not worry," said James to the crowd as the officers led him away. "I am willing to drink the cup that Jesus drank and be baptized with the baptism he was baptized with."

What cup? What baptism?

Nekoda started to reach out, to dare to put a hand on the soldier's shoulder, but Ezra stopped him. "Don't, Abba. We cannot prevent this."

"We can try."

Nekoda followed the soldiers into the streets. One of the guards turned and used his forearm to drive Nekoda back, nearly knocking him off his feet. Ezra caught him.

"Stay back, old man, or we will put you in shackles as well."

Ezra wrapped his arms around Nekoda's waist, restraining him. Then Nekoda noticed several Pharisees and Sadducees watching the spectacle and talking among themselves. His heart dropped when he realized one of them was Hiram.

"Hiram!" Nekoda bolted toward his son.

Hiram stood his ground.

Nekoda spread out his arms. "What is the meaning of this? What are you doing with James?"

"King Agrippa is cleansing Jerusalem of abominations and blasphemies."

"The last person who tried to do that was struck blind on the road to Damascus!"

"King Agrippa is anything but blind. He sees what you are doing! He sees every one of you! He sees, and he acts! None of you are safe!"

"Including your own father? Your own brother?"

"I have no father and brother," said Hiram. Then he turned and followed the soldiers as they hurried James down the street, toward the Antonio Fortress.

The Antonio Fortress dominated the Temple Mount. Herod the Great, Agrippa's grandfather, had constructed the massive fortress on a rock, so it loomed over the Temple grounds like a soldier towering over a priest, always present, always looking, always threatening.

Two aerial bridges spanned from the fortress to the Temple Mount. In times of tumult, Roman soldiers could pour out of the Antonio Fortress and onto the roofs of the porticoes. From this perch, looking down on the Temple grounds, the soldiers could shower arrows on people below.

The fortress was a constant reminder: Rome ruled over Jerusalem.

Nekoda pushed his way through the crowd as the soldiers swept James through the streets of Jerusalem like floodwaters. They nearly lifted James from his feet, rushing for the seat of judgment.

Please, Lord, spare his life. Keep him alive. Keep him with us. He is our voice.

Nekoda prayed constantly as he tried to keep pace with the soldiers. Ezra was only two steps behind. Soon, they arrived at the fortress with its four towers reaching to the sky. This was the lair of the Beast, terrifying and powerful with large iron teeth. The prophet Daniel said this Beast crushed and devoured its victims and trampled underfoot whatever was left.

Daniel also said that no matter how big the fortresses built with human hands might be, the throne of the Ancient of Days was higher still, with a river of fire flowing out before him.

Help us, King of Glory. Throw the Fourth Beast into the furnace of fire! You promised that the sovereignty, power, and greatness of all the kingdoms under heaven will be handed over to the holy people of the Most High. Make that manifest today!

The crowd grew as the soldiers brought their victim to the gate of the Antonio Fortress. Nekoda, a tall man, stood on tiptoes to get a glimpse of James. He caught sight of him, hemmed in on all sides by men in gold breastplates, flashing in the sun. Other soldiers faced the crowd and forced them back at sword point. The crowd drew back, compressing and tightening, until Nekoda thought he was going to be crushed.

Then people began to scatter down side streets, fleeing from the swords. The pressure of the crowd released.

"Do you see him?" Ezra asked. "Do you see James?"

Standing on tiptoes once again, Nekoda searched, but the soldiers were gone and so was James. He had been shoved through the gate. He had been pushed into the jaws of the Iron Beast.

Sveshtari

Sveshtari was victorious once again. It was becoming almost too easy, so he had to force himself not to be complacent. Complacency could get himself killed. In today's combat, he had shown mercy to his opponent, as the crowd had come to expect by now.

When Sveshtari exited the arena, someone handed him a towel to wipe away the sweat and dust plastered to his face. It was a scorching day, and his fight had taken place at the pinnacle of the afternoon.

Sveshtari found a cool corner in his cell. Despite his popularity, he still lived behind bars in Caesarea along with the others forced to be gladiators.

"Someone here to see you, Galilean," growled one of the guards.

Rising, Sveshtari searched the shadows for the visitor, hoping it would be Keturah. He hated it when she saw him caged, but he hated it even more if he didn't get to see her or touch her hand.

But the visitor wasn't Keturah. As a man emerged from the shadows, Sveshtari's stomach dropped. It was Zuriel, the man who had put him here. He hadn't seen Zuriel for almost two years, but he hated him with as much passion as ever.

You have heard that it was said, "Love your neighbor and hate your enemy." But I tell you, love your enemies and pray for those who persecute you, that you may be children of your Father in heaven.

Sveshtari ran Jesus's words through his mind as he gripped the bars of the cage. He was tempted to spit on Zuriel.

Zuriel grinned. "How can you still be alive, Sveshtari?"

Sveshtari didn't honor the question with a response.

"Or shall I call you the Galilean? The fisherman with his nets. You can't survive forever, you know."

Again, Sveshtari didn't answer the question. He responded with a taunt of his own—a reminder of the day he broke Zuriel's nose.

"How is your nose? It looks a bit off kilter."

Zuriel laughed. "Many women like a distinctive nose. So, I should thank you for giving me character. And you should thank me for the character you're developing as a gladiator. You're famous!"

Sveshtari sighed. He was tired of this man.

"If that's all you have to say, then good day, Zuriel."

As Sveshtari began to turn away, Zuriel spoke. "I saw Keturah in the crowd today."

Again, a stomach drop. Sveshtari tried to contain his fury as he slowly turned to face his tormenter. He wanted so badly to reach through these bars and crush Zuriel's head between them.

"If you touch a hair on her head . . ."

"No, no, do not worry, Sveshtari. I simply admired her from afar. She was here with her foolish friends, Asaph and Eliana. I just thought you might like to know she was here to see you live another day."

Sveshtari glanced around his cell, wondering if he could lay hands on a stray piece of stone. Something to hurl into this man's face.

"I know where Keturah sits in the arena. And I know where she lives," Zuriel said.

"If you do anything to her, I will crush you."

"Violent words for a follower of Jesus. Didn't he tell you to love your enemies? And aren't you known for showing mercy in the arena?"

"We're not in the arena."

"But Jesus called you to show mercy wherever you go."

"I can make an exception for you. Killing you would be a minor sin, and I can always ask for forgiveness after slitting your throat."

Zuriel laughed. "Look at you—a lion behind bars, showing your teeth. But I'm on the outside, free as a bird. King Herod is coming to witness the games soon. I hear that he likes to watch women gladiators. Has your Keturah ever fought before?"

This nightmare grew darker. If Zuriel tried to enslave Keturah and sell her as a female gladiator, he would hire an assassin to kill this man. He was surrounded by former criminals. Surely, they could recommend a good cutthroat.

"Keturah is a former slave. And she's beautiful—just the kind of flesh that these crowds eat up."

Sveshtari shot a hand through the bars, grasping at Zuriel. A guard peeled away from the wall and put a hand on Zuriel's shoulder. "That's enough."

Zuriel shrugged away the guard's hand and adjusted his robes.

"If you die in the arena, Sveshtari, then maybe I'll reconsider my plan. Think about it. If you sacrifice yourself, if you die, Keturah will live."

Zuriel strode away, while Sveshtari raged inside his cage.

Nekoda: Jerusalem

James the Apostle, the brother of John, the Son of Thunder, was dead.

Nekoda still couldn't believe it. He didn't think King Agrippa would go this far. Followers of the Way had been murdered before, but this was the first time that one of the twelve disciples had been killed. Agrippa had ratcheted up the pressure by a thousandfold when he had James beheaded. The king discovered he could kill an apostle without stirring up the city's wrath. In fact, many applauded his tyranny.

As the believers scattered and went into hiding throughout Jerusalem, Nekoda and Ezra found refuge in the home of Mary, the mother of John

Mark. Peter also found safety in her house. Rumors raced through the population about other abductions, other deaths.

One morning, Nekoda and Ezra ventured out of the house to track down Hiram in a desperate hope to stop the terror. It was Passover, the day of sacrifice, the day that Jesus had died on the cross. The city was packed, but they knew they could find Hiram if they came to his house in the early hours, since "his house" used to be Nekoda's home.

Nekoda felt strange returning to the home where he and his wife raised their two boys—and knowing that it was no longer his. It remained to be seen whether he was even welcome there. The home's exterior had not changed, although it had deteriorated with age, and Hiram had not kept up with repairs. The outer wall had missing stones, and the door was cracked.

A light rain fell as Nekoda rapped on the door.

"What do you think you're doing, coming to me like this?" Hiram asked when he finally answered the knock. He stood in the doorway; he did not invite them in from the rain.

"We need to talk, son." Nekoda made a move to enter, but Hiram blocked his way.

"How can you disrespect your abba?" said Ezra. "Basic hospitality says to invite us in from the rain."

"If you value your life, you will stay away."

"If you value your soul, you will stop this madness," said Nekoda. How could his son seem so foreign, so utterly different? As a boy, he had been strong-willed, defiant even, but that was normal for a child. Even Ezra could be difficult as a boy. But he expected the sharp edges to be gone by manhood. Instead, Hiram grew more difficult with every year.

"Do you really think I have power over Agrippa?" Hiram said.

"Maybe not you alone. But your leadership has sway. By your silence, Agrippa assumes it is acceptable to use the sword against the Way."

Hiram smiled. "The Way. You talk as if following Jesus is the only Way. The One Way."

The rain picked up in intensity. They were getting soaked. Still, Hiram kept them outside.

"I thought like you did once, Hiram. I only ask that you hear what we have to say, to see the miracles, to feel the power of the Holy Spirit, to listen to Peter."

"Peter? I have no plans on listening to a man in chains."

Ezra took a step forward, crowding his brother. "In chains? What are you talking about?"

"King Agrippa has sent soldiers to arrest Peter."

Agrippa was insane. Was James just a test run? Was he planning on picking off the apostles, one by one? Was Peter the next to die?

Nekoda and Ezra turned and ran back to Mary's house, splashing through puddles as the rain came down harder. They carried a warning, but they knew there was nothing they could do to stop Peter's arrest any more than they were able to stop the soldiers from killing James. Things were spiraling out of control.

Eliana

Eliana dreamt that she had been sent into the arena to face two tigers. She fell on her knees and began to pray as the cage doors slid open with a clang and the tigers leaped out.

As the tigers circled her, growling and preparing to pounce, her dog, Lavi, suddenly came from nowhere, jumping between her and the beasts. Outmatched in size but not in spirit, Lavi snarled and barked, bringing the tigers to a standstill. Eliana called Lavi's name, urging him to stand down. But Lavi charged one of the tigers.

Eliana couldn't watch. She willed herself to wake up, to escape from the nightmare. But as she sat up in bed, a dread came over her. Lavi? Where was her dog?

Normally, he slept at the foot of their bed, but she found no sign of him. Then she heard a scream rise up from Keturah's home next door. It sounded like Babette!

"Asaph, wake up!" Eliana shoved her husband's shoulder until he sat up, rubbing the dreams out of his eyes.

"What?"

"Hurry!" Eliana was already on her feet, throwing on a cloak and slipping on sandals.

Asaph was just behind her as they plunged outside and saw Babette kneeling in the dark in the street. Was she hurt? Why was she awake in the middle of the night?

As Eliana rushed to Babette's side, a horror came over her. Babette knelt over a body, a small body. Her first thought was that something had happened to Keturah's youngest child. But this was not a child's body.

It was a dog.

By this time, Keturah and her other children were awake. "What happened, Eliana?"

"It's Lavi."

Lavi was their first protector. He was the one who rescued Keturah and Eliana on the King's Highway so many years ago. He was the one who faced the wild beasts in their lives. And he never backed down.

Asaph knelt beside Eliana and examined the still body. One of the children had retrieved an oil lamp, shedding light on the bloody scene.

"Babette, do you know how this happened, dear?" asked Eliana, gently.

Babette shook her head. "I woke up and heard Lavi whimpering. I rushed outside and . . . " Babette could get out no more words before she broke down. Keturah crouched and drew her oldest daughter to her side.

Eliana put her face to the ground and wept, clutching her chest. It felt as if her heart had been ripped from her. Lavi was her heart, her protector, her companion, her friend. Lavi had also been her lion, for that is what his name meant. Lion.

She remembered the first time she saw Lavi. He came out of nowhere, a wild dog following them on the road. She threw rocks to drive him away, but he kept coming. It's as if he knew he had a role to play in her life, and he couldn't be driven away. Did God weave animals into the plans of his children? It certainly seemed like it.

The Lord is close to the brokenhearted and saves those who are crushed in spirit. Evil will slay the wicked. The foes of the righteous will be condemned.

That was Eliana's prayer. She prayed that evil would slay the wicked, that the snake would die of its own poison.

"Vengeance is yours, vengeance is yours, Lord," she prayed aloud. She wanted to find out who did this, to take vengeance in her hands, but she knew she had to hand that judgment over to the Lord.

Eliana felt many hands on her shoulders. Keturah's touch. Babette's. Asaph's. Their two families merged into one embrace, one tight fist of grief and sorrow.

I am worn out from my groaning. My eyes grow weak with sorrow. Away from me, all you who do evil, for the Lord has heard my weeping.

With her head bowed to the dust, Eliana noticed a large rock lying next to Lavi's head. The rock had a jagged edge, and it was smeared with Lavi's blood. Surely, this was the murder weapon. Raising her head, she picked up the rock, studied it, and handed it to Asaph.

Asaph turned the rock over in his hands, then looked Eliana in the eyes. "Zuriel."

That was exactly what Eliana was thinking. This was Zuriel's work. She was sure of it.

Nekoda: Jerusalem

Nekoda and Ezra woke up at the fifth hour of the night to take their shift on one of the prayer teams. Jeremiah, a young man in his twenties, roused them from sleep. Nekoda groggily pulled on his robe.

The Feast of Unleavened Bread, which began on Passover, had saved Peter's life. The Jewish authorities were not permitted to execute prisoners during the Feast, so Peter was safe—for now. But only one day remained before the festival ended and Peter met the same fate as James.

Rotating teams of four guards each kept a watch on Peter in the prison. Two of those four guards were chained to Peter, one on each side.

The followers of Jesus had a rotation of their own, making sure that people prayed for Peter continuously throughout the day and night. They too had teams of four or more prayer warriors. But time was running out. Tomorrow, Peter would face the sword.

As Nekoda and Ezra followed Jeremiah into the prayer room, the enormity of the stakes hit him—and depressed him. This was their last chance to prevent Peter, the Rock, from being executed. It seemed like an impossible request. How do you escape when you're chained to two guards with two more standing watch?

True, Jesus rose from the dead while a contingent of soldiers kept guard on his tomb. But that was Jesus.

"We sing in the shadow of your wings," Nekoda prayed, echoing the words of David's Psalms. "We cling to you; your right hand upholds us. Your hand of mercy reaches us, rescues us, and raises us."

God's right hand was his hand of mercy and deliverance, which was why the apostles often spoke about Jesus being at God's right hand. But Ezra balanced out this petition by praying about God's *left* hand—his hand of judgment and fire.

"Smite our enemies with your left hand, O Lord. Wield your sword of judgment to crush the powers of darkness and despair. Break the slave chains with fire and steel."

The images of the right hand and left hand, salvation and judgment, poured out of them, almost without thinking. Their intertwining prayers brought Nekoda to life, giving him hope and energy. In fact, he was so absorbed by the words that he didn't hear the commotion coming from the forecourt of the home of Mary, the mother of John Mark.

Suddenly, the servant girl, Rhoda, barged into their prayer room. Nekoda's first instinct was to rebuke Rhoda for interrupting prayer. But her face glowed in the flicker of the oil lamp in her hands.

Ezra rose from his knees. "What is it, Rhoda?"

"It's Peter!"

Nekoda leaped to his feet. "What happened to him? It's not yet daybreak. King Agrippa should know he can't act against Peter until the Feast of Unleavened Bread has come to a close."

"No, no! Peter is here! Peter is out of prison!"

"You're out of your mind," said John Mark, who had been awakened from bed. So had several other people, including John Mark's mother, Mary.

"It must be his angel," Mary suggested.

"I'm telling you, Peter is here!" Rhoda insisted.

Nekoda and Ezra craned their necks to look behind Rhoda. Had the servant girl gone mad? Was she imagining things? They saw no sign of the disciple.

"So . . . where is he?" said Ezra.

The smile instantly vanished from Rhoda's face. She turned in a circle, scratching the back of her head, as if straining to remember where she had last seen Peter.

"Oh no! I forgot to let him in! I slammed the door in his face!"

"*You what?*"

Nekoda, Ezra, Rhoda, and the others raced back through the courtyard to the forecourt and the gate. Rhoda yanked on the door handle while holding up her oil lamp with her free hand.

Caught in the glow was the big fisherman. Peter had his arms crossed on his chest, mildly amused by Rhoda's absent-minded behavior. He feigned displeasure but then broke into a horizon-wide smile.

"Is this how you greet an escaped prisoner?" he asked, striding through the gate.

Nekoda closed the door quickly after first making sure no pursuing soldiers were following Peter.

The entire household was roused by this time, and they collected in the courtyard to hear Peter's incredible tale.

"An angel of the Lord appeared, and a light shone in the cell," he said, trying to keep his voice to a whisper so he wouldn't draw attention to the house. "This angel struck me on the side and woke me up. 'Quick, get up!' the angel said, and the chains fell off my wrists."

It had to be true, Nekoda thought. How else could he have broken free from the chains and the guards and the bars?

"Then the angel said to me, 'Put on your clothes and sandals.' And I did so. 'Wrap your cloak around you and follow me,' the angel said. I followed him out of the prison, but I had no idea that what the angel was doing was really happening. I thought I was seeing a vision."

Mary handed Peter a cup of water, and he drained it before continuing his story.

"We passed the first and second guards and came to the iron gate leading to the city. It opened for us by itself, and we went through it. When we had walked the length of one street, suddenly the angel left me. So, I came here, where I knocked and Rhoda answered the door—and closed it on my face."

Rhoda covered her blushing face. "I'm sorry. I can't believe I did that."

"That is all right, daughter. It made it all the more real when you shut the door in my face. I knew I wasn't seeing things. I knew without a doubt that the Lord sent his angel to rescue me from Herod's clutches."

Rhoda couldn't stop smiling and blushing.

Asaph

Escorted by guards, Asaph came to Sveshtari's cell in the night. A couple of gladiators in his cell were already asleep, but Sveshtari was on high alert.

"Where is Keturah?" Sveshtari asked, clutching the bars. "Is she safe?"

"She is. Several men are keeping watch over her."

A few days ago, Sveshtari told Asaph about Zuriel's threats against Keturah. And Asaph had told him about the death of Lavi, most likely at the hands of Zuriel.

"Lavi's death is a warning that he can penetrate the security of our homes any time he pleases," Sveshtari said.

"I agree, but I don't think Zuriel will do anything until the games are over. He's too busy with plans for Herod Agrippa's visit."

Tomorrow was the grand celebration of Emperor Claudius's birthday, and Herod Agrippa was already in Caesarea Maritima to host the event. Sveshtari would be fighting in front of Agrippa, the ruler of Idumea, Judea, Samaria, Galilee, Trachonitis, and other territories. The day would be fraught with tension.

Sveshtari sighed. "Make sure Keturah doesn't come to the arena tomorrow to watch me fight."

"We told her she needs to stay home under protection."

"Good. It would be more difficult to protect her in a crowd. But she can be a stubborn woman."

"Eliana will convince her to do what's safest."

"Thank you."

"For now, King Agrippa has other matters on his mind—like these games. Agrippa is also curious about you. The Galilean."

Sveshtari scowled "That isn't good. It's always better to avoid the notice of tyrants."

Asaph agreed. Kings do not tolerate rivals. "I'll pray for an angel to show up in your cell."

"I hear the one who sprung us from prison several years ago isn't doing anything tonight."

Asaph smiled. "Tomorrow, be victorious. The Lord fights for you."

Asaph clasped hands with his friend before slipping away.

Eliana

Keturah was gone.

Eliana walked next door to Keturah's house first thing in the morning to check on her. The two men watching over her led Eliana to Keturah's room. But when she knocked on the door . . . no answer. She knocked two more times before saying, "Keturah, I'm coming in."

The room was empty. The bed had been slept in, but no sign of Keturah.

Eliana confronted the two men who had been on watch through the night. "She's gone!"

"Gone?" The men hustled into the room and glanced around, as if they were going to find her hiding in a corner.

"How could you let her go? You're two men. She's one woman. How hard could it be?"

"I have no idea how it could have happened," said one of the men—Joel.

Eliana had an idea how it happened. The two men probably took turns sleeping and standing guard, but there must've been a moment when both dozed off.

Eliana rushed back to her house where she snagged Asaph, who was just downing a raisin cake. "Keturah is gone!"

"Do you think Zuriel grabbed her?"

"I think it's more likely that she's heading for the arena!"

They had just buried Lavi, and now she feared for Keturah's life. Keturah was walking into the lion's den, where Zuriel lurked. Eliana rushed back outside as Asaph set down his food, threw on a cloak, and tried to catch up.

Sveshtari

This was not a good time to get sick. Sveshtari was about to enter the arena for the most important combat of his gladiator career. Herod Agrippa was in the audience, and the arena overflowed. But Sveshtari's muscles ached, and nausea hit him in waves. He was dizzy, and his heart was racing.

Still, he had no choice but to fight. He weaved a little as he stepped into the arena into the blazing sunlight of the early morning hours.

One of the other gladiators noticed. "Are you all right?"

"I'm not." He tried to keep from vomiting as he marched into the arena with the other gladiators.

"May the Lord Jesus be with you, brother."

Sveshtari cast a sidelong glance at the man. Sveshtari had never seen him before, so he must be a fresh fighter—another net man. "You're a follower?"

"I am. Do not be afraid. When you walk through the fire, you will not be burned."

Sveshtari appreciated the words. But right now, the fire was in his gut, burning him from the inside. The gladiators lined up before the stands where Herod Agrippa would soon appear. Sweat beaded on Sveshtari's face, and he wobbled on his legs.

As he stood there, it dawned on him that the illness had hit him shortly after he drank a goblet of wine. Had he been poisoned?

Sveshtari tried to picture who might have done such a thing, but everything had been chaotic and crowded. It could have been anybody. But he would lay odds that Zuriel had sent somebody to do the deed.

Suddenly, the crowd rose to its feet in unison as Agrippa emerged from the bowels of the arena. He wore a dazzling silver robe that flashed in the sun with blinding intensity. He stretched his arms like wings as if embracing his people. As he did, he moved from side to side, and the morning sun burst on his silver costume.

"A god! A god! A god!" someone shouted, and the crowd picked up the chant.

Soon, the entire arena resounded with the proclamation. "Agrippa the god! Agrippa the god! Agrippa the god!"

The king soaked it up, despite his Jewish heritage. Surely, he knew it was blasphemy to be declared a god. But he embraced the title. He beamed. He preened. Agrippa, friend of emperors, was more Roman in spirit than Jewish.

Sveshtari was dazzled by the silver light flashing from Herod Agrippa's chest. He also noticed a large bird circling overhead and then landing on a rope strung like a garland in the seats behind the king. It was an owl! These birds brought ill tidings, and Sveshtari prayed the evil omen was directed at Herod Agrippa, not at him.

The king was oblivious to the owl as he continued to soak up the crowd's chant. On and on and on it went. Was the crowd afraid to stop cheering? Were they afraid that the first person to stop would be struck down by a bolt from Olympus?

Sveshtari prayed for the crowd to stop chanting because he didn't know if he could remain on his feet much longer. If he collapsed, would they have him killed for disrespecting a god? Probably.

He felt an arm slide beneath his left shoulder, propping him up. It was the new gladiator, the fellow net man.

"Thank you, brother," Sveshtari mumbled. The arena began to spin out of focus. He swallowed bile and held his stomach.

At last, the crowd's chant began to peter out, and no blast of lightning struck the people who eventually stopped their praises to the king. But the owl remained perched above Agrippa, a silent observer. The king lowered his hands as the chants faded into a low murmur.

Let the games begin.

Asaph

Asaph and Eliana drew a volley of hostile stares because they didn't join the chant. But, at last, mercifully, the barrage of blasphemy stopped. Asaph was stunned that the Jewish king had accepted the title of "god," let alone relished it. Herod had spent too much time with Roman elites.

They found Keturah sitting close to where she normally watched the gladiator contests. This was good because it made her easy to find. But it also meant she might be easy for Zuriel to locate.

Eliana kept watch from the vomitorium, the passage where people entered and exited the arena, while Asaph approached Keturah. He squeezed beside her, much to the annoyance of the man to her right. "Keturah, we must go."

Keturah scowled, obviously angry that they had tracked her down. Then she returned her gaze to the arena, where Sveshtari stood among the fighters.

"Do you notice how unsteady Sveshtari is on his feet?"

Asaph followed her gaze. She was right. Sveshtari seemed to be having a difficult time standing erect. His body bobbed like a cork in the ocean. The big man to his left put a hand under his armpit to keep him standing upright.

"Is he sick? He was fine when I talked with him last night." Asaph squinted for a better look. Something was clearly wrong. Sighing, he returned to the task at hand. "Sveshtari would be upset to know you risked coming to the arena. Come, we must get you to a safe location."

"I wouldn't think of deserting Sveshtari now. Look at him. How can he fight in that condition?"

"But if he knew you were in the stands, he might become even more distracted. You do him no favors by insisting you stay here."

Keturah finally made eye contact with Asaph. She appeared to be giving his words some thought.

"No," she finally concluded. "He would be strengthened to know I am here."

Asaph couldn't make a scene by dragging Keturah out of her seat. He glanced back at Eliana, who pointed to her left. Eliana seemed agitated. Swiveling his head, Asaph saw where she was motioning.

She was pointing in the direction of Zuriel. The man stood at another vomitorium, arms crossed with a soldier flanking him on either side. He stared directly at Asaph and Keturah.

Sveshtari

Sveshtari disappeared into the room just off the arena where he would await his turn. He was scheduled to do battle at the peak hour of the festivities. He was the Galilean. He was the highlight of the day, if he lived that long.

He slouched, his head drooping and his stomach churning. Periodically, his core was stabbed by sharp pains. He passed out for a spell but had no idea how long. It must have been for a significant stretch of time because someone was soon jostling him by the shoulder.

"Wake up, Galilean. It's time."

Parts of Sveshtari's legs had gone numb, making it difficult to rise and walk. It was more of a stagger, but he forced himself to shuffle forward. Every eye in the room was fixed on him as he stumbled toward the entrance to the arena. Then he emerged into the sunlight, where the crowd roared his name.

"Galilean! Galilean! Galilean!"

Sveshtari saluted the crowd and turned to face his opponent—an enormous fighter.

As if jealous of the adulation, Agrippa rose to his feet, flashing his silver suit and extending his arms.

Suddenly, the chants of "Galilean" transformed into "A god! A god!"

The king was playing with fire, Sveshtari thought. But at least the chants were keeping him alive a little longer. Once the fight began, he didn't know how he would survive. He prospered in the arena because of his agility and accuracy with the net. He would have none of those advantages today. And if his opponent didn't finish him off, surely the poison in his blood would.

Sveshtari wiped the sweat from his eyes and tried to focus on his opponent. His arms were weighed down with weariness, his legs nearly buckling beneath him.

The battle began. From the start, his opponent could see something was wrong. Sveshtari stumbled as the two fighters circled each other. The circling motion sent him into a spinning fit of dizziness.

The other fighter paused in confusion. He straightened and lowered his sword arm. Normally, this would be when Sveshtari sprang into action. But he could only blink the perspiration out of his eyes and struggle to maintain his footing.

"What is wrong with you, Galilean?" his opponent growled.

"Poison." The word came out slurred.

His opponent glanced around the arena. The crowd could see that something was wrong. Murmuring spread. At this point, Sveshtari would welcome death.

Shrugging, his opponent strode toward him and raised his sword. Sveshtari lifted his head, which was difficult enough. His eyes locked on the sword flashing in the sun like the shining silver on Herod's chest.

Eliana

Eliana watched as Zuriel pushed through the crowd, followed by his two thugs. Zuriel had come for Keturah, and Eliana had to delay him. She had to give Keturah time to come to her senses and get out of the hippodrome.

Eliana ran down the aisle, dodging a man and woman who stood in her path. Then she planted herself directly in front of Zuriel.

He grinned. "Eliana, it is such a pleasant surprise to see you. I thought you'd be sitting with your friend Keturah."

"You will not touch a hair on her head." Eliana spoke with strength, but she knew it must look preposterous—a small, older Jewish woman standing up to Zuriel and his two tree-trunk guards.

"I hear that someone touched the hair on the head of your dog, Eliana." Spoken with a smirk.

Eliana wanted to claw his face. She was prepared to let it all out and hurl herself on Zuriel, like Asaph did when they were children. No matter her age or size, she would turn wildcat on him.

She would've, too, but an inhuman scream suddenly ripped across the hippodrome. Afraid it was Sveshtari being murdered, her eyes locked on the arena. But the combatants looked as perplexed as the crowd.

Then the scream repeated itself, and she realized it was coming from the vicinity of King Herod Agrippa. Was someone assassinating him?

Sveshtari

Sveshtari's opponent snapped his head in the direction of the scream. Something had happened to the king. Herod Agrippa had buckled over, clutching his stomach. Then the king vanished from view as his bodyguards clustered tightly around him like attendant bees.

For a third time, an otherworldly scream erupted from the center of the bodyguards. Some of the guards glanced around for assistance, their faces displaying confusion and panic. The owl, still perched above Agrippa's head, launched into the air and raced out of the theater.

Then the wind began to pick up, lifting the arena sand and spinning it. It was happening again, except on a grander scale. The earth was rising up against a king who called himself god.

Sveshtari's opponent locked eyes on him. "Are you doing this, Galilean?"

"Not me. Yahweh."

By this time, a growing frenzy spread across the spectators. Panicked people shoved and threw elbows as they rushed for the exits. Dozens lost their footing. Some pushed, others tripped. Fists were thrown. Meanwhile, bodyguards rushed the prone body of Herod Agrippa for the nearest exit, lifting him under the arms with his legs dangling, barely touching the ground like the limbs of a puppet. The wind picked up, spinning the sand.

Sveshtari's opponent stood there gawking, his sword arm at his side. As Sveshtari took a few steps toward the gladiator exit, his stomach tightened, and a stab of pain to his chest brought him to his knees.

Groaning, Sveshtari wrapped his arms across his chest and bowed his head to the dirt. If his opponent wanted, he could decapitate him in an instant.

"Come with me, brother." It was the voice of Sveshtari's fellow net man.

Then Sveshtari felt himself being lifted into the air and draped over the man's shoulder. If Sveshtari had been halfway cognizant, he would've been humiliated by being carried out of the arena, half dead.

He closed his eyes and let the dizziness spin his world into oblivion. All that was left were the shattering sounds of chaos and confusion as the judgment of God blew through the arena.

Keturah

Asaph didn't have to tell Keturah to run. She was on her feet in an instant and bolting for the nearest exit.

She wasn't running to elude Zuriel, however. She saw Sveshtari being carried off the field of combat, and she wanted to be with him. For all she knew, her husband was dead, and that was a lifeless body she saw being carried off.

"Right behind you!" Eliana shouted, latching onto Keturah's hand. Asaph moved in front of Keturah and took her by the other hand. They formed a three-person chain, squeezing through the crowd of panic-charged people pushing toward the exits.

A large man to Keturah's right shoved people aside as he plowed through the crowd. He threw his shoulder into Keturah, breaking her link with Eliana and Asaph and sending her tumbling to the ground. She found herself in a forest of legs. Some stepped on her, and others kicked her as they rushed for the exits. Keturah shielded her head and curled into a ball, praying that people wouldn't fall on her and crush her.

"Out of the way!" She heard Asaph's voice above her but was afraid to uncover her head to look. She didn't open her eyes until she felt arms lifting her up. Two sets of hands. Asaph and Eliana. As she rose to her knees, another pair of men came barreling through the crowd, oblivious to the people around her. Asaph acted as her bodyguard, turning to face the men and throwing a shoulder into one of them.

The next moment, Keturah was back on her feet and Eliana gripped her hand so hard it almost hurt. Keturah covered her face to block the wind-blown sand. But by the time they fought their way outside, the wind had let up a bit—enough for Keturah to breathe again without swallowing sand.

"We need to find Sveshtari!" Keturah shouted.

"This time, we're in agreement." Asaph tugged her toward the gladiator entrance with Eliana still holding on.

As they neared the entrance, they were stunned to see a large gladiator emerge from the arena, still carrying Sveshtari over his right shoulder. Keturah had never seen her husband in such a vulnerable position.

Keturah kissed Sveshtari on the lips, which had gone cold. His face was as white as a statue, but he was alive.

"This way," the big man said, ducking down a Caesarea side street. "We're drawing attention."

He was right. Shopkeepers and pedestrians stared and pointed. It wasn't often you saw a gladiator carrying another combatant out of the arena.

"Thank you for your help," Asaph said, trying to keep up with the man. "How did you get past the guards?"

"It wasn't hard." The big man didn't elaborate.

He led them around the corner and ducked down an alley. There, he gently placed Sveshtari on the ground and stepped back. The others swooped down on Sveshtari's prone body, looking for any sign of injury. There was none.

Keturah put a hand to his forehead. "Is he alive?"

Asaph leaned down to assess Sveshtari's breathing. He also put a hand on his chest to see if it was rising and lowering, ever so slightly.

"He breathes."

Keturah kissed Sveshtari once again and put a hand to his cheek.

"Is your friend all right?" came a voice to their right. Standing in the doorway of a rug shop was an older man, as thin as a skeleton.

"We need to get him inside and out of the sun."

"Come with me." The man motioned with his bony fingers, leading them inside his shop. "I'm a rug-maker. I specialize in making people comfortable. Set him here." He pointed to an intricately designed carpet stretched across the floor.

Keturah was amazed the man would encourage them to lay a gladiator on his priceless rug, staining it with dust and sweat. But she wasn't going to argue. The comfort of the rug was more priceless than its threads and colors.

She was also puzzled because the other gladiator, the one who had placed Sveshtari on the rug, was no longer at their side. She glanced around. He was gone.

"You need to find a way out of the city," said the rug-maker, who introduced himself as Jotham. It was obvious to his eyes that Sveshtari was a gladiator. "Is he the Galilean?"

"He is," said Asaph. "You know of him?"

"Of course. Everyone does. He is my favorite. It's a miracle he has survived this long, but I don't think you want to test the limits of survival any further. Do you know what is wrong with him?"

"He wasn't injured in the arena, so it must be something internal."

"Can I pray for him?" Jotham said.

"We would love that," said Keturah.

Keturah, Eliana, Asaph, and the rug-maker clasped hands in a circle. Then Jotham led out in prayer, while Keturah's muddled mind tried to think of a way to escape this city alive.

Asaph

That night, Asaph left Jotham's house and made his way to the home of Abel, who lived on the edge of Caesarea with his large family. If anyone knew how to smuggle someone out of a city, it was Abel. He had worked wonders many years ago when they were trapped in Jericho.

But Asaph never could have predicted that Abel had access to a Roman *carpentum*, a luxurious four-wheeled wagon enclosed with an arched wooden roof. It was pulled by horses and often used by the wealthy.

Never underestimate Abel's connections, he told himself.

Asaph rode beside Abel as the wagon rattled up to the rug-maker's home, just a stone's throw from the arena and the Great Sea. In the dark of the early morning hours, they could hear the lapping of waves nearby.

Eliana and Keturah rushed out to greet them. "Abel, you're a God-send," Eliana said.

Abel smiled and climbed down from the wagon. "It pays to know a former smuggler with many connections. A wealthy friend loaned me this wagon. Anything for the Galilean, she said."

Abel and Asaph hurried into the house, which was dimly lit by several oil lamps. Sveshtari continued to sleep on the beautiful tapestry. "How is he doing?"

"He hangs on," said Jotham.

"Jotham thinks it was poison," said Eliana.

"Monkshood to be exact," Jotham said. "The purple poison. It's been used on spear-tips to poison enemies. But the Galilean is strong. If he hasn't succumbed by now, I think, Lord willing, he will pull through."

"Light is fast approaching," Abel said. "No time to lose."

Working as a team, Asaph, Abel, and Jotham kept Sveshtari wrapped in the carpet as they raised him from the floor. They heaved Sveshtari into the enclosed back of the *carpentum*. Then Asaph helped Keturah and Eliana aboard.

"Thank you for your help," Asaph said, clasping hands with Jotham.

"Shalom, shalom," said Jotham. "Now hurry away."

"First, I need to show everyone the most important feature of this wagon," said Abel. He pulled aside a rug from the bottom of the *carpentum*, revealing a recessed handle below. Gripping the handle, he raised the lid on a secret compartment on the bottom of the vehicle—a hiding place big enough to fit a person.

"Amazing," said Asaph.

Abel grinned. "As I said, it helps to know a reformed smuggler. This vehicle has many compartments, but this is the only space big enough for a person."

Abel and Asaph placed Sveshtari inside the hidden compartment. He was still breathing, but he looked close to death.

"How will he breathe?" Asaph asked.

"There are plenty of air holes. But you can keep the lid open for now to tend to Sveshtari. If we are stopped or face any trouble, you will need to immediately close him in. Do you understand?"

Keturah nodded. "What about our families?"

"That's been taken care of," Abel said. "My oldest son is driving a *raeda* with half of the children aboard, while Eliana's father is driving a second *raeda* with the rest of the children. We're meeting them near the city gates. In fact, they're probably already there, waiting for us."

"Thank you, brother," Asaph said, clasping hands with Abel.

After supplies were loaded and everyone said their goodbyes to Jotham, Asaph and Abel scrambled back into the driver's seat. Moments later, the wagon lurched forward, its iron-shod wheels rattling on the Roman road.

Keturah

Keturah held Sveshtari's hand and tried to rub warmth into his skin. The sun was just rising in a clear sky as their wagon weaved its way toward the city gates. They met up with the two *raedae*, the common four-wheel wagons carrying their families. Instead of the luxurious enclosure of the *carpentum*, these wagons had cloth roofs, but they did the job.

Keturah and Eliana quickly conducted a head count of their children packed into the wagons. Even though they were sizable wagons, carrying a carnival of thirteen children was almost comical to behold.

Keturah transferred her children to the back of the larger *carpentum*, where Sveshtari remained hidden in the compartment. Each vehicle contained a separate family with the three drivers being Asaph, Abel, and Judah.

Keturah snuggled in the back with her youngest child, Esther, age nine. Cassia was eleven, and Ethan was ten but acted like he was thirteen. Asher was twelve, while Babette was fourteen, going on thirty. The compartment holding Sveshtari was kept open, like an uncovered sarcophagus, and Babette knelt at her father's side, holding his hand.

"His hand is still cold, Ima," Babette said, rubbing her father's hand to generate heat.

"Do not worry. The rug-maker said he is healing rapidly."

"What does a rug-maker know about such matters?"

"More than any of us."

Keturah led the family in prayer, but it was a short-lived devotional. Moments after their "amen," the wagon came to a stop. They had reached the city gates. Before Keturah lowered the lid on Sveshtari's compartment, Babette kissed her abba on the forehead. Then she reluctantly drew back her hand as Keturah closed him in.

They listened to the muffled voices of Asaph, Abel, and Judah speaking with the guards. Then the back doors of the *carpentum* swung open, and they found themselves being gazed at like animals in a cage. Two soldiers peered into all corners of the wagon, but Keturah didn't know what they were looking for. Signs of smuggling activity?

"Where is your husband?" one of the guards snapped at Keturah.

Keturah averted her eyes. "He is no longer of this world. I am a widow."

Satisfied that the wagon carried only women and children, the soldiers slammed shut the *carpentum* doors and returned to the front of the vehicle.

"You lied, mother," Babette whispered.

"I had no choice, my lamb."

Besides, in a sense it was true. Sveshtari was buried in the bottom of the *carpentum* like a corpse in the ground. He had the aspect of death, even if he was still breathing. She teetered on the edge of widowhood.

Eliana

The guards crouched to peer beneath their carriage. *They are unusually attentive,* Eliana thought.

"May we pass?" Asaph asked after they completed this inspection.

"Hold your horses," said one of the guards as the two men conferred with a third.

Then the guard returned, shaking his head solemnly. "We will need you to wait until later this day before we can allow you to leave."

"Later this day? But why? Can't you see that we are nothing more than three families? We pose no threat to anyone."

"Since the poisoning of King Agrippa, we have orders to be extra vigilant."

The poisoning of Agrippa? Eliana and the others hadn't heard this news. She prayed that Abel could find a way to get them through this checkpoint—quickly. Surely, alerts had gone out for Sveshtari. If these guards discover they are related to "the Galilean," they will be detained and interrogated. Maybe worse.

At that moment, a fourth guard arrived on the scene—a tall man who moved with authority.

"What is the trouble?" the soldier demanded. His voice was strangely familiar.

When the soldier turned his head to look at their carriage, Eliana had to hold back a gasp. This was the same man who had carried Sveshtari from the arena. *Who was he?*

The man followed the same routine as the other soldiers. He checked the backs of all three wagons, and he looked beneath them to make sure no one was hitching a ride below.

"These wagons carry mostly children. Pass them through."

"But, sir, we have orders to keep the population within the city until Agrippa's poisoning can be investigated."

"I think it's safe to say that these children did not poison Herod Agrippa. Herod was struck down by God, and we have no plans to arrest the Almighty."

The other guards exchanged glances and backed away from the tall man. They seemed afraid, and rightly so. The tall man radiated strength.

"Yes, sir," one of the guards finally said meekly.

Then, trying to muster some authority of his own, the guard waved a dismissive hand at their three carriages. "You heard him. Leave before we change our minds."

"Yes, sir," said Abel, shaking the reins.

As their wagons rolled through the gate, Eliana peered over her shoulder and nodded at the tall soldier. He nodded back before turning and striding into the morning light.

Asaph

Asaph steered their wagon along a minor road that hugged the coast going north from Caesarea. They planned to link up with the major Roman road, Via Maris, and follow it the rest of the way to Antioch. Antioch had become a major hub for followers of the Way, including many leaders, such as Saul. They would find safety there.

Asaph breathed in the sea air—fresh and invigorating. With every moment, he savored the growing distance from the death and blood in Caesarea. The road was narrow and uneven, so Asaph prayed they wouldn't break an axle on the rocks. He would breathe easier when they finally reached the wide, smooth Via Maris. The land along the Great Sea was flat, but they would soon be skirting around Mount Carmel to their right.

"Clouds of dust!" Abel shouted to him from the driver's seat of the second wagon in line. "Look!"

As Abel motioned over his shoulder, Asaph peered at the road behind them. Abel was right. A cloud of dust had kicked up and seemed to be moving in their direction. He prayed it was just dust stirred up by ordinary travelers following the same route north. Nothing unusual in that.

At least that's what he told himself.

"Faster!" Abel shouted.

Asaph and Judah did as Abel commanded, but they were carrying heavy loads. The vehicles behind them appeared to be gaining quickly.

If they're ordinary travelers, they're in an awful hurry, Asaph thought.

"*Essedae*!" Abel called out.

Asaph's heart sped up. *Essedae*. Chariots. There was no way their wagons could outpace chariots.

"How many?" Asaph asked.

"I count four!" Abel shouted.

Asaph had his sling and a sword, while Abel and Judah also carried weapons. But their staunchest defender was tucked away in a hidden compartment, asleep and on the edge of death. If these chariots were coming after them, they were in serious straits.

Asaph understood what it must've felt like for the ancient Israelites under Moses when they saw hundreds of Egyptian chariots racing at them. God had told Moses to camp along the Red Sea, a perplexing command because it backed them up against the water with nowhere to run. It's as if God intentionally stacked the odds against the Israelites, just to show his power. God had done it to show that he will fight for them, even when all the power of Egypt was arrayed against them.

In their case, the Great Sea was to their left, not to their backs, but it seemed just as hopeless as it must have been for Moses and his people. How can three men, one of them elderly, fight off what was fast approaching?

Do not be afraid. The Lord will fight for you; you need only to be still.

God had given those words to Moses, but they seemed too difficult, too threatening. Be still? How could they? When you're still, you are an easy target! Lambs are still when they stand in the Temple, waiting to be slaughtered on the altar.

It also occurred to Asaph that Jesus remained still when he squared off with the powers of this world. He did not fight back when he was brought before Herod Antipas . . . and Pilate . . . and the Roman soldiers. He allowed them to batter his body until it was bloody and torn.

Be still? Impossible!

"We need to form a defensive position," Judah shouted from the third wagon.

I guess that's one way of being still, Asaph thought.

Bringing their wagons to a stop, Asaph retrieved his sling and sword, while Abel brought out his sword and bow and Judah produced a blade. The chariots were almost upon them.

Eliana

Eliana thought it had all been too easy to get out of Caesarea safely. Few things are easy in this world.

"What's happening?" she asked Asaph after climbing from the back of the wagon.

"Chariots." That's all he said. That's all he needed to say.

Keturah emerged from the back of their *carpentum*. "Stay inside," she snapped at Babette when her oldest daughter made a move to climb out of the covered wagon. "And be sure the rest of the children stay out of sight."

"You should stay out of sight as well," Asaph said to Eliana and Keturah. He already had a rock loaded into his sling.

"No," said Eliana.

Asaph glared at his wife, shocked by her blunt rejection of his authority. But at the moment, he had greater problems than an uncooperative wife. All eyes went to the four chariots closing in on them.

"It's Zuriel," Eliana said. *When would they ever be rid of this man?*

The person standing up in the lead chariot was clearly Zuriel. The other three chariots carried two men each, bringing the total of their opposition to seven. Seven was a holy number, but not today.

Abel drew his bow and aimed it at Zuriel. "No farther, Zuriel, or you will be the first to die."

Zuriel smiled as his chariot rolled to a stop. The other three chariots flanked him on either side. "Didn't your teacher say that those who live by the sword will die by the sword?" Zuriel said.

Abel drew back his bow even further. "This is a bow, not a sword."

"Don't be a fool. There are seven of us and only three of you."

"But I only need one arrow to kill you."

That removed the smile from Zuriel's face. "If you give us Keturah, we will let the rest of you go."

"You're a fool if you think we would hand over Keturah," Eliana said, stepping from behind the protection of the covered wagon.

Zuriel's eyes landed on Eliana. He sighed. "Eliana, you tire me. I'll be pleased when you finally leave my life."

"The feeling is mutual. Keturah stays with us."

"You would put your children at risk to protect one woman?"

Keturah stepped out from behind the wagon. "Let them take me," she whispered to Eliana.

Eliana shook her head. She crossed her arms and glared at Zuriel.

Zuriel nodded toward the other soldiers accompanying him. As two of them climbed from the back of their chariot, Asaph and Judah blocked their way, while Abel kept his arrow aimed at Zuriel.

"No farther." Asaph held out his sword.

Zuriel stepped down from his chariot. "If you're not going to deliver Keturah to us, we'll *take* her."

Eliana drew Keturah around the back of the wagon. Once Keturah was inside the wagon, Eliana hurried back to Asaph's side. She got there just in time to see the soldiers overpowering him. Four of them restrained Asaph, Abel, and Judah, while a fifth grabbed Eliana by the wrist. A sixth soldier strode behind the wagon to retrieve Keturah.

Then she heard a cry of alarm.

Sveshtari

When Sveshtari came to, he found himself in a dark box of some sort. His first fear was that people thought he was dead, and he had been buried alive. But when he pounded on the lid, Babette opened it.

"What's going on? Where am I? Where are we, Babette?"

Babette put a finger to her lips. "We're in a wagon, leaving Caesarea. We were stopped by the one called Zuriel and several soldiers. They're coming for mother. I don't think they know you're here."

No sooner had Babette said the word "mother" than the door to the covered wagon opened. In climbed Keturah. When she caught sight of Sveshtari, alive and alert, she nearly let out a shout. She slapped a hand over her mouth to contain her surprise.

"How many?" he whispered.

"Seven counting Zuriel," Keturah said.

Babette handed her father his sword, plus two nets. They had been wise enough to pack his weaponry in another hidden compartment. Sveshtari could hear raised voices from outside as he slipped silently out of the wagon. From the sound, Asaph, Abel, Judah, and Eliana were scuffling with the enemy.

The sudden burst of sunlight flared his headache. He was still groggy and unsteady on his feet, but he was much better than he had felt in the arena. How long ago had it been? It seemed like moments ago—and yet an eternity.

With his mind fogged by the remnant of whatever drug he had been given, Sveshtari started to formulate a plan. But before he had a chance to think, one of the soldiers flew around the corner of the wagon. Acting on instinct, Sveshtari flung his first net over the soldier's head. His reflexes were as sharp as ever, and so was his aim.

The soldier let out a shout and struggled in the net, but he just tangled himself up even more. As a second soldier flew around the corner, Sveshtari shoved the one caught in his net, and the pair of them tumbled backward in a heap. Slamming the butt of his sword against the second soldier's head, he knocked him unconscious. Then he did the same with the soldier caught in the net.

Suddenly, their opposition went from seven to five. Sveshtari would take those odds any day.

Asaph

Asaph was stunned to see Sveshtari come charging around the corner, a sword in one hand and a net in the other. The last time he saw Sveshtari, he was at death's door. Now, he appeared resurrection-ready. These soldiers would've been better off facing an enraged bear.

The soldier holding on to Asaph must've been thinking the same thing because he released his arm, drew his sword, and backpedaled toward his chariot. "The Galilean!"

One of the other soldiers hurled a glare at Zuriel. "You didn't tell us the Galilean was here! I thought we were just coming for the woman!"

"Those fools who inspected the wagons said he was not among them!" Zuriel fumed. He took several steps backward toward his chariot. One of the chariots, carrying two men, had already wheeled around and started back toward Caesarea.

Zuriel jumped back into his chariot and started to wheel it around. But Sveshtari still had one net in his arsenal. He flung it with uncanny accuracy, snagging Zuriel like a fish. Zuriel thrashed in the net, tripping and falling head over heels from the chariot. He landed hard on his head.

The remaining two soldiers had seen enough. They were already racing back to Caesarea, following in the dust trail of the other chariot. Sveshtari and Asaph strode over to Zuriel, who continued to struggle in the net. Asaph had only seen Sveshtari work the net from a distance—from his seat in the arena. It was even more impressive up close.

Sveshtari

Sveshtari put a foot on Zuriel's chest and applied pressure. Zuriel stopped thrashing. Then Sveshtari placed his sword against the man's chest, and Zuriel's eyes went wide. Years ago, before Sveshtari met Jesus, Zuriel would already have been dead. So would the other soldiers who dared to threaten his family and friends.

Now, he was debating whether to finish off Zuriel or not. That was progress, wasn't it?

Zuriel didn't dare move a muscle. He was helpless, still wrapped in a net and lying on his back in the dust. "You are the Galilean. You show mercy to your opponents."

"But my opponents in the arena never tried attacking Keturah and my children."

"I give you my word that I will no longer pursue you or your wife."

"Your word is worth nothing." Sveshtari put slight pressure on his sword blade, cutting through Zuriel's clothing and pricking skin. A slight red blotch appeared against the white cloth.

Keturah appeared at his side. She put a hand on his sword arm. "The prophet Isaiah said that a sword, not of mortals, will devour evil. We have a just God. Let him wield the sword."

Sveshtari did not remove his sword from Zuriel's chest. "I cannot wait that long. I prefer more timely justice."

"Some trust in chariots and some in horses, but we trust in the name of the Lord our God. Herod Agrippa was judged by God. Zuriel will be as well."

Shocked, Sveshtari shot a look over his shoulder to see who had spoken those words. He was stunned to see his oldest daughter, Babette.

Babette continued to quote the words of David: "The evil are brought to their knees and fall, but we rise up and stand firm. Lord, give victory to the king!"

Sveshtari let out a growl. He knew he couldn't kill a man in front of his precious daughter. Babette's presence reminded him that the three wagons carried all their children. He couldn't allow them to even hear the sound of him killing a man.

Sveshtari tossed aside his sword. He could see relief rise in Zuriel's eyes—although the relief quickly transformed back to fear when Sveshtari reached down and yanked Zuriel to his feet.

"What are you doing?" Zuriel asked.

"My daughter reminded me that some trust in chariots and some in horses. I recommend you begin to trust in both because who knows where your horse and chariot will be taking you."

Sveshtari picked up Zuriel, who was still caught in the net, and heaved him back into the chariot. Then he turned the horses and chariot around to face Caesarea. He swatted the flank of one of the two horses, and the animal took off, pulling the chariot and its panicked passenger.

Zuriel's shouts faded into the wilderness as the horse and chariot disappeared into the distance.

"Thank you, Sveshtari." Keturah rushed into his embrace, and so did Babette. Eliana let the other children out of the wagons to stretch their legs and find some bushes to take care of nature's call.

Eliana's father motioned toward the unconscious soldier and the one still caught in the net. "What do we do with these two?"

Crouching, Sveshtari slapped the unconscious soldier a few times, bringing him back to life. The man gasped when he saw Sveshtari looming over him.

"Help your friend get loose and then take your chariot back to the city."

"Thank you, Galilean. Thank you for your mercy."

"Mercy is what I'm known for."

Suddenly, before the men could rise to their feet, their chariot took off without them, the horses running hard and the empty vehicle rattling on the rough road.

"I take that back. It looks like you'll be *walking* to Caesarea. I hope you have sturdy sandals."

"Everybody back on board," Eliana said, rounding up the children like sheep. "We still have a long road to go."

Nekoda: Jerusalem

Nekoda couldn't leave Jerusalem without seeing his oldest son. It could be the last time he laid eyes on him.

"It's too dangerous to visit Hiram," Ezra said. "But if you insist on going, I will accompany you."

"No, let me go alone. I don't want to put both of us in danger. But I must see him one more time."

"I am not about to desert you now."

So, Nekoda and Ezra trudged uphill from the Lower City to the Upper City, finally reaching Nekoda's former home. They paused outside the gate of the compound's outer wall.

"Are you sure you want to do this, Abba?" Ezra asked. "You could be walking into a trap."

Word had reached Jerusalem that Herod Agrippa was dead, but the persecutions still went on. Agrippa died after the crowd in Caesarea declared him to be a god—afflicted by a deadly intestinal sickness that tormented him for five days. He was "eaten by worms," people said. Herod had worn robes woven of silver—beautiful on the outside—while worms multiplied inside his gut. He was a white-washed grave full of everything unclean.

It was a painful death. Even Nekoda had to feel sorry for the man.

Pushing open the gate, he entered the courtyard and knocked on the door. No answer. He knocked again. Still nothing.

"Let us depart." Ezra clearly didn't want to linger at the door of his brother's house.

But as Ezra took his father by the arm and turned, the door opened. Hiram stood on the threshold, mouth agape.

"Abba?"

Nekoda was pleasantly surprised. It had been a long time since Hiram addressed him as "Abba." But Hiram immediately tightened up, stiffening his spine and frowning, as if the word had slipped out unintentionally.

"Son, we came to say goodbye."

Hiram's expression changed again, this time to puzzlement. He furrowed his brow. "Why would you take such a risk to come here?"

"Because you are my son. I know you will not do to me as has been done to James—and as the king tried to do to Peter."

"How can you be sure?"

"Because I raised you."

"But there are others here in this house. They pose a danger to you."

"I warned him not to come," Ezra said.

"You should have stopped him."

When a noise sounded inside the house, Hiram took Nekoda by the arm and hurried him out the gate and back into the street. "Please. I beg you to leave Jerusalem."

"That is what we are planning to do," Ezra said. "But Abba wanted to say goodbye."

Nekoda held out his arms. "Farewell, my son."

He perceived tears in the corners of Hiram's eyes. Maybe there was hope for his son after all. But Hiram did not walk into his embrace, and Nekoda did not want to force his affection.

"We leave today for—"

"Don't tell me," Hiram said. "It is better I do not know."

Nekoda nodded. Shadow feelings came over him, and he bowed his head. He too fought back tears. How could life have made such a turn? Scorned by the son he once held in his arms as a baby. He wanted to bend down, pick up handfuls of dirt, and bury himself. He was bowed down with sorrow.

Then, to his surprise, Hiram gave him a quick embrace. It was over in a moment, but it was their first embrace in years. Nekoda raised his head, and their eyes met.

"Please, do not stay in the city long," Hiram said. "You must go."

"Yes. We must go, son."

As Ezra took Nekoda by the arm and turned him toward the street, Hiram said, "Goodbye, Abba." This time, the word "Abba" did not seem to slip out accidentally. It was consciously chosen. Nekoda turned and smiled. Then he turned away again, for the tears were beginning to flow.

Nekoda and Ezra were traveling to Antioch, north of Jerusalem, even north of Galilee. Many believers were in Antioch, including Saul. However, the apostle Saul now went by a new name, his Greek name.

He was known as Paul.

Eliana: On the Road to Antioch

They camped at the foot of Mount Carmel, which loomed over them in the dark. Eliana had put their children to bed, and she sat on a log next to Asaph and her father. Joining them in front of the fire were Sveshtari and Keturah, while Abel and Hannah busily put their children to sleep.

"Do you think Zuriel will give up his pursuit, as he promised?" Eliana asked.

Sveshtari tossed a stick in the fire. "He will hesitate for a season. But we may not yet be done with him."

"But he has no idea where we are going," Asaph said.

"Judging by the road we're on, he might have already guessed that Antioch is our destination."

Eliana raised her eyes to Mount Carmel, the mountain where Elijah confronted the priests of Baal. "Elijah won a great victory over the priests up there, but that didn't make his life any easier. In fact, it made his life harder because Queen Jezebel vowed to hunt him down and kill him."

"Are you saying that Zuriel is our Queen Jezebel?" Keturah asked. "Will he make our life harder after our victory?"

"I don't know. Jezebel was thrown from a window, so her pursuit of Elijah came to nothing. I don't pray for Zuriel to be thrown from a window, but I pray his pursuit comes to nothing."

"Jezebel was also eaten by dogs," Keturah said. When she realized what she had just said, she added, "But not all dogs are scavengers."

Keturah's words had brought up images of their dog, their protector, Lavi.

"I miss him every day," Keturah said.

"So do I." Eliana wiped her eyes with the back of her hand. She sighed and worked to gain control of her emotions. Her thoughts returned to Mount Carmel.

"God sent down fire on Mount Carmel to show His majesty and power," she said. "We have witnessed the same power, the same fire."

"Keturah told me you had a tongue of fire on your head when you were captive in the cave," Sveshtari said to Eliana. "What was it like. Was it painful?"

"Not at all," Eliana said. "I cannot describe it. The best I can say is that the tongue of fire gave me a feeling of warmth, but not a burning."

"Like our campfire." Sveshtari tossed a stick into the flames.

"Yes . . . and no. It was also a feeling of power beyond my normal capabilities. A holy power. The fire at our feet offers warmth, but not power."

Keturah tossed a large stick into the flames.

"I look forward to some peace in Antioch," Eliana said. "Do you think we'll find it there?"

Judah shook his head. "I don't know. For hardship does not spring from the soil, nor does trouble sprout from the ground," he said, reciting the words of Job. "Yet man is born to trouble as surely as sparks fly upward."

"What is Antioch like do you think?" Abel asked, suddenly appearing at the campfire with his wife, Hannah. They took their places on the ground.

"Large," said Judah.

True. It was the third largest city behind Rome and Alexandria.

"Large enough to get lost in," added Asaph.

"I hear the people there came up with a new name for the followers of Jesus," Sveshtari noted.

"Oh? What is it?"

"Our enemies in Antioch call us Christians."

Abel laughed. "Clever, but it will never catch on."

Eliana smiled. "I don't know. I like the sound of it. 'Christian' is easier to say than 'followers of the Way.'"

She tossed another stick on the fire, sending sparks crackling and swarming into the night. She raised her eyes to watch them fly into the black sky. When the sparks disappeared, she found herself staring at stars—sparks of Creation going back to the First Day.

Asaph leaned in closely and whispered in her ear. "Time to rest, Eliana. We have a long day ahead of us."

Eliana groaned as she rose. She latched onto Asaph's arm and looked again at the night sky. He who made the Pleiades and Orion, who turns midnight into dawn and darkens day into night—the Lord is His name.

Then they crawled into their tent to share their dreams together.

THE KINGDOM COME SERIES

To discover how it all began for Eliana, Asaph, Keturah, and Sveshtari, check out *Thrones in the Desert* and *Swords in the Desert,* the first two parts in the Kingdom Come series.

AUTHOR'S NOTES

SEQUELS ARE NOT A modern phenomenon. Some call Homer's *Odyssey* a sequel to *The Iliad*, although others dispute whether it is a true sequel since many years elapse between the two stories. But without a doubt, the Book of Acts is a sequel to the Gospel of Luke because it picks up where the Gospel ended.

So, when I was writing my two-book series based on the Book of Luke (*Thrones in the Desert* and *Swords in the Desert*), I knew I wanted to follow my story into the Book of Acts. The result: *Fire in the Desert*, which covers the first twelve chapters of Acts.

As with my Luke novels, each chapter of *Fire in the Desert* corresponds directly with a chapter from Acts. Chapter 1 in *Fire in the Desert* corresponds with Chapter 1 in Acts, and so on. The cast of fictional characters gave me the freedom to place them in various key locations, whether it's Galilee where a resurrected Jesus appeared to 500 people, or Jerusalem, where the Holy Spirit swept through the city. (Note: The Bible doesn't say exactly where Jesus appeared before 500 people, but many theologians believe it was Galilee.)

Ironically, the persecution of the early church helped to spread the Gospel as followers of the Way (they weren't yet called "Christians") fled the violence and dangers. My fictional characters are dispersed as well, escaping to Sebaste and then Joppa and Caesarea Maritima on the coast of the Great Sea—the Mediterranean.

The Book of Acts has a natural breaking point at Chapter 12. The first 12 chapters follow Peter and the other disciples, and we see Saul, the persecutor of the Church, converted on the road to Damascus. There's even an ideal climax at the end of Chapter 12, where Herod Agrippa is gripped by a mysterious ailment while delivering a public address and eventually dies a painful death. In addition to following the text of Acts, I based that scene on the account written by the ancient historian Flavius Josephus, who describes Herod appearing at a spectacle dressed in a silver costume that flashed in the sun. Josephus also mentions the ominous owl that perches behind Herod just before he is struck down.

In Chapter 13 of Acts, Saul (who is now Paul) begins his first missionary journey, leaving behind the story of Peter and other disciples. So, that is a natural beginning for the next book in the series.

In the next novel, I plan to have one of my characters accompany Paul as his secretary because it is likely he traveled with a contingent of people. The other characters (Eliana, Asaph, Sveshtari, and Keturah) will remain behind in Antioch on the Orontes, a key location where the early Church was born. It's in Antioch where believers were first called "Christians."

The Book of Acts is longer than Luke, so I was left with a decision. Do I cover Acts with two novels or three? I decided to do it in three novels because, once again, there is a natural breaking point at Chapter 20.

As a result, *Fire in the Desert* covers 12 chapters of Acts, the next book will cover 8 chapters, and the last book will cover the final 8 chapters of Acts. A lot of time is covered over this stretch, so look for the characters to age considerably.

The question is where to go after the Book of Acts. Do I follow my characters and their children into the fall of Jerusalem and the early Church? Or do I progress to Revelation, which would be a tricky book to portray? I'll put that decision off for now.

For my research, I used a library-load of books, prompting my wife to wonder where I plan to store all of them. My two key sources were: *The New International Commentary on the Book of Acts* by F. F. Bruce (1988) and N.T. Wright's *Paul: A Biography* (2018). Other important resources include the following:

Chronological and Background Charts of the New Testament, Second Edition by H. Wayne House (Zondervan, 2009)

Food at the Time of the Bible by Miriam Feinberg Vamosh (Palphot, Ltd., 2007)

Holman Illustrated Bible Dictionary (Holman Bible Publishers, 2015)

Josephus: The Complete Works by Flavius Josephus, translated by William Whiston, A. M. (Thomas Nelson, 1998)

Gladiator: The Roman Fighter's [Unofficial] Manual by Philip Matyszak (Thames & Hudson, 2011)

Lexham Geographic Commentary on Acts Through Revelation by Barry J. Beitzel (Lexham Press, 2019)

Paul: Apostle of the Heart Set Free by F. F. Bruce (The Paternoster Press, 1977)

Handbook on Acts and Paul's Letters by Thomas R. Schreiner (Baker Academic, 2019)

The Message of Acts by John R. W. Stott (IVP Academic, 1990)

The Smart Guide to the Bible: The Book of Acts by Robert C. Girard and Larry Richards (Thomas Nelson, 2007)

The Story of God Bible Commentary: Acts by Dean Pinter (Zondervan Academic, 2019)

Walking in the Dust of Rabbi Jesus by Lois Tverberg (Zondervan, 2012)

ACKNOWLEDGMENTS

Fire in the Desert is my 99th book—just one shy of 100. But an even greater milestone arrives alongside its publication: my 50th wedding anniversary.

Nancy and I were married on May 22, 1976, just a couple of months before our country's 200th birthday. It feels only right to begin here—with gratitude for her. Thank you, Nancy, for putting up with me for 50 years and for faithfully reading my manuscripts (often more than once!) and offering thoughtful, invaluable feedback every time.

I also want to thank both of my gifted sons, Michael and Jason, for being heirs to my heart and for being such committed and caring fathers to our four precious grandchildren, Jackson, Joshua, Tomás, and Sofía. Note: The honor of my 100th book will go to *The Sabotage of '76*, a middle-grade novel co-written with my youngest son, Jason, and due out in October 2026 from Morgan James Publishers.

Also, thanks to . . .

• Seth Kerlin, my pastor at Cornerstone Fellowship in Urbana, Illinois, whose teaching—especially through Luke and now Acts—has helped shape this series.

• Urbana Theological Seminary, for deepening my understanding of the Book of Acts, and Dr. Ken Cuffey for leading a life-changing trip to Turkey and Greece, where I walked the very ground of these stories.

• Alyssa Durst, for her insightful editing of *Fire in the Desert*.

• Kirk DouPonce, for another stunning cover.

• Vincent Davis II, for your wisdom and assistance in marketing.

• My brother, Ric, for taking the time to read and review this manuscript.

• Vern Fein, for also reviewing this story and for your unflagging faith in the Kingdom Come series.

Now, it's on to the next twelve chapters of the Book of Acts. May His Kingdom come!

OTHER TITLES BY DOUG PETERSON

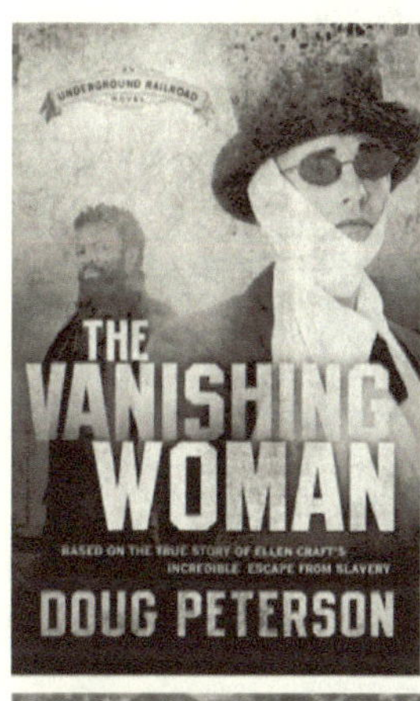

MIDDLE-GRADE FICTION BY JASON AND DOUG PETERSON

Doug Peterson and his youngest son, Jason, are soon releasing the first book in their middle-grade "Time's Up" series—*The Sabotage of '76.* In *The Sabotage of '76*, two middle-school buddies travel back in time to save the Declaration of Independence in 1776, while also saving the Philadelphia 76ers basketball team in 1976. Will they succeed? Only time will tell.

www.ingramcontent.com/pod-product-compliance
Lightning Source LLC
LaVergne TN
LVHW050925080826
845145LV00001B/212

* 9 7 8 1 7 3 5 8 1 5 1 4 5 *